CLONE

M.A. GELSEY

Published by Bifrost Press

CONTENTS

For my family

PROLOGUE

Conscience is but a word that cowards use,
Devis'd at first to keep the strong in awe.
- William Shakespeare, *Richard III*

Finally, after so many years of planning and work, it was time for the birth. Initially, Dr. Edgar Midas had refused to leave the birthing room, determined to see his project through to the end. After the first few hours of watching the surrogate pace and pant and sweat (punctuated by the occasional agonizing wail), he decided to step out for some air. The nurses reassured him that there was still plenty of time, and they'd fetch him at once if anything changed. In the long white hallway, Edgar leaned against the wall and massaged his temples. He'd been more taken aback than he should have been as a scientist by the screams, the smells, the sweat and blood.

After a moment he collected himself and headed to the cafeteria with a vague notion that coffee might do him some good. He texted Caden to meet him there; for some reason he did not want to face the rest of his team until he knew the outcome of the experiment. It was different with Caden, though. With Caden, he never felt the pressure.

He was seated at a corner table near a window, staring at the forebodingly cloudy sky and sipping the vilest cup of coffee in the history of mankind, when Caden arrived. Edgar watched him approach. Caden was the very picture of elegant strength: tall with broad muscular shoulders, yet moving with a grace of a dancer. Caden had thick black hair, bronze skin and kind brown eyes. Nobody had ever held such sway over Edgar before, and he doubted anyone else ever would again.

"Dr. Yang," he said in greeting as Caden slid into the seat next to him.

"Dr. Midas," Caden returned, his mouth quirking into a smile. Using formal titles had become something of a private joke between them, something that had begun during the long hard years when they worked towards their Ph.Ds.

Edgar did not speak, he merely looked at Caden. Without consciously making the decision, he leaned over and kissed him full on the mouth. It was the first time, but Edgar was a confident man, and he knew the feelings were reciprocated. He wondered why he'd never done it before; half-formed fears about upsetting their friendship, their working relationship, all stupid and meaningless. When they finally broke apart, Caden's face was flushed.

"Harlow is looking for you," he stammered out.

Edgar laughed. "Of course he is. Did you tell him where to find me?"

Caden shook his head, and Edgar heaved a theatrical sigh. "I suppose I should go reassure him that his investment is safe." He made to stand up, but Caden caught his arm and pulled him back into his seat for another kiss. Edgar had to fight the urge to drag Caden off into an empty on-call room, but there wasn't time. *Later,* he thought. *It wouldn't do to miss the birth.*

He left the cafeteria with a most undignified grin plastered across his face, too elated to care. He nearly walked right into Damon Aldous Harlow III, his chief investor and a man renowned for being the first to amass a personal fortune of one trillion dollars.

"Knew I'd find you here, Edgar," said Harlow, clapping Edgar on the back in greeting. "I hope you didn't try the heinous coffee, that's just asking for trouble."

"Hello, Damon," said Edgar. Harlow was a short man in his early forties with gray-streaked sandy hair and ice blue eyes that had an almost hypnotic quality to them.

"The press is in the waiting room," Harlow told him, chuckling appreciatively. "You're about to become very rich, my friend."

"You mean *we* are," Edgar corrected. "But it doesn't matter. That's not why I'm doing this, and you already have far too much money."

"You'll never get into the four comma club with that attitude," Harlow boomed. He gave Edgar another jovial pat on the back. "How much longer, d'you think?"

"I'm on my way back to check, but it should be soon."

"Better you than me," Harlow jested. "I've never had any stomach for those sorts of things. Avoided the hospital when all three of my sons were born. Probably would have vomited all over the floor! None of the wives would have appreciated that."

Edgar nodded politely. Harlow had recently divorced his third wife, and rumor had it he was already living with the woman who would likely become number four.

"I'll update you as soon as there's news," Edgar promised.

"See that you do, Edgar. The suspense is killing me," Harlow said.

Edgar returned to the birthing room just in time.

"Baby's crowning," the OB announced. She looked up at the surrogate. "You're almost there."

Edgar quickly approached to look over the OB's shoulder and see the top of the baby's head himself, but recoiled almost immediately. There was no avoiding the surrogate's ear-splitting wails or the nurse's cheerleading as the surrogate performed the final part of her role. Edgar resumed his pacing around the periphery of the brightly-lit, white room, wishing he could un-see what he had just seen. He was full of a bemused admiration for the doctors and nurses who experienced this sort of chaos and mess everyday. He much preferred the controlled elegance of the petri dishes and pipettes in his lab.

He noticed that one of the residents — a gorgeous blonde — was eyeing him over the knees of the screaming surrogate. He gave her a brief smile, but did not otherwise engage. Edgar was used to the attention of women; he was tall and lean-muscled with skin the color of espresso, straight white teeth, and gold-framed glasses that he was told made him look the part of the handsome young geneticist about to make history and win a Nobel prize by creating the first ever human clone.

He had already given advance interviews at several prestigious publications so they could go to print the moment they received confirmation that the birth was successful and the clone was alive and healthy.

As if in answer to this thought, the surrogate screamed her loudest yet, followed by what was possibly the most beautiful sound Edgar had ever heard: the wail of a newborn. Edgar watched transfixed as the OB handed the small, blood-covered infant to the resident at her shoulder, who carried it over to the nurses to be cleaned off. Frozen, Edgar listened to the music of the baby's cries, overwhelmed in spite of himself. When a nurse carried the first ever human clone over to him a moment later, swaddled in blankets and quieter now, Edgar could barely breathe.

Gently, he took the clone baby from the nurse, staring down at his genetic copy and thinking this must have been what he'd looked like thirty-six years earlier when he'd first been pulled out of his mother. Wordlessly, he carried the clone baby down the hallway to the waiting room where the rest of the team was assembled along with the press.

The instant he opened the door, babble broke out amongst the crowd; questions flew at him about the clone, whether it survived, whether it was healthy, whether he'd written his Nobel acceptance speech yet. He held up a hand, cradling the now-calm clone baby in his other arm, and silence fell at once. His eyes found Caden's in the back and he suppressed another huge grin, knowing that if ever there was a moment to look professional, this was it.

"Our names will be remembered as some of the most daring and accomplished scientists ever to have lived," Edgar began, addressing his team. "Your years of hard work and dedication have paid off. I'd like to introduce you to the first human clone. Meet Edgar Prime."

He pulled back the blanket for a moment so the crowd could see the clone baby for themselves, and more than one of them gasped in reverence; he was perfect.

"Today, we've made history." He covered Edgar Prime with the blanket, and the clone baby turned slightly, snuggling against his chest. "The world will never be the same again."

1: ANNABEL

Annabel opened her eyes on the morning of her eighteenth birthday and immediately wished she could plunge back into oblivion. But it was impossible; Ms. Durant was already rapping her knuckles on Annabel's door.

"I'm up," Annabel mumbled. She threw back the blankets and climbed out of bed, shivering in the cold early morning air.

"Breakfast is waiting for you," Ms. Durant said crisply through the door.

"I'll be right down," Annabel called. She pulled on a soft white robe and slid her feet into slippers. Annabel had grown up in a large, lonely house in a small, lonely seaside town in New England. There were enough people during the summer months, but now it was only March and the landscape was as desolate as it was beautiful.

Annabel sighed as she glanced out the window, taking in the gentle slope of the grassy hill that she knew would be full of wildflowers in the coming months, and the rocky beach and ocean beyond. She could hear the soothing roar of waves in the distance from everywhere in the house, which had been built in the traditional New England style of graying wood shingles and white trim with gorgeous old floorboards inside that creaked when Annabel walked on them.

Deciding she'd delayed facing the day for as long as she dared, Annabel glanced at herself quickly in the mirror — braided dark red hair, ocean blue eyes and fair skin — before opening the door to her room and walking down the winding staircase to the kitchen where Ms. Durant waited with her breakfast.

When Annabel entered, Ms. Durant looked up from the crossword she was doing on her tablet.

"Good morning, my dear," Ms. Durant said. "Happy birthday."

"Good morning, Ms. Durant." No matter how she was feeling, Annabel had been taught to always be polite.

She sat down and started eating her almond milk chia pudding with fresh raspberries while Ms. Durant scrutinized her from across the table. A sharp-featured woman with gray hair pulled back into a neat bun and gray eyes, Ms. Durant was the picture of propriety. After a moment, the older woman went back to her crossword, and left Annabel to stare out the large bay windows and listen to the waves.

"We'll go to the church at half past two," Ms. Durant said, not looking up. Annabel clenched her hands in her lap, but said nothing. She knew there was no use arguing. As Ms. Durant always said, Annabel was neither a natural born nor an original, she had been designed by someone to fill a specific purpose, and it was not her place to protest that.

"Ten letters," Ms. Durant said, tapping her tablet absentmindedly. "Unhappy wife of Charles."

Annabel considered for a moment. "Emma Bovary."

Ms. Durant gave an appreciative, "Hmm," then went back to working in silence. Annabel forced herself to finish her breakfast, already feeling sick with nerves. She pushed away the empty bowl and told Ms. Durant she was going to the meditation room to practice yoga for an hour or two before she bathed and dressed for the ceremony that afternoon.

"Don't tire yourself out," Ms. Durant warned. "You've got a big day ahead of you."

"I won't," Annabel said, although she doubted it was the truth. She wanted to stop thinking for a while and that was best accomplished when her muscles were aching and sweat was running down her face and body. She left the table and went back upstairs to the large empty room she used for her practice. Annabel threw open all of the windows despite the morning chill. The humid, salty air that smelled of the sea was soothing to her and she breathed in deeply as she laid out her mat on the floor.

Annabel had never met the man who had commissioned her, but she supposed she would at half past two that afternoon. Ms. Durant, who had been hired before her birth to be her primary caretaker, had told her the story of her creation often enough. A successful young entrepreneur named Rex King had married the love of his life, Annabel Turner. They had six happy years together before she died of brain cancer at thirty.

Just before her death, Annabel Turner consented to be the second person to have a clone made from her DNA. The following year she was born and named Annabel after her original. According to Ms. Durant, Rex King had not thought it seemly for him to be present for her upbringing so that once she reached adulthood they would be able to marry. He had been waiting for her for eighteen years, and it would not do to disappoint him.

This marriage was her *raison d'être*, as Ms. Durant liked to remind her during their French lessons. The original Annabel had spoken French fluently, and so must she. Whenever Annabel showed the slightest frustration over her situation, Ms. Durant sharply informed her that she should be grateful to exist at all, and that less fortunate clones were sold on the black market to have their organs harvested or to be used for a thousand other sinister purposes. Was Annabel not safe and comfortable? How dare she ask for more?

Before long, Ms. Durant was hurrying her into the shower so they'd have enough time to do her hair and makeup before they left for the church. Annabel took as long as she dared, wishing to postpone the moment when she had to don the white dress and walk down the aisle to meet her fate.

Ms. Durant made her sit in front of the mirror for more than an hour as she combed out and dried Annabel's hair so that it fell in long loose waves down her back. Afterwards Ms. Durant applied a few minimal touches of makeup, and had her step into the dress that had been chosen for her.

It was a simple dress, ankle length and cream-colored, cut elegantly without any unnecessary adornment.

"Beautiful," breathed Ms. Durant when she regarded Annabel, fully dressed and ready. Annabel was surprised and a little embarrassed to see tears sparkle in the corners of Ms. Durant's eyes, but they did not fall. She smiled at Annabel.

"Rex will be overjoyed. You look just like she did on their wedding day," said Ms. Durant.

Annabel said nothing, but her thoughts skittered around like frightened birds frantically trying to escape their cages. *Don't forget to breathe,* she reminded herself.

At a quarter past two, a limousine pulled up outside to drive them to the church. Ms. Durant prattled on about how kind it was of Annabel's intended to send the car, while Annabel reflected that the next time she saw the house she'd be married to a stranger. The fact that they would continue to live in the lonely seaside town in the only house Annabel had ever known gave her little comfort. Gravel crunched in the driveway as the car pulled away, and Annabel swallowed the lump in her throat.

The small white church where the wedding would take place was located at the edge of town. Annabel had walked by it dozens of times but had never before ventured inside. The car pulled up and Annabel stepped out onto the pavement. She saw no sign of her intended, and Ms. Durant told her to wait by the front steps while she checked whether they were ready to begin.

Annabel paced back and forth, staring up at the stained glass windows with their intricate geometric patterns wrought in red, blue, green, purple and gold. Within a couple of minutes Ms. Durant returned, gave Annabel a hug, and instructed her to walk down the aisle. Rex was already waiting for her inside with the priest who would perform the ceremony.

Annabel took another deep breath, then crossed the threshold and stepped into the church. Colored light filtered down from the high stained glass windows, creating patterns across the white walls, dark wooden benches, and maroon carpet. The church was empty, aside from two figures at the far end of the long aisle and Ms. Durant, who gave her a quick kiss on the cheek and darted up to sit in the front row.

Knowing she had no choice in the matter, Annabel began to walk. *Don't stumble. He won't like it if you ruin the dress.* There was a tall, tuxedo-clad, gray haired man standing at the alter with tears in his eyes and a white boutonnière pinned to his jacket: her commissioner and her intended, Rex King. When she reached him, he took her hands in his and gazed into her eyes.

"I've waited a long time for you to return to me, my love," he whispered. Annabel's mind went blank and she could not summon a single word to say, but Rex King did not seem to mind. The old priest cleared his throat and began. "Dearly beloved, we are gathered here today ..."

Annabel didn't hear the rest. She was too busy avoiding Rex King's eyes and trying to calm the rapid beating of her heart. At the appropriate time, she repeated her vows, and managed to barely hesitate before sealing her fate with a simple, "I do."

2: JAVI

The morning was thick with tension in the Vasquez house. All of Javi's birthdays were tense. Technically, this birthday didn't even belong to him. He'd never been told the actual day of his birth. His family had always celebrated it on March 15, the day that the original Javier Vazquez had been born and had died.

He supposed a more industrious person might have done some research to learn more about his origins. It wouldn't be difficult — he knew he was the third successful human clone, and surely all kinds of information about his birth would be publicly available, including the date. But he never bothered. He didn't want to be reminded of yet another thing he and the real Javier did not have in common.

Sometimes he wondered if his parents would prefer him if he didn't speak, making it easier for them to believe the lie that he really was the son they had lost instead of an inferior copy. He had seen photos of the original Javier, and they both had the same tall, lanky frame, the same light brown skin, messy black hair and chocolate-colored eyes. Lately, Javi had started growing a wispy beard in an effort to distinguish himself from the specter of his original. But deep down, he knew it wouldn't make any difference.

Today they'd celebrate his eighteenth birthday. Javi had known it would be the strangest of all his strange birthdays because the original Javier had died at seventeen. It was a car accident. He and three friends had missed a curve on the Pacific Coast Highway and driven his new car — a birthday present — off a cliff. In a way, this year was the first birthday that belonged to Javi alone. An observation best kept to himself, he knew.

The conversation over breakfast was stilted, as his father tried to keep things normal by asking him about school and whether he'd heard back from any more colleges (the original Javier had wanted to go to Stanford and it was assumed that Javi did too — in fact he thought he'd prefer Georgetown but he hadn't told anyone that yet).

His mother had been holding back tears since she first greeted him with a tremulous, "Happy birthday, sweetie," and a hug. He supposed he shouldn't feel resentful for that. It had taken his parents thirty-five years to reach their only child's eighteenth birthday.

"I'm gonna go meet up with some friends," Javi mumbled as he got up from the table once breakfast was finished. He felt guilty but had to escape. He hated that they both looked at him and saw someone else.

"We're gonna go out to the vineyard next weekend," reminded his father. "See if they want to come."

"I will," Javi said.

"Be safe," his mother whispered.

"I will," Javi repeated after a split-second pause.

Thirty minutes later he was getting off the bus (he wasn't allowed a car) and walking towards a park downtown. There he met his two best friends Herman O'Flannery and Fred Singh, both even more awkward and nerdy than he was. Herman was pale and slightly chubby with curly orange hair and too many freckles, and Fred was skinny and hunchbacked with glasses, black hair and skin the color of a coffee stain on paper.

The three of them went to their usual haunt, a weeping willow tree with branches that bent all the way to the ground, almost creating a tent with their leaves. Fred lit a joint and passed it to Javi who inhaled gratefully, looking forward to the pleasant warm feeling and mental cloudiness that he always associated with pot. Javi passed the joint on to Herman who took two short puffs and passed it back to Fred.

"Think we'll see Stella today?" Herman asked, peering through the swaying branches of the willow.

"Doubt it," Javi said. Stella Castell was the most popular girl in their school, the one all of them fantasized about. It didn't matter that they all wanted her; she'd never look twice at any of them.

"I think we might," Herman said, unperturbed. "It's Saturday. She likes to come here on Saturdays sometimes. She likes the lake."

"Jesus, Herm. You sound like a goddamn stalker," commented Fred.

They all laughed, even Herman. Fred handed Javi the joint again and he took a long draw, waiting a few seconds before blowing out the smoke.

"D'you know, I think her tits look bigger than before. Do they still grow when you're eighteen?" Herman asked.

"Maybe she had some work done," suggested Fred.

"I'm fucking tired of us all obsessing over Stella," Javi said. "We've gotta broaden our scope if we don't all wanna die virgins."

"Easy for you to say," Herman said, coughing as he took the last puff of the joint and stubbed out the end in the grass.

"Why is that?" Javi asked, although he thought he knew the answer.

"You're a *clone*," Herman said as though explaining the most obvious thing in the world. "That's exotic."

"If by exotic you mean freakish, then yes," Javi snapped, and Fred snorted with laughter. "What does that have to do with girls?"

"Girls like exotic," Herman said.

"Says who?" Javi muttered.

"You're an idiot, Herman," said Fred. "Girls like tall, attractive athletes like Kato Barre. Come to think of it, that's probably why Stella's dating him."

"Stella's got a new boyfriend?" gasped Herman as though he'd never heard such horrible news in his life.

Fred gave him a scathing look. "Like you'd ever have a chance with her."

Herman groaned and lay back on the grass. "That doesn't mean I want her dating someone else. Especially not an asshole like Kato."

"He's not really an asshole," Javi said fairly. "And he's a lot less stupid than her last boyfriend — "

"Todd," finished Herman. "See, I liked her with Todd because I knew it'd never last."

"You've never even talked to her!" Javi said. On that score at least he was doing better than both of his friends. Stella sat in front of him in his Chinese class and every so often would turn around to pass him a test or homework paper. He'd usually say "thanks" and receive no response, but once she'd smiled and said, "no problem." No wonder he was doing so badly in Chinese, he reflected. Too much time spent staring at Stella's perfect blonde hair and perfect shoulders and perfect ass.

"Changing the subject," said Fred. "Either of you get any more college letters?"

"Got into Berkeley," said Herman.

"UCLA and Stanford," Javi mumbled. He didn't want to talk about college.

"Bet they flipped out when you got into Stanford," Herman said, referring to Javi's parents.

Javi shrugged. "Haven't told them yet."

"I got into Berkeley too," said Fred.

"Roomies!" Herman exclaimed.

"Good for you," Javi said, hoping to keep the conversation from circling back to him.

"Why haven't you told them?" Herman asked Javi, pulling another joint out of Fred's backpack and rummaging around for a lighter.

"Obvious, isn't it?" Javi said. "If I tell them I got in, they'll want me to go. Just like *he* always wanted."

The slight awkwardness that followed was broken when

Herman spotted Stella Castell walking around the duck pond across the park hand in hand with Kato Barre.

"Fuck everything," said Herman, lighting the second joint.

3: EDGAR PRIME

"Just one more test Prime, then you can go to class," said Dr. Midas.

Edgar Prime sighed but nodded wearily. "Fine."

He was about three-quarters done with his first year of college. He liked Columbia well enough, despite it being the same university where his original, Dr. Edgar Midas, had gotten his Ph.D. and completed the first stages of his cloning research. After he'd established a name and reputation, Dr. Midas had set up his own lab using private funding. It was where Edgar Prime was conceived, and where new clones were produced to this day.

When Edgar Prime was young, he had fantasized about going elsewhere, somewhere far away where nobody had heard of Dr. Midas and his brilliant science experiment, but it wasn't long before he realized that such a place did not exist. Dr. Midas had friends and colleagues at universities all over the world, and his face was familiar even to those outside of academia. Edgar Prime had been dealing with an odd, reflected fame his whole life, and he often felt like the star act in a circus freak show. There was nowhere to hide.

Dr. Midas had taken to calling him 'Prime' as though it was some sort of endearing nickname, but Edgar Prime took it as further confirmation that he was not expected to develop any identity of his own. While Dr. Midas had insisted on educating him and encouraging him to study hard so that one day he too might do great things, Edgar Prime knew that anything he accomplished would ultimately be attributed to his original, the man to whom he owed his genetic code, his life, and every-

thing else. There was a time when he had considered changing his name so that he might be better able to carve out his
own destiny. But what other name was more appropriate for a
copy, a derivation? Dr. Midas would probably laugh if he knew
that Edgar Prime thought such things — he had never thought
of Edgar Prime as anything more than an extension of himself.

"I'm going to start the slideshow now," Dr. Midas informed
him.

"All right," replied Edgar Prime.

The lights in the lab dimmed, and Edgar Prime tried to pay
attention to the photographs that appeared on the screen in
front of him instead of dwelling on bitter thoughts. He had
done a hundred tests like this before, but as Dr. Midas frequently reminded him the human brain was not fully developed until the mid-twenties. Dr. Midas wanted to study and
catalogue every step of Edgar Prime's development, and as
much as possible compare it to his own.

After the series of photographs designed to elicit various
emotional reactions came math problems, science questions,
and verbal exercises in both English and Spanish. Dr. Midas
never asked him about history during these tests, preferring
to focus on those areas he considered valuable. Edgar Prime
thought this was likely why history was his favorite subject,
even though he had never told Dr. Midas. It felt like something
that belonged solely to him.

After the fMRI was complete, Dr. Midas had his research
fellow, Dr. Patrice Zhao, raise the lights once more. Edgar
Prime stood up and glanced at the clock on the far wall. If
he left in the next five minutes he'd be able to make it to his
World History II class on time.

"Excellent, Prime," Dr. Midas said as he strode over from
behind the panel of computer monitors on which he had been
watching Edgar Prime's brain activity throughout the session.

"I've got a class to get to," Edgar Prime said, not wanting to
hear what Dr. Midas thought of his latest scans.

"Of course," Dr. Midas said. "Same time on Thursday then?

And maybe we can have dinner sometime this week too."

"Sure," Edgar Prime said. The sensation of looking at his older self had disturbed Edgar Prime since he was old enough to understand it. He supposed he should be relieved; Dr. Midas was still handsome and looked much younger than his fifty-five years. But Edgar Prime disliked seeing versions of his own facial expressions playing out on a much older face. Edgar Prime stooped down and picked up his backpack. "I'll text you."

"Enjoy your class," Dr. Midas said. Behind him, Patrice sat down at the computer and began typing furiously, completing her notes and properly cataloguing this round of scans. She rarely talked to Edgar Prime during these sessions, and when she did it was only as a research subject. Never as a person.

Edgar Prime nodded to Dr. Midas and left the sterile white lab. He was grateful to get outside again, able to feel the sun on his face and pretend he was just like everybody else. The illusion lasted only an instant; standing on Riverside Drive outside Midas Labs, he drew a few stares and he knew they knew who he was, or rather *what* he was.

He put his head down and walked briskly back towards campus, already looking forward to losing himself in a lecture on the Greco-Persian Wars for the next couple of hours.

4: ANNABEL

They returned to the house without Ms. Durant. Rex explained that from now on she'd be living elsewhere in town, but that Annabel could see her whenever she wished. Annabel felt distinctly uncomfortable standing on the threshold of the house where she had grown up next to her new husband. He hadn't taken his eyes off her since she first entered the church, as though he was afraid she would vanish if he did. When the priest had said, "You may now kiss the bride," Rex's lips had been too eager and too moist.

"Such a beautiful view," Rex said. She glanced over in his direction, and saw he was looking not at the ocean or the barely-blooming wildflowers, but at her. She looked away quickly, pretending to be fascinated by the vista she had seen every day of her eighteen years.

"Yes," she said, stepping away from him and inside the house. Rex followed, more closely than she'd have liked.

"Are you hungry, my love?" Rex asked.

Annabel shook her head, trying not to cringe at the endearment, one foreign to her ears.

"Are you sure?" Rex said. "You look pale."

"I'm fine," lied Annabel. She went out onto the balcony and watched the ocean break against the waves, wishing she were anywhere else.

Rex was eyeing her with concern. "I'll make us some tea."

Annabel turned and gave him a weak smile, remembering the courtesies that Ms. Durant had drilled into her.

Rex left, giving Annabel a moment of solitude. *He's trying*, Annabel told herself, ashamed at how judgmental she'd been.

She resolved to do her very best to make this work.

Before long, Rex returned with two steaming mugs. She saw that he had put a lemon slice in her tea and accepted the offering, though she preferred almond milk.

"Thank you," she said, barely above a whisper. The joyous look on his face at this tiny gesture of gratitude was heartbreaking.

"Can I get you anything else?" he asked. "Some fruit or a sandwich? I had Mrs. Lennox put a roast chicken on for our dinner, but it won't be ready for hours. She's also making blueberry pie for dessert. Your favorite."

"Tea is fine, thank you," Annabel repeated, almost managing a genuine smile this time. She did love blueberry pie, but found it disconcerting that this stranger knew her dessert preferences so well.

They sat down side-by-side on the two balcony lounge chairs, smelling the ocean, watching the sunlight glint off the water, and listening to the birdsongs and the sound of the waves.

"I missed this view," Rex said.

"Have you seen it before?" Annabel asked, startled.

"Of course," Rex said. "We —" he stopped. The moment of awkwardness hung between them. "I used to live here . . . before."

"Oh," said Annabel in a small voice.

"We'll be happy here again," Rex promised. All Annabel could think was that they had never been a 'we' before, not in her lifetime. She didn't know how to reply to that, so she took another sip of her tea.

5: JAVI

When Javi returned home hours later, he was still stoned. He walked into the living room to find the unwelcome sight of his only living grandparent: his father's mother. An ancient woman with wispy white hair, she was wrinkled from head to toe and dressed all in black. She had come, he knew, to pay her respects at the gravesite of the Javier who had died. It had always been that way. In all of Javi's eighteen years she had never once come for the purpose of seeing him or wishing him a happy birthday.

Immediately upon his entrance she fixed her beady eyes on him, and muttered "El diablo," under her breath, but still loud enough that he could hear it. She had never been shy about condemning her son's choice to clone his dead child, and never failed to mention Javi's "unnaturalness" during her infrequent visits. This would not be the first of Javi's already uncomfortable birthdays that she ruined.

"Mirabel," Javi's mother said reproachfully. She was seated on the couch opposite her mother-in-law, who had taken up her usual spot in Javi's father's armchair. The old woman gave her a sour look but did not comment further.

"I'll be upstairs," Javi mumbled, trying to make his exit quickly. He hoped they couldn't smell the smoke on his clothes or see his bloodshot eyes.

"Come sit with us for a few minutes," his mother said just before Javi was able to disappear down the hallway.

"I've got some homework to do," Javi said without real conviction.

His mother gave him a stern look. Reluctantly, Javi

slouched into the living room and sat down in the chair furthest away from his mother and grandmother.

"Hello, Abuela," said Javi as he slumped back in the chair.

His grandmother merely grunted in response.

"I was just saying you've gotten a lot of acceptance letters in the last few weeks," Javi's mother said in an attempt at normalcy. "Still no word from Stanford, but I'm sure it won't be long."

Javi nodded even as his stomach squirmed uncomfortably. He didn't want to lie about his Stanford acceptance, but he didn't know if he could face their celebration that his original's dearest ambition had finally been accomplished, albeit eighteen years too late.

"Very nice," his grandmother said with a disdainful sniff. Javi averted his eyes from hers, feeling that she could see the lie written across his face.

"What could be taking David so long?" his grandmother asked suddenly, turning back towards Javi's mother. "Call him, will you Josefina? He's been forty-five minutes getting those flowers."

"Sure," said Javi's mother, hiding her grimace well as she stood up to find her phone. Javi's grandmother was the only one who ever called her Josefina; everybody else just called her Jo. That almost-grimace made Javi feel a surge of affection for his mother. She was always the one to reassure him not to take his grandmother's words to heart, that she was old and dogmatic and old-fashioned, and they had to tolerate her eccentricities because before too long she'd be dead.

Before Javi's mother had time to even dial, his father walked through the front door with a large bouquet of white roses clutched in his hand.

"Sorry," he said, before Javi's grandmother could do more than open her mouth indignantly. "Traffic was terrible."

Sensing that he'd be able to sneak off, Javi stood up and walked quietly towards the door that led to a short hallway beyond which lay the stairs to his bedroom.

"Everything good, son?" his father asked as Javi passed him.

"Yep," Javi said. "Herman and Fred will come to the vineyard next weekend they said."

"Great!" said Javi's father, overly enthusiastic to cover the awkwardness of the situation. Javi's mother and grandmother gathered up their purses and went to stand next to his father.

With a glance at the impatience on Javi's grandmother's face, Javi's father said, "We'll be back soon," shooting an apologetic look across the living room to where Javi stood alone.

"No problem," he said. Before anyone had a chance to say anything else to him, Javi turned and trudged down the hallway and up the stairs, closing the door to his bedroom. He lay across his bed staring at the ceiling and listening to the front door gently close, to the sounds of his parents and grandmother getting into his mother's SUV and driving away. Javi told himself he didn't want to go to the grave anyway. He had never been invited, and he was glad of it. He had no wish to see his own name on a tombstone. *Happy fucking birthday to me*, he thought bitterly.

6: EDGAR PRIME

"Make sure to read the rest of Herodotus, we'll be having a discussion on his account of the Battle of Thermopylae next class," Professor Van Willigan reminded them loudly over the sounds of laptops closing and bags zipping. "And don't think you'll be able to get away with just watching the movie *300*. I'll know if you do." He gave them a faux-stern look and a few people chuckled.

"Edgar Prime," said a voice behind him. Edgar Prime turned in his seat to face Celeste Huxley, a pretty girl with very short hair, caramel skin and piercing blue eyes. A glance at her notebook revealed that as usual she had spent most of the lecture doodling complex equations instead of taking notes. She was a junior physics major, only taking World History to fulfill her core curriculum requirements, and she made no secret of her distain for the subject.

"Yes, you can borrow my notes," Edgar Prime said, before she had a chance to ask.

Celeste grinned. "Knew I could count on you. Got any plans tonight?"

"Not really," Edgar Prime said, surprised. He and Celeste had thus far only spoken in the few minutes before and after class, and usually it was only about their assignments.

"Good. I'm having some people over, and you should come," Celeste declared.

"Okay," Edgar Prime said with a surge of joy as they both stood to leave. He had mostly kept to himself since starting college, but spending every night in the library did get tedious after awhile.

"I'll text you the address," Celeste said.

"Okay," Edgar Prime said again. *What an interesting conversationalist you are*, his subconscious sneered at him. He ignored it. "Should I bring anything?"

"Only your glorious smile and winning personality," Celeste quipped, and when he glanced sideways at her she laughed. Her laugh was contagious, and Edgar Prime joined in even though he knew she was teasing him.

Edgar Prime almost said "okay" again but managed to stop himself.

"D'you go out much?" Celeste asked as they exited the building and crossed the quad. The sun was low in the sky and there was a chill wind that made Edgar Prime wish he'd thought to wear a hat.

"Some," Edgar Prime lied.

Celeste grinned at that, and he knew she must see right through him. "Well, good. This won't be a *party* party, just a few friends hanging out. I normally wouldn't invite freshmen to these things, but I'm making an exception for you."

Edgar Prime longed to ask her why, but didn't want to seem pathetic. They reached a fork in the road where they'd be going opposite directions; Edgar Prime to his dorm, Celeste to her apartment.

"I'll email you today's notes when I get home," he said.

"Thanks again, Edgar Prime. You're the best." Celeste hugged him and set off down her path, leaving him to continue on his way while trying to suppress a huge grin. Finally, things were looking up.

7: ANNABEL

That evening, Annabel barely ate any of her dinner, despite the fact that it was comprised of all her favorite foods: roast chicken with lemon and garlic, braised kale and tahini mashed sweet potatoes. Every time she looked across the table at Rex's painfully reverent expression her stomach twisted into knots. Ms. Durant had prepared Annabel for what would be expected of her as a wife, and the thought of it made her nauseated.

After Mrs. Lennox cleared away the last of the dessert plates, Rex suggested they sit together by the fireplace before turning in for the night. Annabel settled herself on the sofa as far away from Rex as she could manage without seeming rude. After a few minutes of awkward conversation, he stood up to stoke the fire. When he returned to the couch, he sat right beside her, close enough that their legs were touching. Annabel crossed one leg over the other to minimize the contact, but she could not escape the press of his hip against hers.

He stretched an arm around the back of the sofa, and let it come to rest around Annabel's shoulder. She almost flinched but managed to stop herself. In order to keep her hands from trembling, she grasped them tightly together in her lap.

"Do I make you nervous?" Rex asked in a quiet voice.

Annabel shook her head but did not meet his eyes.

"Look at me," he commanded.

Taking a deep breath first, Annabel looked. The expression on his face was kind but imploring.

"I want you to feel comfortable around me, Annabel," said Rex. "I know this is strange right now — it's strange for me too.

But in time, you'll realize that we belong together. That's why I didn't want to meet you before now — I wanted only to see you as the woman I love, not as a child. It would have been unseemly had I made contact sooner."

She nodded because she knew he wanted her agreement. Ms. Durant had already explained this to her. Annabel swallowed, her throat dry.

"I understand," she lied, barely above a whisper.

"Good," he said. Rex looked satisfied with this answer. His hand gripped her shoulder slightly, in what she assumed was meant to be a reassuring manner, and she noticed something new in his eyes — a hunger.

"Let's go upstairs," he said. His voice had dropped to a low purr, and he stroked his fingers down her arm gently.

Annabel swallowed again, thinking of what Ms. Durant told her about the less fortunate clones, the ones who were flawed and sent to the black market to be sold to the highest bidder. Was she not safe and healthy? Was she not well-fed and sheltered? What more could she ask for, really? What more did she even deserve? The man who sat before her with desire written all over his face had paid for her very existence, and everything else she'd ever enjoyed in her life. For this perhaps, she owed him a debt. She ought to at least pretend she shared his fantasy of marital bliss.

She forced a smile. "All right," she said. Beaming, he stood up and offered her his hand. It was soft and warm, but his palm was slick with sweat.

8: JAVI

Once his parents returned from the graveyard, they had dinner with his grandmother. Miraculously, they seemed to have finally found a way to subdue her usual muttering and suspicion because she was far more docile than usual — even polite at times. Still, Javi was relieved when it was over.

Just after 9pm he said goodnight to his parents, and waited in his room for an hour until he saw their light go out. Then he climbed out his window onto the thick branch of a large oak tree in the yard, and shimmied down its trunk. He walked to the corner where Fred was waiting in his car, Herman in the back seat.

"What took you so long?" Fred asked once Javi had gotten into the passenger seat.

Javi shrugged. "Had to wait for them to fall asleep, didn't I?"

"Check it out," Herman said, and Javi turned to see Herman pulling a flask out of his pocket.

"You've gotta be fuckin' kidding me," said Javi laughing. "Where the fuck did you get a flask?"

"It's my dad's," Herman said proudly. "He won't notice I took it — I hope."

"What's in it?" Fred asked.

"Whiskey," Herman said. "I think." He unscrewed it carefully as Fred made a left turn, then took a small sip. He coughed and grimaced, almost spitting it out but just managing to swallow. "Definitely whiskey," he croaked as Javi and Fred laughed again.

Herman passed the flask up to Javi who took a longer swig but still couldn't manage to swallow without a shudder. Fred abstained; he was always strict with himself about drinking and driving.

"D'you think Stella will be there tonight?" Herman asked hopefully. He took another swig from the flask, and managed it slightly better this time.

"Doesn't matter, does it?" Javi said. "If she is, she'll be with her boyfriend anyway. Why don't you go for Phoebe Mead instead? She's cute enough. And I bet she'd blow you if you ask her to prom."

"Ugh!" Herman cried in mock-disgust while Fred hooted with laughter. "Phoebe fucking Mead? If you think Phoebe Mead is so cute *you* can take her to prom. Enjoy getting the clap though. I heard she got that shit off Zane Goldbrook last year."

"I'd rather get the clap than graduate a virgin," Javi snapped. "Besides, you can get rid of it with antibiotics. Any idiot knows that."

"You sure know a lot about it," Herman said with a smirk. "Something you're not telling us, Javi?"

"Fuck you," Javi said, laughing. They arrived at their destination and Fred parked on the street.

"I'd rather fuck Stella Castell," retorted Herman.

"You're a lost cause," Fred said as he pulled a paper bag with a bottle of tequila out of the trunk and locked the car. The house loomed large before them and they could hear loud music emanating from the windows along with the clatter of voices punctuated by occasional joyous shouts and laughter.

When they reached the front door Fred had to hammer on it with his fist in order to be heard over the music. A wiry brunette girl answered and her face split into a grin when she saw Fred. She pulled him into a drink-fueled, overly-enthusiastic hug, and jumped up and down giggling when he showed her the tequila.

"Come in!" she shouted after releasing a stunned-looking Fred. The three of them crossed the threshold and she shut the door behind them.

"I'm Violet!" the brunette girl yelled over the music as she led them through the foyer.

"This is Javi and Herman," said Fred loudly. They passed through the living room where fifty people were drinking from red solo cups, dancing, and laughing. Violet led them further down the hallway and behind her back Herman raised his eyebrows and winked at Fred who shoved him and looked down, awkward. Javi thought Violet was pretty although not particularly his type. He suppressed a grin as she grabbed Fred's arm and led him to the kitchen where the booze was. Perhaps one of them would be getting lucky after all . . .

Fifteen minutes later Javi and Herman drifted back into the packed living room armed with screwdriver-filled solo cups (Violet had insisted on mixing everyone's drinks and from the taste of it they were at least 90% vodka). They left the kitchen when Violet had given them a pointed look after handing them their drinks that plainly said she wanted to be alone with Fred.

"How did Fred manage to score with Violet Fisher anyway?" Herman wondered aloud.

"Dunno, they've got class together I guess," Javi said.

"I've got class with her too," Herman muttered, but Javi wasn't paying much attention anymore. His eyes were on Phoebe Mead across the room, and he wondered whether it'd be worth a try to see if she'd live up to her 'serial blower' reputation. She was flirting with Kato Barre, but Javi knew she was wasting her time. No guy in his right mind would go for Phoebe when he already had Stella Castell.

He was just wondering where Stella was — if Kato was here she was sure to be too — when someone bumped into him from behind causing him to spill his screwdriver all over a couple he didn't know who were making out on the couch in front of him.

"Fuck!" he exclaimed as the drenched and furious couple sprang up from the couch and added their voices to the ruckus. Javi whirled around to give the person responsible for the mess a piece of his mind, but his angry accusation died in his throat as he saw Stella Castell standing there looking more beautiful than ever as she repeated apology after mortified apology to him and the couple. Most of the rest of the room was focused on the scene now, laughing and stage-whispering.

The couple both swore at Javi and Stella once more before they made their exit, probably seeking out a bedroom where they could avoid further interruptions. Javi was vaguely aware of Herman standing behind him gaping at Stella, but he only had eyes for her.

"I'm really sorry," she said again. "I'm such a klutz in these stupid shoes." She gestured to the stilettos on her feet.

"They look good on you," Javi said without thinking.

She gave him an odd look. "Right, thanks. Did the drink spill on you also? Can I get you a paper towel or something?"

"No, I'm okay," Javi said. "Actually I think almost all of it went onto that couple. I don't know either of them, thank god."

Stella laughed. Javi thought it was a beautiful sound and marveled that he had been the cause of it.

"It's Javi, isn't it?" she asked.

"Yeah," he said, secretly ecstatic that she knew his name. "And you're Stella?" He thought he heard Herman snort at that, but Stella didn't pay him any attention.

"Yeah," she said. Javi noticed that her hazel eyes had a greenish tinge in this light. He didn't know what else to say, so he merely stared. "Come on," she said finally. "Let's get you another drink."

She started back towards the kitchen and Javi followed her, dumbfounded by this turn of events. He glanced over his shoulder and saw Herman give him a thumbs up. Stella's hips swayed back and forth with each step she took, mesmerizing Javi like a hypnotist's watch. He trailed in her wake, hardly daring to believe his luck.

9: EDGAR PRIME

He took a sip of beer and tried not to grimace, not wanting to look like a stupid freshman in front of Celeste and her friends.

"Shit beer isn't it," said Celeste with a grin. "Come on Edgar Prime, I wanna introduce you to some people." She hooked her arm through his and steered him through the hordes of people crammed into the tiny apartment.

"This is 'just a few friends hanging out'?" he said, unable to help himself.

Celeste shrugged. "It got bigger than I originally planned. But hey, just go with it, right?"

Edgar Prime laughed, vaguely in awe but trying not to show it. He took another sip of beer as they walked, careful not to spill it on himself or anyone else.

"That'll start to taste better when you get to your third or fourth cup," Celeste informed him cheerfully.

"God, I hope so," Edgar Prime said, and Celeste burst out laughing.

"There they are!" She said, pointing across the room.

Edgar Prime looked over and nearly dropped his beer. Coming towards them was the most beautiful man Edgar Prime had ever seen: one of the RAs in his building, Hugo Larsson. He was tall with tousled blonde hair, broad shoulders and glasses that covered intensely green eyes. It was all Edgar Prime could do not to panic and hide, although he doubted Hugo would remember who he was. There were two others trailing behind Hugo, but Edgar Prime barely glanced at them.

Celeste hugged each in turn when they finally squeezed

their way over, and made introductions: the other two were Blake Nejem, a tall dark-haired girl with the largest breasts Edgar Prime had ever seen and George Lange, a member of the crew team with black hair and (according to Celeste) a notoriously sharp tongue. When it came time for her to introduce Hugo however, he interrupted her.

"I already know Edgar Prime," Hugo said with an easy smile. He leaned closer and dropped his voice to a conspiratorial whisper. "Technically, I'm not supposed to be drinking with any freshmen. So do me a favor and don't mention this to the other RAs. Or the other freshmen, actually. We wouldn't want them to be jealous."

He winked, and Edgar Prime's heart beat faster. "I won't."

"Do you have a nickname? Edgar Prime is kind of a mouthful," Hugo asked.

"Dr. Midas just calls me 'Prime'," he said reluctantly.

"But you're not a fan of that one?"

"Not really," Edgar Prime muttered.

There was a pause while Hugo considered him.

"I'm gonna call you Ed," he announced. "Unless you hate that even more than 'Prime'."

Before Edgar Prime could answer, he was interrupted by a peal of laughter from Celeste. She, Blake, and George were in the midst of a debate about whether or not Blake should sleep with a guy she'd met at a party the night before.

"If he judges you for that he's a moron anyway," Celeste said with a shrug. "And a hypocrite."

"Well yes and no," George argued.

"More yes than no," Celeste said. "He'd be doing the same thing, wouldn't he? So if he holds it against her, he's a hypocrite."

"Calm down Ms. Women's Studies," George said, eyes twinkling with mischief. "I'm not saying he should judge her, I'm just saying if he *does* maybe it's because he's looking for someone not like him, which in this case means someone who wouldn't fuck a person the day after they meet."

"That's stupid," Edgar Prime said without thinking, a comment that earned him an appreciative clap on the back from Celeste and a laugh from George and Hugo. Blake was preoccupied with trying to compose a text with the right degree of detached intrigue.

"Your cup is empty Ed," Hugo said suddenly. "I'm gonna get you a refill." He snatched Edgar Prime's solo cup and pushed his way back through the crowd towards the keg. Edgar Prime watched him go.

Blake's favorite song started playing and she dragged them all into the center of the room where people were dancing pressed close together out of necessity from the lack of space in the tiny apartment. Edgar Prime felt self-conscious; he had never been a very good dancer. Hugo rejoined them and Edgar Prime downed his second beer in three long gulps to the raucous applause of George and Blake. He refilled his third himself and by the time he'd gotten to his fourth he forgot to feel awkward and danced with abandon to song after song with the rest of them.

At some point Blake and a drunken George started making out, and Celeste gleefully filled him in on their on-and-off history, despite their joint insistence that they were "just friends". Edgar Prime couldn't remember having more fun in his entire life. At the end of the night he got to walk back to the dorm with Hugo, and was too drunk to even feel nervous about it. Hugo lived on the third floor and Edgar Prime lived on the fifth; just before Hugo exited the elevator he put a finger to his lips and raised his eyebrows, causing Edgar Prime to laugh aloud. It was with mingled fatigue and euphoria that he staggered back to his room and fell asleep as soon as his head hit the pillow.

10: ANNABEL

The bedroom was lit only by a bunch of fat candles lining its periphery, each scented with cinnamon and cloves and other spices Annabel could not identify. She supposed the candlelight was meant to be romantic, but she still felt too exposed and would have preferred total darkness.

Rex undressed her slowly, reverently, and she let him do it, trying not to betray any signs of nervousness. She lay back onto the bed once she was naked, fighting the impulse to try to cover herself again. His eyes never left her the whole time he peeled off his own clothes, and after a moment he was naked too, and crawling into bed next to her. His body was lean and muscular with sandy gray hair across his chest and leading down from his belly button. Her eyes darted downward but she averted them almost immediately — he was already fully erect and the sight was one that Annabel found both curious and unnerving.

She expected him to enter her immediately, but he surprised her, running his fingers gently over her body followed by gentle caresses with his mouth. Despite the fact that she was not attracted to him, Annabel could not deny that the sensation was enjoyable enough. At one point he teased her nipples with his tongue and teeth, and she felt a ripple of pleasure and a wetness between her thighs. He continued to move down her body, and she gasped aloud when he stuck his tongue inside her, massaging her with his fingers as he licked and sucked. Before long she felt heat build inside of her and then release in a sweet explosion that she had only experienced a few times before in her life — and those times it had always been her alone and by accident. Annabel's first reaction afterwards was shock — shock that it had happened and that Rex had been the one to make it happen.

"I haven't forgotten what you like," he murmured. He kissed her inner thigh looking immensely pleased with himself, but Annabel felt shy that he had just witnessed something so intimate. He crawled up and kissed her neck and her mouth. His tongue tasted metallic this time.

Just before he entered her he warned, "This will hurt, but only at first. Are you ready?"

Annabel nodded, although she wasn't sure she was. The first thrust was slow and controlled, but deep. Annabel felt an intense burning sensation, and couldn't stop her sharp intake of breath. Rex groaned with pleasure, sweat already beginning to slide down his back, chest and stomach. She could tell he was trying his best not to thrust too hard or too fast, but after the first few he seemed unable to help himself and each time Annabel felt a jolt through her whole body. Through the pain there was a strange thrumming pleasure too, and Annabel closed her eyes.

"Oh God," Rex whispered hoarsely, his breath hot and moist against her ear. "How I've missed you, my love."

Annabel wished he would stop talking so she could concentrate instead on the curious sensation that coexisted with the burning feeling. More than anything, this felt to her like an experiment. And she found herself wondering what it would be like with someone else, someone to whom she was actually attracted.

She mentally chastised herself for thinking such things as her husband continued to thrust in and out of her, consummating their marriage and making her a woman. He bit her neck and moaned her name again as he finished, sweat dripping off his body and mingling with Annabel's own as he collapsed on top of her. After a moment, he rolled off, wrapped his arms tightly around her, and fell asleep almost immediately.

Annabel lay awake for hours staring at the waning candle-light flickering on the ceiling and feeling like she was being held by a particularly enthusiastic octopus. She wished to twist away from the grip, but didn't know how to do so without waking Rex, or worse, offending him. *I'll get used to it in time,* she told herself, almost managing to believe it.

11: JAVI

Stella poured him a gin and tonic, and even cut a wedge of lime to squeeze into it. Violet and Fred had disappeared from the kitchen, and Javi hoped they were upstairs somewhere or else down in the basement. A vicarious hookup was better than none at all.

She handed him the solo cup and he drank, watching intently as Stella made one for herself too.

"Good?" she asked, glancing up at him.

"Yeah," Javi said. "So good." In truth he didn't notice the taste at all. All his attention was focused on her.

"Can I ask you a question?" Stella said. She finished making her drink and took a sip, looking hesitant.

"Yeah, of course," Javi said. He was astounded that she was still here talking to him but tried desperately not to show it.

"What's it like?" she asked.

"What's what like? The gin and tonic?" He was confused by her question, but didn't care. As long as he got to keep staring into those greenish hazel eyes, he didn't much care about anything else.

"What's it like to be . . . a *clone*," she nearly whispered the last word, leaning forward as though telling him a secret.

"I dunno," Javi said. "I've never been anything else."

"Sorry." She blushed, and it was a beautiful thing to behold. "I didn't mean to offend you or anything, I've just always been curious."

"I'm not offended," Javi said, amazed that she'd ever spared him enough thought to be curious. "I guess it's pretty normal most of the time. Sometimes it's weird when I think too much about my original."

"Your original," she repeated as though trying out the words and finding them as strange as Javi sometimes did.

"Yeah," Javi said. "His name was Javier Vasquez too."

Stella nodded, and it occurred to Javi that she probably already knew that. His story was hardly a secret and had been written about extensively for anyone who cared to search for the information. Herman had told him there was even a whole wikipedia article, although Javi hadn't been able to bring himself to read it.

"Do you ever wish you weren't one?" Stella asked.

Javi shrugged. "More when I was younger than now. I don't really think about it all that much anymore." *Liar,* his subconscious whispered. He pushed the thought aside.

She nodded again like she understood, although of course she couldn't have. Javi didn't care though. He thought he'd explode with happiness that Stella Castell wasn't merely deigning to speak to him, she was actually asking him questions, was interested in him. Not *interested* interested, but still. She found him worthy of her curiosity, and that was more than Javi had dared hope for.

"What about you?" Javi asked.

"What about me?" she repeated, eyebrows raised.

He felt his cheeks heat up but forced himself to continue. "Got any plans for after graduation?"

The knowing look in her eyes told him she knew exactly what he was doing, that he was grasping at straws simply to keep the conversation going, but for whatever reason she didn't mock him for it or come up with an excuse to leave. She answered him.

"NYU I think," she said. "And you?"

"Georgetown," he replied without hesitation. He decided right then and there that his parents' expectations for him could fuck off. Besides, D. C. wasn't so far from New York. "But my parents want me to go to Stanford."

"How come?" Stella asked. "Georgetown is a good school."

Javi shrugged again. "It's closer to home. But mostly because that's where *he* wanted to go. My original." Javi didn't know why he was confiding this in her.

Her eyes widened slightly but she didn't say anything for a moment. Just as he was cursing himself for making her feel awkward and ruining everything she said, "Have you started studying for our Chinese midterm yet?"

"N-no, not really," Javi stammered, thrown by the abrupt change of topic.

"Me neither," Stella said. "We should study together sometime. I'm still not very good at differentiating all the tones."

"Neither am I," Javi admitted. "But maybe it'd be easier practicing with someone else." His heart was hammering and his hands sweating as he handed her his phone to put her number in. When she'd finished she smiled at him.

"I've gotta get back. My boyfriend Kato is probably wondering where I disappeared to," Stella said. "Text me tomorrow and we can figure out when to meet up."

"I will," said Javi, barely concerned with her casual reference to her handsome scholar-athlete boyfriend. She wanted to study with him. Stella Castell had just given him her phone number, like it was nothing.

She threw one more dazzling smile his way then turned to leave the kitchen. He watched her go, eyes roving up and down her long, toned legs and the perfect curve of her ass. The room seemed dimmer when she was gone. Javi closed his eyes for a moment and took a deep breath to suppress the urge to jump up and down and whoop. He didn't stop grinning for the rest of the night.

12: EDGAR PRIME

It had been the best night of his life, but the hangover the next morning was awful. He dreamed he was inside a bell tower that was being rung over and over again until he realized that the noise was just his phone on the floor next to him. It sounded unnaturally loud and he winced as he reached for it, feeling like his head was being split open by a giant with a hammer and chisel.

Patrice Zhao's name lit up on his screen as the phone continued to ring, and he answered it with an aggravated swipe of his finger, letting his head fall back onto his pillow with a groan.

"Edgar Prime?" came Patrice's concerned voice on the other line. "Is something wrong?"

Edgar Prime bit back a scathing remark about how robotic she always sounded when she spoke to him. It wouldn't do to offend Dr. Midas's favorite research fellow.

"I go by 'Ed' now," Edgar Prime said through gritted teeth.

"All right, I'll make a note of that, Ed," said Patrice, unflappably professional as ever.

"I don't want to be rude Patrice, but why are you calling so early?" Edgar Prime asked.

Patrice snorted. "You should be thanking me. You have class in thirty minutes."

"I don't have class 'til 9:15," muttered Edgar Prime. There was no way it could be 8:45 already, was there?

"Up and at 'em," Patrice said. She seemed to be enjoying this.

Edgar Prime sat up and stifled another groan. "Thanks for

the wakeup call, Patrice. Gotta go."

He took the phone away from his ear and hung up even though he could still hear Patrice talking. Knowing she'd call again, Edgar Prime switched his phone to silent and stood up too quickly, fighting off a wave of dizziness. After standing still for a moment, he stumbled down the hall towards the bathroom.

Stepping out of a hot shower a few minutes later, Edgar Prime felt marginally more alert, but it did nothing to calm the throbbing in his head. As he pulled on a pair of jeans and a t-shirt, his phone blinked insistently from where he'd tossed it on his bed, informing him that Patrice had called again and left him a voicemail.

Snatching up the phone and swinging his backpack over his shoulder, Edgar Prime shoved his feet into a pair of flip-flops and left the room, hoping his professor wouldn't notice as he slipped into class late. Edgar Prime listened to Patrice's voice-mail as he strode purposefully across campus, each step accompanied by a surge of pain radiating through his head.

"Hi *Ed*, it's Patrice. You hung up before I could remind you that Dr. Midas is taking you to Zurich next week to present at the International Congress of Genetics, so make sure you tell your professors that you'll have to miss your classes during that time. I've emailed you the itinerary, but please call if you have any questions." A beep signaled the end of the message.

Edgar Prime stuffed his phone into his bag and suppressed yet another groan. This would be the third time Dr. Midas dragged him along to be presented at the International Congress of Genetics. For all the promises about it being a spectacular learning experience and an honor for Edgar Prime to attend, he knew the truth: he was little more than walking, talking evidence of the genius behind Dr. Midas's greatest experiment. The only thing Edgar Prime could honestly say he liked about the I.C.G. was that it only convened once every five years.

With this gloomy reminder hanging over his head, Edgar

Prime slowly pulled open the door to his Elements of Political Theory lecture, which had only just begun. He took care to close the door quietly, the shuffled along the last row and slid into an empty seat as Professor Richards said in a ringing voice, "Thomas Hobbes described the life of man as 'solitary, poor, nasty, brutish, and short'. Cheerful guy, wasn't he?"

A few students chuckled, and Edgar Prime smiled in spite of himself. Professor Richards was a pale, thin man with sandy blonde hair, but despite his unassuming looks he still managed to captivate every last one of the fifty students in his class. He was somehow charismatic enough to make Elements of Political Theory seem sexy. Several girls in the front row were hanging onto his every word, occasionally whispering things to each other that Edgar Prime felt certain they'd be mortified for their professor to hear.

Edgar Prime took dutiful notes on *Leviathan* for the next 75 minutes although he'd have preferred to put his head down on the desk for a nap — he'd only gotten a few hours of sleep the night before after all, and his hangover was worse than ever. Still, he knew that in a less mentally-foggy state he'd enjoy reading more about Hobbes, who he thought must have been the king of all pessimists.

When the class was dismissed, Edgar Prime sighed and gathered up his books before trudging to the front of the room to speak with Professor Richards about having to miss the following week for the I.C.G.

"I understand," Professor Richards said after Edgar Prime had explained the situation. "It sounds like a great honor to be invited."

"I suppose," Edgar Prime muttered, looking down at his feet. He'd just as soon be spared the *honor* and the curiosity.

Edgar Prime glanced up to see Professor Richards giving him a knowing look. "It must be strange for people to be so interested in you for something you didn't ask for or do yourself," he said.

"Yeah," Edgar Prime said. "It's — well, there are a lot of

expectations."

Professor Richards nodded sympathetically.

"Send me an email reminder and I'll give you the slides for next week," Professor Richards said, back to business. "When you get back you can come to my office hours to go over anything you'd like to talk more about. And try to find some time to enjoy Zurich while you're there. It's a beautiful city."

Edgar Prime gave him a small smile. "I will. Thank you."

Professor Richards gave him another amiable nod, and Edgar Prime left the classroom. He made his way to the student-run coffee shop on the ground floor of the building, deciding he needed to get a coffee before his Linear Algebra lecture if he was to have even the slightest hope of staying awake.

While in line, Edgar Prime allowed his thoughts to drift back to the night before. He hadn't realized how much he was missing out on before, but seeing how Blake, George, Celeste, and Hugo interacted with each other made him long for that sort of companionship as well. Of course, they'd all welcomed him into their group but he knew it was most likely short-lived. He didn't deceive himself — at best they were taken with the novelty of spending a night drinking with the first-ever human clone. He knew it was only a matter of time before that novelty wore off.

There had been times while they were all dancing and sweating that Edgar Prime had longed to press Hugo's long, lean body against the wall and kiss him, but he didn't dare. He did not want to face Hugo's inevitable rejection and pity.

"You look like you've seen better days," said a voice off to his right, making Edgar Prime jump. He turned to see Celeste looking statuesque and not at all like someone who had been up 'til 3:00am that morning.

"Yeah," Edgar Prime said. "How is it you look so good? You were up as late as me last night."

Celeste grinned. "Don't tell anyone, but I'm actually a robot. No sleep required."

Edgar Prime snorted at the joke. "Your secret is safe with

me."

"You'd think they'd have made it so you wouldn't need as much sleep as the rest of us when they engineered you," Celeste said. "Then instead of a copy you could be Dr. Edgar Midas 2.0 — the new and improved version. I guess you don't have a Ph. D. yet so maybe we'd have to lose the 'Dr.' part of that..."

"Right," Edgar Prime said. Even though he usually didn't like when people compared him to his original, Dr. Midas, Edgar Prime liked how Celeste mentioned the fact that he was a clone casually, so unlike the awkwardness or the clinical curiosity he usually encountered from people when they broached the subject with him. Her teasing felt comfortable, and he realized it was like the way she spoke to her other friends. *Does this mean we're friends?* Edgar Prime wondered.

"Sorry, am I not supposed to joke about that?" Celeste asked.

"No, it's fine," Edgar Prime said. "I — it's refreshing to hear someone talk about it like it's not a big deal."

"You can always count on me for that," Celeste said. "I never take anything seriously. It drives my parents crazy."

Edgar Prime smiled at that, but it also jogged a fuzzy memory from the night before, of Celeste leaning in and saying to him in a conspiratorial voice, "Hugo likes you, you know." Had she meant that seriously, or was it another joke? Edgar Prime told himself it didn't matter either way, it wasn't like he was going to ruin things now by asking her. She'd probably laugh in his face if he did.

Oblivious to the questions that churned through Edgar Prime's mind, Celeste had begun recounting the story of how she'd overheard Blake and George's awkward drunken hook up through the wall the previous night. Edgar Prime laughed along with her, almost forgetting his exhaustion and the now-dull pain beneath his skull. He told himself firmly that this newfound camaraderie was more important than pursuing something that was surely hopeless with Hugo. It would be best for him to forget all about it. It wasn't a big deal. He was only nineteen after all, he'd meet someone else before long and forget he ever felt anything beyond a platonic fondness towards Hugo. Laughing by Celeste's side at that moment, Edgar Prime almost believed his own lie.

13: ANNABEL

She awoke the next morning naked and sticky with arms squeezing her and something hard pressing into her upper thigh. It took her a few seconds to realize where she was and why she felt a strange aching soreness in her pelvic region. Then the events of the previous day came back to her, and she had to resist the urge to scream. The arms around her tightened a bit, trapping her even more securely in their embrace. Rex's arousal poked her leg more insistently, and his hands began caressing her gently.

With a sigh, Annabel rolled over and allowed him to insert himself inside her again with a grunt and a moan in her ear. It was still painful, but over more quickly this time. Almost as soon as he was done Annabel crawled to the edge of the bed and stood up, not wishing to be ensnared in his arms once again.

"Good morning, my love," murmured Rex.

"Good morning," Annabel forced herself to say, before grabbing her robe and taking refuge in the bathroom.

Rex's things had been moved into the house during the wedding, and Annabel found it strange to see foreign objects like a man's razor, deodorant and toothbrush in her bathroom. He had told her the previous afternoon — apologizing profusely — that the movers had put most of his boxes into the large empty room she used for yoga and meditation. She had lied and said she didn't mind, but the idea that *he* had taken over her small sanctuary twisted inside her like a knife.

Annabel realized she'd been staring at her pale face in the bathroom mirror lost in thought for twenty minutes when she heard a soft knock on the door.

"Annabel my love," came Rex's voice, slightly muffled through the door. "Are you all right?"

"I'm fine," she heard herself say; another lie. "I'll be out in a minute."

Quickly, Annabel commenced brushing her teeth and showering. She made the water as hot as she could stand, and rinsed the dried blood from between her thighs with a wince. She suspected there was a stain on the sheet as well for Mrs. Lennox to scrub out; the thought made her blush. When she stepped out of the shower, she glanced at the foggy mirror once more before she left the bathroom. Everything had changed in the last twenty-four hours, but her face looked the same as always.

When Annabel returned, Rex was mercifully absent from the bedroom. He'd opened the curtains to let in the gentle morning sunshine. Even though it was cold, Annabel threw open the windows to let in the sea breeze. The bed drew Annabel's eye, and she saw that it had already been stripped and remade. The room was all wood beams and white linens, with tall bookshelves along one wall and seashells artfully arranged at the end of each level. As with everything else this morning, it was simultaneously familiar and alien.

Annabel had to force herself to leave the tainted serenity of the bedroom. She arrived downstairs just in time to see dowdy Mrs. Lennox laying plates of food on the table for their breakfast.

"Good morning, Annabel," Mrs. Lennox said as she poured Rex a cup of coffee.

"Good morning, Mrs. Lennox," Annabel said. She felt embarrassed that the older woman had seen her bloody sheet, but Mrs. Lennox behaved with the same detached professionalism as always. She poured Annabel's coffee, and then retreated back into the kitchen, her short black hair sticking up at odd angles as though she'd run her fingers through it too many times.

"I had Mrs. Lennox make your favorite," Rex informed Annabel as she sat down in the chair to his right — he was seated at the end of the long dining table. He smiled an incandescent smile and she returned it, hoping that her happy wife facade would become easier to maintain over time. Looking at the table she saw a much more elaborate spread than usual: eggs scrambled with fresh parsley, cilantro, and green onions, chestnut flour muffins with homemade lemon curd, and a bowl of the reddest cherries Annabel had ever seen.

Rex served them both a generous portion of everything, and they began to eat in what Annabel supposed could be described as a companionable silence.

"I'm going to have to do a few hours of work after breakfast," Rex said with an apologetic note in his voice. "But I thought we could go for a walk on the beach this afternoon."

"That sounds good," Annabel said with more enthusiasm than she felt. Still, at least she'd have the rest of the morning to herself. Once their plates were clean Rex kissed Annabel and went off to his study on the ground floor. Annabel drifted out to the balcony to watch the waves crash against the shore. For the first time, she felt sympathy for the rocks.

After a while Annabel decided to investigate the state of her meditation room in the hopes that there would be a small corner of bare floor she could use for her yoga practice. When she reached the third floor of the house she was pleased to find that there was still enough space for her to lay out her mat, and spent the next hour and a half working herself into a sweat with one sun salutation after another while striving to empty her mind of anything but the present. This proved more difficult than usual, and when Annabel finally lay back in the corpse pose *savasana*, her mind felt as frantic as ever.

From her place on the floor, she noticed that none of the boxes were taped shut. She sat up slowly, ignoring the dull ache in her muscles that always accompanied a good workout, and crawled over to the nearest box.

Without thinking too much about it, Annabel opened it up

and began rummaging inside. Her vague intention was to discover more about this stranger who was now her husband. In the first box, she found nothing but clothes. They all appeared well-made and she recognized some expensive labels. Someone had meticulously folded them all and arranged them according to color. Annabel wondered whether it had been Rex.

Careful to put them back as she'd found them, Annabel moved on to another box. This one was full of books. Almost against her will, Annabel smiled. New paper books were something of a luxury but there were plenty of old ones to be had, ones printed before the conservation laws had been passed heavily taxing the use of trees for such things. There was something romantic about old paper books, even if they couldn't compete anymore with the vast virtual libraries that existed.

Growing up, Ms. Durant had given Annabel access to all of the books owned by her original, and they took up most of the shelves in the master bedroom. The original Annabel had loved authors like Jane Austen, the Bronte sisters, and Charles Dickens. She seemed to have collected nearly everything they'd ever published. Annabel liked them well enough, but her favorite was a small book she'd found on the lowest shelf in the corner, almost out of sight. It was called *Mother Night* and had been written many years ago by Kurt Vonnegut. She found the story of the man pretending to be someone else profoundly moving, and had read it so many times she'd practically memorized it.

Based on the contents of the second box, Rex liked a completely different sort of book; most of the ones he owned were spy thrillers. Annabel ran her fingers over the spines of the complete works of Ian Fleming, Barry Eisler and John le Carré. She wondered whether there were more books in the other boxes, and after resealing the second box she opened a third to see.

This box contained what seemed to Annabel to be random odds and ends. She found a couple of small, black and white abstract paintings carefully wrapped in soft cloth to protect them, tennis equipment, a small collection of signed baseballs each in its own hard plastic case, and a metal box with a handle on one side about a foot-and-a-half by a foot long. She picked up the gleaming box, and placed it carefully on the floor in front of her. It was heavy; much heavier than she'd expect based on its dimensions. The box was sealed with a metal clasp on either side of the handle, and she undid each one with a click. Annabel looked around, suddenly wary and feeling as though she was snooping where she shouldn't, but she was completely alone and after all, she had a right to know more about the man who she had married. She dismissed the feeling, and slowly opened the box.

Nestled inside black foam was a pistol. Annabel just stared at it for a moment. She'd never seen a real gun before — she'd seen plenty of them on the crime shows that Ms. Durant liked to watch in the evenings, but never in person. Her heart beat faster as she reached out an unsteady hand to pick it up, wanting to feel what it was like to hold it. As she lifted it from its foam bed, she was startled again that something so small could be so heavy. There were three empty magazines in the foam indents alongside it, and underneath there was a cardboard box full of bullets. She picked one up to read the small .45 engraved on its base.

Annabel was gripped with a strong desire to know what it felt like to point this gun at something and fire it. She wondered whether it would make her feel powerful and if it did, whether that would just be another illusion. Deciding it would be best to pretend she hadn't looked though Rex's things, she carefully replaced the gun where she'd found it before resealing the cardboard box.

Later in the shower, Annabel pondered how much of a person is revealed by the things they owned. And if a person *could* be understood in such a way, what conclusions could she draw about the man who was now her husband? She came up with no answer, but continued to wonder for the remainder of the day— when she walked along the beach hand in hand with Rex, when they ate dinner, when they watched an old movie. When she lay on her back later in the dark as he plunged into her and moaned in her ear.

Afterward, Annabel tried to ignore the pressing arms around her, stifling her movement and holding her in place. Much as she wished for unconsciousness, sleep was once again elusive, but not for Rex who had begun to snore almost the moment he finished. Annabel stared at the ceiling, hoping she'd one day have the courage to elbow him away from her in bed so that she might be able to shift around more comfortably. *Such a modest fantasy*, she thought to herself. *How small your hopes and dreams have become.* Finally after a long while, she managed to fall into a fitful sleep.

14: JAVI

Monday morning brought with it the daily grind of school. Fred picked him up at 8:15 as usual, and Javi spent the remainder of the short drive being interrogated yet again about his conversation with Stella Castell.

"D'you think if you and Stella start dating she'll set me up with one of her friends?" Herman asked.

"Shut the fuck up, Herman," Javi snapped. "We're just studying together she's still dating Kato Barre."

"For now," Herman said slyly. "I still don't know how you managed to get her to voluntarily agree to spend time with you at all. Maybe you're secretly a wizard."

Javi grinned in spite of himself. He was just as stunned as Herman was that Stella had not only suggested studying together that night at the party, but had confirmed the idea the following afternoon when he finally worked up the courage to text her. He spent twenty minutes trying to phrase it just right and had fully expected her to ignore the text or else respond with an excuse about being too busy. To his astonishment, she simply proposed meeting Monday afternoon in the park. He couldn't have come up with a more perfect plan for their first date if he'd tried.

He knew of course that it wasn't *really* a date, but it was still probably the closest he'd ever come to one with Stella. He spent most of the day vacillating between indulging in wild fantasies and sternly reminding himself that if he acted overly eager Stella would probably be put off. It didn't help that Herman seemed unable to prevent himself from recounting in graphic detail every single porno he'd ever seen involving two people who had met up to "study" and wound up fucking instead.

Fred smirked and chuckled at this, but didn't comment. Aside from telling them that he and Violet had "a nice time" on Saturday night he hadn't given any other details. Herman speculated often and loudly that Fred had lost his virginity that night but promised Violet he wouldn't tell anyone. If it was true (and Javi wouldn't be surprised if it was) then Fred was the first of them to reach that particular milestone. Fred just gave them a knowing smile when Herman floated this theory by him. Javi was torn between jealousy and awe. How did it even happen? He wanted Fred to tell them his secret.

Aside from a cursory greeting, Stella didn't speak to him in their Chinese class, causing Javi to worry she'd changed her mind. When the bell rang, however, she smiled and said, "See you later," on her way out. Javi didn't have time to reply with more than, "Yeah," and mentally kicked himself afterwards for being so awkward.

When the three o'clock bell rang, Javi found Fred and Herman waiting at his locker.

"What are you two doing?" Javi asked, suspicious at the smug looks both of them wore.

"That's not a very nice way to thank the people who are about to give you a ride to the park for your date with Stella," chastised Herman.

"Shh!" Javi hissed. He looked around but fortunately nobody was paying them any attention. He glared at Herman; the last thing he needed was for Stella to hear he'd told people they were dating.

"Don't be so paranoid, Romeo," Herman said with a grin.

"I don't need a ride," Javi said. "I was gonna take the bus."

"Nonsense," Fred said. His expression shifted to sympathetic. "It's on the way. And you don't want to be late, I doubt Stella would wait for you if you were."

"Fine," Javi conceded. He pulled a few things out of the locker and slammed it shut. The three of them started walking towards the parking lot.

"Nervous?" Fred asked.

Javi didn't answer for a moment but then nodded stiffly.

"I don't blame you," Herman said. "It's a lose-lose situation really. Either you make a fool of yourself and Stella tells everyone or you don't and Kato Barre beats you up for trying to steal his girlfriend. One way or another, your imminent future sucks, doesn't it?"

Javi scowled at Herman as they reached Fred's car, but didn't deign to respond. As soon as Fred pulled out of the parking lot, Herman started up again.

"Just tell us, Fred. Did you bang Violet, or not?" he asked.

Fred glanced at him in the mirror with what Javi knew was supposed to be a frown but looked more like a badly concealed smile. Grateful for the distraction from the roiling sensation in his stomach, Javi joined in.

"Come on, Fred. *Something* must have happened. Blowjob? Handjob? Did you at least get to see her tits?" Javi said.

There was a pause — Javi and Herman waited with bated breath.

"Okay, fine. We had sex," Fred said in a would-be casual voice.

Herman and Javi both whooped and Fred started laughing even as his face turned red. Javi had never seen Fred look so pleased with himself, but he supposed if ever there was a time to feel self-satisfied it was when you lost your virginity to a pretty girl.

"What was it like?" Javi asked.

Fred gave him a sly look. "Whatever you think it's gonna be like, it's a thousand times better."

Herman laughed uproariously at that and thumped Fred on the back. Fred swatted his hand away and added, " We're gonna hang out again at Violet's place tomorrow after school. Her parents don't get home 'til 7 or 8 usually."

"Wow," Javi said, awed. The prospect of having sex even once seemed unbearably daunting, and Fred was already going to do it again.

"Who'd have thought scrawny Indian kids were Violet's type?" Herman said, still laughing. "You whip out some Kama Sutra tricks for her or something?"

"Shut up about her, Herman," Fred said and this time he really did scowl. "She's — I really like her. We're not like official or anything yet, but maybe . . ."

He trailed off with a pensive expression on his face. Javi exchanged a shrug with Herman and they drove on in silence. They reached the park fifteen minutes before Javi was supposed to meet Stella. Javi felt his palms start to sweat when Fred and Herman drove off. He wiped them on his jeans and started towards the weeping willow where they usually hung out. He texted Stella telling her where he was and saying he could meet her anywhere she wanted.

He spent the next ten minutes staring at his phone, but she didn't reply. It was making him increasingly tense, and he had just managed to convince himself that she had changed her mind and decided to stand him up when she appeared, pulling aside two of the hanging branches and stepping under the shady curtain towards him.

Javi sprang to his feet, nearly hitting his head on one of the lower branches, and Stella smiled at him but not in a mocking way. "Hi," he said. "D'you want to stay here to study or should we go to the picnic tables by the lake? Or anywhere — whatever you want is good." He almost cringed at how eager he sounded.

"This is perfect," Stella said. Behind her the leaves swayed gently back and forth and she approached him and sat down on the grass near the trunk of the tree. Javi sat down next to her, but not too close. He didn't want to push his luck. Stella pulled her tablet out of her bag and opened a pdf of her class notes. Hastening to mimic her, Javi snatched up his laptop and pulled up his own notes and the exam study guide.

"Where should we start?" Stella asked.

"Anywhere —" Javi cleared his throat nervously. He had to

stop sounding so pathetically worshipful. "Or — or maybe we should just go through the guide from the beginning?"

"Sure," Stella said, oblivious to Javi's self-consciousness. He supposed she must be used to it — probably a day didn't pass without some guy making a fool of himself as he struggled to impress her.

Throat dry, Javi read out the first section of their study guide, and from then on it became slightly easier to talk to Stella without worrying that he might humiliate himself with an uncontrollable boner or an accidental confession of love. For the next two hours, they took turns quizzing each other and discussing particularly challenging translations. Javi barely dared think it, but it seemed to him when they reached the end of the guide that things had actually gone well.

Stella seemed in no hurry to depart, however, and Javi took his cue from her and dawdled in packing up his things.

"I think we'll be fine," Javi was saying. "At least it'll be over in a couple days. I hate exams."

"Oh!" Stella said suddenly, making Javi jump. "There's something I wanted to show you, I almost forgot." It seemed she hadn't been paying much attention to what he'd just been talking about, but Javi didn't care. She typed something into her tablet then handed it to Javi. It was a blog article entitled, "INTERNATIONAL CONGRESS OF GENETICS TO CONVENE IN ZURICH". He glanced questioningly at Stella, and she read his hesitation correctly.

"The article says Dr. Edgar Midas — the father of human cloning — is going to be one of the keynote speakers," she explained. "Do you know him?"

Javi gave a short laugh, slightly bewildered. "Never met him."

"But he's the one who made you, isn't he?" Stella pressed.

"I guess," Javi said. He really didn't like to think about how or why he was 'made'. Not that he ever managed to forget for long.

"I'm sorry, I know I keep bringing this clone thing up, you're probably tired of it. I'm just — I kind of like science and lately I've been thinking a lot about the ethics of things like cloning, robotics . . . technology in general really. Sorry, I'm sure you don't want to hear about that kind of stuff." She looked down at her lap and actually blushed.

Javi was so floored that she thought there was anything she could say that he wouldn't be interested in that it took him a moment before he said, "No, it's fine. You're right, that is interesting. I guess I never thought of it that way. Maybe I should go meet him someday, this Dr. Midas."

He was almost ashamed to admit it to himself, but he'd never thought of Stella as being a person with actual *interests*. She'd always been more of a concept, a Platonic Form to be admired from afar but never truly known or understood. Not that he understood her now, of course. But he was just beginning to come to terms with the idea that she might have a lot more depth than he had ever imagined.

She had already begun speaking again, much more freely and enthusiastically than before, and Javi hastened to listen so she wouldn't think he was another one of the many guys who only cared about her looks.

"And really, there's the whole question of ownership too — somebody is paying a lot of money for a clone to be made, but you can't *own* a human. It's kind of strange when you think about it. A pretty risky investment," Stella said.

"Yeah," Javi said, slightly uncomfortable again. This was always something that had bothered him about his parents. Growing up he had wondered more than once if they regretted spending so much money on his creation, when no matter how hard he tried he couldn't live up to the memories of their original son.

"Have you ever met another clone?" Stella asked.

"No," Javi said. "Or at least, not that I know of. But I guess it's possible. It's not like we walk around with the word 'CLONE' tattooed on our foreheads."

Clone

Stella laughed at that, a musical sound that made Javi want to laugh too out of sheer joy.

"Of course," she said. "I mean, I'd never have known you were a clone if we just met on the street. The fact that they can do that is pretty miraculous. The scientists, I mean."

"It's not the easiest thing to step into though," Javi said without thinking.

"What d'you mean?" Stella asked.

"Oh I dunno," Javi said, wishing he hadn't spoken. "It's just — I'm sure you've heard the story of why my parents commissioned me."

"Yeah," Stella said, and a faint crease appeared between her eyebrows, like he'd brought her attention to something that had never occurred to her before. "How old were you when you found out?"

Javi shrugged. "I must've been really young, because I can't remember anyone actually telling me. So it's like I've always known. I dunno if that's better or worse than finding out later." He tried his hardest not to sound bitter, but wasn't sure he succeeded.

For a moment, Stella just looked at him. Then she rummaged through her bag and pulled out a small baggie with several joints and a lighter. Javi raised his eyebrows, not sure why he was surprised.

"D'you smoke?" she asked, opening the baggie and putting one of the joints between her perfect pink lips. Javi nodded, unable to tear his gaze away from her mouth. All of the dark thoughts he'd been pondering fled in an instant, and he was transported to a world where he was a regular person, sitting under a tree with the girl he liked sharing a joint. This would probably be the best afternoon of his entire life, and he didn't want to waste it brooding.

Stella lit the joint and took a long draw, then passed it to Javi. Her lip gloss had left a mark on the light brown paper and Javi covered the same spot with his own lips as he inhaled the smoke. He couldn't wait to see the look on Herman's face when he heard about this.

15: EDGAR PRIME

"Come on, Prime, you need to focus if we're going to get through this before we leave for Zurich tomorrow," Dr. Midas drawled.

"How do you know I'm not focusing?" Edgar Prime asked through gritted teeth. He had an itch above his left ear, but the EEG sensors glued to his head prevented him from scratching it. Dr. Midas raised an eyebrow while Patrice reset the experiment without comment and waited dutifully for Dr. Midas to begin again.

Dr. Midas picked up the white pawn and moved it forward two spaces while Patrice clicked a timer and began typing notes into her laptop. As with most of his experiments, Dr. Midas hadn't bothered to explain to Edgar Prime what he hoped to learn from their chess match. In truth, Edgar Prime had been holding back. No matter what he said, Edgar Prime knew Dr. Midas hated losing. Edgar Prime sighed and moved one of his knights. Patrice clicked the timer again.

"Aggressive," Dr. Midas commented. Edgar Prime shrugged. Dr. Midas clicked his tongue and made his next move. Edgar Prime tried to ignore the sound of Patrice's frantic typing and the clicking of the timer whenever one of them moved. For the next fifteen minutes they played in silence, until Edgar Prime maneuvered himself in a position to take Dr. Midas's queen. The older man stared at the board with a furrowed brow then after a few moments he smiled grimly.

"I knew you had it in you, Prime," Dr. Midas said. He moved to take one of Edgar Prime's pawns after ascertaining that nothing could be done to save the queen.

"I go by Ed now," Edgar Prime said as he took the white queen with one of his knights.

Dr. Midas burst out laughing. "I always hated people calling me 'Ed'." He moved one of his bishops to take Edgar Prime's knight.

Edgar Prime shrugged again. He had long ago learned it was often better to make a neutral gesture for Dr. Midas to interpret than it was to try to explain himself. He was equally likely to be misunderstood either way, and shrugging took less effort.

"Ed," said Dr. Midas, enunciating as though testing out the sound of the word. He wrinkled his nose. "No, I can't call you Ed. Too strange. It's like I'm talking to myself but using my least favorite nickname. No, you'll always be Prime to me." He gave Edgar Prime what was clearly supposed to be an affectionate smile.

"Checkmate," announced Edgar Prime, moving his castle into position. He kept his face blank, but inside he was scowling. Dr. Midas threw his hands up theatrically, but he was unaccountably pleased despite his loss.

"Very impressive, Prime. I can't wait to show you off at the International Congress of Genetics. This will be an exceptional year, I think." He looked at Edgar Prime expectantly, as though waiting to be asked why. Edgar Prime did not indulge him, instead stooping to pick up his backpack.

"Are we done?" he asked. "I've got a lot of homework. I'm trying to get ahead since I'll be missing this week."

"Of course," Dr. Midas said. He looked slightly bemused, and Edgar Prime knew when he left Dr. Midas would confer with Patrice to brainstorm possible causes of his moodiness. "A car will pick you up at half past four tomorrow morning. Be sure to pack that suit I got you."

"I know," Edgar Prime said wearily. It wasn't as though this was the first I.C.G. Dr. Midas had dragged him to. Patrice began unsticking the EEG sensors from his head.

"Good luck with your work," Patrice said. Edgar Prime

glanced up at her in surprise. She usually didn't say anything at all to him, and when she did it was only to do with whatever experiment Dr. Midas was running at the time.

"Thanks," Edgar Prime said, eyeing her with vague suspicion. It felt strange for her to speak to him as a person rather than an experimental subject. "Good luck with . . . whatever you're working on too." It was only an empty courtesy to him, but she seemed appreciative nonetheless. He supposed praise might be hard to come by working for Dr. Midas.

"Thanks Ed," Patrice said, giving him a small smile. Edgar Prime only just managed not to drop his jaw in shock. She removed the remainder of the sensors in silence. Edgar Prime stood up and stretched, rubbing at some remaining stickiness behind his left ear. He nodded to Patrice and Dr. Midas in farewell, and left the lab to get back to his dorm.

The sun was low in the sky when Edgar Prime reached the street. He noticed three protestors holding signs and marching back and forth in front of the building. Two of them were women, each holding signs with anti-cloning slogans. Their hair was tangled and down to their waist. The third protestor was a man with a thick, bushy beard. Their clothes were all earth tones, loose-fitting garments that Edgar Prime suspected were deliberately mismatched to recall the hippie styles of the 1960s.

He watched them for a few seconds — none of their signs were particularly witty or original — then turned in the direction of campus. A shout stopped him and he looked back towards the protestors. One of the women with dirty blonde hair and skirts that brushed the sidewalk was pointing at him.

"There he is! The first clone, copy of the man who made it all possible," she called. A few of the passerby glanced in his direction, but nobody stopped or said anything else. "Come join us, unnatural test tube creature. Surely you want to save others from your fate."

Edgar Prime turned around and headed back towards campus. Behind him, the woman continued to shout.

"You can walk and talk and think and dream, but you'll never be one of us! You're the canary in the coal mine, Edgar Prime. Even your name is sinister."

Edgar Prime hunched his shoulders and shook his head, even though nobody was paying him much attention. The woman's rant became unintelligible, and soon he couldn't hear it anymore at all.

16: MIRA

The cockroach scuttled out from underneath the refrigerator, startling Mira so much she gasped and dropped the mug of coffee she'd just poured, splashing the expensive mahogany cabinets, the marble floor, and her shoes.

"Fuck," Mira muttered, as the thing darted back underneath the fridge before she had time to do more than look around wildly for something to kill it with (preferably something with a long handle so she wouldn't have to get too close). She cursed herself for not having the stomach to leap over and smash it with her shoe — she hated the crunch they made and the way the guts would later have to be scraped off. The very thought made Mira shudder.

"Fuck," Mira said again. She dialed the exterminator, and supposed she should consider herself lucky that she'd been the one to find the roach instead of her boss. If Harlow had seen it, she'd likely be out of a job. After offering the exterminator double his usual rate to come later that afternoon, she grabbed a handful of paper towels and crouched down to clean up the spilled coffee. She was more jittery than usual and kept whipping her head around when she thought she saw something move in her peripheral vision. When she finished she left quickly, not even bothering to refill her coffee mug. Even here, in a multimillion dollar high-rise office building, they weren't immune to vermin.

Back at her desk, Mira hastily added "Exterminator" to her calendar, although she doubted Harlow would notice either way. She'd only been working as his assistant for just under three weeks, but he rarely checked up on her — he just expected things to be done.

She spent the remainder of the day running his errands and finalizing his meetings for the following week. Towards the end of the day, a dull throbbing pain had developed at her temples and the base of her skull. Her computer screen seemed too bright even on its dimmest setting. She was just about to pick up the phone to confirm Harlow's restaurant reservation for a dinner that evening, when a voice behind her made her jump.

"You'll get a hunchback leaning over the computer like that, Miss Behzad," Harlow said.

"You startled me," Mira told him unnecessarily.

Harlow grinned. "Apologies."

Mira waited. When Harlow wanted something, he didn't need prompting. And if he had just stopped by to chat, she didn't want to encourage him.

"You know, you really should smile more." Harlow told her. Mira barely managed to stop herself from rolling her eyes at that. Instead she gave him a smile, as though his comment was flattering rather than annoying as hell.

"There, now! That's better. You're much prettier when you smile." Mira heard an echo of her mother in that sentiment, and had to fight the urge to throw her empty coffee mug at Harlow's back when he turned away to head towards the elevators. Once he'd rounded a corner, the smile slid off Mira's face. While harmless, Harlow's regular comments about her looks rankled. She supposed she was pretty enough; short black hair, brown skin, a nice smile. *It took two years of braces to get that smile. You earned it.* Perhaps she was a bit more muscular than some men liked, but she didn't care, she had more important things to worry about. Inside her head, a voice that sounded suspiciously like her mother began to protest that thought loudly, but Mira pushed it away and started packing her things up for the day.

After waiting another ten minutes — she didn't want to run into Harlow by the elevators or in the lobby — Mira took her leave. As she passed by the kitchen, she saw the exterminator on his knees, strategically placing glue and poisons in various crevices. She willed herself not to shudder again, and made her way outside.

Mira glanced up and down Park Avenue, taking in the usual bustle of Upper East Side rush hour. She set off towards the 59th St - Lexington Ave subway station, and took the 6 train to Canal Street while keeping a careful eye on those around her. She walked the rest of the way to a boarded-up storefront on Mott Street in Chinatown. The entrance was covered by a sign that read "Closed For Renovations", but Mira ignored it and slipped inside. The space had a cramped feel: two low-ceilinged windowless rooms connected by a doorframe with no door.

Three people were seated at a large rectangular table working on laptops when she entered.

"You're late," Jack Sterling informed her. "He's been antsy for the last couple of hours."

"I can hear you!" bellowed Warren Watson from the second room. "Don't test me, Sterling!"

Liesel Warner stifled a laugh from beside Jack. She was blonde and fair with blue eyes and dimples. *Harlow wouldn't need to ask her to smile more*, Mira thought, immediately ashamed of spitefulness. She liked Liesel, and holding her beauty against her was such a pathetic cliche.

"What did you do?" Mira asked Jack.

Jack shrugged. From Liesel's other side, John Fitzgerald leaned over and said quietly, "Apparently Jack isn't as charming as he thinks. His mark broke things off with him today. We aren't sure if it's because she made him, or if he failed to please her in... other ways."

"Fuck you, it wasn't that," Jack said, an irritable bite to his voice. John smirked. The two of them looked like they could be brothers; both had dark eyes, dark hair, and aquiline noses. John was paler than Jack and had a spray of freckles across his face, but both were handsome in their way. And Jack had the sort of deep baritone voice that could make women shiver with pleasure. *Stop that,* Mira chided herself. *Don't be stupid.*

"You'd better hope it *was* that," Liesel told him. "It'll be much worse for us if it's because she found out who you really are. That could set us back months."

Jack opened his mouth to retort but was drowned out by Warren calling, "Mira, get in here!" from his office.

Mira hastened to obey, not wanting to find herself on the receiving end of Warren's notoriously prickly temper. The second office was larger than it seemed from the outside, and Mira found Warren pacing the periphery with a feverish look in his eye. With his stocky build and gray hair, Warren looked like an aging boxer. As he paced, he ran his hands through his hair several times in quick succession.

"Where are we with Harlow?" he asked.

"Things are going well enough. He's had me out doing a lot of his random errands lately. Nothing overtly connected to the black market, but it's possible we'll get a lead from it. He doesn't suspect me at all."

"Good to know not everyone on my team is incompetent." Warren cast a sour look towards the door as though he thought Jack would be able to feel his wrath emanating through the wall. There was a pause.

"It may not have been Jack's fault. Maybe he just wasn't her type," Mira wasn't sure why she was defending Jack.

"That's no excuse," Warren grumbled. "His job was to *become* her type. Sterling is entirely too cocky. Thinks he's God's gift to women. Ha!"

Mira couldn't disagree with that, so she didn't say anything. Warren shook his head in disgust, then crossed the room and left the office. Accustomed to his taciturn moodiness, Mira followed. When Warren sat down at the head of the table, Liesel smiled at him and he appeared to soften slightly. Liesel had always been his favorite.

"Have a seat, Mira," Warren said gruffly. "Apparently Liesel and these two clowns have a report for us."

Mira sat. Jack smirked, but kept his retorts to himself. John cleared his throat, then began.

"We already knew that Harlow's multinational owns a string of shelters designed to provide care for clones that are deemed defective, either by the producer or the commissioner. These shelters are government funded, but privately owned. We also know that sometimes these clones are adopted by third parties, and we suspect this may be a cover for Harlow's black market sales. We can infer that these purchases result in everything from illegal organ sale to sex slavery. So far, we've been unable to trace any of the financial transactions associated with these clone adoptions." Warren huffed at this, and John took a deep breath before continuing. "However, Liesel has been cataloguing the details of these purchases. Many of the clones are taken overseas shortly after leaving the shelter, which makes keeping tabs on them more difficult. As with traditional human trafficking, they find themselves in a strange place, completely dependent on their captor." John paused, and turned his computer screen to show them all what looked like a passport photograph. The man was pale with black hair and distinctive bronze eyes. He appeared to be in his late twenties or early thirties. The corner of his mouth curled upwards in the tiniest ghost of a smirk.

"On paper, all the adopted clones are placed with different people. The ones from overseas flew in specifically to retrieve their clone. But when we looked at airport security footage from all the arrivals, this man showed up multiple times using different aliases." John paused, to let this sink in.

"So you're saying..." Warren frowned in concentration, and even his hostility towards Jack seemed to have been forgotten.

"He appears to act as a courier," Liesel said. "The purchase is made — we think there are darknet auctions, but we haven't been able to access them yet — then the clone needs to be transported to his or her new legal guardian. While it seems that some of them do pick up the clones themselves, others don't want to be associated with the transaction at all. So our friend here comes to get them, using a different name each time. It's likely he's not the only one fulfilling this courier function. There's a lot of data to get through, but we expect to find others who travel under multiple names as well. And this isn't even taking into account the ones who remain in the U.S."

They all digested that for a moment.

"Do we know this guy's real name?" Warren asked.

"We're working on it," Liesel said.

"The connection with Harlow himself is pretty thin," Mira said. "But it's a good start."

"I think we should pick him up," Jack said. "Let's see if we can flip him."

"And if we can't?" Mira countered. "It'll alert Harlow to the fact that his people are being investigated and he'll change up the routine."

Jack shrugged. "No reward without risk."

"Listen, cowboy," Warren said in his gravelly Texan accent, "This is the FBI, not a nursery. The director may have stuck me with you, but so help me, if you do anything reckless that blows this investigation I'll make sure you spend the rest of your career doing clerical work in the Quantico basement. Do you understand me, Sterling?" He spat the name, his distain palpable.

Jack yawned ostentatiously. Everyone knew the threat was an empty one; Jack's father had been with the bureau for over thirty years, and was a longtime friend and golf buddy to the director. Warren, on the other hand, was not. He'd made a splash early in his career for catching Paolo and Lucrezia Leone, heads of the most notorious mafia family of the twenty-first century. But that had been many years ago now, and things had taken a definite downturn for Warren since then as a result of him refusing to play the political game. Considering Warren's well-known animosity for Jack's father (rumor had it there'd been an affair with Warren's ex-wife), having Jack assigned to his task force was just the latest in a string of slights carried out by those he had offended over the years.

To add insult to injury, their operation was badly under-funded; Mira suspected that without Warren's bullheaded persistence they wouldn't be investigating the clone black market at all. The potential for political fallout was too great, success too unlikely. Warren liked to grumble that the suits had grudgingly granted him this task force after he put in dozens of requests, but gave him so little funding that he was almost certain to fail and ruin what was left of his career. Mira had always liked Warren, and had privately vowed to do everything in her power to prevent that from happening.

"Have you ever seen him, Mira?" John asked.

She thought for a moment, staring intently at the photograph. "No," she said finally. "Harlow would never have someone like that around his office. He'd want to keep that connection as invisible as possible."

Warren grunted in assent. "Given time, maybe he'll slip up and send you on an assignment that has to do with his other business, Mira. Until then, we'll watch and wait, and hope one of our other leads bears fruit." Warren turned towards Jack, with a scowl. "Let's have your report now, Casanova. What went wrong with your mark?"

Jack's mouth twisted, then he shrugged. "Her name is Deirde Kirke. She's in her fifties, wealthy. We came across her in the records as someone who'd adopted a thirteen year old clone from Harlow's shelter a couple of years ago. At the time, Deirdre's daughter was the same age, and needed a heart transplant. Her prognosis was serious, but not quite bad enough for her to top the transplant list. Shortly after the clone was adopted, the three of them spent several months in Thailand. Officially, the clone died in a car accident there. When they returned, the daughter had been miraculously cured."

Mira felt a chill go through her. All of them waited for Jack to continue.

"Deirdre likes jazz, and there are a few clubs she goes to

regularly. I approached her at one of them. She seemed interested at first, but after a few weeks she tells me out of nowhere that she can't see me anymore. I tried to ask her why, but she wouldn't explain. And that was it."

Warren harrumphed at that.

"It wasn't totally useless," Jack said defensively. "I copied the hard drive of her laptop and I cloned her phone. We might get something off one of them."

"That remains to be seen," Warren said mulishly. Mira thought he was letting his personal resentment towards Jack cloud his judgement. After all, it was entirely possible they'd find something helpful on her hard drive, something about the clone auctions or some link to Harlow. It was really the best they could hope for under the circumstances.

Mira left shortly after the meeting concluded, carrying a small bag of equipment that John had finally managed to procure for her. She thought about their poorly-funded operation — her first time going undercover. It was different than she expected; easier in some ways and harder than others. She was nearly at the subway when Jack caught up with her. When he lightly grabbed her arm she whirled around, just stopping herself from kneeing him between the legs. She mentally cursed herself for allowing him to catch her off guard. He regarded her with a smirk as she yanked her arm out of his grasp.

"You startle too easily," Jack informed her. "Gotta work on your situational awareness. Daydreaming will get you killed."

"What d'you want, Jack?" Mira was angry, but more at herself than him. She knew he was right.

Jack shrugged. "Thought you might want some company."

"Company?" she repeated, wishing the idea didn't cause her stomach to flutter pleasurably.

"Sure. Let's get a drink."

It was Mira's turn to smirk. "So you can drown your sorrows? It's gotta be rough, being rejected by a mark."

"You have no idea." Jack's voice was low, seductive. His eyes glittered in amusement, and she found herself torn between desire and annoyance. They were coworkers, it wasn't a good idea.

Mira took a step back. "Another time. I have to be up early tomorrow."

"Come on," Jack said. "You know you want to."

"Goodnight, Jack." Without waiting for an answer, Mira turned away and walked briskly towards the subway entrance. She didn't look back, and he didn't try to stop her.

When Mira arrived home to her messy, poorly lit studio apartment, she pulled some leftover Chinese takeout from the fridge and ate it while listening to the three voicemails her mother had left her from her cousin's wedding, each drunker than the last.

"Mira my dear, I can't believe you would want to miss this for some silly job, the ceremony was *beautiful*," her mother crooned. "The next time you come home, I'm going to introduce you to the son of Sylvia Nuri, my friend from the Mahjong club. She tells me he's very, very handsome, *miraculously* single, and he just started his own production company. You two would really hit it off." Mira scoffed at that. Her mother was in a state of continuous bafflement that Mira would choose to work for the FBI instead of settling down with some nice man to start a family like her older sisters all had. As far as her mother was concerned, her career was little more than a phase. Every time Mira returned to the Beverly Hills home where she'd grown up, there were several new suitors for her to meet, courtesy of her mother's friends. It was endlessly tedious, which was perhaps why Mira had not returned home in almost a year.

Deciding she could wait until tomorrow to call her mother back, Mira brushed her teeth, stripped off her clothes and fell into bed, exhausted. The next morning, Mira woke earlier than usual. She arrived at the office while it was still dark and deserted. She went straight to Harlow's office, and set about installing the small bugs John had given her throughout the room: under Harlow's desk, under his sofa, behind his filing cabinet. This part of the operation was meant to commence weeks ago, but it had taken ages for the grinding bureaucracy of the FBI to obtain the necessary warrant from a judge. When Mira finished, she went downstairs to visit the coffee shop in the lobby. She drained the last of her caramel macchiato as Harlow passed her desk with a jovial smile and a joke about how she worked too hard.

A short time later, Harlow's first meeting arrived, and Mira led him into Harlow's office. When she returned to her desk, she saw a text from Warren that read, "Nice work." The bugs were in place, and the trap was set. It was only a matter of time before Harlow blundered into it.

17: BOB

Bob was almost entirely sure the man following him was with Interpol. He'd noticed the tail half an hour ago, but hadn't bothered to shake him yet — he still had two hours before his meeting, and he figured if he was lucky his inaction would lull the man into complacency. Surveillance was dull work for the most part, and his tail looked young and was likely inexperienced.

Rome was the perfect city for losing a tail — the cobblestoned streets were an endless maze, mobbed with tourists and street vendors to run interference while he slipped away. Bob sat sipping his macchiato at an outdoor cafe near St. Peter's Basilica and pretending to read a newspaper. He noticed a pretty, olive-skinned woman at the next table eyeing him with interest, and suppressed a smile. He toyed with the idea of chatting her up — he had an easy way with women, generally — but he knew it would pique the attention of his shadow and he didn't want that. On the pretense of glancing around the square in a bored manner, Bob snuck a look at his tail. He could practically feel the waves of frustration pouring off the man — Bob suspected he'd be reckless. *Good.*

After another hour, Bob stood up lazily and made his way towards the street. He didn't have to turn around to know his shadow had mirrored his movements. He wove through the crowds expertly, until he ducked down a narrow alleyway, partially blocked by a fruit cart. he made an immediate left then right, picking up his pace. When he emerged, it was a diagonal two blocks from where he'd left the street. His tail was nowhere to be seen.

To be safe, he walked a little further, then repeated the process down a different network of alleys. This time just before he came out on the street again, he shoved his windbreaker into the fanny pack he was wearing and pulled on a baseball cap before starting a surveillance detection run. For over an hour he meandered through the streets of Rome, changing speed and direction frequently, looking for all the world like a lost American tourist.

In truth, he was indirectly making his way towards the Spanish Steps. Once he was certain he was not being followed, he approached the building where his meeting was to take place. It looked much like all the others on the cobblestone street: demure, graceful, and frozen in antiquity. He used the key he had received for this assignment, and stepped into an elegant lobby. The rickety elevator in one corner had a sign that read, "Out of Order" in Italian. Bob took the polished mahogany stairs up to the fifth floor. Without knocking, he used a second key to enter the penthouse apartment.

The inside was sleek and modern, and seemed dissonant with the baroque exterior of the building. Bob closed the door softly behind him, and made his way to the terrace where a man was waiting for him, looking out over the city. The man didn't turn around until Bob was a few feet away, but appeared entirely unsurprised at his arrival. He was younger than Bob had expected, no more than early-forties. He had black hair and a neat beard, both flecked with gray. There was something cold about his eyes.

"Bob Smith." He held out his hand.

His contact eyed it with suspicion. "That's far too generic to be your real name," he said.

Bob waited another few seconds, then dropped his proffered hand. "My name doesn't matter. Neither does yours."

"No," the man said. "I suppose it doesn't."

"You've received our instructions about payment?"

"If I hadn't, I'd have asked what the fuck you were doing in my apartment, wouldn't I?" The man had an unpleasant, nasally voice. Bob pitied the clone who'd end up with this one.

"Good. It's important that you follow the instructions precisely. My employer expects the money before the delivery next week."

The man gave him a long, sour look. "Are you this patronizing to all your buyers? You're not the only market in town you know. I've half a mind to look elsewhere."

Bob knew the threat was an empty one. None of the other sellers were half so reliable. "Remember," he said. "Payment before delivery. You have the account information to make the bitcoin transfer."

The man gave him a vague nod, and turned to lean once more on the ornate terrace railing. As he gazed out over the city, apparently lost in thought, Bob reflected on the fact that rooftops made him wary. *All it takes is one sharp shove . . .*

"It goes without saying that I expect the utmost discretion," the man said, interrupting Bob's train of thought.

"Of course." Bob did not ask the man what he intended to do with his clone. He'd found that it was better not to know.

18: ANNABEL

"Here you go," Ms. Durant said, handing Annabel a steaming mug of coffee. "Almond milk and honey just the way you like it."

"Thanks," Annabel said. They were seated on the windy balcony, but the sky was a brilliant blue and the sun kept them comfortably warm. For a moment they each sipped their coffee in companionable silence.

"Wildflowers are beginning to bloom," Ms. Durant observed, gesturing down at the lawn where buds of all colors peeked through the tall grass.

"Yes," Annabel said. She could feel Ms. Durant's eyes on her, but did not acknowledge the scrutiny.

"Marriage seems to suit you," Ms. Durant said finally.

"Yes," Annabel said again. It hadn't been long since the wedding, but the lies came more easily now. "How do you like your new house? Next time I'll have to visit you instead."

"It's a lovely cottage in town," Ms. Durant said. "Small, but one person doesn't need a lot of space. Rex was very kind to arrange it for me."

"Very kind," Annabel echoed. She supposed he was kind in his way. She knew she should be satisfied with that.

"Indeed," Ms. Durant said.

"What have you been doing since the wedding?" Annabel asked. The idea of Ms. Durant having a life outside of how Annabel had known her was strange to contemplate.

"Oh, just settling in. Going on walks, cooking meals. Reading. Going to my knitting club. Many of the same things I did for the last eighteen years. I have missed your company. But you've grown up and I know my place is no longer by your side."

Annabel nodded although she didn't feel very grown up — she felt like an impostor, always pretending.

"Will you find another job?" she asked.

"Not for the time being," Ms. Durant said. "Rex has promised me a generous stipend for life — he said I needn't seek other employment unless I wish to. For now, I'm enjoying things as they are."

"How did you come to work for Rex originally? Did you know him before I was born?" Annabel asked. These questions had never occurred to her growing up, but her new reality had pushed them to the forefront of her mind.

"I did know him, and I knew the original Annabel too. But not very well. We all went to school together. I was a teacher before I became your caretaker."

"What kind of teacher?"

"The best teacher there ever was," said a voice behind them. Annabel turned to find Rex standing just inside the screen door smiling fondly at her. He slid open the door and came out to join them on the balcony. Annabel looked over to see that Ms. Durant's cheeks were faintly pink.

"I'm not sure I'd go that far," Ms. Durant said, looking up at Rex. He glanced at her with a benevolent smile before seating himself next to Annabel.

"I would. That's why I hired you, Helena," Rex said. It was strange to hear Ms. Durant called by her first name.

"As you say," Ms. Durant replied.

Rex turned back to Annabel. "We grew up in Boston. You and I should take a trip there sometime, it's only a couple hours away. It's a beautiful city, but not as beautiful as here. I can show you all my favorite places."

"That sounds lovely, doesn't it, Annabel," said Ms. Durant before Annabel could comment.

"It does," Annabel said, truthfully. She'd never traveled anywhere — the town where she grew up was her entire universe. Ms. Durant had taught her geography and history, of course, but she knew it wasn't the same as actually going places.

"When's the last time you went back, Helena?" asked Rex.

"Oh, not for many years. Not since before Annabel . . ." Ms. Durant trailed off. Annabel realized she was referring to her original, the first Annabel. She shivered suddenly at what had been unspoken: before Annabel died.

"Are you cold?" Rex asked her, misinterpreting the cause of her shiver. "Here, take my jacket." He pulled off the jacket and draped it over Annabel's shoulders. She had been about to say she wasn't cold at all, but she didn't want to explain the real cause of her shiver so she accepted the jacket with a quiet "thank you."

A movement on the lawn below them caught Annabel's eye, and what she saw there made her stare. It was a new gardener, much younger than the previous one. He was tall and well-muscled with olive skin and black hair, and he wore jeans, boots and nothing else. Annabel couldn't take her eyes off his bare chest, strong arms and broad shoulders. She felt a fluttering in her stomach that radiated down below and made her feel pleasantly warm. She crossed one leg over the other, thinking that if she kept watching she'd probably leave a puddle on her seat.

It was only then that Rex, who had been asking Ms. Durant about her new living arrangements, noticed the direction of her gaze. His face darkened, and he stood up and walked to the railing at the edge of the balcony.

"Who are you?" Rex called down to the shirtless gardener. When he came closer, Annabel noticed sweat glistening on his torso and a light dusting of black hair across his chest that trailed down below his belly button and disappeared under the waistband of his jeans.

"Leon Floros," the gardener said. "Are you Mr. King? Pedro sent me. I'm your new gardener."

"And what happened to Pedro?" asked Rex cooly.

"Guess he's moved up in the world," Leon said with the trace of a smile. "Don't worry, I know what I'm doing."

Rex glanced over at Annabel then returned his attention to Leon. "I'm sure you do," he muttered. Leon had followed his gaze and stared at Annabel now. She stared right back, wishing that Ms. Durant and Rex would vanish. Instead, Rex waved his hand dismissively.

"Get back to work, then."

Leon nodded and gave Annabel a small smile, then turned away to begin weeding the vegetable garden. Annabel watched him for another moment before she became aware that both Rex and Ms. Durant were watching *her*. Hastily, she fought to make her face blank and indifferent, but the balcony was already thick with tension.

"Let's go inside," Ms. Durant said. "You've got such fair skin, Annabel, we wouldn't want you to get burned out here in the sun."

"Yes," Rex agreed. He cast another angry look in Leon's direction as Annabel reluctantly got to her feet and followed Ms. Durant into the cool shade of the house. Not long after that Ms. Durant took her leave. Rex was sure to keep Annabel occupied for the remainder of the day. He went out in the late afternoon to talk to Leon as he packed up his truck. She couldn't hear what was said, but as she surreptitiously watched them through the curtains it seemed to her that Rex was angry and Leon was defensive. Maybe Rex had ordered him to wear a shirt the next time. It wouldn't matter if he did — even that couldn't make Annabel un-see what she had already seen.

That night in bed, Rex's hands gripped her tighter than usual, and there seemed to be a desperate possessiveness in the way that he touched her. When he flipped her over she was grateful not to have to look at him or feel his hot, panting breath on her face. Instead, she closed her eyes and imagined it was Leon the gardener behind her. That night, she did not have to fake her climax, and for the first time since the wedding she fell asleep before Rex did.

A few days later, Annabel was sitting on the balcony waiting to see the shirtless gardener again. She scanned through articles on her tablet to pass the time. After a few minutes, one of the headlines caught her eye and she stopped to read it more carefully. It was a blog piece about the International Congress of Genetics in Zurich, and the keynote address by the father of human cloning, Dr. Edgar Midas. It was vaguely unsettling to read about the man who she knew was responsible for her existence. She had never met him, but still they were connected. The article said that the first clone he ever made used his own genetic code. *How strange it must be for him*, thought Annabel. She couldn't decide if having an original who still lived would be better or worse.

Annabel heard a truck pull up in front of the house. The ignition died, and there was the sound of two doors opening and closing. Her whole body buzzed with anticipation, but she did her best to feign stillness. Then two women carrying gardening tools came into view. They exchanged a few words, pointing out various tasks to be performed, then they both began to wander around the yard pulling up weeds and trimming bushes.

Annabel felt her heart drop. He wasn't there. She had taken extra care with her appearance that morning in the vain hope that he would notice her. Now she was sitting outside like a fool whose idiotic fantasy had been crushed. She realized with a jolt that it was obvious what Rex had said to Leon when they spoke by the truck at the end of his last shift. Annabel felt a sudden urge to fling her tablet off the balcony, or better yet into the driveway where she'd be able to see it smash into a thousand pieces. For a moment she sat wrestling with this impulse, then she took a deep breath and decided to do what she knew Ms. Durant would say was the grown up thing.

She hovered outside her husband's office for a moment before knocking softly.

"Come in," he called. She opened the door, and he regarded her with a surprised smile. "Annabel, what is it? I'll be done in a couple hours, I was thinking we could go see a movie later at that vintage theater in town."

"That sounds nice," Annabel said. She stood there for a moment, suddenly feeling awkward.

"Do you need something?" Rex asked.

"I — I was just wondering. What happened to the other gardener? Is he sick or something?" Annabel asked in what she hoped was a casual voice.

She knew immediately that Rex wasn't fooled for an instant. His demeanor changed from affectionate curiosity to icy dismissal. Rex looked back down at his laptop and began typing away.

Just when she thought he wasn't going to answer her, he said, "I fired him."

"But why?" Annabel asked, as though she did not already know the answer.

Rex looked up at her then, and his eyes were cold. "I'm working now, Annabel."

His tone of voice sent a chill through her, and she hastily left the room and went back out onto the balcony. The beautiful vista had dimmed, and even the bright sun wasn't enough to warm Annabel anymore.

19: JAVI

Javi looked at the A- on the faintly glowing screen of his tablet with a sinking feeling in the pit of his stomach. He knew he should be happy — it was the best grade he'd ever gotten on a Chinese exam — but all he could think about was whether this meant his study sessions with Stella were at an end. As if in answer, Javi's phone buzzed.

It was a short text: '*Best I've ever done on a Chinese exam.*'

Javi flung the phone back onto the bed. He supposed he should respond with congratulations or something else to demonstrate pleased detachment, but he couldn't bring himself to do it just then. She hadn't even bothered to ask how he did. Or anything else to indicate she wanted to start a conversation rather than make a simple statement of fact.

Javi locked his bedroom door and threw open the window on the opposite wall. He knew it was risky to smoke while his parents were home, but at that moment he didn't care. He rolled himself a thick joint and sat on the floor next to the open window, watching the smoke curl and dissipate as he slowly inhaled and exhaled it. The room was messier than usual, dirty clothes thrown carelessly in a pile on the floor, bed unmade, the wires of various chargers jumbled into a cluster of loose knots. The walls were white, the floor cherry wood. The bed was a large four-poster complete with royal blue curtains.

The room had been much the same when it belonged to its previous occupant, Javi's original. He had learned long ago that to propose a change in decor was tantamount to heresy. The message from his parents was clear: Javi was there to fill the place of their beloved dead son, not to formulate his own independent identity.

A knock on the door interrupted Javi's brooding, just as he was taking another draw on the joint. Startled, Javi began to cough. He tried to stifle the sound unsuccessfully as he leapt to his feet, frantically stubbing out the joint and waving his arms around to clear out the smoke.

"Javi?" came his father's voice through the door.

"Just a second," Javi choked out, still trying to control his coughing fit. He put the makeshift ashtray and the stub of the extinguished joint into a drawer, took a deep breath and held it for a second, then exhaled slowly. He cast a nervous glance around the room but he didn't notice anything else that might draw suspicion. *Except for the smell, you idiot* said a small voice in the back of his head. Ignoring this, he opened the door, trying to feign a calm boredom.

His father regarded him for a second. "Were you smoking pot just now, Javi?" he asked without preamble.

"W-what?" Javi stammered, thrown by the abruptness of the question.

"I'm not an idiot, Javi. I know what pot smells like." The stern look on his father's face twitched for the briefest of moments, like he wanted to laugh but stopped himself.

"I got into Stanford," Javi blurted out, grasping for something that would distract his father. He regretted the confession immediately, but the damage was done. His father's eyes widened and he broke out into a grin.

"That's wonderful! Congratulations!" He clapped Javi on the back affectionately. "I can say this now, but your mother and I were starting to get a little worried. Normally they send out their acceptances earlier and we were thinking maybe you'd been rejected and just didn't want to tell us. That's such fantastic news. I'm so proud of you."

"Yeah, thanks," Javi said. His mind was still fuzzy from the weed. "Listen Dad, I've got some homework to do."

"Of course, of course." His father was beaming. "Your

mother will be *thrilled*. Want to wait 'til tomorrow morning to make the official announcement? No doubt she'll want to celebrate."

"Yeah, great," Javi mumbled. How could he have been so stupid as to let the news slip like that?

"My lips are sealed 'til then. Good luck with that homework."

"Thanks," Javi said. He took a step back and was about to close his door when his father reached out a hand to stop him and leaned in closer.

"And don't worry about the smoking. Our little secret. I think it's fair to say you've earned a little lenience, and I can't pretend I don't indulge from time to time too. Just don't tell your mother I told you, she'd never let me hear the end of it." With a wink, his father reached for the doorknob and gently closed the door himself.

Once he was alone again, Javi let out the breath he hadn't realized he was holding. He was torn between dismay that he'd now have to contend with his parents relentless pressure that he live up to the dreams and expectations they had for the original Javier, and laughter that his father had finally confessed what Javi had suspected since he was ten: the hours his father spent in the backyard shed weren't only about his woodworking hobby. Javi wondered if he'd be invited the next time his father snuck back there to smoke. It was a bizarre idea but not without appeal.

Javi sighed and went back to his bed where he lay down on his back on top of the rumpled covers. In truth, he had already finished his homework. He put on his headphones and for a time lost himself in the gentle tingling that radiated up and down his body in time with the rhythm of the music. He'd been staring at the ceiling for an unknown amount of time — if pressed Javi would have guessed an hour but he really had no idea if that was accurate — when his phone blinked and vibrated from where he'd tossed it earlier. Without sitting up, Javi groped a hand around until he found it, then lifted it to his face to read the new text on the screen.

'I hope we can keep studying together. Maybe a couple after-noons a week? You're my good luck charm now :)'

Javi sat up abruptly as a jolt of adrenaline coursed through his body. She wanted to see him again. She had called him her good luck charm. That had to mean something — didn't it?

Heart pounding, Javi carefully typed out his response: *'Sure, I'd like that. Thursday at 4 in the park?'*

He only had to wait a few seconds; she agreed, and Javi went to sleep that night smiling.

On the way to school the next morning, Javi was still bask-ing in the glory that was Stella Castell's attention. He lost no time in recounting the text exchange to Herman and Fred. Herman was awed, Fred merely amused.

"Okay, now you really do have to tell me your secret," Her-man said as Fred pulled into the parking lot of the Starbucks across from school. They were early for once, and Fred wanted coffee to get him through AP Calculus.

"There is no secret. I'm just . . . I dunno the way I always am. Guess she likes that," Javi said. He was unable to keep a proud smile off his face, causing Fred to shake his head in mock dis-gust when he noticed.

"I don't see why she would," Herman said, and Javi shoved him playfully. "You must be saving all your charm and wit for her."

"Dunno why you think he'd waste it on you," Fred said, pulling open the Starbucks door. "You're not the one he dreams about sticking his dick in." Herman burst out laugh-ing.

"Don't talk about her that way," Javi hissed. "It's not about that. Or at least it's not *only* about that."

"Right," Fred said just as Herman said, "Bullshit."

"Can we not talk about this here? I don't want her to think I talk about her," Javi said in an undertone, looking around fur-tively. The last thing he needed was for some friend of Stella's to overhear this conversation and tell her — she'd think he was a freak and never speak to him again.

"Don't be so paranoid," drawled Fred, but he relented after Javi glared at him for a moment. "Fine. I'll talk then. Violet and I did it again yesterday afternoon. On the living room sofa while her parents were out. It gets better every time." Javi could tell he was trying to play it cool, but he looked immensely pleased with himself.

"No shit," Herman said in reverent tones. "Weren't you afraid of getting caught?"

Fred gave a cavalier shrug. "Part of the fun, I guess."

"Whoa," Herman said. Javi was impressed too, but he didn't say anything. A tall brunette woman had caught his eye by the register. She looked like she might be in her thirties, but something about her was immediately appealing to Javi. When she accepted her cup from the barista and turned to leave, her eyes met Javi's and she stopped in her tracks. The coffee in her hand seemed to fall in slow motion, spilling its contents everywhere as it bounced off the ground.

Shock and horror were etched on her face — it was as though she'd seen a ghost. There was a flurry of movement around them, people yelling and jumping out of the way of the scalding latte, the barista sending the janitor to fetch the mop and clean up the mess, and hushed speech as people looked on and speculated with their neighbors what had happened.

Javi was too stunned by her reaction to move or speak. Some of the coffee had splashed onto his shoes but he barely noticed. He continued looking at the woman and she continued looking at him. Even in his bewilderment, Javi noticed she had a pretty face framed by waves of brown hair cascading to her shoulders, perky full breasts, and long legs. She seemed to realize what had happened a moment later when the janitor started mopping around her feet and the barista came out to offer her a replacement. She nodded and the barista hurried back behind the register. All the time she kept her stormy gray eyes locked on Javi's. The janitor handed her the sunglasses that had fallen off her head and she took them from him word-lessly. She stepped closer and Javi noticed Herman and Fred exchange baffled looks off to his right. He wanted to ask the woman what was going on, but the words stuck in his throat.

The woman stared intently as though she was inspecting him, making Javi feel awkward and exposed. He was vaguely aware that everybody else in the Starbucks was still watching them, obviously expecting to witness a scene even more dra-matic than what had just happened. Finally, she spoke.

"You look just like him," she said softly. Before Javi could think of anything to say to that she rushed out, not even wait-ing for the barista to finish making her drink.

20: EDGAR PRIME

Edgar Prime laid the suit that Dr. Midas had forced him to buy on his bed. His limbs felt heavy and slow, like he was walking through molasses. He knew that he should hurry up—the only thing that would result from him dragging his heels like this was sleep deprivation before his early flight the next morning. But still, the thought of standing up in front of all those geneticists and reporters again like a trained circus act filled Edgar Prime with dread.

He was packing his underwear when he was interrupted by a soft knock on the door. Hugo was the last person he expected when he yanked it open, and for a second the surprise robbed him of speech.

"Hugo," he finally managed, mentally berating himself for getting so easily flustered. "Hello. Hi. Um, how's it going?" He barely managed to stop himself from cringing, but Hugo pretended to be unaware of his awkwardness.

"I'm going for a drink at Celeste's place," Hugo said. "She made me promise to bring you along."

"Oh," Edgar Prime said, torn between being pleased that Celeste thought he was worthy of hanging out with again, and disappointment that it had been her rather than Hugo who wanted to see him.

"Nothing crazy, just a classy glass of wine Celeste said." Hugo's green eyes twinkled.

"You're a terrible RA," Edgar Prime said with a half-smile. "Encouraging underage drinking like this."

Hugo's eyes widened for a moment, then he burst out laughing. "So true," he said. "But to be fair I don't encourage it in all my residents. Did you hear about the puke in the stair-well last weekend? We never did find out who that was."

Edgar Prime laughed, considering the offer. "I wish I could, Hugo. I've gotta pack tonight. Zurich tomorrow."

"Come on, Ed," coaxed Hugo. "Not even for an hour?"

Edgar Prime hesitated, but hearing Hugo casually say his nickname like that was too much to resist. "I guess an hour couldn't hurt. I'll just finish this off then I can come meet you."

"It's okay, I don't mind waiting," Hugo said and he smiled that beautiful golden smile. "Unless you'd rather be alone, that's fine too. Whatever you want."

I want you, Edgar Prime thought to himself, but he did not dare speak the words aloud. "Sure, okay. Come on in," he said with as much nonchalance as he could muster.

He held the door open for Hugo who walked into the tiny room and sat down in Edgar Prime's desk chair. Edgar Prime noticed him looking at the underwear stacked in the open suitcase and hurriedly pulled out his sock drawer and threw several pairs of black socks on top. Hugo didn't comment, instead roving his eyes across the room. There was very little for him to see; Edgar Prime kept his possessions meticulously organized and spare. He noticed Hugo's eyes lingering on the posters he'd hung on the wall, the only part of the dorm room that was personalized.

"Picasso and Matisse?" Hugo asked after a moment.

"I saw an exhibit once where the two of them were displayed side by side to show how they'd influenced each other," Edgar Prime explained. "I like Picasso better, but they're complementary."

"Really? I prefer Matisse," Hugo said. "He's gentler than Picasso."

"But less powerful," Edgar Prime said, folding a few business casual outfits to add to the suitcase. He thought he'd take Professor Richards' advice and try to see a bit of Zurich on his own. The last time he'd been compelled to attend an I.C.G. he'd been fourteen and had barely left the hotel room except for the compulsory lectures where he'd served as a glorified prop for Dr. Midas. He had decided that unpleasant as the conference itself was likely to be, he wasn't going to waste the rest of this trip playing virtual reality games and wishing he was somewhere else.

"True," Hugo agreed. "Have you taken any art history?"

Edgar Prime laughed. "Dr. Midas thinks it's a waste of time to study art. And history."

Hugo raised an eyebrow. "Does he know you want to major in history?"

"Not yet. I'm planning to avoid telling him 'til after I declare next year."

"Probably smart." Hugo turned his attention back to the posters. "If he doesn't like art, who took you to see the Picasso/Matisse exhibit?"

"It was a school trip," Edgar Prime said. "Fifth grade. Ms. Caine. She was great. She used to do all these impressions of old politicians when we studied U.S. History — she did Nixon's 'I am not a criminal' and Clinton's 'I did not have sex with that woman' except instead of saying the word 'sex' she just said 'hmm-hmm'. I guess she thought a room full of eleven year olds couldn't handle hearing the word 'sex' without pandemonium erupting."

Hugo chuckled. "Wish I'd had a teacher like that. Most of mine were either straight out of college with no clue how to deal with kids or super old and just didn't give a fuck. I wound up reading in the corner most of the time I was in school."

"Bet you had lots of friends, though," Edgar Prime said without thinking.

A curious look appeared on Hugo's face as Edgar Prime shoved his dress shoes into the bag and zipped it up.

Hugo shrugged. "I guess I did. Didn't you?"

"Not really," Edgar Prime said. *Not unless you count Dr. Midas's research assistants trying to build rapport while they conducted his experiments.*

"Well, I can't imagine why that would be the case," Hugo

said. Edgar Prime glanced up at him from the drawer where he was fishing out his passport expecting to see sarcasm, but was instead met with sincerity. He felt his cheeks growing hot and was grateful that his dark complexion kept this barely noticeable.

"Should we go?" Edgar Prime said, stashing his passport in the outer pocket of the bag and picking up his keys and phone.

Hugo stood and walked to the door, holding it open for Edgar Prime. As they made their way down the stairwell and through the lobby, Hugo told Edgar Prime the latest about Blake and George's dysfunctional non-relationship.

"So right now they're just pretending the other night never happened?" Edgar Prime asked. They reached the bustling courtyard and began walking across campus to Celeste's apartment.

"As far as we know," Hugo said. "Celeste says they've been acting weird around each other, a little more formal than usual. So maybe it went badly and they agreed not to talk about it again, I dunno. But if they're awkward tonight, that's why."

"Got it," Edgar Prime said. "What's Celeste's deal?"

Hugo looked at him curiously. "I'm not sure even she knows," he said. "A different night a different guy. But then she goes months where she's fed up with dating in general. Why, are you into her or something?"

"Wha — no, of course not." Edgar Prime was surprised Hugo would even ask him this. As far as Edgar Prime was concerned his interest in Hugo was blatantly obvious to the point of being embarrassing.

"Are you sure?" Hugo asked. "If you are, it's okay. I won't tell her."

"No, really," Edgar Prime said firmly. He knew his disappointment was unmerited. Why should he think that Hugo would mind if Edgar Prime liked Celeste or anyone else? For all Edgar Prime knew, Hugo could already be involved with someone.

When they reached Celeste's building, she buzzed them in and they walked up to the fourth floor. They could hear music playing from all the way down the hall. They found her door unlocked and entered a mood-lit living room covered by a haze of marijuana smoke and populated with around ten people including Celeste, Blake and George.

"Ed!" Celeste cried when she saw him. "Come in, come in! I made sangria!"

She stumbled slightly when she stood up and used George's shoulder to steady herself, laughing. She crossed to where Edgar Prime stood with Hugo and gave them both a sloppy hug.

"Everyone this is Ed! Ed, everyone." She waved a hand in the general direction of the living room's other occupants, one of whom was in the process of taking a hit on a water bong. They all nodded in greeting and Hugo went over to speak to a few of them by the window.

"Let's get you a drink," Celeste said, leading Edgar Prime by the hand through the living room and into the minuscule kitchen.

"Thanks," Edgar Prime said. "I can't stay too long, I've got an early flight tomorrow. But I did want to stop by."

"Flight, shmight," Celeste said with a giggle. "Live a little."

Edgar Prime shook his head with a smile. Celeste placed her hand on his chest and gave him a tiny shove, then turned to the fridge. She pulled out a pitcher full of dark red liquid with slices of orange, lemon and lime floating in it.

"I made it from scratch," Celeste explained as she poured him a full solo cup.

"It looks good," Edgar Prime said. She handed him the cup and he took a sip. "Really, really good. Strong."

"There's lots more where that came from." She threw open the fridge to replace the now half-empty pitcher and stepped back to reveal two more just like it.

"Wow," was all Edgar Prime could say. Celeste giggled again and gave his arm another playful shove.

"What are we drinking?" Hugo said from the doorway to the kitchen. Edgar Prime felt his stomach leap and Celeste turned her sly smile in his direction.

"Sangria, baby," she said, waving her solo cup at him. "Help yourself."

"Nice," Hugo said, and he squeezed past Edgar Prime and Celeste to open the fridge. He poured a healthy measure into a blue solo cup. "Cheers," he said, raising the cup to Celeste and Edgar Prime before taking a long sip. "Damn, that's good."

"Why thank you," Celeste said. "I do try."

Up close, Edgar Prime could see that Hugo's eyes were dilated and he deduced that he must have made use of the water bong in the living room. Edgar Prime had never smoked pot before, and the thought of doing so filled him with both trepidation and curiosity. He wasn't sure what he'd do if Hugo offered him the chance to try it, but it turned out Hugo had other things on his mind.

"Let's go up to the roof," he said, giving them both a mellow grin. Edgar Prime looked to Celeste for guidance.

"Sure, why not?" Celeste said. They followed her out of the kitchen through the living room and out of the apartment to the stairwell. Two flights up and they came out on top of the building, The air was crisp enough that they could see their fogged breath but not so cold as to be unpleasant. Edgar Prime looked out on the city lights stretching infinitely ahead of them, and wondered why he had never before noticed their beauty.

21: ANNABEL

Just breathe, Annabel reminded herself over and over again. Sometime in the next thirty minutes she and Rex would welcome his old friends, Phineas and Veronica Hawthorne into their home for dinner. Annabel almost couldn't believe how nervous she was. *It doesn't matter what they think of you,* she told herself, but even as she thought it she knew it was a lie. Phineas and Veronica had both known her original quite well before she'd died, and for this reason she had no idea how they'd react to her. Surely they'd be polite, for Rex's sake if not her own.

Nonetheless, Annabel had taken extra care with her appearance that night. She wore a knee-length silk tiered skirt the color of the ocean at dusk, and a sleeveless cream-colored blouse. Her makeup was minimal, and the only jewelry she wore was a platinum anchor pendant necklace and her wedding ring. Rex wore jeans and a navy linen button down shirt with the sleeves rolled up. Even though he told her not to worry, she could tell that he was nervous too. *He thinks you won't live up to their expectations*, whispered a sneering voice in her head. It was almost a relief when a knock at the door ended the anticipation. Rex gave her a reassuring smile, then strode across the living room to greet their guests.

Phineas was of middling height and build with warm brown eyes and salt and pepper hair. He dressed in all black and wore a small diamond stud in his left ear. Veronica was all color; she had blue eyes, strawberry blonde hair that Annabel suspected was fake, and wore a 60s-style halter dress with pink and green stripes. She coordinated her nail polish to her outfit, wore bright cherry red lipstick, and stood a few inches taller than her husband. Both Hawthornes were deeply tanned, and their trim physiques suggested that they spent a considerable amount of time on the tennis courts.

"Rex, darling!" Veronica squealed, as her husband clapped Rex on the back and she embraced him.

"Hello Veronica, Phineas," Rex said, grinning. "It's been too long."

"Too right it has, old friend," Phineas replied.

Annabel stood behind Rex, watching the reunion and fighting the urge to bolt. Veronica's eyes flickered to her and widened slightly.

"Annabel, my dear," Veronica exclaimed. Annabel felt herself redden, as everyone's attention shifted to her.

"Annabel, this is Veronica and Phineas," Rex said, putting an arm around her waist. The glance that passed between the Hawthornes was not lost on her; it was as though they were saying *This one looks just like her*. The next instant the moment of strangeness passed; Veronica and Phineas both hugged her in greeting, and they all crossed the threshold to sit around the fireplace while Rex offered everyone martinis. Annabel had never had one before, and nearly choked after her first sip.

"Takes some getting used to, doesn't it?" Veronica said kindly. Annabel smiled ruefully, and took another, smaller sip, fighting back a grimace. For the first hour, Annabel didn't say much. Veronica and Phineas regaled them with tales of their recent visit to Chile. By the time they settled around the table, laden with steamed lobster, tubs of melted butter and lemon juice, fresh bread and a large caesar salad with homemade croutons, Annabel felt pleasantly fuzzy from the martinis, even though she had only drank half as many as the others. As the lobsters were cracked and the Sauvignon Blanc was poured, Annabel felt at ease enough to ask Veronica about where else they'd traveled, and which places were their favorites.

"Oh, I couldn't possibly choose!" Veronica said. "Could you,

Phin? We did have a marvelous time climbing the Sydney Harbor Bridge in Australia last spring. But few things can compete with the Great Wall of China, can they? Such a magnificent view, and a fascinating history." Veronica took a sip of wine, and Phineas weighed in.

"The UK was fun too," he commented. "All those castles. Funny to think people actually lived in them, once."

"Admit it, Phin, you spent that whole trip pretending to be a student at Hogwarts," Rex said with a sly grin.

"Fine, fine, you got me," Phineas said. He held his hands up in mock-surrender. "It's not my fault I've got a more active imagination than you do."

Rex and Veronica guffawed, and even Annabel gave a hesitant chuckle.

"Then there are the adventures closer to home," Veronica said, finishing another glass of wine and picking up the bottle for a refill. "We had plenty in Cambridge. That time you two clowns decided to spend a semester earning a few extra dollars by volunteering for psychology experiments, remember? You spent a whole month sleeping in a lab with electrodes glued to your heads. All so you'd have the money to build a working replica of C-3PO."

"Hey, we almost succeeded there," Rex said while Phineas laughed at his side.

"Where was this?" Annabel asked. She was almost starting to enjoy herself, and grinned as she took another sip of wine.

"When we all lived in Simmons Hall, you remember dear, you were there too!" Veronica exclaimed. The instant it was out of her mouth she realized her mistake and shot a nervous glance at Rex, whose face had turned to stone. Annabel froze too and Phineas's gaze traveled from his wife, to Annabel before finally resting on Rex.

"Makes me feel old to think about how long ago that was," Phineas said gruffly. The tension eased, but did not quite dissipate. "How about we open another bottle of wine?"

Rex stood up so quickly that there was a loud scraping

noise as the chair slid back over the floor. "I'll go grab one," he said. When he left, Annabel looked down at her lap so she wouldn't have to see the guilty look on Veronica's face, or the pitying one on Phineas's. When Rex returned they made a show of steering the conversation back onto neutral ground, but Annabel remained on edge for the rest of the evening, and was not at all sorry when Phineas and Veronica finally took their leave. Rex went straight off to sleep, foregoing sex for the first time. While Annabel wasn't sorry about this, it still took her hours to drop off to sleep beside the snoring stranger who was her husband. *Everything you are and everything you have you owe to Rex King,* she told herself. *Never forget that.*

22: JAVI

Javi was unusually quiet at the lunch table that day. He'd barely paid attention in his morning classes — his thoughts kept returning to the woman from Starbucks. There was something haunting in the way she had stared at him, the tremulous softness of her voice when she'd said Javi looked just like *him*. For the last few hours, Javi found himself wondering over and over again who she was and how she'd known his original. She must have known him well to have such a strong reaction to seeing Javi.

The more he thought about it the more he found himself vacillating between curiosity and frustration. Why should he care about the people who'd known the original Javier? He was his own person! But even these reassurances were hollow. It seemed the lies he had told himself so many times before had fallen away, leaving only the ugly truth.

"D'you want to eat that?" Herman asked, pointing at Javi's chocolate bar. Wordlessly, Javi pushed it towards him. "Thanks," Herman said, unwrapping it with gusto and taking a large bite.

"Did you hear about Phoebe Mead?" Fred asked. "She and Zane Goldbrook got caught in the janitor's closet yesterday."

"What were they doing?" Herman asked, eyes wide.

Fred shrugged. "What d'you think? Anyway, they're both suspended for the rest of the week."

"Lucky them," Herman muttered. Javi let out a humorless laugh and turned back to his chicken sandwich. He felt a prickle of annoyance when he noticed Fred and Herman exchanged concerned looks.

"Look," Herman began, leaning forward. "About that woman this morning. You know what they say."

Javi scowled at Herman's expectant look. "What's that?" he muttered, to speed the end of the conversation.

"Bitches be crazy," said Herman, quirking an eyebrow.

"You're an idiot, Herman," said Fred with a snort.

Herman ignored this and leaned forward again. "Any idea who she was?"

"Nope," Javi said shortly.

"Are you curious?" Herman asked. He seemed much more tentative than usual.

"Nope," Javi lied.

"Really?" Herman said. "I'd wonder about that stuff if it were me. I'd probably have googled all about my original if I was a clone."

"Good for you," mumbled Javi. He was getting angrier by the minute, and he wasn't even sure why.

"Have you ever? You do know his name, after all." Herman never knew when to keep his mouth shut.

"No," Javi said through gritted teeth.

"Never? Not even once?" Herman looked flabbergasted. "How is that possible?"

"Will you just shut the fuck up about it already," Javi snapped. He found he was breathing heavily, and had to fight the urge to turn over their table and throw his chair at the wall. Suddenly, sitting became too much to bear. He stood up, feeling a savage pleasure at the startled looks on Herman and Fred's faces.

"I'll see you later," he muttered, and stormed off without even bothering to throw away the remnants of his lunch.

There weren't many places to hide in the school, so Javi headed for the library, thinking that even if Herman and Fred tried to find him they'd be unable to talk without the old librarian throwing them out for disrupting the silence she prized so much. He needn't have worried; he spent the remainder of the lunch hour alone and uninterrupted, wishing he could silence his thoughts as easily. For most of the afternoon he continued to obsess about the woman while simultaneously trying to convince himself that he was indifferent to her. By the time he saw Herman and Fred again he felt more weary than angry, and he regretted his earlier behavior.

"Ready?" Herman asked nervously, as though expecting Javi to lash out again.

"Yeah," Javi said. "Look, about before —"

"Don't worry about it," Fred cut in. Javi nodded gratefully and slammed his locker shut, falling into step behind the other two as they walked out to Fred's car. Neither of them broached the subject of the mystery woman again, and they instead heard more about Fred and Violet's budding relationship. He told them proudly that they'd tried sixty-nining the night before, but that it was something they liked more in theory than in practice.

"Whoa," Herman said after Fred gave them a brief description. "What did she taste like?"

Fred laughed at the question, but Javi found he was curious too even though he'd never admit it. "So fucking good. But hard to describe, it's different from anything else."

"Whoa," Herman said again.

Fred parked the car and they went over to their usual weeping willow tree. Herman was digging around in his backpack for the joints he'd stashed when they heard a female voice off to their left.

"Javier?"

All three of them whipped around to look at her; it was the woman he'd seen at Starbucks that morning. Javi stared up at her, dumbfounded. For all his wondering, he'd never expected to see her again, and certainly not here or so soon.

"Can I have a word?" she asked, shifting from one foot to the other. Without consciously making a decision to do so, Javi got to his feet. Herman and Fred looked similarly bewildered.

For a moment, Javi considered telling her to fuck off, but curiosity won out and instead he mumbled, "Let's go over there." She nodded and he led her to the empty picnic benches by the lake. They sat across from each other, and there was an awkward pause before either of them spoke.

"How did you know I'd be here?" Javi asked finally.

"I called your parents," she said. "I wanted to apologize and they told me you go to the park a lot after school."

"Oh." His insides boiled with anger again. Now he'd have to talk to his parents about this too. The thought made him want to knock himself out with a large rock.

"I guess you're probably wondering who I am," the woman said.

"Yeah," Javi admitted grudgingly. He wished he could honestly say he didn't care.

"My name is Imogen Shaw." Javi noticed she wasn't meeting his eyes, instead staring down at the table or out at the lake. "Javier and I — we knew each other quite well."

"Oh," Javi said. He didn't know how else to respond. Imogen bit her lip as though torn over whether or not to say more.

"He was my first boyfriend," said Imogen quietly.

"Oh," Javi said again. He cleared his throat. "It must have been hard for you when . . ." he trailed off. *When he died,* Javi thought, but he couldn't bring himself to say it aloud.

Imogen nodded. Javi noticed her eyes seemed overly bright, but none of the tears fell. Neither of them spoke for a moment, but then Imogen took a deep steadying breath and looked up at him for the first time.

"Anyway, this morning was just a shock. I knew about you, of course, but I guess it hadn't occurred to me that we'd ever run into each other. Kind of stupid in hindsight."

"I — it's fine," said Javi uncomfortably. He shifted in his seat. "You don't need to apologize for anything."

"It was like seeing a ghost," Imogen said.

Javi couldn't help but frown at that. To his surprise, Imogen burst out laughing.

"What?" Javi asked, alarmed at her abrupt change in mood.

"I'm sorry," Imogen said. "It's just — that face you made. He used to make that face too when he was annoyed about something but didn't want to admit it."

"Huh," was all Javi could say to that. *She's beautiful when she smiles.* It was only then he noticed a diamond ring on her left hand. "Have you been married long?" he asked, without thinking.

Imogen looked surprised but answered him all the same. "Just over eight years. Theo and I met our last year of college. We've got two kids now — Bryony is seven and Poppy is three." Talking about her children seemed to have cheered Imogen somewhat.

"That's . . . nice." Javi glanced back towards the tree to see what his friends were doing. This conversation was making him antsy, and he'd prefer to be getting high than walking on eggshells as he spoke to the former girlfriend of his original. Imogen followed his glance and looked at him shrewdly.

"Sorry," she said, standing abruptly. "Your friends are waiting for you."

"No, it's okay," said Javi, but he stood too.

Imogen held out her hand formally, and the two of them shook. "It was good to see you again," Imogen said. "I mean — to meet you." She blushed, and Javi found himself thinking it made her look adorable. She really was very pretty for someone twice his age.

"Nice to meet you too," Javi said. She dropped his hand, nodded and set off, striding towards the parking lot. Javi watched her go filled with the strangest feeling that he'd like to see her again. After a moment he mentally shook himself and turned to head back to where Herman and Fred were waiting. When he ducked between two particularly low-hanging branches, pushing aside the curtain of leaves, both stared up at him expectantly.

"What?" Javi said flatly. He threw himself down on the ground and took the half-smoked joint from Fred, who exchanged a look with Herman.

"What was that about?" Herman asked, as though it was the most obvious thing in the world. Which in a way, it was.

"She just wanted to apologize for this morning," Javi said, blowing out the smoke he'd inhaled. "That's all."

Herman persisted. "But who was she? Or who is she I guess I should say."

Javi handed the joint to Herman. "She knew my original," he muttered. "The first Javier Vasquez. They . . . they used to date in high school."

Fred blew out a low whistle and Herman began to cough, having been halfway through an inhale.

"No shit," Herman said, continuing to sputter.

"I thought it might be something like that," Fred said. "Didn't I say?"

"Yeah," Herman said. He turned to Javi, still wheezing slightly. "He did say that."

"It's no big deal," Javi said. Both Herman and Fred looked like they wanted to keep discussing it, but before either of them could speak again, Javi changed the subject. Reluctantly, the other two let it drop and allowed the conversation to be steered back to the pros and cons of sixty-nine.

Alone in the shower later that night, Javi's thoughts drifted back to Imogen Shaw unbidden. He tried for a moment to push them away, but eventually gave up and began stroking himself rhythmically while imagining her gorgeous mouth wrapped around his cock. Afterwards he felt unsettled and vaguely guilty, but he dismissed this, reminding himself that it really didn't matter. It wasn't as though he'd ever see her again.

23: EDGAR PRIME

The knock at the door was as gentle as a butcher's knife. Edgar Prime woke in a fog, head pounding. He had almost managed to convince himself that he should just go back to sleep — the knock had been merely a dream — when it happened again, and louder. Edgar Prime groaned as he crawled out of bed and stumbled to open the door.

Outside he found Patrice Zhao, dressed in smart black trousers, a short-sleeved periwinkle blouse and sensible flats, one of which was tapping impatiently on the floor while she waited. For a second she took in his disheveled appearance — he realized too late he was dressed in nothing but his boxers — and then her lips twitched as though suppressing a smile.

"You might want to put some clothes on," she said.

"Right," he muttered, wishing she would go away and leave him in peace. "Can you give me a few minutes?"

"No more than five," she said, checking the time on her phone. He grabbed his towel from the hook by the door and hurried down the hall to brush his teeth and have a quick shower, ignoring the throbbing in his head. It took close to ten minutes before Edgar Prime was dressed and ready to go. He found Patrice sitting cross-legged in the empty common room looking vastly out of place despite only being eight or nine years older than he was.

The minute she saw him she sprang to her feet, picked up a large faux-leather handbag and wheeled her suitcase into the hallway.

"Rough night?" she asked as they waited by the elevator. He was surprised to see the hint of a smile on her face.

"No, just a late one. Studying, you know," Edgar Prime lied. In truth he'd had far too much sangria, and had only the blurriest memory of getting back to his dorm and passing out.

"Studying," Patrice repeated. They wheeled their suitcases onto the elevator and Patrice jabbed the L button.

"That's right," Edgar Prime said. He glanced sideways at her and found himself slightly miffed by the ghost of a knowing smirk on her face. He had to stifle a wince at the soft ding of the elevator as it opened. It sounded much louder than usual for some reason. There was a car waiting outside. Once they were comfortably seated, Patrice dug around in her handbag and pulled out a bottle of coconut water.

"Drink this," she said, handing it over to him. "It'll help."

"Thanks," he said in as dignified a voice as he could manage. She was right though it *did* help, and by the time they'd reached JFK airport he was feeling marginally more alert. Fortunately for him, Dr. Midas only flew first class so they were able to avoid waiting in security lines and soon found themselves settled in the executive lounge.

Dr. Midas hadn't arrived yet, and Edgar Prime curled himself into a wide arm chair for another nap. Patrice shook her head in amusement but did not comment, instead pulling out a tablet and beginning to read. Within seconds, Edgar Prime fell back into a deep sleep.

"Morning Patrice, morning Prime," boomed Dr. Midas, causing Edgar Prime to jump so much he nearly fell out of his chair. It felt like he'd only been out for a few minutes, but the clock on the wall informed him that it had been just under an hour. He stretched his stiff legs out in front of him and rubbed his eyes.

"Good morning, Dr. Midas," Patrice said.

"Morning," mumbled Edgar Prime.

"Don't worry, Prime," said Dr. Midas with a good-natured expression on his face. "Plenty more time for you to sleep on the plane. Our presentation isn't until tomorrow. We can have an early night tonight, and wake up refreshed and ready to go."

Edgar Prime sighed, but did not comment. Dr. Midas looked downright ebullient and Edgar Prime knew nothing good would come of him voicing his distaste for the I.C.G. — it wasn't as though his participation in it was optional. Patrice was quick to divert Dr. Midas's attention, informing him that she'd been reading the other papers being presented at the conference this year and recounting what she believed to be the relative merit of each. Edgar Prime closed his eyes again, but before he could fall into another stupor Dr. Midas turned back to him.

"You ought to read those papers too, Prime," Dr. Midas chided. "If you're ever going to take over my lab you'll need to be on top of all the research being done in the field."

Take over the lab — it was Edgar Prime's worst nightmare, but something that Dr. Midas had always assumed would be a foregone conclusion.

"Maybe I won't be the one to take it over," Edgar Prime said. "Maybe it'll be Patrice instead, and I'll do something different."

Dr. Midas let out a great "Ha!" at that, guffawing as though Edgar Prime had made a great joke. "What else could you possibly want to do? You're *me*, remember? What future could be more fitting for you than to take over my life's work?"

"I don't know," Edgar Prime said more coldly than he meant to. "But it won't be that."

He expected Dr. Midas to be angry at his attitude, but he merely looked bemused. Patrice appeared poker-faced, and Edgar Prime wondered if she was offended by Dr. Midas's reaction to the idea that she could one day take over his role as director of the illustrious Midas Labs. He realized he didn't actually know Patrice at all despite the countless hours he'd spent in her company over the last few years. He was almost surprised that it had never before occurred to him to wonder about the person behind the lab coat.

"Don't worry, Patrice," said Dr. Midas in a stage whisper, "I had a rebellious streak when I was younger too, but I grew out of it, and so will Prime. He'll come around."

Patrice raised an eyebrow at Edgar Prime, but he merely shook his head in disgust and closed his eyes once more. The next forty minutes weren't particularly restful — he was stuck listening to Dr. Midas hum contentedly while getting a neck massage in the adjacent chair. Just as Edgar Prime began to finally drift off, he was shaken awake once more by Patrice so they could board. He shuffled miserably after Patrice and Dr. Midas, reminding himself that soon he'd be able to enjoy close to eight hours of uninterrupted sleep.

They were the first aboard, greeted by a smiling blonde flight attendant who immediately asked if they'd like anything to drink. Something in his face reminded Edgar Prime of Hugo, and he had to smile as he slid into the second row window seat and requested another coconut water. Patrice took the seat next to him and Dr. Midas settled himself across the aisle next to an attractive older man with salt and pepper hair, dressed in jeans and a black t-shirt. It took less than a minute before the man recognized Dr. Midas, and immediately engaged him in conversation, extending a hand to shake that Dr. Midas accepted with a benevolent smile. For all his talk of the work, Edgar Prime knew Dr. Midas also loved the fame, enjoyed nothing more than the awe and reverence of strangers. It eclipsed everything else, except perhaps the money.

The blonde flight attendant returned with Edgar Prime's coconut water and a coffee for Patrice.

"My name is Elliott if you need anything else," he told them with a warm smile. Edgar Prime suddenly found himself much less inclined to go right back to sleep. Patrice noticed his eyes on Elliott's back as he brought drinks to the other first class passengers.

"He's handsome," Patrice said in an undertone. Edgar Prime looked at her in surprise; it was the first time he'd ever heard her talk about anything that didn't directly pertain to Dr. Midas.

"He reminds me of . . . someone I know," Edgar Prime muttered.

"Is it serious? she asked.

"Serious?" he said, looking at her with genuine confusion. "Oh! No, no, it's not — we haven't — nothing's happened yet. Or maybe it never will, I dunno." Edgar Prime stared down at his feet trying to get a grip. Dr. Midas's research fellow was the last person he wanted to discuss his feelings for Hugo with. He didn't want Dr. Midas to find out and somehow interfere.

"Don't worry, I won't tell him." It was as though Patrice had read his mind. "He looks a bit like my boyfriend too. The flight attendant, I mean."

"You have a boyfriend?" Edgar Prime repeated stupidly. He didn't know why he hadn't expected that. Patrice was very smart and very pretty — of course she was bound to have someone. She laughed at his question.

"Don't look so flabbergasted," she said. "I don't live at the lab, you know."

"Oh, I didn't think you did," he said unconvincingly.

"It's okay. I should take that as a compliment. I obviously come across as dedicated to my job."

"How long have you been with your boyfriend?" Edgar Prime asked.

"Five years. We've lived together for four. He's been proposing a lot lately," Patrice commented. Edgar Prime couldn't tell if she was happy about this or not.

"Congratulations," he said hesitantly.

Patrice laughed again. "We're not engaged. I don't believe in marriage, Wilbur just thinks if he keeps asking maybe I'll change my mind."

"Wilbur?" he said, raising both eyebrows.

"His mother was a massive fan of *Charlotte's Web*." Patrice rolled her eyes. "It's partly for her sake he wants us to get married. She's not religious or anything, just a sucker for old fashioned romance."

Edgar Prime wasn't sure what to say to this apart from, "Hmm." Other passengers filed past them towards coach, and the cabin was filled with overlapping conversations.

"And you don't think you'd ever marry him? You know, to make her happy?"

"No," said Patrice simply. "If I ever get married, I'd want it to be for me. Besides, what difference will a piece of paper make? If Wilbur and I are meant to last, we will. Marriage certificate or no."

"That's . . . an interesting perspective."

"You want to get married?"

"I dunno," said Edgar Prime. "I've never really thought about it." This was the truth. He was far more concerned with his immediate situation than he was with what might happen a decade or more into the future.

Across the aisle, Dr. Midas and the silver fox were laughing together, their faces closer than necessary, given the wide seats of first class.

"Wanna make a bet on how long it takes for the two of them to disappear into the bathroom together?" Patrice muttered so quietly Edgar Prime could barely hear her. Now it was his turn to laugh, because he had been thinking along those lines too. Patrice grinned at him but Dr. Midas was oblivious to them both, focusing all his attention on his new companion.

"Five hours in," Edgar Prime said finally. "By then everyone will be too zoned out to notice."

"I'd say no more than three," Patrice said. "But probably less than two. After they clear away the food would be my guess."

Patrice won the bet. Across the aisle, Dr. Midas and his companion flirted through a meal of endive pear gorgonzola salad, creamy mushroom pasta and quite a bit of red wine. They even shared the chocolate mousse dessert. Once the dishes had been cleared away, they barely waited fifteen minutes. Dr. Midas got up first, walking discretely behind the curtain to the restroom. A moment later, his companion followed, something that Elliott the flight attendant seemed to notice but did not comment on.

Edgar Prime and Patrice laughed together, Patrice joking that he should have been able to predict Dr. Midas's actions better than she because of their identical DNA. Twenty minutes later when they made their staggered return to their seats with matching satisfied expressions on their faces, Edgar Prime thought for the first time that maybe he ought to observe Dr. Midas in these situations more closely. He had never bothered to hide his many dalliances from Edgar Prime, no doubt assuming they'd be as identical in this respect as they were in appearance and intellect. But Edgar Prime was still a virgin at almost nineteen, and still felt awkward and fluttery whenever Hugo was around. He didn't know the first thing about how to go about turning his fantasies into reality the way Dr. Midas seemed to do with such ease.

It was far from the first time Edgar Prime felt envious of Dr. Midas, but for once he wondered whether maybe this was something he too could learn. After all, if Dr. Midas could do it, logic dictated that so too could Edgar Prime. One final glance at the pair across the aisle allowed this notion to further crystallize, and Edgar Prime lay back and closed his eyes thinking of the many things he'd like to do to Hugo once he solved the mystery of how to make the first move.

24: ANNABEL

It was overcast and breezy. Annabel sat at a spindly out-door cafe table in town, staring across the street at the park while she waited for Ms. Durant. She had arrived first despite taking the long but more picturesque route into town, walking around the bay across rocky beaches with dry seaweed that crunched beneath her feet. After about thirty minutes of that she'd cut through the tall grass that grew beyond the sand and found the narrow, curved footpath leading into town. She could have been driven, of course, but she preferred the solitude and the freedom of her walk.

She spotted Ms. Durant hurrying up the sidewalk, handbag swinging back and forth with each step.

"Annabel, darling," said Ms. Durant when she reached her. "Have you been waiting long? I always underestimate how long it'll take me to do this walk."

"No problem," Annabel said. "I just got here." Ms. Durant settled into the seat opposite to catch her breath. After a few moments a waiter came to take their orders: a jasmine tea for Annabel, and an espresso and soda water for Ms. Durant. As always, Ms. Durant began by asking Annabel if she was happy in her married life.

"I'm not sure," Annabel confided. "I think maybe it would be different if I had something to *do* during the day."

"Oh hush," Ms. Durant chided her. "Be grateful that your husband can provide for you. Many aren't so lucky."

"I am grateful," Annabel protested. "But I'd just like to feel like I'm contributing somehow. I've been thinking of getting a job."

"What kind of a job?" Ms. Durant asked. She had a skeptical look on her face, and Annabel scowled.

"I don't know," Annabel said. She wasn't sure what she was really qualified for — she had a high school diploma but nothing else.

"That's not a very good place to start, is it?" Ms. Durant said.

"I suppose not." Their drinks arrived and Ms. Durant took a delicate sip of her espresso.

"Hmm," she said, pursing her lips. "Not up to their usual standard. Certainly doesn't hold a candle to the espresso I had in Italy."

"When have you been to Italy?" Annabel asked. Her jasmine tea was too hot to drink, but Annabel inhaled the delicate floral scent of the steam rising from the cup while she waited for it to cool.

"I studied there for a year in college," Ms. Durant said. "In Rome."

"You never told me that!" Annabel's tone was almost accusatory.

"You never asked," Ms. Durant replied, taking another sip of the espresso. "This is growing on me, I think."

"That's not fair," Annabel chided. "I didn't know enough to know I should ask about that. Does that make sense?"

"It does," Ms. Durant said. "I was only teasing. But there is a lot you don't know about me."

"What else?" Annabel asked.

"Nothing you need to concern yourself with, young lady," said Ms. Durant primly. "Some things would be inappropriate for a caretaker to share with her ward."

"But I'm an adult now. Married and everything," Annabel said, even though she did not really feel like an adult.

"That is true," Ms. Durant conceded. "But you're still quite young. I would not want to shock you."

"Shock me?" Now Annabel was really interested. "I bet you couldn't."

"Bet I could."

"You'll have to tell me so we can figure out who wins the bet," Annabel said.

Ms. Durant considered her for a moment before answering. Then she leaned forward and spoke in a conspiratorial voice. "I hitchhiked a few times when I was in my twenties. Also — I used to smoke."

"What?!" Annabel said. "You were a smoker who hitch-hiked?" Annabel couldn't even picture a young Ms. Durant, much less one with a cigarette in her mouth and her thumb out to signal she needed a ride.

Ms. Durant shrugged. "Everybody makes bad decisions when they're young."

"What else?" Annabel asked.

"Nothing abnormal," Ms. Durant replied. "Occasionally drinking too much, staying up all night. The sorts of things you do for no reason other than to prove you can."

"I've never done any of that," Annabel said in a small voice.

"Be grateful for it," Ms. Durant said. "You've been spared the need to experience that all firsthand. All it'll get you is a hangover."

"But maybe —"

"Not buts," Ms. Durant said firmly. "I only told you this because as you said you're a married woman now, and I thought you were mature enough to hear about my youthful mistakes without wanting to emulate them."

"Have you ever been in love?" Annabel asked. A faint frown line appeared between Ms. Durant's eyes, and she did not answer immediately. She sipped her espresso, looking as though she was lost in thought. Annabel waited.

"I have," Ms. Durant said finally. "Many years ago. It didn't work out."

"Why not? Who was he?" Annabel asked. She wondered what it was like, having never experienced it herself.

"Someone I went to school with," Ms. Durant said. "We were both young and stupid. Then after we broke up, he met someone else. For a long time I hoped he'd come back to me, but it wasn't to be."

"That's so sad," Annabel said.

"It was hard," Ms. Durant admitted. "But I'm grateful I had the good times, even though the end was painful. After a while, I moved on."

"Has there been anyone else?" Annabel asked.

"There have been a few over the years," Ms. Durant said. "But none of them lasted."

"Oh," Annabel said. She wanted to ask if Ms. Durant was lonely, but she couldn't quite bring herself to do it.

"Don't worry about me, my dear," Ms. Durant said, correctly interpreting the look on Annabel's face. "I've had plenty of joy in my life, and anyway I'm not dead yet."

That made Annabel smile.

"And what about Rex? You knew him when you were both young. Was he very different?"

Ms. Durant took a long while to answer, draining the last of her espresso then taking a sip of her soda water.

"Flat," she said, making a disappointed face as she put the glass back down. Annabel waited, watching her expectantly. "In many ways he was just the same," said Ms. Durant. "He loved *you* for one thing. And he still does." There was a pause during which the word *you* hung between them, unacknowledged by either for its inaccuracy.

"But was he — more fun back then?" Annabel asked in a tentative voice. She wished Ms. Durant could tell her something that would make the stranger who was her husband seem more lovable to her. *Is it possible to make yourself love someone?*

Ms. Durant turned the question back on Annabel. "He's not fun now?"

"It's — of course he is," Annabel lied. She couldn't bring herself to tell Ms. Durant the truth of their relationship. Ms. Durant continued to scrutinize Annabel for another moment before she nodded, apparently satisfied.

"Good," she said. "You're very fortunate, Annabel. Do you

know how many other women would kill to be in your place?"

"I am grateful." Annabel had lost count of how many times the word "grateful" had come up in this conversation. She drank the last of her tea quickly, then made her excuses.

"I'm sorry. I really should be getting back. Rex wants to have lunch with me." This wasn't the case; in fact Rex had told her he was likely going to be working until dinner. But as much as Annabel had previously craved company, now all she wanted was solitude.

"Of course. Please give him my regards." Both women stood up and gathered their things.

"I will." Annabel laid some bills on the table. Ms. Durant hugged Annabel briefly, then they parted ways. Annabel made her way slowly back to the trail that would lead her the long way home around the bay. Once Ms. Durant was out of sight, Annabel considered circling back to wander for a while. If she was lucky, maybe she would run into the shirtless gardener, although she didn't have the faintest idea what she'd do if she got her wish. All of her fantasies about him conveniently skipped over the initial contact and started mid-tryst. Annabel couldn't even bring herself to feel guilty for having them. It wasn't as though she expected them to ever become a reality.

She reached the trail that led back to the house without seeing many people — it was still the off-season for the New England beach town — and she began trudging through the grass, taking care to avoid any poison ivy. The walk back seemed to take no time at all. Annabel ate lunch alone when she returned, then spent the rest of the afternoon laying on the balcony with a book. She was rereading *Sense and Sensibility* in the hope that she'd learn something worthwhile about love and duty. She found herself more moved by the characters than ever before, particularly the fact that marriage was the only solution they had to remedy their unfortunate circumstances.

Inside she could hear the sound of a Roomba vacuum

slowly making its way over all the wooden floors of the house while Mrs. Lennox prepared dinner. The aroma drifting out the wide kitchen windows suggested paella, one of Annabel's favorites.

Rex made his appearance just as Marianne was cast aside by Willoughby. They sat down to dinner, and Rex asked about her morning with Ms. Durant. Annabel told him it was enjoyable but did not elaborate. Rex didn't seem to mind. After a few minutes of silence, Annabel took a deep breath and decided to broach the subject of her possible employment.

"I was thinking," she began in a tentative voice. " I might try to find a job. At least part time, so I'll have something to do during the day."

Rex looked up from the mussel he'd been removing from its shell. For a second he looked surprised, then he burst out laughing. Annabel shifted uncomfortably in her seat — this wasn't the reaction she'd been expecting from him.

Through his laughter Rex said, "But why?" as though it was the most hilariously preposterous suggestion he'd ever heard.

"I don't know," Annabel said stiffly. "I just thought it would be good for me to contribute."

"Oh my darling, there's no need for that!" Rex exclaimed, his mirth still evident in every line of his face. "We've absolutely no need for any additional income. You're already contributing more than enough."

"I just thought —" she began.

"— it would be fun?" Rex finished for her shrewdly. He still looked amused. "Trust me, a single day working in some boring shop will cure you of that notion. It's a great privilege not to have to work. Most women appreciate having that sort of security from their husbands."

"I do appreciate it," Annabel said. "It was just an idea."

"Tell you what," Rex said. "Instead of getting some silly little sales job or whatever you were thinking about, why don't you enroll in online university? You've always been interested in art history, haven't you? Might give us some new things to talk about."

Annabel considered the suggestion. She had never expressed any interest in art history before, but she assumed that he must be remembering something the original Annabel had liked. Annabel wasn't even bothered by his confusion — instead she felt excited for the first time in ages. *Something new.*

"I'll enroll tomorrow," she said. Rex smiled and lifted his wine glass to toast her decision.

25: JAVI

To Javi's pleasant surprise, neither of his parents brought up Imogen Shaw during the next couple of days. He had been dreading that painfully awkward conversation from the moment she'd said she called them. His dread was compounded by the fact that she had somehow become his new go-to masturbation fantasy. Try as he might, Javi couldn't figure out what it was about her that he found so arousing — sure, she was pretty but not exceptionally so. Maybe it had something to do with the fact that after their meeting he'd been dreaming of her — not just sexually but in all sorts of ways. She seemed to make at least a cameo appearance in just about every dream he could remember, no matter how much he tried to fight it. Then he'd wake up sweating profusely, usually with a rock-hard boner.

At breakfast on Thursday morning, Javi found himself once again dwelling on thoughts of Imogen. Irritated, he pushed them away while picking at his avocado toast, trying to focus instead on the study date he had that afternoon with Stella.

"Did you send Stanford your deposit yet?" his mother asked as she poured herself a cup of coffee. Javi grunted non-committally. She sat down across from him at the kitchen table and fixed him with a penetrating stare.

"What does that mean?" she asked.

"Not yet," he mumbled. Javi still hadn't talked to his parents about how he'd rather not follow their dead son's dream of attending Stanford, and that he'd prefer to choose his own school.

"Why not?" came his father's voice from the foot of the

stairs. His father strode through the living room into the open plan kitchen where he poured his coffee and sat down next to Javi.

"I just haven't yet." Javi hunched his shoulders. He did not want to have to deal with this over breakfast.

"Don't forget," cautioned his mother.

"I won't," Javi said.

"We should do something to celebrate," his father declared. "What d'you say?"

"That's a wonderful idea," chimed his mother. "What d'you think, honey? You've earned it."

Javi took a deep breath and let it out. "That sounds nice," he said tonelessly. He noticed his parents exchanging a look.

"You could show a *little* enthusiasm, sweetie," his mother said. "You've wanted this forever and now it's finally happened!"

"I wasn't the one who wanted it," mumbled Javi so quietly he wasn't sure if either of them heard.

"What are you talking about?" asked his father. A small crease appeared between his eyes.

"Nothing," Javi muttered. Silently, he reminded himself that it wasn't worth the argument right now. In fact, he'd been toying with the idea of not telling them until after he'd already sent his deposit to Georgetown. Then they wouldn't be able to force him to change his mind.

"No, go on, tell us. We're your parents," his father said with a slight edge to his voice.

Javi closed his eyes for a second then opened them. "I don't want to go to Stanford." He braced himself for the explosion.

"What — what d'you mean you *don't want to go to Stanford*?" His mother said, a dumbfounded look on her face. "You've wanted this since —"

"I wasn't the one who wanted it," Javi repeated, louder this time. His mother looked like he'd slapped her in the face.

"We *never* forced you into anything," she said, chin trembling and eyes tearing up. "Never. You're our son, our baby boy."

"I'm your replacement." Javi shoved his chair back and stood up, suddenly furious. Much slower and more calmly, his father stood up too. They were almost exactly the same height, and in his father's eyes Javi saw agony. The kitchen was silent apart from his mother crying, and thick with tension. It only took a moment before Javi's anger receded, replaced by shame and self-loathing. But even then, Javi still couldn't let go of his resentment. He felt guilty for hurting his parents, but he knew what he'd said was the truth.

"You're going to be late if you don't hurry," his father said softly, his jaw clenched so tightly Javi thought he might crack a tooth. Javi's throat was too constricted to speak so he just nodded and left the room. His mother wouldn't even look at him as he passed her, and tears flowed freely down her face.

Fred and Herman were waiting outside for him. He barely spoke on the drive, and just before they pulled into the parking lot Herman said, "You're quiet today."

"Just tired," Javi lied. Herman opened his mouth ready to inquire further when Fred shook his head, causing Herman to reluctantly let the matter drop. Javi was grateful, having no desire to discuss what had transpired that morning. He brooded for most of the day, but he could tell that by the time the last bell rang his friends were growing fed up with his moodiness. He made an effort to join in their plans to do a marathon of classic sci-fi movies that weekend starting with *The Matrix* trilogy, but his heart wasn't in it.

Fred dropped Javi off at the park again to meet Stella. He felt less nervous today, although he couldn't say whether it was because he was so preoccupied, or whether he was finally becoming used to her presence in his life.

He arrived at their usual spot in the shade of the willow tree a few minutes early. Stella wasn't there yet, and Javi lay on his back and stared up through the branches at the overcast sky wishing he had thought to bring a joint with him. He wasn't sure how much time had passed — he'd been zoning out and trying not to think of Imogen — when he heard leaves rustling. Stella dropped her bag and unceremoniously plopped down beside him, sitting cross-legged. The extra material of her short, flowing skirt pooled between her thighs. With effort, Javi pulled his gaze up to her face.

Luckily for him, she had been rummaging in her bag and hadn't noticed how long he had stared at her legs and what was between them. She seemed preoccupied too, and Javi sat up and shifted slightly so he could lean his back against the trunk of the tree.

"Not much for us to practice today," he said.

"No, I guess not." Stella tossed her tablet onto the grass between them, and typed furiously into her phone for a few seconds jabbing the "send" button much harder than was necessary.

"Should we maybe go over the new vocab from this week?" Javi suggested. Stella's phone beeped three times in quick succession with text notifications. She ignored it.

"Sounds good."

"Okay," Javi said, glancing at her phone uneasily. It beeped twice more. "D'you need to check those? I don't mind."

"No," Stella said in a tone that brooked no argument. Her lips were pursed in what Javi thought was suppressed anger, although it did not seem to be directed at him. He wanted to ask what was going on but figured she'd say if she wanted him to know. A second later as Javi was loading his notes from the last few days of lecture, Stella snatched up her phone, evidently having changed her mind about checking the messages. Whatever she saw obviously displeased her, since she sucked in an indignant breath and looked as though she was seriously considering flinging the phone away.

"Un-fucking-believable," she muttered to herself, clicking the screen off without replying. "My boyfriend," she said in answer to Javi's questioning look. Unbidden, Javi's pulse began to beat more quickly.

"Are you guys — have you been having problems?" Javi

asked, trying not to sound too hopeful.

"He's an idiot," Stella replied. "A jealous fucking idiot. I mean, we're just *friends*."

"We?" Javi asked, bewildered for a second.

"You and I," Stella clarified. "Kato doesn't like me spending time alone with you, as though he gets to have any say in what I do and with whom."

"Right," Javi said, sure his face would betray him and he'd inadvertently enrage Stella further with his euphoria. The idea that Kato Barre considered him a rival worth arguing with Stella over was so thrilling it made Javi momentarily forget his lingering resentment.

"I mean, I've told him it's ridiculous," Stella continued, oblivious to his suppressed happiness. "He obviously doesn't get the concept of platonic friends."

"Yeah, no," said Javi. "Stupid." Although he didn't admit it, Javi didn't think it was stupid at all. Of course Kato had to know he didn't just want to be Stella's friend, not really. What mesmerized him though, was that Kato apparently believed there was a chance she felt the same way about him. Not that Javi had any delusions that she shared this view — hadn't she just said repeatedly that they were only friends? Still, *someone* thought the idea of Stella Castell wanting him wasn't too crazy to contemplate, and that alone gave Javi a serious self-esteem boost.

"How long have you guys been together?" Javi asked, since she didn't seem eager to begin studying.

"Not long at all," Stella said. "We met over winter break but he didn't ask me out til a few weeks ago. Before that we just hung out whenever our groups of friends got together."

"Guess he must be the possessive type," Javi said.

"I guess," Stella looked dejected. "I thought he was different."

"Different how?" Javi asked.

"I dunno, just different."

"And that's . . . a good thing?" Javi hazarded a guess.

Stella gave him a look. "Yes."

"Am I different?" Javi asked. He thought he was probably pushing his luck since she was already in a mood, but her scowl softened when she looked at him and was replaced by a half-smile.

"Maybe. I haven't made up my mind about you yet."

"Really?" His heart was beating so fast now it was as though he'd been running for miles and miles.

"Is that so hard to believe?" Stella raised an eyebrow. She leaned back on her hands and her skirt rode up even higher. He couldn't stop his eyes from roving up her body, over her taut stomach to the swell of her breasts, to her slender neck, finally reaching her face — the full lips curved into a beguiling smile and the green-tinged hazel eyes watching him watch her. Javi's throat was dry, and he had to shift positions to hide his growing arousal. Somewhere in the back of his mind Javi wondered — was she flirting with him? Hadn't she just said they were only friends? But then he realized it didn't matter either way. He had wondered if she knew he wanted her, and now he seemed to have his answer.

The moment was broken by Stella's phone beeping again. She took her eyes off his, and read the message. With a sigh, she typed back a response. When she looked up her expression was content once more, and she seemed to be fighting a smile.

"Never mind," she said. "He's apologized."

"Oh." Javi felt himself deflate like an old balloon.

"Let's get started on that vocab," Stella said, all business. She picked up her tablet and began opening her notes.

"Okay," Javi said hollowly. He was the world's biggest idiot.

A few hours later, he returned home to find his mother brushing away tears and hurrying from the kitchen at his arrival. His father gave him a look that could almost be apologetic, then followed her upstairs to their bedroom. He could hear them arguing through the wall, but their words weren't clear enough to make out. Javi felt like screaming and throwing things, but he controlled the impulse. This was *his* life after all, they couldn't tell him what to do with it. Still, he hated himself for hurting them the way he had at breakfast that morning. A dead weight had settled somewhere between his chest and his stomach, and hadn't lifted all day except for the few minutes he'd been stupid enough to entertain the notion that Stella might reciprocate his feelings. The situation with his parents was fucked, and he didn't know if things would ever go back to the way they'd been before. He didn't even know if he wanted them to.

Upstairs in his bedroom, Javi found a note on his desk. It was in his mother's handwriting, and parts of it were slightly smudged as though she'd cried again while writing it. His stomach twisted itself into knots, and he considered knocking on their door to beg forgiveness. Instead, he read the note, going over it three times before he felt like he'd understood it properly. There had been a phone call that day from a reporter, someone from *2100* magazine named Arthur Blair. They were doing a piece on cloning, and they wanted to interview and profile the first three clones — the only ones who were over eighteen. There was a phone number at the bottom of the note.

Javi crumbled the paper in his fist. Why would anyone think he'd want to be paraded around like some sort of freak show for regular people to stare at and gossip about? He almost threw the crumpled note across the room into the small trash can by the door, but then he hesitated. Maybe it was pointless for him to try to blend in with everybody else. Maybe no matter what, he'd always be seen as different; an aberration from nature, a science experiment. Maybe he should accept who — what? — he was instead of living in denial. Where had denial gotten him, after all? Nowhere anyone wanted to be.

26: EDGAR PRIME

There were few things Edgar Prime found more tedious than spending the evening dodging geneticists clad in cocktail attire who wished to speak to him at the reception following the ICG keynote. He could feel their eyes following him as he refilled his wine glass and moved across the opulent ballroom to stand in the corner with Patrice.

Dr. Midas, on the other hand, was in his element. His keynote address had been a smashing success, and he'd had Edgar Prime assist him by using a laser pointer to indicate which part of each slide he was discussing when he shared the results of their latest experiments. Edgar Prime supposed it was charitable of Dr. Midas to refer to them as "our experiments" as opposed to "my experiments" but they both knew that was more for PR than any true involvement on Edgar Prime's part in designing them. Dr. Midas stood in the center of the ballroom while the rest of them hovered around him like vultures over an animal carcass, waiting to take their turn shaking his hand, asking their questions — even breathing the same air as the father of human cloning. It was this that caused Edgar Prime to refill his wine glass for the third time.

"I'd go easy on that if I were you," Patrice said mildly. She looked nicer than usual; instead of being thrown into a messy bun, her black hair fell in loose waves around her shoulders and she had lined her dark eyes with kohl.

Edgar Prime took a long sip of his red wine before answering. "You're not me," he said. He didn't know much about wine, but this one was smooth with a spicy finish. Patrice shrugged.

"Guess you know what you're doing."

"I do, thanks," Edgar Prime said. He was vaguely annoyed by the whole situation, but he didn't want Patrice to leave because then he'd have no excuse not to talk to the others. He cast about for something to say, his mind drawing a blank.

"Hello, Prime," said a deep voice off to his right. Startled but endeavoring not to show it, Edgar Prime turned to find a man he'd met a few times before, but couldn't honestly say he liked. Damon Aldous Harlow was in his early sixties but well-preserved: compact but muscular with a healthy, natural-looking tan, artfully tousled gray hair and a five o'clock shadow that made him look almost ruggedly handsome. Edgar Prime was well familiar with the way his ice blue eyes drew people in, the pitch of his mesmerizingly persuasive voice, and the way he always seemed fully engaged in whoever he focused his attention on.

Harlow was the world's first-ever trillionaire, Dr. Midas's most prominent financial backer and the Chairman of the Board of Directors for Midas Labs. As the living embodiment of one of Harlow's many investments, Edgar Prime always felt uncomfortable around him.

"Hello Mr. Harlow," said Edgar Prime stiffly.

"Hello Mr. Harlow," Patrice echoed.

"Excellent presentation today Prime, excellent," said Harlow. "Hello to you too, Patrice. Your work at the institute is invaluable. Don't know what Edgar would do without you." He nodded to where Dr. Midas was laughing with a small cluster of colleagues.

"Thank you, sir," Patrice said. She seemed surprised and flattered that Harlow was familiar with her work. Edgar Prime had heard that he made it his business to know about everyone employed by the institute, and all those who made use of its services. Information was power, and all that.

"How are you getting on at university, Prime?" Harlow asked. Edgar Prime could see his small knot of surreptitious observers leaning even closer.

"Good," Edgar Prime said.

"Got a favorite class? Let me guess — genetics!" Harlow guffawed at his own joke.

"Actually, I'm really enjoying my world history class," Edgar Prime said.

"History?" Harlow seemed incredulous. "What's history good for? Just a bunch of dry old men rattling on about things that no longer matter to those of us who live in the here and now."

"I like the stories," Edgar Prime explained. "And they say history repeats itself."

"Pah!" Harlow said. "Pish posh balderdash is what I say to that. The future belongs to those who take it, not those who spend their days looking behind them. I'd have thought you'd know that, Prime."

Edgar Prime didn't reply, instead draining the rest of his wine. Patrice looked like she wanted to laugh but was trying hard not to.

"I'm gonna get a refill," Edgar Prime said, holding up his empty glass.

"Good to see you, Prime," Harlow said. As Edgar Prime walked off, he saw Harlow lean in towards Patrice, no doubt hoping to charm and co-opt her like he seemed to do with everybody else. Moodily, Edgar Prime handed his glass back to the bartender and requested it be filled up to the top.

"Prime!" cried a jubilant voice behind him just as the bartender handed Edgar Prime his now-full wineglass. Edgar Prime turned around to find Dr. Midas standing there with his oldest friend and occasional lover, Dr. Caden Yang. Behind them stood several others Edgar Prime didn't know, hanging on to Dr. Midas's every word. Dr. Midas threw an arm around Edgar Prime's shoulders, effectively trapping him there.

"Skulking around by the bar I see," Dr. Midas said with a grin. "Very prudent, Prime. Take advantage of the lower drinking age in Europe while you can." The others chuckled appreciatively. Dr. Yang's dark eyes glittered with amusement, and he gave Edgar Prime the smallest of winks.

"Like original, like clone." Dr. Yang declared.

Dr. Midas threw his head back and roared with laugher. He turned towards the others and said in a conspiratorial stage whisper, "Caden here knew me before I became respectable. Oh, those were the days."

One of the clustered sycophants edged forward; a chubby man in his late twenties. He had auburn hair, a goatee, a pointed nose and a sweaty sheen on his forehead that he mopped away with his sleeve before extending his hand to Edgar Prime.

"Arthur Blair, *2100* magazine. Dr. Midas was kind enough to agree to an interview on your behalf for our upcoming feature about the first three clones."

Edgar Prime blinked, but after a second got a hold of himself and shook Arthur Blair's hand. He couldn't say he relished the idea of talking to a reporter, but agreeing would require less effort than arguing the point with Dr. Midas.

"You'll all have that to look forward to next month!" Dr. Midas said to the crowd.

"Yes, it'll be timed with the nineteen year anniversary of the birth of human cloning," Blair said. "Or as I'm sure you think of it, *your* birthday, Edgar Prime!"

"Right," said Edgar Prime.

"You can call him 'Prime' for short," Dr. Midas said. "Although lately he's preferred being called 'Ed' for some unfathomable reason."

"Whichever you like," Blair said graciously.

"Ed is fine," said Edgar Prime, shrugging Dr. Midas's arm off his shoulders.

"Asserting his independence," commented Dr. Yang with a smirk.

"As well he should!" Dr. Midas said.

Edgar Prime couldn't remember him ever being in such a jovial mood.

"He'll be the one to take up the mantle once I'm gone, so

to speak. Independent thought and intellectual curiosity are essential to the heir apparent of Midas Labs. Edgar Prime has both in spades — and small wonder since he's an exact genetic copy of the man who created him! You can quote me on that," Dr. Midas told Blair.

"Why, thank you," Blair said. Edgar Prime restrained himself from rolling his eyes with difficulty, and began tiptoeing away from Dr. Midas. It was possible that Dr. Yang noticed this and decided to help Edgar Prime out with a diversion, because he chose that moment to ask Dr. Midas whether he'd heard about the scandalous divorce of one of their old MIT fraternity brothers, and immediately launched into the story which featured a multi-billion dollar settlement and reciprocal attempted murders.

Edgar Prime made his way back into the corner where he found Patrice flirting with one of the panelists due to give a talk the following afternoon. She winked at him over the man's shoulder, and shortly thereafter the two of them disappeared together, sharing a taxi back to the hotel. Not sure what to make of this considering what Patrice had told him on the flight about her long-term boyfriend, Edgar Prime circled the room aimlessly. Alone in the crowd, he thought maybe he'd stayed long enough to be polite and could slip away unnoticed too. It seemed that he was not the only one thinking along these lines. Dr. Midas and Dr. Yang were leaving as well, and as he exited the building Edgar Prime saw them kiss in the back of a taxi as it pulled away from the curb.

"What happens at the I.C.G. stays at the I.C.G.," Harlow said from behind him with a hearty guffaw. Edgar Prime jumped, not having heard his approach.

"I guess so," Edgar Prime said.

"You don't seem to be taking advantage of your rock star status, Prime. Intimidated by all the fine researchers around us? Ha! You shouldn't be. They're only human, after all." Harlow chuckled at that.

"Nobody here thinks I'm a rock star," Edgar Prime said.

"You need to sharpen up your observation skills," Harlow said. "The hangers-on have been lurking after you all night. You could go home with any of them in an instant if you wanted to."

"And what about you?" Edgar Prime said. "Why aren't you enjoying the — the scenery?" He stepped closer to the curb and stuck his arm out to hail a taxi.

"Who says I'm not?" Harlow's eyes gleamed.

A taxi pulled up. Edgar Prime stood by uncertainly, thinking that it might be bad manners for him not to offer the first taxi to Harlow.

"Your ride is here kid," Harlow said. A stretch limousine pulled up behind the taxi. "This is me."

Edgar Prime clambered into the taxi as the door to Harlow's limo automatically swung open for him. He saw Edgar Prime looking and gave him a mock salute before climbing into the limo and driving off into the night. It was only then that Edgar Prime noticed the small knot of anti-cloning protesters watching him from a square across the street with their homemade signs. For a moment, he forgot where he was going, but after the automated voice asked him twice he blurted out the name of the hotel, and stared back at the protestors' silent vigil in the taxi's wing mirror until they disappeared from view.

27: ANNABEL

At first, Annabel thought Mrs. Lennox handed her the envelope by accident. She had heard the mail carrier drone make the delivery, but had assumed it belonged to Rex. For a moment after reading her own name above the address, Annabel only stared — she had never gotten a single piece of mail her whole life — but then she clutched the letter to her chest and hurried outside to the balcony without even saying thank you to Mrs. Lennox. In her favorite chair facing the bay she tore open the envelope quickly, burning with curiosity.

Inside was a short typed letter, inviting her to be interviewed for *2100* magazine as part of a piece about the first three clones. The letter was signed by somebody named Arthur Blair. It was strange to think that there were others who knew about her, that a major magazine even wanted to interview her for an article that who knows how many people would read.

Accompanying the article would be a photo shoot with the three clones together. That was what really piqued her interest. Not the idea of being photographed, which made Annabel feel vaguely uncomfortable, but the prospect of meeting the others. She had always wondered about her fellow clones, but had never before had an opportunity to meet one. The thought was exciting and nerve-wracking at the same time.

She pulled out her tablet and did a quick search. The only information she was able to find was about the first-ever clone, a copy of the father of human cloning, Dr. Edgar Midas. He had named his clone 'Edgar Prime' and was still conducting research with him at Midas Labs. The name made Annabel shiver slightly as she realized that this was the place where she had been conceived. It was strange to contemplate.

Annabel next tried searching her own name, but the only things that came up were about her original — the first Annabel King. While Annabel already knew a fair amount about her original through Ms. Durant, it was learned in the context of shaping Annabel into the clone wife that Rex had paid for, a copy of his lost love. But this was different somehow, reading about her on google. Before, she had only thought of her original in relation to Rex but here, Annabel saw, there was evidence that she was her own person as well. There wasn't much — a small piece here or there about an opening at her art gallery, some blog posts she'd written reviewing various artists — but it made her seem real in a way she never quite had before.

There was nothing readily available that mentioned Annabel the clone though. Obviously some people had to know about it since the *2100* magazine reporter had requested an interview, but it seemed her existence was not widely acknowledged. Annabel supposed the people who paid so much to have a clone made might not want publicity. It was then that she began to feel wary about Rex's reaction to the interview invitation.

The more she thought about it, the more she knew he'd be opposed to the idea. Would he go so far as to forbid her to participate? It wasn't outside the realm of possibility. She knew she'd have to be careful how she brought it up, find a way to persuade him that it was a benign idea — one that would not reflect poorly on him. She thought about it for a time and decided her best strategy would be to feign nonchalance and downplay the invitation as much as possible. Having decided, Annabel turned to her online Arts of Renaissance Europe class. It was one of several she had enrolled in; the others were International Relations and Intro to Physics. Rex had scoffed slightly at the last one and reminded her that she hated science. She didn't argue but added it to her course schedule anyway, reasoning that just because the original Annabel had hated science didn't mean she would too.

Annabel listened to a lecture on Artemisia Gentileschi and watched the painting slide show diligently, but she wasn't as engaged as usual. Underneath, she kept thinking about the interview, the prospect of meeting two other clones, and the apprehension of trying to convince Rex to allow her to do it. Her stomach clenched and unclenched as her plan ran through her mind over and over again on an endless loop despite her best efforts to focus on the art history lecture. Annabel switched to a physics lecture, but didn't have much more luck learning about Newton's Three Laws of Motion than she had learning about *Judith Slaying Holofernes*.

Mrs. Lennox called her in for lunch, and she kept the envelope with the letter clutched in a sweaty palm. Rex seemed preoccupied when they sat down, and Annabel saw her opening.

"This came today," she said in as casual a voice as she could muster. She tossed the envelope onto the table as though it was of no real importance to her.

"What is it?" Rex asked, ladling some of the miso soup Mrs. Lennox had prepared into their bowls.

Annabel shrugged. "Some reporter is writing an article about the first three clones, and he wants to do an interview. Nothing big, I don't think. Most of it will probably be about the scientists behind it all."

Rex's spoon froze halfway to his mouth. "Out of the question."

"But —"

"What is wrong with you, Annabel? Our private affairs have no place in — which rag wanted to do the story?"

"*2100* magazine," Annabel said reluctantly.

Rex made a disparaging noise and gulped down another spoon of his soup. "What nonsense."

"But what's the harm —"

"Didn't you hear me?" Rex's eyes narrowed. "It's out of the

question. I don't want to hear another word about you talking to any reporters. Ever. Is that understood?"

Annabel choked on her frustrated shame in silence. With a short nod she let the subject drop.

28: JAVI

Neither of Javi's parents spoke to him about the argument for the rest of the week. His mother didn't speak to him at all, and his father only spoke about the most superficial of topics: the weather, his favorite TV shows, march madness — always in a falsely jovial voice. Most of the time, they both seemed to avoid him. He supposed they thought it was easier that way. Javi spent a lot of time in his room listening to metal and watching porn.

The guilt of his confrontation with his parents was eating Javi alive, but he couldn't bring himself to apologize for it. He hadn't even told them about the phone conversation he'd had with Arthur Blair after impulsively deciding to do the interview. Blair's assistant had answered the phone on the third ring.

"Arthur Blair's office," he said in a bored but professional voice.

"Um," Javi said. "My name is Javier Vasquez. I'm returning Mr. Blair's call —"

"One moment," said the assistant.

There was a click, and Blair introduced himself almost immediately. "I'm very glad you called, Javier. Do you go by Javier, or something else?"

"Javi usually," Javi said.

"Javi it is!" Arthur Blair had a painfully eager voice that made Javi want to cringe. "I'd like to fly out and conduct your interview in person sometime next week if that works for you."

"Okay," Javi said nervously.

"Don't worry, I'll work around any school commitments you have," Blair said. "But it's always best to get a sense of the environment a subject inhabits — gives the whole thing more color."

"Right," Javi said, not sure he knew what the man was talking about.

"Then we'll have you fly to New York for a weekend to do the photo shoot with the other clones."

"I — what?" Javi thought he'd misheard. *The other clones?*

"If you're unable to come, we can photograph you closer to home and digitally insert you in with the other two being profiled," Blair said. "But if possible we'd really like to do the shoot with all three of you together so that you can meet and interact naturally for the pictures. And of course we'll cover your travel expenses."

"Um, okay," Javi said, barely aware of what he was agreeing to. He wasn't sure why the casual mention of other clones was so jarring — he had always known he wasn't the only one.

"Excellent!" Blair said. "I'll have my assistant contact you to finalize the details."

"Okay," Javi said again.

"I look forward to meeting you, Javi." It was only after they hung up that Javi began to wonder what he had gotten himself into.

All of this together left Javi moody and withdrawn for the rest of the week, and he found himself alone at his computer on Friday afternoon. He wasn't sure what made him search for her home address, but before he knew it he was putting it into his phone's GPS and heading outside. He had just missed the bus, but the walk was only about twenty minutes. The time passed quickly, and suddenly he was standing outside a single story Spanish style house. The front yard was a large vegetable garden replete with tomatoes, several types of squash, strawberries, and various leafy greens, with a winding path leading up from the sidewalk to the front door. There was even a lemon tree that gave the air a clean, pleasantly tart scent. Javi hesitated, then took a deep breath and walked up to knock.

For a moment there was no answer, and Javi wondered if she was out. Then the door opened to reveal a little girl, no more than seven. Javi's mouth fell open and he mentally kicked himself for not realizing — she'd mentioned that she had kids when they spoke in the park after all.

"Who are you?" the girl asked. She looked up at him quizzically. She had the same gray eyes as her mother, but her hair was sandy blonde.

"I — my name is Javi. Is your mom here?" Javi heard himself asking. He sounded calm, despite his inner panic. Part of him wanted to flee, but something kept him rooted to the spot.

"Who's there, Bryony?" Imogen called from the back of the house.

"Someone named Javi!" yelled Bryony. For a moment she studied Javi, and he felt uncomfortable under her scrutiny. "He says he's here to see you," she added, twisting around to yell back to wherever her mother was. Just like that, she lost interest in Javi and wandered off, leaving him alone on the front step with the door hanging open.

Somewhere inside the house he could hear the sound of a robot vacuum, and the joyous shrieks of two small children raucously playing together. Javi had almost convinced himself to turn around and leave when Imogen appeared, wearing charcoal leggings and a loose-fitting pink shirt, her hair wet presumably from a shower. There was a long pause; she just looked at him.

"D'you want to come in?" she asked finally. "I just made lemonade."

"Um," Javi said, mentally kicking himself for acting on this stupid impulse. "Lemonade would be great, thanks." He followed Imogen across the threshold and closed the door behind him. She led him through the house and into the kitchen where she poured homemade lemonade for him and iced green tea for herself.

"I didn't expect to see you again," she said, as they sat down together at the gleaming cherrywood table.

"I — yeah, I dunno what I was thinking, I'm sorry. I'll go." Javi made to stand up, but Imogen placed a hand on his arm to stop him.

"No need to rush off. You haven't even tried my lemonade yet."

Javi relaxed back into his seat and took a sip. It was the perfect balance of tart and sweet, everything lemonade should be. "It's good," Javi said, and she smiled appreciatively. He took another sip. There was a brief silence, but it wasn't as uncomfortable as before. Eventually Javi said, "This is a nice house."

"It is, isn't it? We bought it last year when we moved back here."

"Where did you live before?" Javi asked.

"All over," Imogen said. "Edinburgh, Shanghai, Buenos Aires, Sydney, L.A. Theo and I both have location independent jobs so we moved every few years. But since the girls are getting to be school-aged we thought it would be good for them to have some stability. Both our parents live nearby so the girls can spend time with their grandparents . . . good decision all around."

"It must have been cool — living in all those places."

Imogen shrugged. "We ended right back where we started." Javi couldn't tell whether she was relieved or disappointed.

"Are you going to tell me why you came?" Imogen asked. She fixed him with an intense stare, and he found couldn't meet her eyes for more than a couple seconds at a time. He imagined that beneath the curiosity and a strange sadness there was longing in Imogen's gaze, but he dismissed this. The last thing he needed was to confuse the Imogen he fantasized about when he was alone with the real, living, breathing one — he doubted he'd survive the humiliation of her finding him out. He swallowed and took a deep breath.

"My parents aren't speaking to me," Javi blurted out.

"Because of me?" Imogen asked, furrowing her brow.

"No, no, it's nothing to do with you. It's because I don't want to go to Stanford."

Imogen gave him a twisted half-smile. "Javier — your original, I mean — he'd wanted to go since he was a child. The day he got in we —" she blushed suddenly, and dropped her eyes to the table. "Well, anyway. It meant a lot to him. But I don't think that they'd really stop speaking to you over it. You're all they have now."

"They want me to be *him*," muttered Javi.

The look Imogen gave him was not unkind, but it was clear that she didn't understand what he was trying to say. "But you are him. You're just like him. You may not want to hear that, but it's true. I knew him better than almost anyone."

Javi felt a morbid curiosity all of a sudden. "Do you still miss him?"

"I do." She said it without hesitation, and for a moment, Javi couldn't breathe. It brought back the crushing weight of his parents' expectations, and reminded him of what a failure he was. Every thought in his head, every word that came out of his mouth, every action he took — they were all wrong. Whatever Imogen said, he wasn't the same as his original. At best he was a poor imitation, but more often he was an endless disappointment.

"I'm not him." Javi didn't know if he meant it to be regretful or defiant.

"Does it really matter?" she asked.

He frowned. "I don't know." That answer felt wrong, but he couldn't think how to articulate himself better— whenever Imogen leaned forward he could see down her loose-fitting shirt, and the sight of her cleavage made him feel fuzzy and distracted. Javi's hand was resting on the table next to his lemonade glass, and she placed her hand over his. He froze; a jolt of adrenaline shot through his body at her touch.

"He was a wonderful person," she said, tracing his fingers softly with hers. "When people compare you to him, it's a compliment."

Javi gave a curt nod, not trusting himself to speak. *What is she doing?* As if in answer, she grasped his hand and gave it a little squeeze. His fingers curled around hers involuntarily. He couldn't meet her eyes, instead staring at their interlocked fingers. The temperature in the kitchen had been ratcheted up by thirty degrees or more. Javi chanced a glance at her and saw that she too was staring at their hands. She looked up then and met his eyes for the briefest of seconds, before she leaned over and softly brushed his lips with hers. At first he was too stunned to react, but when she broke the kiss and pulled back he leaned towards her without meaning to, stopping once his mind caught up to his body.

Heart thudding in his chest, Javi stared at her lips as they curved into a small smile. Every cell in his body was screaming for him to act on his desire, but before he could work up the courage, Bryony burst into the room giggling, followed by another girl who looked a lot like her except a few years younger.

Imogen snatched her hand away from the table as her daughters bounced over carrying a large and messy collage between them that they'd made with colored paper.

"Look Mommy, look!" squealed the smaller of the two girls.

"It's beautiful, Poppy," Imogen said. There was a faint blush on her cheeks and Javi felt a strange surge of pride at having been the one to put it there.

"I helped!" exclaimed Bryony indignantly.

"Of course you did, sweetie," Imogen said with a smile.

"Your face is all red," Bryony informed Javi, and he reflexively looked down at the floor in an attempt to hide it.

"Bryony, it's not polite to say that to someone," Imogen chided gently.

"But it *is*," Bryony insisted.

"Yeah," Poppy chimed in.

"Hush," Imogen said. "Why don't you girls go ahead and make another collage so we can hang one in each of your rooms? That way Mommy can have some time to talk to Javier."

"That's *boring*," Poppy said, yawning theatrically.

"Poppy," Imogen said in a warning voice.

"Boring, boring, BORING!" Poppy shouted gleefully, jumping up and down before swatting at her sister and screaming, "You're it!" then running off with Bryony in hot pursuit. Javi heard the sound of a screen door opening as Poppy and Bryony took their tag game out to the backyard.

"That should keep them occupied for a little while at least," Imogen said with a mischievous look in her eye. "Come with me." She grabbed Javi's hand and jerked him to his feet, leading him out of the kitchen and down a long hallway into the master bedroom on the opposite side of the house. Javi didn't have time to react to his shock before Imogen reached behind him to push the door shut and click the lock into place.

Javi barely had a chance to register her nearness — her soft breasts brushed against his chest and her face was only inches from his — or the fact that he was standing in the bedroom she shared with her husband, before she pressed her lips to his again and wrapped her arms around his neck. He returned the kiss with a desperate fervor he didn't realize he had, and snaked his arms around her waist to pull her closer. There was no space between them now — Javi couldn't wrap his head around what was happening and didn't care to try.

Imogen broke the kiss and leaned back to say, "We don't have long." She pulled off her clothes deftly and Javi stood there gaping at her naked breasts, swaying this way and that with every motion. She chuckled at his dumbfounded look and yanked his shirt off over his head before grabbing his hands and placing them on her. He ran his thumbs over her nipples, his mind strangely blank and calm, even as his boner painfully throbbed against his jeans. Imogen unbuttoned and unzipped his pants and yanked them down along with his boxers. She took him in one hand and squeezed his ass with the other, leading him to the bed without waiting for him to step out of his pants or take off his shoes. When his knees hit the edge of the bed she pushed him onto his back, crawled on top of him, and kissed him before unceremoniously guiding him inside her.

His body was on fire, a thrumming vibration of ecstasy as she rode him and it was only a few of seconds before he exploded inside her with a groan.

"Shh!" Imogen whispered, playfully putting a hand over his mouth and laughing musically. "The girls will hear." She leaned over and kissed him, their tongues intertwining before she moved down to nibble his ear and kiss his neck. He ran his hands over her back, her breasts, her ass, her legs. After a little while he felt himself stiffen again — when Imogen felt him poking her inner thigh, she looked down and grinned.

"So soon," she murmured. She guided him inside her once more, and this time he flipped them over so he was on top. She raked her fingernails over his back, not quite breaking the skin, and with her instruction he found a rhythm. The second time lasted longer, and just before he came she gasped and he felt her contract around him over and over and over again. When he finished he collapsed on top of her, sweating and panting.

Just before he rolled off her, Imogen whispered into his ear, "God I've missed you, Javier."

29: BOB

The air was colder than it should've been for April. Bob zipped up his leather jacket as he stepped out of the car and made his way briskly up the front walk. Everything from the neat brick building to the sprawling, well-maintained garden that took up much of the ground between the street and the front entrance was a testament to the generosity of Damon Aldous Harlow III. No one could claim that the clones at this shelter weren't well cared-for.

Bob shivered as the wind whipped through his short black hair and made its way under his collar. Truth be told Bob hated this part, but he was nothing if not dutiful. He had never been one to shrink from an unsavory task.

The front door opened almost immediately when Bob rang the bell, as though the smiling attendant who answered it had been waiting for him. Bob stepped across the threshold into the familiar hallway that led off towards classrooms on the ground floor and dormitories upstairs. As with the exterior, the building was plain but well-maintained.

"I'll be right back, Mr. Smith," said the middle-aged woman who had let him in.

"Please Angelica, call me Bob."

Angelica giggled, then retreated down the hallway. He thought she was swaying her hips more than usual for his benefit.

A few moments later, Angelica returned, leading a small girl by the hand. The girl was probably five years old with blonde hair and clouded, unseeing eyes. Bob's brow furrowed. No one had told him the girl was blind. He supposed the buyer must have requested her especially . . . but no, it wouldn't do to go down that road.

"Dolores, this is Mr. Smith. Remember how we talked about you going on a trip?" The false enthusiasm in Angelica's voice was painful. It was all Bob could do not to wince.

The girl turned her sightless eyes vaguely in his direction. "Are you going to take me to my new family?" she asked him.

Bob coughed. "Yes. We'll need to fly on an airplane to get there. Have you ever been on an airplane before?"

"No," she said quietly. Bob could tell she was afraid but was trying to appear brave. He knelt down in front of her.

"It'll be an adventure," he told her. "You'll see."

She gave him the tiniest of smiles.

"I've got her luggage here," Angelica prattled, wheeling a small suitcase over to him. "It's got her white cane, although she's still learning to use it. You'll need to hold her hand to keep her from bumping into things or getting lost."

"No problem," Bob said. He stood up, and Angelica passed Dolores' hand to him. "Is this okay?" he asked her.

Dolores squeezed his hand tighter and nodded.

"Bye-bye, Dolores!" Angelica chirped.

"Bye, Angelica," the girl replied with a sniffle.

"Ready to go?" Bob asked her. They needed to hurry up if they wanted to make their flight to Rome.

"Yes," Dolores said solemnly.

Bob took the suitcase in his free hand and wheeled it out, careful to walk slowly enough that Dolores could keep up. When they reached the car, he opened the door and helped her into the back seat.

"Newark Airport," he told the computer.

"Destination: Newark International Airport," replied a cool, robotic voice as the car pulled away from the curb. "Estimated arrival time: 5:27pm."

"Who's that?" Dolores asked.

"It's the car," Bob explained. "I tell it where we want to go, then it drives us there."

"How does it know where to drive?" Dolores asked.

"It's got a computer that follows a map."

Dolores seemed to mull that over. "Oh," was all she had to say in response.

Bob settled back against the seat, expecting Dolores to remain silent. She barely lasted two minutes.

"How far away is Newark Airport?" she asked.

"Not too far," Bob said. His head had started throbbing, just behind the eyes. "A couple of hours."

"What's it like to ride on an airplane?"

"You'll find out soon. Let's play the quiet game. You can look out the window or something." The instant the words were out of his mouth, Bob realized his mistake. Confusion then sadness flitted across Dolores's face. The throbbing in Bob's head increased in tempo.

"I'm sorry," he said. "I just meant —"

"It's okay," Dolores said. "Angelica always says I talk too much."

"No, it's not you," Bob lied. "I had a fight with my sister earlier and it made me cranky." *Why did I tell her that?* Bob wondered. It was the truth. They'd argued (again) about Harlow. Just thinking about it caused Bob to clench his teeth. It wasn't the first time he resented Rebecca — *Jane now*, he mentally corrected — for getting him involved in this mess, but whenever he brought it up, she always managed to Jedi Mind Trick him into agreeing that it was really the best thing.

"I understand," Dolores said solemnly, although of course Bob knew she couldn't possibly. He felt absurdly grateful for her attempt at empathy, however.

She didn't talk much for the rest of the ride, and he was grateful for that too. Once they arrived, they approached the check in counter where Bob produced two forged passports (today they were Peter and Eloise Hayes) and a notarized letter from Dolores's "mother", giving him, her "father" permission to bring Dolores out of the country, ostensibly to visit her godparents in Rome. The airline attendant looked over all their documents carefully, but she was all smiles as Bob chatted amiably with her, and they were sent on to security without any trouble.

After they finished checking in, Bob had one of the female attendants take Dolores to the bathroom. They went to the gate together afterwards, and he guided her into a leather chair in the first class lounge. Her legs were too short to reach the floor, and she swung them back and forth.

"Are we on the airplane yet?" she asked him.

"No. We're waiting to board. It won't be long now, maybe fifteen minutes."

"Can you tell me about where we're going?"

"We're going to Rome. It's . . . a very beautiful city. The food is better than anything you've ever tasted before. Have you ever had ice cream? They have something like it there, but better. It's called gelato."

"I like ice cream," Dolores said. "Especially chocolate."

"The chocolate gelato you'll have in Rome is the best in the world," he told her. *It's not a lie,* he told himself. *It might not be a lie. You don't know what he's planning.*

The time came for them to board. They settled into the first row, with Dolores on the window seat. When the captain announced that they were taking off, she grabbed for his hand, groping frantically over the arm rest. Bemused, he reached over to her, and felt her tiny fingers grip his.

"I'm scared," she whispered.

A punch to the gut would've hurt less. "It's okay," he lied. "It'll all be okay."

She continued to squeeze his hand for duration of the take-off. Once the plane leveled off, she loosened her grip but did not let go.

"Are we flying?" she asked him.

"We are," he replied. "Not so bad, is it?"

"Not so bad," she agreed.

It wasn't too long before she drifted off to sleep. Bob tried to sleep as well, but instead found himself watching her. He told himself it was a stomachache that kept him from sleeping, but he knew the lie was hollow. She wasn't the first clone he'd escorted to an overseas buyer, but this one felt different, somehow. Perhaps it was the buyer himself. There was something about that man's eyes that made Bob's skin crawl. He thought about his parents then, and how his mother would slap him and tell him to toughen up if she were around to hear his thoughts. Hesitation was a weakness, and weakness had no place in their world.

When the plane landed in Rome, Bob took Dolores's hand and led her through the airport, outside to their waiting car.

"Your hand is sweaty," she informed him.

"Sorry." Bob's stomachache had gotten worse, and the dull throbbing behind his eyes had started again. *It's because I didn't sleep. Not anything else.*

Bob told the car their address and it pulled away from the curb. Dolores hummed to herself excitedly. The ride seemed to take no time at all. As Bob helped Dolores out of the car, he thought, *this is your last chance to change your mind.* He ignored that, and walked towards the building entrance. It was like moving through molasses, through quicksand. Each step required an extraordinary effort.

When they reached the penthouse, Bob fumbled in his pocket for the key. He slid it into the lock and turned. The door swung open to reveal the buyer, seated on the couch where he could watch them enter. The look on his face was predatory, and there was greed in his cold eyes. *He's not even trying to hide it. She can't see him so . . .*

"Hello, Dolores," said the man. "I'm your new Daddy."

"Hello," Dolores said shyly. She still clung to Bob's hand.

The man stood up and approached them. Dolores took an involuntary half-step behind Bob. The man's eyes flicked over her, not failing to notice. Far from being put-off, her fear seemed to excite him further. He reached out and snatched her hand from Bob. She let out a little yelp in surprise, and turned her head from side-to-side, as if trying in vain to see what was going on. The look on her face shattered Bob's heart in a million pieces.

"That'll be all," the man told him. "We're fine here."

Bob stood where he was, staring dumbly. A hand found its way onto his shoulder and another gripped the crook of his elbow. He turned to see an armed security guard, and when the hands tugged him towards the exit, none too gently, he didn't resist. As the door was slammed behind him, he heard Dolores whimper.

He didn't have a very clear memory of making his way outside. The next thing Bob knew, he was vomiting in an alleyway as disgusted tourists gave him a wide berth and a few locals screamed insults at him from their balconies. No doubt they thought he was just another drunk American, sloppy and pathetic. With each retch, Bob heard that whimper repeated in his head over and over and over again. He wanted nothing more than to lie down on the ground, curl up in a ball and sleep, never to wake again. *Weak,* a voice in his head whispered. It sounded uncannily like his father. *You've always been weak.* Bob knew it was the truth.

30: EDGAR PRIME

"Dr. Edgar Midas is a genius," Harlow said to a small knot of reporters gathered on the steps outside the conference center. "A visionary. But some credit must go to the lawmakers — legalizing human cloning was the best thing our congress has done in years. The people spoke, and for once congress listened." Harlow gave a guffaw at that, and the journalists holding the microphones tittered.

Harlow continued, "It has allowed the United States to once again lead the world in science and technology. Dr. Edgar Midas has done more than advance the field of genetics — in creating the cloning industry he has solved the problem of grief. In doing so, he has joined the great pantheon of those who have irrevocably changed our world, whose contributions will continue to echo for generations, for centuries. I am honored to have been able to facilitate his work in my own small way. After all, even the greatest researcher needs funding, doesn't he!" The press around Harlow smiled indulgently, but Edgar Prime shook his head in disgust and walked off before Harlow could continue — he had heard more than enough of Harlow's pontificating for one day.

He made it to the building entrance before he stopped. His arms and legs had turned to lead, they weighed him down and each step was more difficult than the last. Even after all these years, the feeling of being a lab rat had never abated — he knew they were always studying him, observing the subject of a grand and ongoing experiment.

Edgar Prime stood outside the door for another minute while other I.C.G. attendees cast curious glances in his direction as they passed. *Fuck it*, he thought savagely and he turned away from the conference center without a backwards glance. Harlow had decided it for him — he'd already OD'd on self-congratulatory pomp for the day. Edgar Prime crossed the street and headed through the square opposite with a heady rush of euphoria at playing hooky from the conference. He grinned, forcibly suppressing the desire to laugh aloud for fear of scaring a large group of Japanese tourists strolling past.

A female voice with an American accent drifted over the square, and Edgar Prime saw a couple hundred people clustered together on the far side. The first words that Edgar Prime could make out were, "And what kinds of rights do these clones even have?" The grin faded from his face and he slowed, hesitating. Without consciously deciding to do so, Edgar Prime turned and began to walk towards the protestors. He could see the woman speaking better as he approached — she was so short that she was barely visible over the heads of the crowd despite standing on a park bench. She looked to be in her mid-twenties and had olive skin, freckles, clear blue eyes and dark reddish brown hair.

"Clones are expensive — when somebody spends thousands and thousands of dollars to have one made, does that give them the right to treat the clone like their property? The first clones are just now reaching the age of majority. Can they vote? Can they run for office? Could we one day have a clone president?" she yelled, her voice strong and clear. She seemed like a person who was born to lead this kind of rally — something in the way she spoke was stirring, and each time she made a point the protestors who stood listening would verbalize their assent. Many carried signs and wore t-shirts with various slogans like "Clone Rights = Human Rights" and "We Will Not Remain Silent". Edgar Prime stood in the back of the crowd listening.

The woman finished her speech shortly thereafter, and although Edgar Prime still didn't quite understand why they were protesting, he felt strangely energized about participating in the next part of the rally. Edgar Prime watched the woman leap down from the bench and followed when she led the way across the square back toward the conference center. Exuberant chatter broke out in the crowd, and the other protestors waved their signs at passing pedestrians and vehicles. They were nonviolent and (for the most part) respectful, milling around on the opposite side of the street as they waited for the conference attendees to exit the building. Edgar Prime slowly edged through the crowd and approached the woman who had been speaking.

"Great speech," he said when he reached her, and she turned and looked up at him. It only took a split second before he saw recognition in her eyes.

"You're Edgar Prime," she said.

"I prefer Ed." He wasn't surprised that she'd recognized him.

"Noela Kearney," she said, sticking out her hand. "Co-Founder and President of the Clone Advocacy Network. CAN for short."

Edgar Prime shook her hand and she gave him a cordial nod. "I've never heard of the Clone Advocacy Network," he admitted.

"We've only been in action for the past year or so," Noela said. She waved over a man in his early twenties with black eyeliner, black hair, lively brown eyes and deeply tanned skin. Both he and Noela wore dark jeans and black t-shirts that read, "Not For Sale". The man was shorter than Edgar Prime by several inches and when he spoke, his accent was also American.

Noela made the introductions. "This is Luken Ochoa. We founded CAN together in our last year at Columbia." No matter what she was talking about, Noela somehow exuded charisma.

"Edgar Prime," said Luken, also recognizing him on sight.

"He prefers Ed," Noela told him.

"Nice to meet you Ed," said Luken, extending his hand as Noela had. "Is it true that Dr. Midas calls you 'Prime'?"

"Yeah," Edgar Prime said, taken aback for a moment that he'd know to ask that. Then it occurred to him that Dr. Midas had given hundreds of interviews over the years, and that anyone at all inclined could learn all kinds of things about him; the information was freely available. He tried not to let his discomfort show on his face.

"Can I introduce you to them?" Noela asked suddenly, gesturing toward the crowd. "Don't worry, I won't make a big thing of it." Although the thought made Edgar Prime vaguely nervous, he nodded.

"Everyone!" Noela called, and the other protestors turned to listen. "This is Ed. He is a clone — the first ever human clone. He's here with us to advocate for basic human rights for others like him." A whoop went up at this, along with brief cheering. When it subsided, Noela added, "That's all. I just wanted you all to know — we are doing good and important work and it is not going unnoticed!" Another cheer. Within a few minutes, Edgar Prime found himself facing a small cluster of people close to his age, all vying to introduce themselves first.

"Ed, welcome. I am Jordi —" he was tall, dark, and thin, and spoke with a Catalan accent.

He was elbowed out of the way by two fashionable blonde girls, one of whom said, "I am Madeline and this is Valerie. We are both students at the Sorbonne in Paris. We have read a great deal about —"

She was interrupted again by Jordi who said, "My field of study is Philosophy and Ethics. Do you feel that cloning is ethical?"

"Can we have your autograph, Ed?" asked Valerie. She had a thicker French accent than Madeline.

"Calm down," Noela cut in sharply. "He's a person, not a circus freak."

Madeline, Valerie and Jordi looked chastened, but Luken laughed.

"It's not so surprising they're acting like they've met a celebrity, Noela," said Luken. "We've all been following Ed's story for ages, haven't we? He's really the only clone we know anything about, and even still it's indirect knowledge courtesy of the esteemed Dr. Midas."

The way Luken said Dr. Midas's name held just the faintest hint of mocking, and Edgar Prime's mouth twisted involuntarily into a small smile.

"I'm not all that interesting to be honest," Edgar Prime said. He had never particularly liked being the center of attention.

"Now that I don't believe," Jordi said, with an easy grin. "You are undoubtedly more interesting than the rest of us." Madeline and Valerie both smiled and nodded in agreement.

"And you all — you traveled here for the I.C.G.?" Edgar Prime knew they must have, but he found it hard to comprehend.

"Of course," Luken said, looking slightly reproachful that Edgar Prime would ask such an obvious question. "Some of us didn't have far to come, like Jordi, Madeline and Valerie here, but Noela and I knew this was too important an opportunity to miss — all the scientists doing this sort of work in one place, all the press. We had to come to get our message out."

"And — what message is that, exactly?" Edgar Prime asked them.

"We get confused with the anti-cloning lobby a lot but what we do is totally different," Noela said. "As an organization, we don't take sides about the ethics of cloning itself. What we want is for there to be both national and international statutes protecting the rights of clones."

"What rights?" Edgar Prime asked.

"Because clones are paid for, some people make the mistake of thinking that they're owned," Noela said. "They treat their clones like property instead of like autonomous people. Most often they're purchased to replace someone who's died, and they don't get a say in whether they want to fill that person's role or not. We learned recently that the second clone — the first after you — was created to replace a man's deceased wife. She was raised by a caretaker and on her eighteenth birthday, the man married her. Do you think she had any choice in the matter?"

Edgar Prime blinked. He hadn't ever really spared the other clones much thought, but he knew there must be hundreds by now, maybe even thousands. The idea that some of them were trapped in situations far more restrictive than his made Edgar Prime feel ashamed. Yes, his upbringing had been far from traditional, but at least Dr. Midas had given him a lot of independence from an early age. He hadn't been forced to marry anyone or do anything he didn't want to, aside from the experiments. Now he was even studying history, bemused though Dr. Midas was with that choice. He'd been so consumed with bitterness at his own lot in life that he hadn't considered the possibility that he might actually be one of the fortunate ones.

"That's awful," he said quietly.

"It is," Noela agreed. "Which is why we are here with our signs and our bodies, to show the world that not every step forward constitutes progress."

Edgar Prime nodded, slowly at first then more vigorously. Valerie offered him one of the two signs she carried, and he accepted. The sign was bright green with white lettering that simply read, "Equality For All" with a peace sign beneath it. Edgar Prime lifted it high even though none of the press who had stood fawning around Harlow were outside any longer.

The next two hours passed in a pleasant blur for Edgar Prime. He enjoyed everything about the protestors — their fierce optimism, their mingling languages and accents, their awareness. By the time the I. C. G. attendees started trickling outside during the lunch break, Edgar Prime was as fired up as he'd ever been his entire life. They all waved their signs and marched and chanted, but barely anyone gave them a second glance.

Still, to Edgar Prime, it was exhilarating. None of the "major players," as Noela called them, emerged during the lunch break — no doubt they were enjoying an expensive catered meal courtesy of the conference sponsors. Just as people began filing back inside for the afternoon presentations, Edgar Prime received a text from Patrice, asking where he was, to which he replied, *'outside'*.

She came out a couple minutes later, scanning the street with a confused expression on her face. Edgar Prime almost laughed aloud as she looked back and forth, twice glancing towards the protestors without noticing him. When she saw his wave, her eyes widened in surprise and she crossed the street to meet him.

"Come inside, Ed," she said without preamble.

"I'd rather not," said Edgar Prime cheerfully. Noela and Luken stood on either side of him, both eyeing Patrice with distrust. "Patrice, I'd like you to meet Noela and Luken, the founders of the Clone Advocacy Network." Patrice gave them each the briefest of nods, focusing back on Edgar Prime.

"I'm serious, Ed. This isn't funny anymore. Come inside," Patrice said.

"He doesn't have to listen to you," Noela said loudly.

"Yeah," Luken said.

Patrice spared them an exasperated glance. "Harlow isn't happy."

"Why should I care?" Edgar Prime said, emboldened by his initial rebellion that morning. "You heard them. I don't have to listen to you."

"What has gotten into you, Ed?" Patrice asked.

"Harlow is a corporate pig who would happily throw Ed here into a wood chipper if he thought it would make him a bigger profit," Noela said. She glared at Patrice with open distain now, eyes narrowed, hair wilder than ever, like a fiery halo. Other protestors had noticed the confrontation and were staring now, and Patrice took a step closer to Edgar Prime and spoke to him in an undertone.

"Come on, Ed. Please. I don't want to get fired over this." The look on her face was so imploring, Edgar Prime felt himself soften with sympathy, followed by a rush of resentment. He tried for a second to convince himself that Dr. Midas wouldn't really fire Patrice because of his disobedience, but he knew that wasn't true. Dr. Midas was exacting when it came to his research fellows and assistants, and he did not tolerate failure in any form. Much as he told himself it didn't matter, that it wasn't his problem, Edgar Prime's kinder nature won out and he found himself heaving a great sigh and giving a single resigned nod. He wondered dully whether Patrice's attempts to befriend him had been a calculated move for just such a moment as this — even if that were true he couldn't bring himself to feel indifferent about the consequences his actions might have on her.

"I've gotta go," he mumbled to Noela and Luken.

"But —" Noela started indignantly, before Luken caught her eye and shook his head. Reluctantly, she shut her mouth, scowling at Patrice.

"You've got our contact info," Luken said, clapping him on the back. "Don't be a stranger."

"I won't," Edgar Prime said. Noela hugged him, then he walked back across the street to the conference center a half-step behind Patrice all the way. The lobby seemed dark and gloomy in contrast to the sun outside, and it took a few seconds before Edgar Prime's eyes adjusted. He followed Patrice to the auditorium where he was assailed once more by Arthur Blair.

"Prime!" he called out jovially. "How are you enjoying the conference this year? Can I get a quote?"

"No," Edgar Prime said shortly. He slouched into the auditorium and sat in the row behind Dr. Midas, Dr. Yang, and Harlow. Patrice sat down at his side, casting a curious glance at him but not commenting. Edgar Prime tried to keep his expression neutral, not wanting to answer any questions. Before long he had zoned out, thinking again of Noela and Luken. His mood improved by a fraction. True, he was in here rather than outside with them, but they were based in New York, and he'd be able to connect with them again after the conference. He wished there was something he could do to contribute — something more than simply showing up and enjoying himself.

He suddenly realized that there *was* and got up quickly, telling Patrice he'd be right back. Edgar Prime found Arthur Blair in the lobby, pacing and recording a list of reminders into his phone.

"Don't forget to stop at CVS for that prescription. Also, follow up with that girl from the bar — Sally? Sylvia? Figure out her name first. Or just don't say it on the message. Then prep for the interviews and —" Arthur Blair turned to find Edgar Prime behind him and stopped mid-sentence with a comically startled look on his face. He clicked off the recording and put his phone into his pocket. "Prime, how are you? Can I help you with something?"

With difficulty, Edgar Prime suppressed his snort of derision. "I have a condition. For the interview."

"Name it," Blair said. "We're happy to accommodate anything you might need."

"I'll only talk to you if you do a story on the Clone Advocacy Network first. If I like that article, then you'll get your interview with me."

Blair scratched his pointed nose, and stroked his auburn goatee nervously. "That's a lot to ask, for me to have it done *before* my article with you. What if I interviewed this, er, group, and put them in your feature as well?"

"I don't think so," Edgar Prime said. "That doesn't give me any guarantee you'll actually do it."

"But — I don't have any names, contact info — how can I do this on such short notice?" blustered Blair.

"They're right across the street." Edgar Prime pointed through the glass entryway. "Noela Kearney and Luken Ochoa are the CAN founders. I have their phone numbers. Tell them I referred you."

Blair's forehead began sweating again. "This is quite a tall order."

"Then I guess you'd better get started."

Blair gave him a reluctant nod before he headed out to meet the protestors. Edgar Prime watched him go, then re-entered the auditorium with a strange and intoxicating feeling. He had to mull it over for half the panel discussion before he could correctly identify the sensation, as he had experienced it only rarely before. What Edgar Prime felt in that moment was *power*.

31: MIRA

"I'm worried, Damon." The man said it flatly, without emotion. "What if something happened?"

"If something happened, we'd know," Harlow said.

There was a pause, and the sound of two drinks being poured. Mira shifted her earbud from the right ear to the left. The man in Harlow's office was Solomon O'Brien, a business associate in both the legitimate and (it was believed) black market arenas. He had been glowering when he passed by Mira's desk; though he and Harlow were similar in age, O'Brien looked several decades older. He had thin white hair, sallow skin, reddish eyes and the saggy jowls of a bloodhound.

O'Brien coughed. "Is there a plan in place if there *is* a problem? We can't have Smith singing the wrong tune if he gets picked up."

"Do you really think you need to ask me that question, old friend?" There was reproach in Harlow's voice. "I'd like to think you know me better than that."

There was a pause. "I suppose you're right."

"I'm always right," Harlow said. "You let me worry about Smith. You worry about your end."

"Dorcas Pryce is acting up again. She gave a speech on the senate floor about how cloning is an abomination and how congress needs to pass a law banning it. It's getting a lot of play in the media."

Harlow laughed. "Fortunately everyone's too busy gawking at her tits to take her seriously. We should thank whoever dresses her. Those things deserve their own PR agent."

"You're entirely too blasé about this, Damon. Her support

161

base grows every day. You know campaign contributions only go so far when the fear of being voted out of office is looming over their heads like the sword of Damocles."

"Campaign contributions are what get them elected in the first place. People are sheep, Solomon. They might bleat a bit when they're being steered, but in the end they have no choice but to move along in the direction the dogs lead them. Dorcas Pryce is no threat to us."

"I'd feel more comfortable if she weren't such a loose cannon," O'Brien said. "What does she care about?"

"Cloning, apparently," Harlow quipped. "It's an affront to her deeply held religious beliefs. Whether she can be persuaded to be less vocal about it —"

"— is something we need to discover."

"If you insist. I'll send my finest ambassador with an offer."

"Perhaps one of our allies in Washington could deliver the message," O'Brien suggested. "Do you think she'd be more amenable to being approached by a woman or a man?"

"I've heard she prefers the company of women," Harlow said. "But that's unconfirmed. She's notoriously private."

"Fine. Send whoever you think will do the job best. This is all about subtlety. If the pass is fumbled, Ms. Pryce will have a field day telling the press how the cloning industry tried to buy her."

"It's as good as done."

O'Brien gave a wheezing cough. "Did you read that article in *2100*? The Clone Advocacy Network aired a lot of their 'concerns' about the lack of regulations and the dangers of the black market."

"I saw the headline. They're just a naive bunch of kids," Harlow said dismissively.

"I'm not sure you're right about that, Damon. They seem organized to me."

Harlow snorted. "Solomon, you're a born conspiracy theorist. There's no way some dumb kids and a reporter who's out for clickbait are any threat to us."

"They've got Midas's clone with them now. That Edgar Prime."

This seemed to give Harlow pause; he didn't reply to O'Brien immediately. Mira leaned forward in her seat reflexively, holding her breath as she waited for his response.

"That is... interesting. To say the least. I'll handle it."

"Handle it how?"

"You don't need to know that, Solomon. Just rest assured, it will be dealt with, and quickly."

Shortly afterward, O'Brien took his leave. He gave Mira a once-over as he passed her desk, and grunted with what might have been approval. It took less than a minute before her phone rang. When she answered, she heard Harlow's voice.

"Mira, get in here." Harlow hung up without waiting for a reply.

Mira scrambled to her feet and hurried through the heavy mahogany doors into Harlow's office.

"Yes, sir?" she asked. He gestured to the seat across from him, and she sat.

"What do you know about a group called the Clone Advocacy Network?"

Mira decided not to feign ignorance; she had read the *2100* article too. "Not much. They're a group that focuses on clone's rights. I'm not sure how clear their demands are. I really only skimmed that article in *2100*."

"I'd like you to reach out to them."

"Sir?" Whatever Mira was expecting from this conversation, it wasn't that.

"You'll send them an anonymous message, saying that you're a black market insider, but you've become disillusioned. Tell them you can gain them access. But you have a condition. You first want to know what they're planning."

"Yes, sir." Mira tried to mask the unease in her voice.

"You're to report back to me when they reply. This is a big responsibility, Mira. It's important that you're convincing. We can't afford any mistakes here." Harlow surveyed her over his steepled hands, as though weighing her worth. He nodded, as if in approval, then dismissed her.

"I'd like this out by the end of the day, Mira. And remember: come to me immediately when you have a response."

"I will, sir."

"Stocks are already taking a hit across the cloning industry because of all this Dorcas Pryce nonsense. We don't need any more bad press because a bunch of upjumped students fancy themselves vigilantes."

"I understand." She didn't, but no good could come of telling Harlow that.

"Get to work." Harlow didn't wait for a response; he turned back to his computer and Mira left his office, closing the door behind her with a snap.

It took Mira over an hour to draft an appropriate message for the Clone Advocacy Network, and she sent it off with trepidation. She couldn't tell whether she was worried for the naive CAN members, unaware of how out of their depth they were, or herself if this failed. Harlow was well known for his intolerance of failure, and often fired employees who displeased him. Mira's mission would be compromised if that happened, and she couldn't let her team down, whatever the cost.

It was quite late by the time she arrived at the seemingly abandoned Chinatown building that served as their headquarters for this operation. Nonetheless, the whole team was there waiting. Jack wordlessly handed her a large coffee when she took her seat at the large table, and she smiled in thanks.

John was leaning towards Liesel with a warm smile on his face.

"Did you get teased a lot growing up because of your name?" he asked her.

"Oh God, yes, *constantly*," Liesel laughed. "I was so embarrassed I used to tell people in school that my name was really Lisa."

"Did people think your parents named you after *The Sound*

of Music or something?"

"Number one, I'm kind of surprised that you know that reference, very interesting," Liesel said. John laughed and his cheeks turned slightly pink. Jack glanced over at Mira and rolled his eyes.

"And number two, sadly the people who thought I was named for *Sound of Music* were completely right. I was so angry with my mother when I first saw it because that girl is such an idiot."

They all joined in the laughter that time, and Mira thought perhaps she should put John out of his misery and tell him that his clumsy attempts at courtship were pointless: Liesel had been living with her girlfriend for the last five years and they were planning to get married.

"All right, all right," grumbled Warren, never able to direct his hostility in Liesel's direction. "It's late, let's get this godforsaken briefing over with."

Mira took a sip of her coffee. It was surprisingly good, even without any sugar.

"Solomon O'Brien sounded worried," mused Liesel, and Warren nodded in approval.

"We should consider placing someone with him as well," John said, in a tone that suggested he thought he'd be the best candidate for the job.

Warren ignored the hint. "We won't need to if we can get Harlow. He strikes me as the sort of man who'd be eager to cut a deal. Anything to save his own ass."

"There's something else." Mira told them about Harlow's instructions regarding the CAN, and the reasons he'd given her. When she finished, they were all frowning.

"That doesn't make any sense," Jack said flatly.

Warren agreed grudgingly. "It seems ridiculous that someone like Harlow would concern himself with a silly student group."

"He didn't seem interested until he learned that Edgar Midas's clone was involved. I guess he's worried they'll get more of a platform because of that," Mira said.

"For good reason," Liesel said. "Still, it's a risk for him to get involved personally. I suppose if you got caught, he'd deny knowing anything about it. Should we warn them?"

"Who?" Warren seemed genuinely confused by her question.

"The students," Jack said, before Liesel should speak. "This whole thing just got a whole lot more dangerous now that they're on Harlow's radar."

Warren scoffed. "Their plan is to take on the black market! That was always going to be dangerous for them. This is an opportunity for us. Harlow is worried. People who are worried are more likely to make mistakes."

"But the —" Jack began, but Warren cut him off.

"The subject is closed, Sterling. We're here to investigate a pervasive criminal organization that has thus far remained three steps ahead of us. There was always risk involved. That's the nature of the beast."

John cleared his throat. "We do actually have some good news as well. Deirdre Kirke was far more careless than we could ever have hoped. She had a password-protected file called 'Salvation'. It took a while, but we managed to break into it. Inside, there was a file with a bunch of cryptic numbers and terms all jumbled together. Long story short, we've found the darknet market she used. We think its just one of several where Harlow's clones are auctioned. Liesel's work."

Liesel gave a satisfied smile, Jack clapped John on the back and Warren thumped his hand on the table in exaltation. Mira was stunned that they'd had such a stroke of luck. She hoped it wasn't lost on Warren that this breakthrough would not have been possible if Jack hadn't copied the hard drive for them to begin with.

"When's the next auction?" Warren asked eagerly.

"We're not sure, but we'll keep monitoring it," Liesel said.

"Fitzgerald, I want you and Sterling to start visiting some of these shelters tomorrow. See if your badges can scare the administrators into talking. They probably don't know the whole story, but they might be able to provide us with a more solid link to Harlow."

"Got it," John said, and Jack nodded as well.

"Liesel, you'll run point on the darknet angle. Mira, keep up the good work."

The meeting broke up shortly thereafter, and Jack was the first to leave. Mira tried not to feel disappointed that he didn't ask her to grab drinks with him again. *It's better this way,* she told herself, wishing she could believe it.

32: ANNABEL

"You'll help me, won't you?" Annabel asked Ms. Durant anxiously over tea and lemon squares at the older woman's new cottage.

"I don't know, Annabel. I don't want to get between you and your husband." Ms. Durant spoke stiffly. Annabel knew asking for Ms. Durant's help was a risk, but it was a calculated one. Rex would be far more amenable to her request if Ms. Durant was involved as she would effectively function as a chaperone.

"But this really should be my decision, shouldn't it? Rex is wrong to tell me not to do the interview if I want to," Annabel tried.

"Not necessarily, dear. Marriage requires compromise, and taking the other person's views into account. You're still young, but you'll learn that lesson before too long. It's the secret to harmony."

Annabel frowned at that. What would Ms. Durant know about it anyway? She wasn't married and never had been. "I think there's more to it than that."

"Oh, do you?" Ms. Durant hooted, suddenly amused.

"Yes," Annabel said, trying her best to ignore the ridicule. "I do."

"Why do you want to do this interview anyway, my dear? Your words will be distorted, you'll be used to make a point for some politician somewhere while humiliating your husband in the process. It's not worth it." Ms. Durant picked up a lemon square from the plate and took a refined bite.

Annabel couldn't even bring herself to feel guilty for the

168

surge of pleasure she got at the thought of humiliating Rex. "I don't care. It's my story to tell. I won't even talk about Rex. I met him less than two months ago, I barely have anything to say." The lie hung between them, but Ms. Durant did not remark on it.

For a moment, Ms. Durant looked like she was suppressing a smile. Then she sighed and said, "On your own head be it. I'll help you, but I don't want to hear any complaining afterwards when it goes badly, as we both know it will."

Annabel squealed and hugged Ms. Durant, who gave a surprised laugh. "Thank you," she said, and she meant it.

"So, a women's spa retreat weekend? And if he realizes I'm not the type to go to such a place, eh?" Ms. Durant chuckled at this. "He's known me a long time."

Annabel didn't hesitate. "Don't worry, I'll convince him."

Ms. Durant took another nibble of her lemon square, followed by a long sip of tea. "I don't doubt you will, my dear."

An hour later, Annabel left Ms. Durant's house in high spirits. The air was thick and heavy with moisture, and the day overcast; Annabel knew it was likely to storm later, but she didn't mind in the least. There was something powerful and primal about a thunderstorm that Annabel had always been drawn to.

She walked through the near-empty town humming to herself, nodding courteously at the few people she passed. Just before she reached the footpath that would lead her home along the bay, she saw a familiar pickup truck parked on a nearby lawn. A fluttering started in Annabel's stomach, but the owner of the truck was nowhere to be seen. Annabel felt a mixture of disappointment and relief; she didn't know how she'd look him in the eye after the way she'd been fantasizing about him lately. She drew level with the truck, glancing around in spite of herself, her desire outweighing her embarrassment. And suddenly, he appeared.

Annabel slowed her pace reflexively when Leon Floros walked out from the backyard of the small wood-shingled house. His eyes snapped to her immediately, and she blushed when she noticed him looking her up and down with a half-smile on his face.

"Good to see you again," He commented, coming closer until they were only a couple of feet apart. The fact that he remembered her made Annabel feel far more giddy than it should.

"You as well," Annabel said. She was distracted by the sweat that was sliding down his muscular bare chest, and she found herself wanting to run her fingers over the fine dark hair he had there.

There was a knowing smile on his face when she brought her eyes back up to meet his, and she knew he was fully aware of where she'd been looking.

"What's your name?" he asked. He had the faintest hint of a lilting accent, although Annabel couldn't even hazard a guess as to where he'd gotten it.

"Annabel," she said, trying not to sound breathless.

"Annabel, Annabel. In your kingdom by the sea." He chuckled. "It suits you."

Annabel blinked, confused.

"Poe," he said, as though that explained everything.

"Oh, of course." Annabel had no idea what he was talking about, but laughed along with him as though she did.

"I'm Leon," he said.

She bit back the "I know" that almost escaped her lips and said instead, "Nice to meet you."

From the backyard came a sweaty, balding man dragging a sapling with a large burlap sack covering the roots and the dirt around them.

"Some help here, Leon?" the man called over his shoulder. "These trees ain't gonna plant themselves." He stopped to mop his brow, and when he noticed Annabel he gave Leon a dark look before turning back to his task.

Leon gazed at her for another moment before speaking. "See you around, Annabel Lee." He winked and turned away, striding back to where his co-worker was huffing and puffing over the sapling. Annabel watched him for a few more seconds, then wrenched herself away and continued on home.

Annabel waited until Rex was almost asleep that night before broaching the subject of her weekend away with Ms. Durant. There was a soothing rain pattering outside, drumming gently on the roof and running down the dark windows. Rex lay on his back, a sleepily-satisfied smile on his face. That night Annabel had taken pains to be more enthusiastic than usual about her nightly duties, and she could tell Rex both noticed and appreciated this change.

"Rex?" Annabel began tentatively.

"Mmm?" Rex didn't bother to open his eyes.

"I saw Ms. Durant this morning, and she told me about this women's spa retreat she was thinking of doing next weekend. She asked if I wanted to go along with her."

Rex's eyes snapped open.

"You want to go away with Ms. Durant?" He sounded almost hurt.

"Only for a weekend. I don't think she wants to go alone, and I'd like to do something for her since she's always been so kind to me."

Rex mulled this over. "Can't you do something else? Something here?"

"I suppose," Annabel pretended to agree to placate her husband's fragile ego. "She just seemed very excited about this particular weekend trip. I think if I don't go she'll still do it, but just won't have as good a time."

It was a moment before Rex spoke again, but Annabel could tell she was getting to him. "I don't want other men ogling at you in a towel."

"I wouldn't be comfortable with that either," Annabel lied. In truth, what he'd described sounded exciting. "But it's only other women. None of the staff are men either, Ms. Durant said."

"Where is this place?" Rex asked.

"The Hamptons," Annabel said. "Right by the water. Just like home."

"How could you feel at home without me there?" Rex said, playfully nuzzling her neck.

"You know what I mean," Annabel said.

Rex sighed, and Annabel felt his shoulders relax. "All right," he said in a grudging voice. "I suppose if you really want to go, I can't think of any reason why not. I'll miss you."

"And I you," Annabel said, trying to keep the triumph from her voice. "But it's only a weekend. Ms. Durant will be so pleased."

"She deserves a little happiness," Rex murmured, closing his eyes again.

"She certainly does," Annabel agreed. *And so do I.*

While Rex was working the next morning, Annabel went for a walk and called Arthur Blair's office.

"Annabel King calling for Arthur Blair," she said, slowly making her way around the bay. She was only on hold for a moment, and when Arthur Blair answered she could hear the suppressed excitement in his voice.

"Mrs. King. Thank you for getting back to me, I was starting to worry you weren't interested."

"I don't have much time, Mr. Blair. I'll be in New York next weekend — you can have your interview then. Don't contact me under any circumstances — I'll call you when I arrive. My husband can be . . . jealous and if he sees you calling me he may not let me come."

"I understand," Blair replied. "Please let me know once you arrive in the city and we can do the interview at your first convenience. We'd also like to do a photo shoot that weekend with you and the other two clones we're featuring."

Annabel nearly jumped up and down in excitement, but controlled the impulse.

"That'll be fine," Annabel said in as calm a voice as she could manage. "I'll call you when I arrive next weekend. I — I look forward to it." She realized as she said it that it was the truth.

33: JAVI

"Whoa," Herman said when Javi finished describing how he'd lost his virginity in the bed Imogen shared with her husband.

"I know," Javi said, feverish in his glee. They were sprawled under their usual weeping willow tree in the park after school the next day. Javi had been bursting to brag about what had happened with Imogen from the minute he'd left her house, but had restrained himself—he'd wanted to be able to tell the story uninterrupted, and he finished it just as Herman took the last few puffs of the joint they were passing around and stubbed out the ashes in the grass.

"And her kids were running around in the backyard?" Fred asked. "That's fucking weird, man.'"

"She started it," Javi said defensively. "It's not like I planned for things to go down that way."

"Fucking *awesome*," Herman said, awed.

"Fucking fucked up is more like it," Fred said.

"And it's not fucked up that you and Violet fuck in her parents bed sometimes?" Javi retorted, scowling. Fred could be such a hypocrite.

"Violet isn't married with two little kids," Fred said, as though explaining to a petulant first grader that 2+2=4.

"Fuck you, Fred," Javi said. "Jealousy doesn't suit you."

Fred gave a scornful laugh. "Jealous? Of what?"

"She is pretty fuckin' hot," Herman pointed out. "If she threw herself at me I'd fuck her too."

"You'd fuck anyone who'd have you, Herman." Fred said with a snort.

Herman grinned. "You say that like it's a bad thing."

There was a moment's pause, then all three of them cracked up.

"Look man, do whatever you want," Fred said to Javi. "Just hope her husband doesn't find out."

Javi nodded, belatedly remembering that Fred's parents had split up when he was young after his mother repeatedly cheated on his father. She had moved to Belize and Fred only saw her once a year, if that. *That has nothing to do with this*, he told himself, almost believing it.

"Are you gonna fuck her again?" Herman asked eagerly.

Javi shrugged. "If I'm lucky."

Herman hooted with laughter, and even Fred cracked a smile.

"Can I have Stella now that you have Imogen?" Herman asked.

"Sure," Javi said sarcastically. "All you'll have to do is get rid of Kato Barre."

"Ah fuck. I forgot about Kato," Herman said, heaving a theatrical sigh.

Fred rolled his eyes. "Of course you did."

"One of you has to wingman for me now," Herman said. "I can't be the *only* virgin when we graduate."

"Somehow I doubt Imogen has any friends looking for an awkward eighteen-year-old ginger to fuck," Javi said. "Maybe Violet does, eh Fred?"

"Excuse me, I take issue with the word *awkward*," Herman said, mouth twitching in amusement. "But I can't argue with the rest of that description."

Fred heaved a great sigh. "I guess I can ask her."

"Bonus points if she's blonde like Stella," said Herman. "But really —"

"— you'll take what you can get," finished Fred.

Javi's phone started vibrating and he jumped up and fished it out of his pocket, swiping a finger across the touch screen to answer without even bothering to check who was calling.

"Hello?" he asked, hoping against hope it was her.

"Hi Javi, Arthur Blair here."

Javi suppressed a groan. He'd forgotten all about Arthur Blair. "Oh, ok. Hi," Javi said in as polite a voice as he could manage, shaking his head in response to Herman's mouthed question about whether he was speaking to Imogen.

"I wanted to confirm our interview for tomorrow afternoon. Where should I meet you?" Arthur Blair got right to business.

"Oh . . ." Javi's mind was a blank. He still hadn't told his parents about Arthur Blair and the thought of doing so now when they were already on such rocky terms made his stomach twist into knots. He also wanted to steer clear of anyone from school he might run into. "There's a coffee place on the corner of Main Street and Blossom Hill Boulevard. It's called House of Sumatra." It was a bit of a trek, but Javi was banking on Fred giving him a ride in exchange for a latte and a piece of gingerbread.

"I'll be there. How's 4 p.m.?"

"That works," Javi said, already dreading it.

He hung up and turned to Fred. "I need a favor."

When Javi got home that night, he wasn't sure what to say to his parents, if anything. He knew he'd have to broach the subject before the following weekend, when he was supposed to fly to New York City for the photo shoot. He'd only visited once before — years ago, with his parents — and the idea of losing himself once more in the anonymous crush was highly appealing.

Javi found his father in his study, a small but cozy room with old books lining the walls on shelves and cluttering every available surface except for a small area in the center of the desk where he kept his computer. His father was leaning back in his massive chair — the only place to sit in the room — with his bare feet perched on the edge of the desk and his head bent over his tablet. Javi had never met anyone who loved to read more than his father.

When he stepped tentatively into the room, Javi's father looked up with a warm smile, and the words Javi had been planning to say to him stuck in his throat.

"What are you reading?" Javi asked instead.

"*A Feast for Crows*," his father replied.

"Haven't you read that like twenty times already?" Javi asked with a half-smile. His father reread the entirety of *A Song of Ice and Fire* every other year it seemed.

"Never gets old." His father laid down the tablet. "I learn something new each time."

Javi had always considered his father's practice of rereading all his favorite books so many times he'd probably memorized them endearingly eccentric. But he hadn't come to talk about books.

"I was thinking I'd spend next weekend at Stanford," he blurted out. "Fred's neighbor is a junior there. He said I can stay with him. Fred is going too, he can drive me."

His father's surprise was evident on his face. "I thought you wanted to go somewhere else."

"Figured I should give it a bit more consideration," Javi lied. "Just to be sure."

It was obvious that his father was trying to hide his enthusiasm for this idea. "Very wise, son. Don't worry about your mother, I'll tell her. And we can all talk about it more when you get back."

"Okay," Javi said. He turned to go, worried his father would see through the lie if he stayed.

"Javi," his father said, stopping him at the door. "I'll be proud of you no matter what you decide. Your mother as well. You know that, right?"

Javi's throat felt too constricted to answer, so he just nodded, and ducked out of the study. Back upstairs in his room, Javi paced incessantly, his mind a confused jumble; Arthur Blair, the lie he'd told his father, his mother's continued silent treatment, and his college decision all battled for his attention. Every couple of minutes, Imogen's naked body interrupted his thoughts. He felt himself start to grow hard whenever this happened, and it took all of his effort to wrench his mind back to the problems at hand.

He was seized by the desire to *do* something — all this thinking was making Javi's head hurt. Impulsively, he sat down at his computer and logged onto his email. He found the message from Georgetown, congratulating him on his acceptance. Without giving himself time to reconsider, he clicked the 'submit deposit' link and filled in his bank account information — he had just enough saved up from various birthdays and Christmases over the years to cover the amount. He submitted the non-refundable deposit with a thrill of nerves mingled with a surge of defiance, then slammed the laptop shut and threw himself down on the bed to think about Imogen again and jerk off.

Javi approached the House of Sumatra with trepidation the next afternoon while attempting to feign cool indifference. The second he walked through the door, a man in his late twenties stood up and waved. Arthur Blair had reddish hair with an awkward goatee and a pale, pointy face. He was the sort of man who could stand to lose twenty pounds — at least. When Javi reached his table in the back, Blair stuck out his hand for Javi to shake. His palm was slightly sweaty, and he stared at Javi a little too avidly as they sat down.

"So good to finally meet you, Javi. We have so much to discuss. Would you mind if I record our conversation? To ensure I quote you accurately, of course." Blair patted his phone for emphasis.

"Uh, sure," Javi said, not feeling sure at all.

"Excellent, excellent. Can I get you something to drink? To eat? Coffee? Biscotti?" Blair's voice was a rapid staccato, making Javi more tense by the minute.

"Uh … a mocha I guess. Extra chocolate," Javi said.

Blair sprung up from his seat the instant Javi finished

speaking, and bustled over to the barista to place their orders. Javi drummed his fingers on the table awkwardly, and tried to pretend he wasn't regretting his rash decision to participate in the interview. In what seemed like no time at all, Blair returned with two large mugs. He placed the mocha in front of Javi and kept the black coffee for himself. Not sure what to do, Javi took a sip of his mocha. Even though he always ordered it with extra chocolate, today it tasted too sweet, and Javi placed it down on the table with a *thunk*.

"Is it okay?" Blair asked.

Javi nodded, but Blair barely seemed interested, focusing instead on firing up the phone app that would record their conversation. Silently, Javi reminded himself to think before he spoke. He didn't want to make a fool of himself any more than necessary.

"Shall we get started?" Blair was plainly trying to conceal his eagerness, but Javi could see it anyway. He nodded again, and Blair's face spasmed into a grin before he managed to return to a more professional demeanor. "I'll just dive right in then, shall I?"

"Sure," Javi said. *Let the interrogation begin.*

34: EDGAR PRIME

The Clone Advocacy Network profile was published the day of Edgar Prime's return flight from Zurich. Dr. Midas was more subdued than usual. Edgar Prime had watched him saying goodbye to Dr. Yang that morning by the hotel elevators. From a distance, it had almost looked like an argument — yet still nothing that hadn't happened a hundred times before.

Edgar Prime was in a good mood. Not only had Arthur Blair delivered on his promised article publicizing the work CAN was doing, but Edgar Prime had plans to meet up with Noela and Luken once they were all back in the city. And of course he'd also see Hugo soon, a thought that made Edgar Prime's stomach flutter no matter how many times he told himself to get a grip.

Patrice and Dr. Midas both slept for most of the flight, and Edgar Prime used the time to catch up on his political theory homework. When the plane landed at JFK airport, Edgar Prime's phone began buzzing, and he saw three texts from Celeste and one from Hugo inviting him to Celeste's apartment for drinks later that night. There was also an email from Arthur Blair asking whether he'd be free on Thursday for the interview.

Edgar Prime quickly typed a response to Hugo — *'yes!'* — then a slightly longer message to Arthur Blair with his Thursday class schedule and availability. Nobody spoke much in the limo back to Manhattan, and Edgar Prime sighed with relief when he was dropped off on the curb outside his dorm. An hour later he was greeted at Celeste's door by a scream — she threw her arms around him, spilling champagne down his back from the bottle she clutched in one hand.

"Good to see you too, Celeste," Edgar Prime said with a grin. She laughed and closed the door behind him, before handing him the bottle of champagne. As was often the case, the apartment seemed mostly full of random people Edgar Prime had never met before. The air was smoky and smelled like pot, and there was a pleasant cacophony of voices intermixed with trance music. Edgar Prime took a swig of champagne while weaving through the dancing crowd with Celeste, and some of the liquid bubbled down his chin and dripped onto the floor. Celeste didn't seem to mind in the slightest.

"More!" she said, giggling. They reached one of the two couches crammed into the living room, where George and Blake sat side by side. Edgar Prime was amused to note that George had his arm around Blake — apparently they'd reconciled while he was gone.

"We started early," explained George with a nod to the empty beer bottles strewn across the coffee table. "How's it going, man?"

"Not bad," Edgar Prime replied. He took another long swig of the champagne. "How're you doing, Blake?"

"Better than Hugo," she said, pointing. Edgar Prime felt a rush of mingled joy and nerves as he turned to look. There was a tall boy beside Hugo with bronze skin, black hair and startlingly blue eyes, standing closer than Edgar Prime would have liked. They seemed to be having a disagreement, but the room was too loud for Edgar Prime to hear what was being discussed.

"Who's that?" Edgar Prime asked, not taking his eyes from the boy's chiseled features.

"Hugo's ex," Blake said. "They broke up six months ago, but I guess it's complicated."

Edgar Prime didn't say anything, glaring at Hugo's offensively handsome companion with increasing dislike.

"He's an asshole," Celeste said in a matter-of-fact voice. "But Hugo told me they were going to try to be friends." She rolled her eyes and added sarcastically, "Wonder how that's going?"

Edgar Prime forced a laugh, and wrenched his eyes away from Hugo. He knew he had no right to be jealous, but he had to fight the sudden impulse to pull the Abercrombie model away from Hugo and break his perfectly sculpted nose. Instead, Edgar Prime hit the bottle, finishing off Celeste's champagne in a surprisingly short amount of time. This was followed by several rounds of tequila shots, accompanied by salt and lime. By the time Hugo made his way over to them, Edgar Prime was halfway through burping the ABCs. His laughter soured when he saw that Hugo's pretty ex had followed and was waiting to be introduced.

"Ed, how was your trip?" Hugo asked, as though he didn't have a wraith standing beside him.

"Oh, excellent," Edgar Prime said in a louder and more disdainful voice than he'd intended. Hugo's ex pursed his lips in disapproval, and Edgar Prime sneered at him in return. Hugo caught the ex's eye, frowned and shook his head slightly. Reluctantly it seemed, the ex's face smoothed out into a more neutral expression.

"Ed, this is Gerard Pierson," Hugo mumbled, barely meeting Edgar Prime's eyes.

Edgar Prime grunted in response and gave a tiny jerk of his head that a forgiving person might have termed a nod of acknowledgement.

"So *you're* the clone," pretty Gerard drawled.

To Edgar Prime's disgust, Gerard had a deep, sexily posh British accent. Edgar Prime wasn't sure if he wanted to howl with insane laughter or puke at the revelation that in fact there was no contest between him and his 'competition'. A few girls who were standing nearby turned at the sound of Gerard's voice and eyed him with interest. He winked at them, clearly enjoying the attention.

"Shut up Gerard," Celeste snapped.

"Why should I, Celeste?" Gerard retorted.

"Your puss face pisses me off. Time for it to relocate." Celeste dismissed him with a wave. Hugo looked uncomfortable but didn't defend Gerard, something that gave Edgar Prime a savage pleasure.

Gerard glared at Celeste for another few seconds before turning to Hugo. "Let's go," he said.

Hugo appeared torn. "I dunno . . ." he trailed off.

"Celeste doesn't want me here, so I'm gonna leave. Are you coming or not?" Edgar Prime waited with baited breath. Hugo was staring into Gerard's ridiculously blue eyes. He gave a small nod, and Gerard looked triumphant.

"Laters, children," he spat.

"See you guys," muttered Hugo. He followed Gerard out, wedging their way through the crowd to the door. Edgar Prime noticed he wasn't the only person frowning at their retreating backs.

"Pathetic," Celeste said. "What a little cunt Gerard is."

"Hugo doesn't think he's a cunt," Edgar Prime said in a dazed voice. He felt like a beetle that had just been stomped on.

"He does," Celeste said. "He *knows* Gerard's a cunt. Hugo's just weak when it comes to puss-face Gerard. He was his first love and all that bullshit."

Edgar Prime suddenly realized he desperately had to pee. He stood up and was so dizzy he nearly fell over, using Celeste's shoulder to prop himself up again. "Whoa there," she said, chuckling. He stumbled over to the bathroom infinitely grateful that there was no line. He slammed the door shut and turned the lock, fumbling with the zipper on his pants. Finally free of them, he groaned in relief, not concerned about the stray droplets of urine that sprayed onto the seat due to his unsteady aim. Afterwards he clumsily flushed and washed his hands, staring at his reflection in what looked to him like a funhouse mirror. *I'm not drunk*, he told himself. Even then he knew it was a lie.

When Edgar Prime opened the door, he found Celeste

standing outside blocking his path. She stepped inside and closed the door again behind her, turning the lock with a click.

"Celeste, what —" his question was interrupted by her lips on his. Vaguely a part of his mind protested — she wasn't who he wanted, not really — but damn if her warm, wet tongue didn't feel good. He let her push him roughly against a wall, grateful for the additional support, and she pressed her body against his. He felt her unbutton and unzip his pants and reach her hand inside his boxers.

Someone pounded on the door and he and Celeste both froze, staring at each other. "Use the other bathroom!" yelled Celeste and amidst the grumbling from the other side of the door, they both cracked up. It occurred to Edgar Prime that never in a thousand years had he thought he'd laugh so hard while a girl's hand grasped his erect penis. The laughter subsided and they resumed their making out, with more urgency this time. Celeste pushed his boxers down to his mid-thigh and squeezed his ass with her free hand.

A condom came from somewhere, and she slid it over him as though she'd done it a hundred times before. Edgar Prime stared down at her hand feeling as though he was in a dream about to be slapped awake. An instant later the feeling passed, or didn't matter. She yanked her jeans and thong down and bent over the sink, reaching back to deftly guide him inside her and his brain melted. He moved in and out of her clumsily, watching their distorted images in the funhouse mirror and embracing the blankness of his mind — the only thing that existed was the building sensation in his body, but he couldn't quite find release. He didn't have a clear sense of how long it went on for, but after awhile Edgar Prime stopped, panting in frustration.

"What's wrong?" Celeste asked him.

He shook his head and slowly pulled out of her. Time seemed to skip a few beats — the next thing Edgar Prime knew he was bent over the toilet, vomiting up all the champagne and tequila he'd drunk while Celeste stood over him watching. He hadn't even bothered to pull his pants up, and the tiled floor pressed into his bare knees uncomfortably. Afterwards he managed to stand and zip himself up without falling over. He stared at his bloodshot eyes in the mirror, and accepted the mouthwash Celeste handed him without comment. She left the bathroom first, and he had to resist the urge to smash his head against the wall.

Later, he found himself in the kitchen with a beer in his hand. George was standing across from him with a knowing grin on his face. Edgar Prime blinked.

"How did I get in here?" he asked.

George snorted. "My guess is by putting one foot in front of the other." He was drinking from a water bottle, and Edgar Prime wondered if perhaps he should follow George's example.

"Hmm," Edgar Prime said. He wished the fluorescent lights above them weren't so harshly bright, like needles stabbing his retinas. He felt his pocket vibrate, and realized after a second that it was his phone. He pulled it out and squinted at the tiny words on the screen — a text from Hugo.

It read: '*Sooooo sorry about Gerard. Should've told you about him, but I was trying to not see him or speak to him or think about him. Never thought you'd meet. Anyway, just want you to know it's OVER. Really over. Not sure why I'm telling you this. May've had some drinks. So. There you go. Gerard and I are DONE. You looked cute tonight. Probs gonna regret sending this in the morning.*'

Edgar Prime had to read the message three times for it to really sink in. By the time he looked up at George again, the guilt was burning a hole in his gut. It made his head feel slightly clearer.

"I've gotta go," he mumbled. George opened his mouth to speak, but Edgar Prime didn't give him the chance. He left his beer on the kitchen counter and crept towards the front door, trying to avoid Celeste. Unfortunately for him, most of the people had cleared out and he saw her sitting with Blake talking quietly across the living room. She smiled at him and waved him over when they made eye contact. In a moment of irrational panic, he simply stared at her dumbly for a second, then turned and walked out of the apartment without a word.

The next morning, a sledgehammer went through Edgar Prime's skull as he awoke with a groan. He glanced down at his phone and saw that he'd slept two hours past his alarm — he'd be late to meet Noela and Luken if he didn't hurry. Edgar Prime sat up and cringed at the abrupt increase in intensity of the pain in thrumming in his skull. He stayed still for a moment, waiting in vain for the pain to subside, and gritted his teeth as he slowly stood up and dragged himself down the hall to shower.

Thirty minutes later the throbbing in Edgar Prime's head continued as he stepped onto the subway. He clutched a pole and willed himself not to vomit on the ground. The swaying motion was almost unbearable, and every time the cars turned and the wheels screeched Edgar Prime felt the pain in his head crescendo. Fortunately he only had to go three stops, and he exited gratefully, ascending the steps from the filth and roar of the subway to the filth and roar of the street. Once aboveground, he walked a short way to the corner and crossed the street to the cafe where Luken and Noela were waiting for him at an outside table under a rust-colored umbrella.

"You look terrible," Noela said by way of greeting.

Edgar Prime barely managed to crack a smile. "Rough night," he muttered, wincing at a particularly violent throb above his left eyebrow.

"We've all had those," Luken said with a smirk.

A purple-haired waitress with heavy eyeliner and tattoos poking out from her collar and sleeves approached them and asked if they were ready to order. Noela ordered for both herself Edgar Prime; bacon cheddar omelets with hash browns and green goddess juice.

"I'm not sure I can eat anything," Edgar Prime said, his voice sounding croakier than usual.

"You'll feel better if you do," Noela informed him.

"Maybe I can handle some coffee," Edgar Prime said.

"Coffee will just dehydrate you more. Don't you know that's what causes hangovers?" Noela pursed her lips and shook her head, but somehow looked more sympathetic than stern.

They didn't talk much until after the food came. Edgar Prime downed his first juice and ordered a second. He managed a few tentative bites of hash browns and omelet, and had to admit that Noela knew what she was talking about.

"We have some news," Noela said as the waitress refilled their water glasses. He glanced up and noticed for the first time that she was practically bouncing with excitement.

"Oh?" he asked.

"That article you had Arthur Blair write," Luken said. "It's been more useful than we realized at the time. We've been approached."

"Approached by who?" Edgar Prime asked.

"Someone who says she has information about the black market clone trade. She says she can get us inside," Noela said. "A *whistleblower*."

Edgar Prime didn't speak for a moment. "Is she for real?"

"We don't know," Luken said. "We haven't met her. 'She' just sent us an encrypted message. For all we know it could be from some bored hacker who thought we'd be fun to fuck around with."

Noela gave Luken a reproachful look. "She sounds legit. And anyway, there's only one way to find out whether her information is good."

"But — wouldn't that be dangerous?" Edgar Prime said. His fork was heaped with egg, suspended halfway to his mouth.

Noela shrugged. "Danger is a point of view."

Edgar Prime couldn't say that he agreed with this statement, but decided not to argue. "What are you going to do?"

"We'll have someone pose as a buyer, but go in with a hidden camera. We're going to expose them for what they are," Noela explained in a low voice. She leaned forward in her excitement, and Edgar Prime felt his apprehension rising. For the first time since waking that morning, he didn't even notice his hangover. He glanced at Luken and saw his own doubts reflected back at him, but Luken didn't say anything.

"Look. The black market is *illegal*. These people — they're real criminals. What do you think they'd do to whoever goes in there if they found the camera?" Edgar Prime asked, trying to keep himself from shivering at the thought.

"They won't find the camera," Noela said.

"You can't know that," Edgar Prime insisted. "They aren't going to just *allow* you to collect evidence that could be used to send them to jail for the rest of their lives. People kill for less than that."

Noela fixed him with a stare of such intensity, Edgar Prime felt as though it scorched him to the core. "I'd have thought you'd have more sympathy for your fellow clones. It was just by chance that you got to be educated and cosily brought up by the father of modern genetics, instead of being foisted off on the black market. If you'd been 'defective', do you think the venerated Dr. Edgar Midas would have kept you?"

"You don't know what you're talking about," he said in a low voice. "Being Dr. Midas's lab rat hasn't exactly been a picnic."

"But think how much worse it could be — how much worse it *is* for so many other clones," Noela said earnestly.

Edgar Prime shook his head. "You'd never understand. Either of you. You can't imagine what it's like."

"Maybe you could try to explain it to us, then." Noela said. "Because no matter how you look at things, you're one of the most privileged clones ever made."

"Privileged," Edgar Prime spat the word, not realizing he was capable of such vitriol until that moment. "I'm a vanity project, the worst manifestation of narcissism in existence. I'm a successful experiment. Nothing more." All the resentment he'd ever felt towards Dr. Midas had bubbled to the surface like poison; once awakened it refused to be suppressed again. His only value derived from reflected fame — by himself, he was nothing, no one. It was a bitter pill to swallow, but Edgar Prime knew it was the truth. "Neither of you have any fucking clue what you're talking about," he snapped, glaring at both of them.

"Hey, this wasn't my idea," Luken muttered, holding his hands up in mock-surrender. Noela shot him a dark look, and he let them fall back into his lap, cowed.

"You're right, we don't. But neither do you, Edgar Prime." Noela's use of the name Dr. Midas had given him stung, as she'd intended. "I'm gonna send you some stuff on the clone black market. You need to educate yourself before you say that what we're doing isn't important enough to take a few risks."

They stared each other down for a few more seconds, and Edgar Prime broke eye contact first. He shrugged, feeling the anger seep out of him as quickly as air left a punctured balloon. He had no more energy to fight, and was already beginning to feel ashamed of his outburst. The guilt reminded him of his *other* recent transgression, and he had to struggle not to grimace. He was the biggest fool who had ever lived, and he wasn't sure he'd ever be able to face Celeste or Hugo or any of them again. Did they all know? Surely Celeste would have spread the story of what happened in the bathroom. Edgar Prime felt sick all over again at the idea of Hugo hearing about it. *Why should Hugo care?* asked a small voice in the back of his head. *He doesn't want you anyway. No one does. You're only a clone, after all.*

35: MIRA

They arrived in Washington an hour before Harlow was due to meet with Senator Dorcas Pryce. It was Mira's first time on a private jet — Harlow had told her at the last minute she'd be accompanying him after he'd fired two of his more senior assistants in the space of a week. Whatever she thought of Harlow, she had to admit there were certain perks to this assignment. Rather than wait around in the Senate offices until the meeting, Harlow had the driverless limo take them to the Lincoln Memorial. Mira trailed after him, slightly bemused as he ascended the steps and stood gazing out at the reflecting pool towards the Washington Monument beyond.

A warm breeze rifled through Mira's hair, keeping the humid air from becoming unpleasant. The sky was brilliantly blue and cloudless, and cherry blossoms were blooming all around the National Mall. The petals fell like pink and white snow, blanketing large swatches of the grass.

Harlow paid no mind to bustle of the tourists around them, speaking many different languages and pointing excitedly to their guidebooks and to Lincoln's imposing statue. Mira leaned against a massive white column beside him, uncertain whether he wanted her there. He had an oddly introspective look on his face.

"I grew up here, you know," Harlow said.

"Oh, really?" Mira already knew that of course, the information was available on Harlow's wikipedia. But people liked to talk about themselves, so Mira feigned ignorance in the hopes he might reveal something interesting.

Harlow nodded. "Row house in Georgetown. All this was

my backyard." He waved a hand out at the National Mall laid out in front of them. "It's a strange place. Most of the time you can forget that you're neighbors with the most powerful people in the country. Well, nominally the most powerful anyway."

"Does your family still live here?" Mira ventured.

"Oh yes. My parents are still in the same house, and two of my sisters live nearby as well."

And yet, you aren't taking the time to visit any of them. Mira filed this information away. She could ponder it later.

"Is this one of your favorite spots?" Mira asked.

"It is." Harlow smiled fondly. "When I was a teenager my friends and I used to sneak out late at night and come here, usually with some stolen liquor. By two or three in the morning it's completely deserted. Best place in the world to ponder the mysteries of the universe and plot our glorious futures. We thought we were awfully sophisticated, back then."

"Do you still keep in touch with them?"

"A few. One of them was Tabitha O'Brian. You saw her older brother Solomon in the office not too long ago. God, I had such a crush on her." He chuckled to himself. "Simpler days."

There was a pause. They both looked out across the reflecting pool towards the Washington Memorial.

"You know, I went to prep school with Paolo Leone." Harlow said it casually, but Mira's eyebrows shot up in surprise. *This is new.*

"The mafia boss?" Mira the FBI agent knew who Paolo Leone was, of course, but Mira the silly assistant wouldn't be as well-informed about famous criminals.

"The very same," Harlow said.

"Did you know him well?" Mira asked.

"Somewhat," Harlow said. "He had the most wicked sense of humor."

Mira waited, but he didn't elaborate. She didn't want to push him; it wouldn't do for him to find her questions uncomfortable or impertinent. She was lucky Harlow liked to talk.

Her job was hard enough without adding a taciturn subject.

"We'd best be going," Harlow said. "It wouldn't do to offend the intractable Senator Pryce by being late to our meeting."

Mira followed him down the steps and back to the limo. Shortly thereafter they were dropped off outside a four- or five-story white building with row upon row of large vertical windows decorating its sides. The aesthetic was clearly meant to recall columns, in accordance with the ones framing the front entranceway. Mira found all the pristine white buildings in Capitol Hill ironic, given what went on here.

They went through the metal detectors and took the elevators to the third floor where Senator Pryce had her office. She made them wait for nearly twenty minutes before her interns were allowed to admit them. Mira was sure she had done it on purpose, to send Harlow a message about who held the power during this meeting. Harlow seemed unperturbed however, and graciously took the seat the senator offered to him as if he were settling down on a throne.

Mira sat beside him, placing his briefcase on the floor between them. Senator Dorcas Pryce was a blonde woman in her early forties, with sharp gray eyes and a slightly-too-large nose. Her hair was short and stylishly cut. While not exactly pretty, she was striking in a severe way. She was eyeing Harlow with open dislike, and Mira guessed that she had somehow been strong-armed into taking this meeting.

"Mr. Harlow," she said. Her voice was deep and melodious. A good voice for making speeches with. "A pleasure."

Harlow smiled at that, knowing full well what a lie those words were. "Senator Pryce," he said in feigned deferential tones. "An honor to meet you at last. It has been quite difficult setting up this meeting. You're obviously a busy woman."

"I am." She said it brusquely, not even pretending to be courteous. It was obvious that she thought Harlow was wasting her time.

"I'll get right to it then. You've been very vocal about your opposition to cloning."

Senator Pryce raised an eyebrow. "And you're unhappy about it."

"I would prefer if you turned your talents towards less hopeless endeavors, yes." Harlow gave her a winning smile. "Surely there are other more urgent issues that require your attention."

"If there were, they'd have my attention. Cloning is an abomination. It's shameful that this country has tolerated it for the last nineteen years."

"A time during which hundreds of clones have been born. What do you propose we do with them, if cloning is outlawed?"

"My bill clearly defines their legal status, something your people seem reluctant to do."

"And what of the people who commissioned clones? Will they be at risk for prosecution under your new bill?"

"They would not," Senator Pryce conceded reluctantly. "If I had it my way though, every last one of them would be in jail, along with you and Midas and all your cronies."

"Surely you can understand that they did it for love? For grief? The cloning industry fulfills a very important role in our society, Senator Pryce. It offers the impossible: a second chance." Harlow sounded so earnest that even Mira was almost convinced. She had to remind herself that the true reason for Harlow's interest in cloning was money.

"Some things are impossible for a good reason, Mr. Harlow. It's never a good idea to play God."

A half-smile flitted across Harlow's face before he spoke again. "And yet, that's exactly what you're doing with your sister's treatment, isn't it, Senator Pryce? How lucky that she was able to get that liver transplant before it was too late."

Senator Pryce paled; Mira could tell she didn't think even Harlow would stoop to use her family's tragedy against her. "That's not the same thing at all."

"Isn't it?" Harlow mused. "They seem quite similar to me. Scientific innovation trumping the will of God. If you believe in that sort of thing."

Senator Pryce had balled her hands into fists, but Mira could see they were still shaking. "How dare you," she said.

"I can't imagine what's got you so upset, Senator Pryce. I merely pointed out that you and I are more similar than you think."

"We are nothing alike." She steadied herself, and took a deep breath.

"Nonetheless, my corporation wishes to set you up with a Super PAC, run by a person of your choosing to be used for any purpose you like *except* to undermine the cloning industry. All you have to do in exchange is withdraw your anti-cloning bill and get your voting bloc to stop talking about this issue. The question of cloning was decided nearly twenty years ago. Find something new to focus your energy and considerable influence on."

"If you think I can be bought so cheaply —" Senator Pryce began, but Harlow cut her off, raising his voice slightly to drown out her protests.

"There is another alternative, of course. You can reject my kind offer, and we can part as adversaries rather than allies. If that's your choice, you might find yourself with an uncommonly well-funded and well-liked opponent during your next election cycle. You could take your chances against such an opponent, of course, but if I remember correctly, you won your seat by a rather small margin. And many in your state remain dissatisfied that you spend your days railing against cloning instead of addressing the issues they *really* care about. It would be quite a risk for you, I must say."

Senator Pryce opened her mouth to retort, then closed it. She looked as though she'd just been asked to swallow battery acid. And yet she did not throw the offer back into Harlow's face again. As any shrewd politician would, she recognized the truth in what he'd said. It appeared that cloning wasn't such an important issue to Senator Pryce that she'd be willing to risk her seat for it.

"Now, Senator," Harlow said, with a smile that cut like a knife. "What's it going to be? The carrot or the stick?"

36: ANNABEL

Ominous clouds the color of steel wool loomed overhead when Annabel and Ms. Durant arrived at JFK airport. Their flight had been short but turbulent, and Annabel had spent much of it clutching the armrests and praying, despite the fact that she'd never identified with any particular religion and didn't even know whether she believed in God. There was just something about the prospect of plummeting to the earth and smashing into oblivion that made her want to hedge her bets in the spirituality department.

"Is it always like that?" Annabel asked Ms. Durant as they screeched to a halt on the pavement.

"No," Ms. Durant said. "But occasionally you do feel like popcorn rattling around inside a pot."

Annabel and Ms. Durant were the first to disembark the plane, and Annabel tried not to think about the fact that she'd be getting on another one in three days time. Instead, she reminded herself why she was here, and refocused her attention on that. She had three whole days and nights without Rex, and she had a chance to tell her story. By the time she and Ms. Durant exited the airport to hail a taxi, she was already thinking of the tumultuous flight as the first part of a grand adventure.

She had never before seen so many people in one place — yelling, laughing, honking at the traffic jam. The clamor was overwhelming and when Annabel took a deep breath to steady herself, she began coughing at the smog.

"I detest the air in this city," Ms. Durant said with a sniff. "Something about it makes you feel like you're getting coated in grime."

"Have you been to New York before?" Annabel asked.

"Of course, my dear," Ms. Durant said. "I lived here for a couple of years in my youth. In a cockroach-infested closet-sized studio apartment in Brooklyn." She paused and allowed herself a small smile when she noticed Annabel gaping at her. "I wouldn't recommend it," she added in a stage whisper.

"At least you didn't have to marry anyone," Annabel said without thinking.

A hurt look flashed across Ms. Durant's face for an instant but was replaced almost immediately by a reproachful one. "Annabel, we've been over this. You're very lucky. I hope this trip gives you some perspective on just how lucky you are."

"I know. I — you're right." Annabel glanced down at her feet to hide the fact that she'd just told another lie. They reached the front of the cab line then, and a pale driver with too much gel in his dark hair put their suitcases into the trunk and opened the rear door for them. Annabel blushed when she noticed the appreciative look on his face as his eyes scanned her body. She clambered into the seat, mentally berating herself for losing her cool so easily. The driver closed the door behind her and walked around to his seat.

"Where to, ladies?" he asked, watching Annabel in the rear-view mirror.

"Manhattan. Fifty-seventh and Park, please. The Four Seasons." Ms. Durant's clipped tone made it clear that the driver's wandering gaze had not escaped her notice either, and that she did not approve in the least.

"You got it," the man said, turning around and slamming his foot on the gas pedal, sending Annabel sprawling sideways into the door when he abruptly jerked the car into the next lane. She hurriedly buckled her seatbelt, bracing herself as he wove in and out of traffic.

Annabel stared out the window as they approached the skyscrapers, and before long they were slowly making their way through the densely packed streets. Even when she craned her neck to look almost straight up, Annabel couldn't see the tops of the buildings they passed. She watched the people milling around on the sidewalks like so many ants, some striding purposefully along, some strolling as though they had all the time in the world. Rain began to fall then, fat drops splattering on the front windshield of the cab, but it made little difference to the foot traffic, except that some people opened umbrellas as they hurried by. The taxi driver muttered profanities under his breath when the rain started, but Annabel was grateful for it. The sound of the rain had always soothed her, and the sheer scope of the city was overwhelming.

After an hour, the cab finally pulled to a stop in front of a building made of off-white stones and an ornate glass entrance framed by a couple of trees poking up from the sidewalk. As Ms. Durant settled the bill with the driver, two uniformed men rushed forward from the hotel entrance to meet them. One held a black umbrella large enough to shelter four people comfortably, and the other attended to their luggage. They were escorted inside and while Ms. Durant checked them in, Annabel looked around the lobby. There was gleaming marble everywhere, high sweeping ceilings, and designer lamps emitting a soft glow. The plants that stood in the lobby's four corners offered a small but appreciated sense of familiarity. Awed as she was at the endless bustle of New York, she wasn't sure she loved the exchange of grassy, wildflower-dotted fields for concrete and steel.

The same man who'd wheeled in their luggage led them upstairs to their suite. Like the lobby, it was carefully lighted and decorated in such a fashion that no one could fail to call it luxury — the large windows offered stunning views of the city and Annabel walked right up to them and stared out at the dusky sky, trying to keep in mind that each of the tiny lights she could see represented a room with people in it, living their lives alongside millions of others. *Does it make them feel less alone?* she wondered. *Or more?*

"Well my dear, we've arrived." Ms. Durant settled down on

the couch and smiled fondly at Annabel. "I must say, this is a far nicer place than where I spent my nights when I was here last."

"I'm glad," Annabel said, tearing her eyes away from the window and moving to sit in the arm chair adjacent to Ms. Durant.

"Why don't you change for dinner? You've got your big interview in the morning and then that photo shoot afterwards. We should have an early night," Ms. Durant suggested.

"You're right," agreed Annabel, although she doubted she'd be able to sleep, so thrillingly surreal was the situation in which she now found herself. They went to a sushi restaurant around the corner that Ms. Durant picked where Annabel had miso soup, seaweed salad and an exceptional spider roll. On the way back to the hotel, Ms. Durant showed Annabel a chocolate shop and bought them both lavender cardamom truffles for dessert.

Back in the hotel suite, Annabel's mind was buzzing when she climbed into her king-sized bed. She savored the feeling of having it all to herself — she hadn't slept alone since before the wedding. Annabel stretched her arms and legs out wide, taking up as much space as she could, and gazed out the window at the multitude of city lights until she drifted off to sleep.

The next morning, Annabel woke up before her alarm went off, riddled with doubt. She dismissed the uneasy feeling, telling herself it was too late to back out now, and that it was normal to be nervous. It wasn't as though she'd made this decision alone — Ms. Durant was here with her, complicit in her plan. Surely that had to count for something.

Annabel showered and dressed simply in a short-sleeved navy blue cotton dress that brought out the color of her eyes. She did not bother with makeup, and combed out her hair but left it to air dry, not wanting to seem like she'd put too much effort into her appearance. When she went into the common room of the suite, she found Ms. Durant seated on the couch reading from her tablet. It gave Annabel a strange feeling of nostalgia for her childhood, when it had been just the two of them.

"Ready to go?" Ms. Durant asked.

Annabel nodded. Ms. Durant put away the tablet and gestured towards the door, indicating that Annabel lead the way. Annabel took a deep breath and held it for a split-second before releasing it in a *whoosh*. She squared her shoulders and walked through the door, determined not to appear afraid.

A man wearing a hotel uniform ran outside when they reached the lobby to hail a taxi for them. Within minutes, they were speeding across the city towards the cafe where they were to meet Arthur Blair and do the interview over breakfast. Annabel was silent for most of the ride, while Ms. Durant recounted various pieces of trivia about New York landmarks. In what felt like no time at all, the cab stopped outside a beautiful old building with ivy growing all along its front. Ms. Durant paid the driver, and they stepped out. Annabel looked around. A sweaty-faced man with a pointy nose and poorly cut ginger hair approached her, thrusting out a hand when he was a few feet away. He wore a rumpled white button-down shirt and faded jeans that were too baggy for him.

"Mrs. King, I'm Arthur Blair," he said with a wide smile. "So pleased to finally meet you."

"Likewise," Annabel said. She shook his hand, trying not to squirm at the name he'd used. Unpleasantly, his palm was as sweaty as his forehead. "Annabel is fine."

"Annabel it is! And you are . . ." Arthur Blair asked Ms. Durant, who had been hovering at Annabel's shoulder with an appraising look on her face.

"Helena Durant," she said. "Annabel's —"

"Friend and travel companion," Annabel cut in. For some reason she did not want Ms. Durant to be the one to tell Arthur Blair about her role in Annabel's upbringing.

"Charmed," Mr. Blair said, extending his hand politely to

Ms. Durant, who shook it. "Shall we go in? I made a reservation so our table should be ready."

Annabel followed Mr. Blair into the restaurant. It was bright and airy, with white linen table cloths and impressionist still-life paintings lining the walls. A blonde hostess who appeared to be around Annabel's age led them to a table for four next to a window after Mr. Blair persuaded her that the reservation listed for two was really meant to be three and that it was the restaurant's mistake. Annabel noted that his skill at subterfuge far exceeded his skill at personal grooming.

Mr. Blair began by making made polite small talk about their flight, their hotel accommodations, whether they might have time to do any sightseeing the following day before they departed the city. Mostly, Ms. Durant answered these queries while Annabel hid behind her menu, until they ordered and the waiter took away her shield.

"How about we get started on the interview, then?" Mr. Blair said, suddenly all business. "Do you mind if I record it? Just to ensure I quote you accurately, of course."

"Oh!" Annabel said. "Um, okay."

Mr. Blair tapped the touch screen of his phone a few times, then looked back up at her with an encouraging smile. "Excellent. Why don't we start with your childhood? Where did you grow up? What was it like?"

"Oh, um. I grew up in a small beach town in New England. It was . . . pretty normal, I guess." Annabel said.

Mr. Blair made a politely incredulous sound. "Come on now, Annabel. You had no parents. You were raised by a caretaker hired by the man who was married to your original. The man who became your husband on your eighteenth birthday? There's nothing normal about that upbringing." He gave Ms. Durant a look that said he'd known exactly who she was from the beginning.

"I don't like your tone, young man." Ms. Durant glared at Mr. Blair, cutting in before Annabel could even begin to think of a response.

"It's okay, Ms. Durant. He's just doing his job." Annabel gave Arthur Blair a faint smile, chewing her bottom lip and trying not to appear flustered by what she realized was a fair assertion.

"Humph," Ms. Durant said, sitting back in her chair with her arms crossed. She kept her eyes on Arthur Blair who fidgeted uncomfortably in his seat but did not apologize or retract the question.

"You're right," Annabel said. "It was unusual. But it was the only upbringing I had, so I'm not sure how to even begin comparing it to anyone else's. And as you can see, Ms. Durant and I are still close. She was a wonderful caretaker." Ms. Durant seemed mollified by that, but the tension did not completely leave her shoulders.

"Yes, of course. Very touching." Mr. Blair said, wiping his sweaty forehead with his sleeve. He even seemed like he meant it. "But was there ever a time when you wished you were just like everybody else? Maybe sometime at school or...?"

Every day of my life. "Not really," Annabel lied. "I am who I am. There's no point in wishing I was somebody else."

"Hmm," Mr. Blair said. "I suppose that's a mature outlook to have."

"Annabel is a very mature girl," Ms. Durant said with pride.

"I should think so," Mr. Blair countered. "Being that she's already married and all."

Ms. Durant's eyes narrowed. "Watch yourself, young man. She doesn't have to keep talking to you if she doesn't want to."

"Funny, I don't hear her making any objections to me at all." Mr. Blair looked at Annabel and she reddened, not wanting to be caught in the middle of their argument.

"It's fine." She turned to Ms. Durant. "Maybe I should do this on my own, and catch up with you later? After the photo shoot."

Ms. Durant's jaw dropped in shock, but she recovered quickly. "Now Annabel, my dear, is that really —"

"Don't worry about me. I can take care of myself," Annabel said in quiet but firm voice.

For a tense moment, no one spoke. Then Ms. Durant picked up the cloth napkin in her lap and threw it down on the table. "You know, I'm not very hungry after all. I'll leave you to it." She stood, not meeting Annabel's eyes. Guilt twisted in Annabel's stomach for a moment, strangely mingled with triumph.

"I'll see you tonight," Annabel said. Ms. Durant nodded, then cast one final scowl in Mr. Blair's direction before she took her leave.

"Well then," Mr. Blair said, as though there had been no interruption. "Where were we?"

The breakfast went on for two full hours. Annabel found herself getting more and more comfortable with the affably awkward Mr. Blair as the time wore on, but she never forgot to whom she was speaking and for what purpose. Part of her was still worried about what Rex would do when he discovered that she'd spoken to a reporter after he'd expressly forbidden it. She had no desire to justify his inevitable anger with carelessness.

Mr. Blair gave her the address where the photo shoot would take place that afternoon when they parted at the restaurant. Annabel stood outside on the pavement for a moment, watching his receding form as he headed to the corner and down the steps that led to the subway. She had over an hour to herself now, and she wandered along a side street lined with art galleries.

The spring air was brisk and smelled like car exhaust and fried food. Small trees poking up from the sidewalk were well on their way to regrowing the leaves they'd lost during the winter. As Annabel strolled past each gallery window, she saw everything from paintings to sculptures to photographs to video installations. When Annabel reached the end of the block, a shockingly rebellious thought occurred to her. She was alone in a strange city, entirely anonymous. What was stopping her from staying here, or else going off somewhere else on her own? Would Rex track her down? Surely he would try, after spending so much money to commission her creation. What would happen if she refused to return to him?

The thought was fleeting, the sort of wild fantasy that she knew would never come to pass, like slaying a dragon or learning to read minds. She did not know whether one day she would have the courage to leave Rex, but she knew today was not that day. With a sigh, she resolved to enjoy the rest of the weekend away, and not to waste any more of it thinking about her husband.

Twenty minutes later she walked into the five story brick building where the photo shoot would take place. Mr. Blair was waiting for her in the lobby next to a large desk where a bored-looking secretary typed away and paid them no mind.

"Annabel, right on time. You're the first to arrive. Let me show you upstairs."

"Thank you, Mr. Blair."

"Arthur, please," he said as the two of them stepped into the elevator.

"Arthur," she repeated. She felt strange calling him by his first name, but she resolved to try. He had asked her to do so repeatedly.

The elevator had no doors, merely a criss-crossed iron grating that Arthur pulled across and clicked into place. He pushed the button for the second floor and they lurched upwards, initially in fits and starts, then more smoothly. They ground to a halt one floor up, and Arthur unlatched the iron grating and pushed it aside, holding his arm out to indicate that Annabel should disembark ahead of him. She stepped out of the rickety elevator into hallway. Arthur led her to the door at the end, which opened to reveal a large open room with a black drape covering one wall.

There were about ten people bustling around with lighting equipment in a corner, plus a couple setting up large mirrors and unloading makeup on a small table. A few nodded to

Annabel in greeting, but quickly resumed their tasks.

The room contained a few pieces of mismatched furniture, and Arthur led Annabel to an armchair facing an empty fireplace and a large window overlooking the alley.

"Can I get you anything? Water? Tea? Coffee?" Arthur asked.

"Tea please, if it's not too much trouble." The armchair where Annabel sat was lumpy, but she did not want to be rude by pointing it out.

"Be right back." Arthur hurried through an archway on the opposite side of the room which led to the tiniest kitchen Annabel had ever seen. He put an old kettle on the stove and a few minutes later carried over a steaming mug of green tea which he handed to Annabel. She blew on it before taking a sip; it wasn't as good as the tea she had at home, but it was better than nothing.

"I'm going to head down to see if anyone else has arrived," Arthur said. "I'll be right back."

Annabel stood up and paced the room, careful not to spill the tea. She felt awkward being largely ignored by the room's other occupants, but they seemed intent on what they were doing and she did not wish to interrupt. Instead she paced in a small circle around the room. It had high ceilings, crown molding and dark wooden floorboards that creaked when she stepped on them. A few minutes went by before she heard the elevator groaning as it ascended, then the clattering as the iron grating was pushed aside. Arthur had returned with two other people: a tall boy who looked to be about her age with dark skin and a preoccupied expression on his chiseled features, and a woman about fifteen years her senior with a messy blonde pixie cut, copious tattoos, and a camera.

Arthur was practically bouncing with excitement as he shepherded the two new arrivals across the room towards Annabel.

"Annabel, allow me to present Edgar Prime. The first-ever clone. Edgar Prime, Annabel."

Annabel explored him with her eyes. He was one of the

handsomest men she'd ever seen. She almost asked what it was like to have a living original, but that seemed too personal a beginning, so Annabel settled for, "Hi."

"Hi," he mumbled. "It's Ed, by the way. Not Edgar Prime."

"Hi, Ed." Annabel flushed at how tongue-tied she felt, but Ed didn't seem to notice.

"And over there is Beatrice," Arthur said, pointing at the tattooed woman who, without greeting anyone, had strode across the room and begun inspecting the preparations her team of assistants had made, while they waited for her comments with bated breath. She began to rattle off instructions and immediately they jumped into action.

"I'll be right back," Arthur said, hurrying once more to the elevator. "I'm sure our third guest of honor will be here shortly." He stepped into the elevator and clattered back down to the ground floor.

There was a momentary silence during which she and Ed merely stood together awkwardly, completely ignored by Beatrice and the others, who were repositioning the lights so they formed a semi-circle facing the sheet on the far wall.

"Have you ever met another clone?" Annabel blurted out, mentally cursing herself for how eager she sounded.

Ed looked up from the spot on the floor where he'd been staring. "I don't know," he said, but did not elaborate.

She wondered if he was always this standoffish or if it had something to do with her. Uncharacteristically, she decided she didn't care, and allowed her curiosity to trump courtesy.

"What's Dr. Midas like?" she asked.

A scowl flitted across Ed's handsome face. The hostility she sensed seemed to intensify, then it melted away as suddenly as it had come.

"Challenging," he replied. Once more, she waited for him to elaborate, but he didn't. Instead he asked a question of his own. "Who made you?"

"My husband," she said. She noticed his brow furrow slightly as he considered her words; for the first time, he seemed to be giving her his full attention. Before he could say anything else however, the sound of the elevator creaking up from the ground floor interrupted them, indicating a new arrival.

37: JAVI

Javi's flight had been delayed by two hours, and consequentially he was fifteen minutes late for the photo shoot. He'd checked into his hotel with barely enough time for a shower (air travel always made him feel grimy but never more so than this flight, his first ever experience in coach) and it took him longer than he'd expected to hail a cab. While the driver was weaving in and out of traffic, Javi called his dad's cell phone. It was a calculated move, to keep his parents from becoming suspicious or worried about his whereabouts — even though his mom was still upset with him, he knew she would want to know he had arrived safely. He was banking on the call going unanswered since he knew his dad had been planning to spend the day golfing, and he always preferred to have his phone on silent so he could more easily "get in the zone".

He left a short message about Stanford, and said he'd text when he and Fred were on their way back the following night. Guilt battled for his attention, but he pushed the feeling away. He was legally an adult, after all. He didn't have to be honest about everything if he didn't want to be.

When the cab stopped in front of a brick building he hastily paid his fare and ran inside where Arthur Blair was waiting for him.

"Javier, so glad you found us!"

Javi merely grunted in response, but Blair was already yammering on about Javi's one chore during what would otherwise be a completely free weekend.

"Modest building for a photo shoot, I know, but Beatrice Bosch is a true artist. We were lucky to get her."

Javi nodded politely, wondering if Blair was aware how little all of this interested him. Blair beckoned, stepping back to allow Javi to climb into the most ancient elevator he had ever seen. Blair followed him, slid the iron grating in place with a rattling click, and pressed the second floor button.

It was only while the elevator was ascending that Javi's thoughts returned to the other two clones. He felt a strange flutter of nerves in his stomach, mingled with what he supposed he could call excitement. Now that the moment of meeting was upon him, the whole situation seemed surreal. The elevator ground to a halt and Blair unlatched the iron grating and slid it off to one side, leading the way into the large room where the photographs would be taken.

"Allow me to introduce Edgar Prime Midas and Annabel King," said Blair, gesturing to two people standing just inside the entrance. Javi gave Edgar Prime the briefest of nods in greeting, but found it difficult not to stare at Annabel King. She had long, dark red hair that he wanted to run his hands through, porcelain skin, clear blue eyes, and pink lips that were curved into a small smile. She was tall and slender, but curvy in the right places.

"Uh," Javi stammered, mentally cursing himself. "Hi. I'm Javi." He forced himself to glance towards Edgar Prime as he said this so that Annabel wouldn't realize how dumbstruck she'd made him. *Ha, too late for that.*

"I go by Ed, actually," said Edgar Prime. When Javi tore his eyes away from Annabel again to shake Ed's hand, he realized with dismay that there was no way Annabel would look twice at him with someone like this guy around. Ed was the very definition of 'tall, dark and handsome'. He noticed a couple of the younger women across the room shooting Ed appreciative looks while they adjusted the lamps.

"Nice to meet you, Javi," said Javi's newest crush. She looked at him curiously, and he tried to arrange a more nonchalant expression on his face and not stare at her so intensely. *Nothing like coming off like a gawky fucking loser to make a girl fall for you. Get it together, idiot.*

"Hi," he said again. "Sorry I'm late. My flight was delayed." *Like they care.*

"Not to worry, not to worry," Blair cut in. "Let's get started. This is Beatrice, she'll be photographing you." He indicated a thirty-something woman wearing all black who stood in the corner attended by her cluster of eager-looking assistants. Beatrice's visible skin was covered with tattoos, her hair was short, spiky and platinum blonde, and she wore dark red lipstick and a lot of eyeliner. Instead of speaking she merely raised the camera she was holding, pointed it at them and clicked.

"Well then!" Blair cried out, clapping his hands enthusiastically. "Let's get started, shall we?"

Beatrice snapped her fingers and the assistants sprung into action, guiding the three clones over to the area in front of all the lights while fiddling with their hair and dabbing on small bits of makeup. Annabel was placed in the center, flanked by Javi and Ed. Javi thought he must have ruined half the shots by looking sideways at Annabel instead of at the camera. He couldn't help but notice that her hair smelled like lemons.

"How weird is this?" Javi muttered to the others while Beatrice fiddled with the settings on her camera.

Ed barely spared him a glance, then went right back to glaring at the floor. "Weird," he said shortly.

"Have either of you done anything like this before?" Annabel asked, turning to face them.

"Nope," Javi said.

Ed didn't say anything for a moment, then shrugged one shoulder. He looked embarrassed. With a stab of annoyance, Javi noticed Annabel watching *him*.

"I guess this probably seems pretty normal to you," Javi said, barely able to keep the hostility out of his voice. In middle school Fred and Herman had convinced Javi to find out more about where he came from, and they'd come across a number of articles profiling the illustrious Dr. Edgar Midas, none of which failed to mention that his scientific breakthrough was proved when he successfully made a clone using his own DNA. Under other circumstances, Javi might have reflected on how strange Ed's upbringing must have been. But it was hard to have sympathy for someone so disgustingly good-looking.

Ed didn't answer for a moment, then mumbled, "It'll never be normal."

"Did your parents commission you, Annabel?" Javi assumed most clones were, like him, created to replace the prematurely departed children of the wealthy.

"No," Annabel said, but she did not explain further. He wondered whether he'd imagined the glance exchanged between Annabel and Ed, a glance that made Javi feel irrationally jealous. Maybe Ed already knew her story — come to think about it, he probably knew all about Javi as well. Javi scowled, but didn't have a chance to say anything more because Beatrice was ready to resume.

The photo shoot was one of the most uncomfortable experiences Javi had ever had; even though Beatrice was perfectly courteous and patient with them, it was tedious to stand posing while a camera flashed in your face over and over again. Beatrice took a number of group shots, followed by individual portraits. There wasn't much chance to talk with Beatrice clicking away and calling out instructions for them to modify their facial expressions and postures. When she finally announced she had what she needed, Javi sighed audibly in relief.

They all climbed into the elevator together, leaving Beatrice and her assistants to put away the lighting equipment and pack up the camera. As the elevator rattled down to the the ground floor and they stepped out into the lobby, Javi checked his phone and saw that his father had texted, telling him to have fun and be safe (his mother's addition, no doubt). Emboldened by his successful deception, Javi looked up at Annabel who was standing awkwardly as though she was unsure of whether to leave or not.

"D'you want to grab a coffee?" Javi blurted out.

Annabel looked surprised, but gratified. "Sure, okay. What about you, Ed?"

Javi tried to hide his annoyance that she had invited his rival along; he'd been hoping she'd take his invitation as more of a date, but he supposed that was too much to expect.

Ed sighed in what he probably thought was a convincing show of regret. "I'm sorry, I can't. Got plans already this afternoon. But it was nice meeting you both."

Suppressing a grin at his good luck, Javi shook Ed's hand and with an equanimity he would have found more difficult had they not been about to part ways. He even managed to watch Ed shaking Annabel's hand (and holding onto it slightly longer than necessary in Javi's opinion) with only minimal displeasure. Arthur Blair hovered around them, smiling a cloying smile and babbling about how pleased he was that they'd all hit it off. Javi was impatient to leave the reporter behind with his sweaty face and clamoring interest.

With one final nod in their direction, Ed walked off down the street. Javi immediately turned to go the opposite direction with Annabel in order to avoid them all having to share the sidewalk. In truth, he didn't have the faintest idea where they'd go next; he hadn't planned anything out beyond getting away from handsome Ed and sycophantic Blair.

He and Annabel didn't speak for the first block or so, and Javi was more self-conscious than usual of everything from the length of his strides to the way his arms hung at his sides. They strolled in an unhurried way, and Javi tried his hardest to appear relaxed.

"D'you know a place near here?" Annabel ventured.

"Um." Javi stuck his hands in his pockets, the illusion of cool assurance shattered. "No," he admitted. "I live in California, so I don't know the city all that well. I visited a long time ago with my parents but . . ." he trailed off.

"I don't know it either," Annabel confessed. "This is my first time in New York. It's my first time anywhere, actually."

"We could just . . . wander around?" Javi almost cringed at how juvenile he sounded, but stopped himself when he saw Annabel's smile.

"I'd like that," she said, and Javi was quietly elated.

38: EDGAR PRIME

Edgar Prime left the photo shoot in a foul mood. Part of him wished he had never agreed to Arthur Blair's stupid story, and had never had to meet his fellow clones. Disgusted as he was to admit it to himself, the truth was that he resented them. They reminded him of how even among the clones, he was an anomaly. Unlike the others who had been made for love and grief, he was nothing more than the experiment of a narcissist.

There was also the fact that he couldn't help but feel uncomfortably responsible for any hardship incurred by Javi and Annabel — a perverse sort of guilt by association. Were they happy to have been created to fill the roles of the dead, or did their lives consist of one disappointment after another when they couldn't live up to the expectations of their creators? Worse, this had started him wondering about all the others; he didn't even know how many had been made over the last eighteen years. He had never given much thought to Dr. Midas's policy not to ask any questions of his clients, but now he wondered whether that was nothing more than a lame excuse. *Just like everything about him*, thought Edgar Prime. *And I'm his copy — if he can do this, what does it say about me?*

Before the photo shoot, he'd met with Arthur Blair and told him a pack of lies that satisfied the PR requirements laid out for him by Dr. Midas by way of Patrice. *Yes, he was honored to have been an integral part of the history of genetics. Yes, he had learned a lot from Dr. Midas's mentorship. No, he had no reservations about cloning or any of the other genetic experiments carried out at Dr. Midas's lab.* All lies. But it was easier than telling the truth.

The fact that he had neither seen nor spoken to Hugo or Celeste or any of them in over a week was weighing on him too. Edgar Prime knew he should reach out to Hugo at least, but he couldn't bring himself to do it. No matter how many times he took out his phone and stared at it, willing it to ring or buzz with a text notification. Willing himself to make the first move in contacting them, but never doing it. He knew now that he was a coward, and he hated himself for it.

When the photo shoot ended and Arthur Blair shook all their hands and thanked them profusely for their participation, Edgar Prime was relieved. After a curt goodbye to Annabel and Javi, Edgar Prime walked away from the building and began striding through the streets with no clear purpose. For over an hour he walked, not paying much attention to where he was going and it was only when he turned a corner and saw the outline of a familiar building several blocks up that he realized where he was headed.

He stood at the entrance and allowed the scanner to capture his retinas. There was a click and the bulletproof glass door swung open to admit him. Inside, Edgar Prime waved to Charlie the blonde security guard, wishing his golden hair looked less like Hugo's. Charlie nodded to him in greeting, and watched solemnly as Edgar Prime used his thumbprint to unlock the elevators.

Dr. Midas was right where Edgar Prime expected him to be, in his office reading over the latest data reports from Patrice's research while strolling along on his treadmill desk. When Edgar Prime entered, Dr. Midas smiled an avuncular smile and his eyes twinkled as he regarded the living embodiment of his genius.

"This is a pleasant surprise, Prime."

"Do you ever wonder what becomes of them?" He spoke in a rush, without preamble. Dr. Midas furrowed his brow in confusion.

"Of who?"

"Of all of them. Your *children*." He spat the word.

Dr. Midas raised an eyebrow. He didn't need to ask who Edgar Prime meant again; he knew. His mouth curved into half a smile. "They are not my children. Nor my responsibility. None of them but you."

"Maybe they should be. Your responsibility."

"Maybe," conceded Dr. Midas. "But they aren't. What I do is perfectly legal. If I didn't do it, someone else would. Others do, in fact. They just don't do it as well as me."

"Legal because of Harlow," Edgar Prime said. He wasn't sure why he was bringing Harlow into this. Nobody had ever confirmed Edgar Prime's suspicions about Harlow's role in legalizing human cloning, but there had been many hints over the years, most from Harlow himself. Harlow was a man who loved to bask in his own glory, and loved that his influence extended to the highest levels of government.

Any hope that mentioning Harlow would rattle Dr. Midas was quashed; he merely chuckled. "That's just speculation, Prime. But as you know, Damon Aldous Harlow is a powerful man with powerful friends. He's been a loyal patron of my research for a long time."

What was left unspoken floated in the air between them for a moment. "You never answered my question," Edgar Prime said finally. "Do you ever wonder about them? Your clones."

"They are not 'my' clones. So to answer your question, no. It is not my place to wonder, no more than it is yours to judge." Dr. Midas sounded stern now. "I don't know what has gotten into you lately, Prime. Cavorting with this Clone Advocacy Network seems to have mixed up your priorities."

"My priorities are fine," Edgar Prime said through gritted teeth.

"Your priorities are even more muddled than one would normally expect from a person your age," Dr. Midas countered.

Edgar Prime did not answer. Dr. Midas was eyeing him with pity, as though this whole line of questioning was the silliest thing he'd ever heard. Suddenly feeling like he couldn't stand to be in the presence of his maker for another second, Edgar Prime shook his head with as much scorn as he could muster and turned to go. Dr. Midas called after him.

"Good seeing you, Prime. As always."

The only answer Edgar Prime gave was to slam the lab door behind him as he stormed out into the hallway. He jabbed the elevator button and paced while he waited, trying to stop himself from punching the wall. Why couldn't he have inherited Dr. Midas's boundless confidence along with his bone structure? Where did his self-loathing come from, if not his original?

The elevator dinged softly and Edgar Prime stopped pacing and stood right in front of the doors in his impatience. When they opened he nearly barreled into Patrice, who yelped in surprise.

"Ed! You startled me," she said unnecessarily.

"Sorry," Edgar Prime muttered.

"It's okay," Patrice said, stepping off the elevator into the pristine hallway. Edgar Prime was about to get on when Patrice touched his arm gently. "You look upset."

"I'm not," Edgar Prime said shortly. The elevator dinged again and the doors tried to close, but Edgar Prime flung his arm into their path and they re-opened.

"If this is because Dr. Midas isn't being as supportive of your history major as you'd like, you just have to give him time. He finds it difficult to imagine that his genetic copy would have different goals and ambitions than he did."

"How does he even know I want to major in history?" Edgar Prime snapped, thrown off by the change of topic.

"He's a smart man," Patrice said.

"Does it ever bother you?" Edgar Prime found himself asking. "Don't you ever wonder where they all wind up? The clones you make."

"Sometimes. But why would it bother me? Unless you mean — the defective ones?" She said the last part in a hushed whisper, as though worried who might overhear and pass judgment on her.

"That wasn't what I — how many defective ones are there?" Edgar Prime was ashamed once again. He hadn't even been thinking about *them*.

"Far fewer here than at other labs. But even Dr. Midas isn't perfect."

"And what happens to them?" Edgar Prime wasn't sure he wanted the answer.

"It depends on whoever commissioned them. Sometimes they're kept, even with their imperfections. Sometimes . . ." Patrice frowned, but did not finish her thought. Edgar Prime knew she must be alluding to the black market where defective clones were bought and sold for various purposes — everything from illegal medical experimentation to organ sale to trafficking. The horrors of humanity were boundless.

The elevator dinged again in its agitation at being held open for so long, but Edgar Prime ignored it.

"How can you do it then? What you and he do?" Was Edgar Prime hoping she'd have a comfortable answer for him, something to assuage his own guilt?

Patrice answered immediately, as if she'd considered the question before. "It's a kindness. We help people who are grieving find solace."

"Rich people," Edgar Prime shot back.

Patrice shrugged. "Cloning is expensive. At least here we do it right. Dr. Midas produces far fewer defective clones than any other lab. If we didn't do it, it would still be done. Just not as well."

Edgar Prime regarded her coolly. She seemed concerned for him, and he stepped into the elevator to escape her probing eyes.

"I've gotta go," he lied.

"Bye, Ed. Have a good night."

He didn't answer. The elevator doors closed and he was carried downward, away from her, away from *him*. But Edgar

Prime could not escape the questions that plagued him.

Later that night, after downing most of a bottle of gin, Edgar Prime steeled himself and went to Hugo's apartment. It was too unbearable to be such a failure at everything, and he judged the Celeste problem more easily fixed than the cloning conundrum. At Hugo's he knocked and knocked, leaning heavily against the doorframe and contemplating laying down in the hallway for a little nap. Everything swam and blurred before him, and he was on the point of passing out when the door was jerked open, causing him to fall in a heap on the ground just over the threshold.

Hugo stood above him, regarding him coldly. "I should write you up for this."

Edgar Prime struggled unsteadily to his feet, clutching the handle of the door to pull himself up. "That thing that happened. With Celeste. It was a mistake. Just a mistake." His words slurred, and he thought he saw a flash of hurt in Hugo's eyes before they hardened again.

"It was shitty of you to leave like that, and not to call her after." Hugo crossed his arms, indifferent to Edgar Prime's imploring look.

"But, you know I — you know she — it didn't mean anything. It just happened." Edgar Prime felt bile rising in his throat and fought to keep himself from vomiting all over Hugo's floor. "She started it. If she hadn't cornered me ..."

"Oh *fuck you!*" Celeste yelled from inside the apartment. Swaying more than ever, Edgar Prime watched in horror as Celeste stepped up behind Hugo. "You didn't fall and slip on a banana, *Prime.* We had sex in my bathroom then you fucking ran away like a scared little boy. Fuck you."

He quailed under her glare. "I — I didn't mean —"

"You should go." Hugo's voice was soft. He didn't even sound angry. Just sad.

"But Hugo —"

"No," Hugo cut him off. "You should go. Now."

Edgar Prime looked from Hugo to Celeste, a solid wall of

crossed arms and icy cold eyes that cruelly judged him without mercy. Edgar Prime staggered backwards and away down the hall. He heard the door slam but didn't look back. He managed to make it to a bathroom before he collapsed next to the toilet to empty the contents of his stomach, wishing he were dead.

39: ANNABEL

Annabel laughed again — she couldn't seem to stop laughing around Javi Vasquez. They were seated next to the window in a small cafe called Verona. It had a cozy fireplace across the room and was decorated with mismatched vintage furniture and Toulouse-Lautrec prints on the walls; the perfect blend of strange and familiar.

"Okay, how about that lady over there?" Javi said in an undertone, jerking his head to the right towards a woman in her seventies with wispy bubblegum pink hair that looked like it was made out of cotton candy. She wore a hot pink tracksuit that bulged a bit in the belly and carried a fluffy white pomeranian in her handbag. They were playing a game that involved making up stories about other cafe patrons. Annabel had been reluctant at first, but it wasn't long before her reservations melted away.

"Can we steal that dog?" Annabel whispered, thinking she'd never seen a more tiny or adorable animal.

"Why not? I'll accidentally-on-purpose spill my coffee on the pink lady, and while she's distracted by my charming apologies you can snag the bag." They grinned at each other.

"What should we name her?" Annabel asked.

"Princess Pom-Pom?" His eyes twinkled with mischief. "Oh, you meant the woman! I thought you were asking about our dog."

"*Our* dog? You mean my dog, don't you?" Annabel said playfully, but she felt her cheeks warm at the idea of the two of them caring for a dog together. The thought was strangely romantic, and it confused Annabel. She did *not* feel that way, not about Javi.

Javi clutched his chest as though she'd stabbed him in the heart. "I see how it is, Annabel. You use me to help you steal her, then cast me aside the second she's yours. That's cold." His laughter belied any hurt he might have felt, and soon enough, Annabel was laughing again too.

"Not sure how I feel about the name Pom-Pom," Annabel teased. "She's more dignified than that."

"*Princess* Pom-Pom," Javi corrected. "The 'princess' part's essential."

Annabel regarded the pomeranian, whose owner was now lovingly feeding her a treat. "Yeah," she said, fighting off another bout of laughter. "You're right. It's perfect."

After the coffee, they continued meandering around the city, until Javi suggested they go see the Museum of Natural History. He'd visited when he was young, and he wanted to show her something. Annabel agreed, not wanting her afternoon of freedom to end. When they arrived, Annabel insisted they stop to examine all the fossils and artifacts instead of racing right to the room Javi wanted to see. He looked on, patiently bemused, as Annabel experienced her first museum. She'd done virtual tours of many of the exhibits, of course, but somehow seeing them in person was different. When they finally reached the entrance to Javi's favorite room, her eyes were drawn upwards to a giant squid model above them. The passed underneath it to find themselves standing on the second level of the life-sized blue whale exhibit.

Annabel gasped. The whale curved gracefully, suspended from the ceiling by heavy cables that were all but hidden from view by its massive bulk. They walked all the way around it, then went down to the bottom level and explored it from beneath.

"Amazing, isn't it?" Javi murmured beside her. They had both been speaking quietly since entering the blue whale exhibit, as though they were in some kind of temple.

Annabel nodded. She read the plaque explaining that the

blue whale was nearly extinct; before much longer, this scale model would be all that remained of what was once the largest animal ever to have lived. A resigned sense of gloom settled over Annabel, putting a damper on her previous glee. They stayed for a long while, walking around and around, studying the whale from all angles. Or at least, Annabel was studying it. More than once she'd caught Javi's gaze turned towards *her* instead of the exhibit. It made her nervous, but not entirely in a bad way.

When they finally left, it was growing dark outside. Annabel felt a bewildering mixture of emotions — simultaneous exhilaration and melancholy. The thought of going back to the hotel room to have a lonely dinner with Ms. Durant made her stomach clench painfully.

"Hungry?" Annabel asked, surprised at her own daring.

"Starving." He grinned at her, an easy grin that made her heart beat faster.

They got on the subway again and went to Chinatown, where they found a restaurant with a brick facade and wooden beams on its high ceiling. Amid the babble of talk and laughter, they drank jasmine tea from a clay pot and shared the most delicious array of dumplings Annabel had ever tasted: crab and eggplant, steamed lobster, crunchy vegetable and peanut, four mushroom, shrimp and snow pea leaf, and butternut squash with walnuts and ginger. Afterwards, they walked to Rice to Riches for cardamom ginger rice pudding. Annabel was skeptical, but was glad to be proved wrong when she gave into Javi's insistence that it was much better than it sounded. It was spicy and creamy and just the right amount of sweet. The most glorious ending to a glorious dinner.

They wandered along afterwards, finding themselves on a street lined with sex shops and bars in the west village. Incongruously, they turned a corner and came upon a tiny pet store with several fluffy puppies frolicking in the window. For a long moment, they couldn't tear their eyes away and stood oohing and aahing while they watched the puppies at play.

"I wish I didn't have to leave tomorrow," Annabel said before she could stop herself.

Javi glanced at her, then turned his eyes back to the pet store window. "Neither do I. Maybe we should just stay."

Annabel gave a humorless laugh. "My husband would go ballistic."

"You're *married*?" Javi burst out. He gazed at her with incredulity etched all over his face.

Annabel found it difficult to meet his eyes all of a sudden. "Yes."

"But you're only — how can you be married already? Didn't your parents flip out and try to stop you?"

"I — it's complicated." Annabel wished she hadn't mentioned Rex; he was casting a long, dark shadow over what had otherwise been a perfect day.

"Complicated how?" Javi raised his eyebrows suspiciously.

"It's not important."

"How could you go the whole day without telling me you're married? You're not even wearing a ring." His tone had turned accusatory.

"It's not like that. I took it off because I didn't want to think about — the reason my parents didn't object to the marriage is because I don't have any. My husband was married to my original and had me cloned when she died of cancer. We got married on my eighteenth birthday."

"Shit," Javi said. For a moment, he seemed unable to process what she had just told him. "You know that's seriously fucked up, right?"

"I mean — he didn't *raise* me or anything, I had a caretaker named Ms. Durant. We didn't meet until the day of the wedding." She had no idea what was compelling her to defend Rex when she knew Javi was right. Perhaps she was downplaying it so that he wouldn't think of her as tainted or weak. For one day, she had wanted to pretend she was a normal eighteen-year-old girl.

Javi was still goggling at her. "But that doesn't — that

shouldn't make it — how could you go along with that? With an old man you'd never even met before! Eugh!"

Annabel's eyes narrowed and she glared at him. "D'you think I *wanted* to go along with it? D'you think I had a choice?"

"But you did!" Javi had inadvertently raised his voice, and they were drawing curious glances from other passerby. "You could have walked away instead of walking down the aisle."

"Why do you even care?" Annabel snarled back. "It's not that simple. You just be grateful it was your parents who commissioned you and not some grieving ex-spouse. I'm going to go. I don't want this whole day to be ruined by *him*." She stuck her arm out in an attempt to hail a passing taxi.

Just like that, all the inexplicable anger went out of Javi's face. "Look, I'm sorry. I was just — surprised. You're right, I shouldn't judge you."

A cab drove up, but Annabel waved it on and dropped her arm. Even though neither of them mentioned Rex again, the mood had shifted. They spent another three hours walking together, talking about everything and nothing, but the previous pull Annabel had felt coming from Javi had been dampened. When he finally dropped her off in front of the hotel with a look that might have been pity, Annabel knew the earlier magic was gone and could never be recovered.

She crept into the dimly lit hotel suite and darted into her room before Ms. Durant could wake up from where she'd been dozing on the couch with her tablet precariously perched next to her, clearly waiting up for Annabel. The prospect of being questioned about her whereabouts was not one Annabel cared to face at the moment (or ever), so she closed her door loudly enough to indicate to Ms. Durant that she was home safe and had no wish to talk. Annabel brushed her teeth and washed her face in the en suite bathroom like a zombie, then pulled on a nightgown and fell into the large, soft bed where she stared at the darkened ceiling for a long while before the tears finally came.

40: JAVI

When he arrived at the airport the following afternoon, Javi couldn't help but look for her. Realistically, he knew it was a futile effort; the chances of running into one person amid the crowds at JFK were practically nonexistent. But that didn't stop him from looking. Whenever he saw a flash of red in his peripheral vision, he'd whip around, hoping against hope that it was her hair. Disappointment followed like a mocking wraith, cackling silently at him for his stupidity.

Javi barely noticed the many indignities of coach this time; he sat in the uncomfortable waiting area and allowed himself to be herded meekly to the twentieth row. Fortunately, his seat was on the aisle. *Small mercies,* he thought wryly. He felt more conflicted about Annabel than he should, considering he'd probably never see her again. The revelation that she was not only married but had been commissioned by her husband specifically for that purpose had been a punch in the gut. It made Javi's difficulties with his family seem insignificant by comparison, and filled Javi with shame at all his feeble complaints about what he'd endured over the years. More than anything though, Javi wished he'd kissed her.

There had been several times when the urge to touch her was overwhelming, but even at her most unguarded she still had walls to keep him — and presumably everyone else — out. Not that he could blame her for that, considering ... but it had been frustrating all the same. On the one hand, they'd undeniably had a great time together. *No,* he corrected himself, *'great' doesn't even begin to describe it.* On the other hand, he couldn't read her well enough to know whether she saw him as a friend or something more. He knew he should have given it a try anyway, pride be damned, but his courage wasn't quite up to the task. *Coward.*

Just before takeoff, Javi's phone buzzed with a text from Imogen that read: *'Meet me tonight?'* He replied in the affirmative barely sparing a thought for the logistics — was her husband out of town? — then turned off his phone as instructed by a passing flight attendant. At least he had that to look forward to. Javi spent most of the flight reading a mediocre spy thriller, interrupted at regular intervals by intruding thoughts of Annabel and Imogen, sometimes together, sometimes apart. Once or twice Stella Castell put in an appearance too.

By the time they landed in SFO, Javi was somehow both weary and on edge. He waited impatiently for his turn to deplane, striding down the narrow aisle and through the terminal. On his way outside, Javi stopped in a Duty-Free store to buy a pack of cigarettes and a cheap lighter. He didn't smoke tobacco, but thought this might be a good time to start.

When he turned his phone back on, he received a text from Imogen telling him to meet her at a motel near the airport. Javi took this to mean her husband was home, and replied to say he'd be there in half an hour. In the cab, Javi felt a vague sense of guilt about the bewildering pull he'd felt towards Annabel over the weekend, but just as soon dismissed it. After all, Imogen was the one who was married, not him. He didn't have anything to feel guilty about. And besides, who *wouldn't* have been interested in Annabel with that red hair and unassuming beauty?

Any thoughts of guilt were driven from his mind as soon as he arrived at the motel. Imogen was louder than usual, and he realized it was because for once her children weren't playing in the backyard.

After they finished, he got up and rummaged through his backpack for the cigarettes. Imogen watched him with a mixture of lust and bemusement on her face, and he lay back down next to her and tore the plastic wrap off the cigarette pack. He offered one to Imogen and she shook her head with a half-smirk. He put a cigarette between his lips and fumbled with the lighter for a moment before he successfully managed to light it.

Even though Javi didn't like the taste of the tobacco much, he did feel awfully sophisticated smoking a cigarette naked in bed with a woman he'd just fucked. When he glanced to his right, Imogen seemed to be holding back laughter with difficulty. Javi scowled.

"What?" he asked defensively.

"What d'you mean 'what'?" she said.

"What's so funny?"

"I didn't know you smoked."

"I smoke all the time!" Javi said indignantly. "Only pot 'till now."

"I'd stick with pot if I were you. Quitting tobacco is a bitch."

"Did you smoke?"

She shook her head. "Theo smoked a pack a day during college. It was brutal for him to break the habit."

The casual mention of her husband left Javi feeling cold. It was one thing to know in the abstract that she had a husband, another to hear about him as a person. "I don't want to hear about your husband."

Imogen scoffed, and snatched the cigarette from him. She took a long, slow drag on it and blew the smoke towards the ceiling. "You've always known about Theo."

"Still. I don't want to think about him."

"Lucky you. I don't get that luxury." She took another drag on the cigarette, and he hated himself for still finding her so sexy.

"I'm not the one who married him!" Javi's temper flared. He planted his feet firmly on the floor and leaned down to search through the jumble of clothes for his boxers.

"You're not leaving already?"

His only answer was to stand up and begin to dress. Imogen's face softened and she stubbed out the half-smoked cigarette in an ashtray on the bedside table. He turned his back on her but heard the creak of the bedsprings as she stood as well. With a quiet sigh, she wrapped her arms around him from behind. He almost shrugged her off when her left hand slipped downwards and his annoyance melted away.

After the second time, Javi was sweaty and winded. He looked at the clock on the bedside table and groaned; if he didn't leave soon his parents would be wondering why he wasn't home yet. He rolled off the bed and took a two minute shower, hoping he wouldn't pick up a foot fungus from one of the motel's other occupants. Imogen called a cab for him while he got dressed, not bothering to get up from the bed. He gathered up his things and leaned down to give her one last lingering kiss before he left.

He needn't have worried about his parents. When he got home only his father was awake, reading in his study. Javi stopped by the half-open door on his way upstairs. His father laid aside his book — Javi was amused to see it was paper and ink not digital — and greeted him with a smile.

"How was Stanford?"

Javi shrugged. "It was fun. Fred's friend was a good host."

His father beamed and Javi felt a twisting feeling in his gut. "Well, I'm happy to hear it. I know you're probably tired . . ."

Javi seized on this excuse. "Yeah. Didn't get much sleep."

His father chuckled at that. "Can't say I'm surprised. Go on then."

"Goodnight, Dad." Javi walked upstairs, brooding. The lie was taking its toll, far more than Javi had expected. He knew that his parents would find out the truth when the article came out, and he wondered what he'd been thinking. The stupidest part was that they'd probably have been fine with it if he'd just *asked* them. And things with Imogen weren't helping. Now that she wasn't there to distract him, he found himself unable to stop thinking about her husband, home with their

M.A. Gelsey

young kids while she was in a cheap motel fucking the clone of her dead high school boyfriend.

A weight pressed down on Javi, the weight of certainty that he was the worst person in the world. He was a liar and a cheat — a defective copy of someone who a lot of people had loved. With only this heavy knowledge for company, it took many hours before Javi was able to drift off into a fitful sleep.

41: MIRA

With dismay, Mira read the latest message she'd received from the Clone Advocacy Network. They were growing increasingly bold, but Mira didn't see how she could warn them off without arousing Harlow's suspicions. He had something planned to deter them from investigating further, but hadn't shared the specifics with Mira yet. For their own good, of course. The thought made her uneasy. *Don't they understand who they're dealing with?*

Like a good assistant, Mira showed Harlow the message. It outlined a plan to infiltrate the black market with a hidden camera, to show the world what really went on. Their naiveté took her breath away. They didn't seem to understand that there was no one physical place that represented the black market. It was a vast web of seemingly unrelated pockets that communicated through the darknet, frighteningly well-financed and organized. Harlow chuckled to himself when he read the email, and instructed Mira to write back revealing their identities and requesting a meeting with Edgar Prime. The meeting was to be with Harlow himself, and the proposed topic was to discuss his interest in supporting their endeavor. When she was done, he had an errand for her to run.

Once the request had been sent, Harlow gave Mira a package and asked her to bring it to the Central Park carousel. A man would be waiting there to accept the delivery. Mira found the instructions odd, but knew better than to question them. The box Harlow handed her was small, the same size as one that might contain a necklace or a pair of earrings. It had been neatly wrapped in brown paper, and it rattled faintly when she shook it. Before leaving the office, Mira took a detour to the bathroom. Inside the stall, she carefully unwrapped the paper, taking care not to tear it. She opened the box to reveal a flash drive. Knowing she had neither the time nor the skill to break the encryption, Mira texted Jack in the hopes that he'd be able to meet her on the way to Central Park and somehow copy the flash drive before she handed it over to whoever she was due to meet. Ordinarily for an undercover operation like this she'd have a whole surveillance team backing her up, but their poorly-funded task force didn't have the resources for that — Mira was on her own. She didn't have time to go down to their Chinatown base of operations, and would be cutting the meeting close as it was. Quickly, Mira wrapped up the package again and set off towards the elevators.

Mira spent the entirety of her walk to Central Park anxiously checking her phone for a response from Jack. She got one as she was entering the park, saying that he was still in Chinatown but could be there in half an hour. Cursing under her breath, Mira told him not to bother. She had no choice but to hand the flash drive over un-copied, or risk blowing her cover.

The sky was overcast as Mira wound her way through the park, habit causing her to scan the perimeter for any suspicious activity. Noticing nothing of importance, Mira made her way to the carousel. She leaned on an iron fence and waited.

Within a few minutes, she noticed a short man with black hair and bronze eyes approaching her. It only took Mira a split-second to realize where she'd seen him before: he was the one they'd called "The Courier". He'd been caught on airport security cameras coming through customs using a variety of aliases. They had speculated that he was responsible for delivering auctioned clones safely to their overseas buyers. She noticed him looking her up and down as he sidled up next to her.

"You have something for me, Mira?" he asked. She couldn't

keep the surprise from her face when he used her name.

"Do I know you?"

"Not yet," he replied, with an easy smile. The pitch of his voice was soothing, the sort of voice you might hear on a guided meditation podcast. Mira handed him the package, and he stuffed it into his jacket pocket.

"It's not really fair that you know my name but I don't know yours," Mira commented.

"Bob Smith." He held out a hand for her to shake. She took it, thinking that the name was probably another alias, but it was still better than nothing. Mira thought he'd make his exit to deliver whatever was in the small box, but he didn't appear in any great hurry.

"Do you like jazz?" he asked her.

"Sure," Mira said, thrown by the question.

"Will you meet me at Cadence Bar tonight? Best live jazz in the city."

"That's quite a claim."

"I don't make it lightly."

Mira considered him. She was still uncertain how they'd arrived here, but she knew she'd have to meet him. The potential chance to gather information was too great.

"Okay. Nine?"

He grinned. "Perfect." Then he walked away, leaving a bemused Mira in his wake.

That night, Mira sat in a corner booth at Cadence, waiting for the enigmatic Bob Smith to arrive. Jack was acting as her backup for the evening, sitting at the bar and nursing a whiskey and soda. Mira felt a stab of jealousy when she noticed several nearby women eying him appreciatively. She pushed the thought away, angry with herself. Why should she care if other women found him attractive? It didn't matter to her either way.

The room was stuffy and dimly lit with an unpainted brick wall on one side, and exposed metal beams lining the high ceiling. It smelled of liquor and marijuana smoke and sweat.

The band was set up in the corner opposite Mira's booth, and there was a large open space between them and the bar where a few people were dancing enthusiastically to the jazz.

Mira noticed Smith walk in wearing a black leather jacket that she thought made him look marginally sexier. Instead of taking the seat across from her, he slid into the booth next to her, so close that their knees were touching. *Get a grip*, Mira silently berated herself as she blushed. *You're here to work.*

Smith leaned toward her. "What're you drinking?"

"Gin and tonic with extra lime," she said with a smile.

"Can I get you another?" Smith asked, nodding towards the bar. She agreed, even though she knew she should probably watch how much she drank that night. Smith strode up to an open spot at the bar right next to Jack, who was chatting up a pretty girl with blue hair and heavily tattooed arms.

Smith returned as the band began to play a new song. For a while they just sat together sipping their drinks and making the occasional offhand comment about the music or the venue. After their third round, Smith stood up, gave an exaggerated mock-bow, and held out a hand with a nod towards the half-full dance floor. Mira was feeling pleasantly tingly all over, and she gave an uncharacteristic giggle and let Smith pull her from the booth.

While they swayed together, Mira was too drunk to feel awkward about the fact that she was a couple of inches taller than him. She could see Jack smirking at her over the head of the blue-haired woman who was still keeping him company. Suddenly, Mira felt angry with herself. What had she learned from this outing? Not a damn thing, except a reminder that she couldn't hold her liquor. *You're building rapport*, a voice in her head pointed out. *That's not nothing. Maybe next time he'll tell you something useful. He'd be suspicious if you asked him anything tonight.* Grudgingly, Mira admitted to herself that this may well be the case. Smith pressed himself even closer and kissed her, lightly at first. The kiss deepened, and for a time Mira allowed herself to enjoy the sensation and forget about her failings as an undercover agent. Later, Mira found herself outside the bar, with Smith whispering into her ear that he'd like to go home with her. She mentally shook herself, but the world remained hazy.

"I don't think that's a good idea tonight," Mira told him. He was disappointed, she knew, but accepted her decision graciously.

"I want to see you again," he told her. "But I have to go out of town for a few days. Can I call you when I get back next week?"

"Of course." Mira gave him her number. Something about what he'd just said registered as important, but she wasn't in a state to figure out what it was just then. Mira got in a driverless cab alone, and fifteen minutes later stumbled into her apartment, kicking off her shoes and tossing her bag on a heap of dirty clothes in one corner of the floor. She groaned as she sank onto the bed without bothering to undress, knowing she's have a horrible hangover in the morning but not quite caring enough to go through the effort of staying up to eat something and drink copious amounts of water.

A loud knock on the front door sent a jolt of adrenaline through Mira; it was almost two a.m. and her first thought was that mild-mannered as he'd seemed, Smith had followed her home. Mira fumbled in the nightstand for a moment and withdrew her gun. As she made her way to the door, she clicked off the safety and pulled back on the slide. Her whole body was tense as she leaned in towards the peephole, but when she recognized Jack on the other side of the door she exhaled the breath she didn't realize she was holding and pulled open the door.

"Jack, what the fuck?" Mira asked, as he strode into her apartment without invitation. He turned towards her and took note of the gun in her hand with a raised eyebrow. She shut the door and slid the deadbolt into place, then removed the magazine and the bullet from the chamber of her handgun. Jack just watched her, and the moment she put the unloaded gun down on her coffee table he took two steps towards her and kissed her full on the mouth.

She was too startled to react immediately, but after a second she kissed him back, tasting the whiskey on his tongue.

"I hated watching you with him tonight," Jack mumbled, and Mira could tell that he was as drunk as she was.

"You seemed to be doing just fine with that blue-haired girl," Mira said, biting his lower lip hard enough to draw blood. His hands trailed down her back and he grabbed her ass roughly and pulled her even closer. She grinned and pulled off his shirt, grabbing hold of his belt buckle and dragging him to the bed. Seeing the way he looked at her, Mira was tempted to use the belt to tie him to the bed and make him beg. *Maybe next time*, she thought, as they tore off the remainder of their clothes. The sex was the frenzied, uninhibited sort that comes from being drunk, and afterwards they lay side-by-side panting, covered in sweat.

Mira was grinning. "I like you when you're jealous."

"I could tell."

She tossed a pillow at him that he was too lazy to deflect; it hit him full in the face. He just laughed.

42: BOB

Bob walked slowly home from the bar, thinking about what a waste of time the evening had been. When Jane first told him that Harlow needed him to check out his new assistant, he'd leapt at the assignment. Harlow wanted to know whether Mira was a corporate spy for one of his rivals, and Bob wanted a distraction. Now though, Bob had an entirely new dilemma to obsess over. He was almost certain that Mira was law enforcement — her scowling backup at the bar had been a dead giveaway — but he was strangely torn about passing the information along to Harlow.

Once upon a time, he wouldn't have thought twice about it. But that was before. Now, he wondered whether it might not be better to let things take their natural course. Harlow might be arrested. His syndicate would be in disarray, or maybe even dismantled. He had to suppress a shudder as he imagined his father's reaction to such thoughts. Bob had only seen his father get angry a handful of times in his life, but each one was etched into his memory as if with a chainsaw. His father never yelled; instead he spoke in a chillingly quiet voice that inspired terror in even the most fearsome of men. *No doubt that's why Harlow likes him so much.*

Lost in thought, Bob found himself surprised to have arrived at his building. He trudged up the steps and took the elevator to the eleventh floor. When he opened his front door, the apartment was quiet, and pitch black.

"You're home early."

The voice sent a jolt of adrenaline through Bob as he flipped on the light switch. His sister sat on the couch, pointing a gun at him and smiling.

"Fuck, Rebecca," he said.

She lowered the gun and put it down on the coffee table in front of her. "You're lucky it's just me. If it'd been someone else, you'd be dead."

"It wasn't someone else."

"It easily could've been. You're slipping."

Bob snorted and pulled off his coat. He took his time hanging it up in the tiny hall closet. When he was done, he sat down across in the armchair from her.

"Well?" She raised an eyebrow.

"Are you really here for my report?"

"If it's interesting, yes."

"It's not." The lie came easily, and went unremarked.

"I heard there were some . . . issues with your last drop."

"Who told you that?"

She just looked at him.

"I want out." He didn't know what made him say it.

She laughed. "Don't be ridiculous."

"I'm serious."

"There is no 'out' for us. This is what we do, it's in our blood."

"Not in mine."

"Is that so, Michael?"

It was the first time she'd used his true name since they were children.

"It is."

She laughed at him again. "I'm sorry, I thought I was speaking to Michael Leone, son of Paolo and Lucrezia Leone —"

"— both currently in jail —"

"— both temporarily incarcerated, but still running the family business from behind bars."

"Michael Leone is dead. He died in a car crash twenty years ago." After spending so many years as Bob, the name 'Michael' felt foreign to him. He and Jane had been given new identities as children, when their parents were first sent to prison. Their mother liked to say it was to give them a blank slate, but Bob knew it was so that they could operate without the surveillance that all known adult members of the family endured.

"You can't just walk away from this thing they built, Michael. That's not how it works."

"And what if I do? They'll kill me?"

She didn't answer immediately. He knew she was wondering the same thing he was. "Harlow might," she said finally. "If he thought you'd turn on him."

"He doesn't have to worry about that," Bob said, not without bitterness.

"You need a vacation," Jane said. "That's all."

"That's not the problem." He was weary. His sister could argue for hours, days. It never ended until he told her what she wanted to hear.

"I'm serious, Michael. Some things are developing. Harlow needs us."

Bob's head had started to throb, just behind the temples. "Fine."

Jane looked suspicious at his abrupt change of tone. "So you'll forget about all this nonsense?" She always double checked, even after winning an argument.

"You've convinced me."

"I hope you're not lying to me, Michael."

I hope so too.

43: MIRA

The next morning Mira woke to the sound of a woman's voice. Blearily, she opened her eyes and looked around for the source. Jack was standing naked in front of the television, drinking coffee and watching a news report about Senator Pryce withdrawing her support from the bill that would ban human cloning. Mira had only a moment to admire the view before Jack noticed she was awake and slid back under the covers with a grin. He leaned over to kiss her, but she pulled back.

"I'm sure I've got really horrible morning breath right now," she muttered.

"I don't care," he said, and that was that.

It was slower and sweeter in the morning, beginning in bed and moving into the shower despite it really being too small for two people. Afterwards Mira was tempted to go back to sleep, but they had a briefing with Warren in an hour and Jack convinced her that the time could be better spent tracking down a good breakfast. They ate at a diner around the corner from Mira's apartment, and arrived at their meeting with Warren together.

Warren cast a suspicious glare in Jack's direction, and Mira tried not to blush. Surely Warren noticed Jack's rumpled clothes (the same ones he had been wearing the day before), but mercifully he didn't deign to comment. Mira hoped he'd assume Jack had spent the night with someone else. She had told Jack that she didn't want the rest of them to know, and he didn't argue. Once they were all assembled, Mira cleared her throat.

"There wasn't much opportunity for me to question Smith last night," she began. "But he did mention one potentially useful piece of information. He said he'd be going out of town for a few days, and that he'd call me when he got back next week." She half-glanced in Jack's direction and silently cursed herself for it. "It's possible that there's going to be another auction, and that Smith will once again be the one to escort the auctioned clones to overseas buyers. It might even be worth trying to tail him."

Warren grunted. "Not sure we have the resources," he muttered. "I'll put in a few calls."

"I can try to get his flight information," Liesel volunteered. "It's difficult because he always travels under different names but the clones —"

"—might not," Warren finished for her. He looked impressed, a rare sight. "Good, *very* good. John, you'll assist Liesel."

Ever the team player, John nodded, but Warren barely glanced his way. Instead he turned to glower at Jack. "Got anything to contribute here, Sterling?"

Jack scowled, but didn't otherwise allow himself to be provoked. "I was Mira's backup last night with Smith," he said. Mira bit the inside of her lip to keep from smiling. "And I was thinking I could go down to D. C. to meet with Senator Pryce. We know Harlow strong-armed her into killing that anti-cloning bill. If we can get her to turn on him —"

"We'll accomplish very little," Warren snapped. "We *already* have a witness to that little exchange, remember? And revealing that will likely hurt Pryce more than it will Harlow. I want to nail the bastard, and to do that we need some charges with teeth. Not some wimpy bullshit about bribing a member of congress when we both know that'll never stick." Warren had worked himself into a rant, and broke off panting as though he'd just run a marathon.

"Fine," Jack said. "I'll keep tabs on the clone shelters then. See if there's a spike in adoptions. Presumably they'll be smart enough to only do a few from each one, so they don't draw too much attention. Still, their records might reveal a pattern."

They all took Warren's lack of criticism as approval. Jack gave Mira the smallest of winks. Mira looked away from him, again telling herself to get a grip.

"Harlow's also got a meeting with Edgar Prime coming up — there was an email this morning confirming it. He told me he's got a plan to convince the Clone Advocacy Network that their time would be better spent elsewhere, but he hasn't shared it with me."

Warren waved this off impatiently. "Most likely he'll just try to impress upon the boy how dangerous the black market is, and how ill-advised they are for meddling with it. Let's just hope they're smart enough to take the hint. Idealistic college students can be remarkably pigheaded about these things."

"But if they don't —" Mira started.

"—you'll be in the loop to pick up the pieces," Warren finished. "This isn't our primary concern. Harlow's a ruthless bastard, but he's not stupid. Anything too overt from him will arouse suspicion, and the last thing he wants is to have investigators sniffing around in connection with an attack on Edgar Midas's clone or one of his friends. Harlow wouldn't be so bold."

Mira disagreed, but saw no purpose in arguing this point further; the look on Warren's face told her that he wouldn't be convinced. She felt a deep sense of trepidation for the unsuspecting CAN students, and it was with this in mind that she tried one more approach.

"But if *we* warned them —"

"Out of the question." The others agreed with Warren, even Jack. The idea that she'd be reduced to sitting on the sidelines waiting for the hammer to drop filled Mira with bitterness, but she was a professional. She knew how to follow chain of command.

44: EDGAR PRIME

The subway car rattled and swayed, but Edgar Prime was too preoccupied to notice. His meeting with Harlow was set for later that afternoon, and Edgar Prime was already feeling deeply uneasy about it. *Don't be paranoid*, he told himself for the thousandth time. *No harm in hearing him out.*

To further complicate matters, Luken had refused point blank to take part in Noela's plan at the last CAN meeting. He and Noela had a huge fight over it, but they eventually reached a detente, and had left it up to CAN members whether or not they wanted to participate in what they all agreed would be their most dangerous initiative to date.

There were only a handful who had agreed to work with them: Zelda Lisner with her mass of strawberry blonde curls, Carter Riggs, a slightly chubby boy with wiry dark hair and several days of stubble, Victor Healy who had the worst acne that Edgar Prime had ever seen, and Noela's younger brother Omar, who shared her reddish hair, olive skin, and freckles. It was Omar who had volunteered to go undercover with a hidden camera. Noela's mouth had tightened slightly when he offered himself for this task, but she didn't try to dissuade him; Edgar Prime knew she felt hypocritical for wanting someone other than her brother to take on that particular danger — she'd sooner do it herself, but she was known to be the co-founder of the CAN and they couldn't risk anyone recognizing her.

Edgar Prime nearly missed his subway stop, but realized just in time. He walked around the corner into Illyria Cafe, where Noela was already waiting for him at a corner table, looking uncharacteristically solemn.

"Do you trust Harlow?" Noela asked without preamble. "If we go through with this, we'll be putting a lot of faith in him."

Too much, Edgar Prime thought. "We don't really have a choice, do we? It could take years for us to get access otherwise."

"You're right. And anyway, this is too important for us to ignore." She sounded as though she was trying to convince herself. " I just wish we knew *why* he'd offer to help us."

"I'll try asking him about it later," Edgar Prime promised. He was as curious as Noela about Harlow's motivations.

She nodded at that. They sat in silence for a few moments; Noela stared out the window, seemingly watching the pedestrians go by but really, Edgar Prime thought, considering their predicament. She took a gulp of her steaming black coffee and immediately spat it back out, cringing.

"Fuck!" she exclaimed. "That is way too hot. Fucking fuck, fuck." Her eyes watered and she grimaced.

"I'll get you some ice," Edgar Prime said, springing up to ask the barista for a cupful. When he returned she popped a cube into her mouth, still clearly irritated at herself for burning her tongue.

"Have you talked to Luken?" Edgar Prime asked, hoping to distract Noela until the pain subsided.

Her face darkened into a scowl. "No. But I've known Luken for a long time and he's always been stubborn. I'm not worried about it."

"How did you two meet?"

She shrugged. "In college, at some stupid party our freshman year. We started talking and realized we lived in the same dorm. Then one thing led to another, and within a few weeks, we were best friends."

"Just friends?" Edgar Prime didn't know what made him think otherwise. Perhaps something in the way she said his name — affection mixed with exasperation.

She gave him a look as she began sucking on a second ice

cube. "Not exactly. But that's all we are now."

Edgar Prime waited for her to elaborate; when she didn't, he let the subject drop.

"I should go," he said. "Don't wanna be late."

"Keep me posted on Harlow."

"Of course." Edgar Prime got up and left the cafe, heading for the subway. *Better not fuck this up.*

Edgar Prime had never visited the building where Harlow worked before. He was greeted by an elegant blonde receptionist, and almost immediately led back to Harlow's large corner office. Everything was meticulously designed (apparently courtesy of Harlow's fourth wife, an interior decorator); all wood and leather and clean geometric lines. Expensive, yet understated.

"I'm sorry for having my assistant do that whole cloak-and-dagger routine," Harlow said as Edgar Prime took his seat. "But you know how I appreciate dramatic effect. And more importantly, I wanted to see how serious you were before I revealed myself. We've all got reputations to uphold, after all."

Edgar Prime nodded, unsure of how to respond to that.

"Can I offer you a cigar?" Harlow pulled two out of his desk drawer and held them up.

"No, thank you," Edgar Prime said.

Harlow shrugged, and set about cutting and lighting his cigar. The longer the silence stretched on, the more uncomfortable Edgar Prime became, but he was determined not to allow Harlow to rattle him. Finally, after taking a puff and blowing foul smelling smoke in Edgar Prime's direction, Harlow spoke. "Don't you want to know *why* I asked you to come here, Prime?" He seemed amused by the situation.

"Yes," Edgar Prime managed, choking back a cough. He wondered whether Harlow had told Dr. Midas about this meeting.

"Call me sentimental, but the article your friend Arthur Blair wrote about those clone advocacy people really got to me. So here we are."

Edgar Prime's eyebrows shot up before he could stop them. Since when was Harlow interested in the greater good?

Harlow chuckled at Edgar Prime's silence. "Why so surprised, Prime? Once upon a time, I helped a promising young scientist who was convinced he could make history by producing the world's first human clone if only it were legal."

"But that was an investment," Edgar Prime said before he could stop himself. He didn't know why he was arguing this point with Harlow, when he'd already agreed to help. "This is different."

"Is it?" Harlow asked. "Bad publicity is bad for business, and the black market is starting to get traction in the media. Better to stomp it out before it starts affecting our profits."

Edgar Prime didn't buy it, but he couldn't for the life of him come up with an alternative explanation for Harlow's actions. He tried to keep the skepticism out of his voice with only moderate success.

"And you think the Clone Advocacy Network really has a chance to do that?" Edgar Prime asked.

"Why not? Your friends sent a message about their hidden camera idea. That might help motivate law enforcement to look into the matter a bit more expediently. If a group of teenagers can infiltrate the black market, they'll look like buffoons if they don't at least manage a raid before the end of the year."

"And how would you even get us access?" Edgar Prime asked.

Harlow laughed again. "You know, for such a smart person you can be remarkably naive, Prime. Corporate espionage is part of the game! Access is the easy part."

"Then why not take care of it yourself?" Edgar Prime challenged. "Why trust us with something so important?"

Harlow just smiled. "Are you interested, or not?"

45: ANNABEL

Annabel spent the whole of the all-too-brief return flight from JFK with tears streaming silently down her cheeks. She knew that Ms. Durant noticed but was too tactful to say anything. Luckily, Annabel managed to compose herself before de-planing in Boston, because no sooner had she stepped into the waiting area than she ran into Veronica and Phineas Hawthorne.

"Annabel, darling!" Veronica cried. She threw her arms out wide as if initiating an exaggerated embrace, forcing a grinning Phineas to step back from her side in order to avoid being smacked in the face.

Annabel froze, too stunned to say anything for a second. She felt rather than saw Ms. Durant tense next to her. Veronica and Phineas looked much the same as the last time Annabel had seen them: she was all blonde hair and 60s retro fashion (today her dress and nails were turquoise), and he was gray-haired, twinkle-eyed and clad head-to-toe in black. Annabel noticed that Phineas had swapped his diamond ear-stud for an ruby.

"Veronica, Phineas, hi. Good to see both of you," Annabel said, recovering herself. She allowed both of them to hug her briefly.

"What on earth are you doing *here*, darling? With Helena too — how are you, my dear? Didn't see you there at first. Looks like retirement suits you." Veronica said.

"We're just getting back from a spa weekend in The Hamptons," Annabel lied, half-glancing towards Ms. Durant.

"Charming, charming. You ladies and your beauty routines,

I must say they baffle me. I don't understand half of what goes on at such places." Phineas chortled at his own feeble joke, while Veronica rolled her kohl-lined eyes at him. "I'm sure Rex missed you terribly."

"Where are you off too?" Annabel asked, ignoring his last comment.

"Tuscany," Phineas said, patting his flat belly as if in anticipation of all the food and wine he would soon enjoy. "Got a time share with some friends. I asked Rex if you'd care to join us but he turned me down, the old fuddy-duddy."

"I'm sure it'll be lovely," Annabel said. It was news to her that she'd been invited to visit Tuscany, and had it been her decision she most certainly would have taken the opportunity, even if it meant sharing a villa with Phineas and Veronica. This knowledge made her return to normalcy (such as it was) even less welcome than before. There was a moment of silence interrupted by an announcement on the intercom that first class passengers for the 3:50 flight to Tuscany could now board, prompting a startled squeal from Veronica.

"That's us! Must dash! Wonderful to see you again, Annabel. And you too of course, Helena." Veronica hugged her again, followed by Phineas, then they were off, rushing to the adjacent gate. Ms. Durant seemed irritable for the remainder of their trip, but did not explain why, nor did Annabel ask. When Ms. Durant finally dropped Annabel off at the house, she was filled with trepidation. Just as she feared and expected, Rex was there waiting to greet her with a wet kiss and a bone-crushing hug that soon turned into something else as he led her upstairs to their bedroom for what he called a "proper reunion".

A few days later, Annabel found herself sitting on the balcony and staring out at the gentle waves of the bay as they rocked the boats moored in the harbor the way a mother might rock her infant. The air was warm and sticky, but there was a nice breeze that smelled of salt and lifted Annabel's hair off her neck. Nothing at all had changed, and yet everything had.

Since returning from New York, Annabel's days and nights had been characterized by an overwhelming sense of listlessness. Things she had previously enjoyed: practicing yoga, her online college courses, walking into town now held little appeal. She still did them as before, but in a rote manner, deriving no pleasure from anything. At first, she thought of Javi frequently, wondering what might have happened if they'd met under different circumstances, if they'd had more time, if she'd been brave enough to lean over and kiss him, an idea that simultaneously enticed and repelled her. After all, he wasn't handsome the way Leon Floros was handsome, wasn't the type of man she liked to imagine herself with. But nonetheless, there had been a pull of some sort. An attraction.

It was only after a week had passed that she realized it wasn't Javi she was mourning, not really. It was freedom. She had never really had any control over her life, having spent her first eighteen years closely supervised and regulated by Ms. Durant, the remainder by her husband. But for a day, she'd been able to do what she wanted, go where she wanted, when she wanted. For a day, she'd been free. It was almost unbearable to go back to the way things were before.

Except things weren't the same, not exactly. Since Annabel's return from New York, Rex had grown more possessive, and one time Annabel overheard him on the phone talking in hushed tones about his suspicions that she'd taken a younger lover. Annabel would have laughed aloud at the suggestion except that there was nothing funny about it. Even though outwardly he behaved much the same towards her, she could sense something had shifted during her brief absence. She debated coming clean with Rex about the article — he'd surely find out once it was published — but something stopped her, a cold, clenched sensation in her stomach as though an invisible hand had grabbed hold of her insides and twisted. She had no idea what his reaction might be, but she doubted it would be good. *What could he do, really?* she thought, trying to reassure herself. The answer came to her in an instant, accompanied by a chill running down her spine: *Plenty.*

Despite all this, Annabel tried her best to pretend that everything was fine. She recounted the story of how she and Ms. Durant had run into Veronica and Phineas at Logan Airport, omitting the information she'd acquired about her almost-trip to Tuscany. She prattled on about her art history class even though she'd lost interest, and every day the struggle to make herself keep studying intensified. It was during one such session on the deck, under a cloudless sky and a warm morning wind that Annabel realized there was only one thing she could do. The time had come to plot her escape.

This was easier thought than accomplished, however. Rex was in possession of all of her important documents, along with all of the money. The only way for her to access either of those things was through him. Of course, perhaps she could leave anyway. Perhaps she would. But no sooner had the defiance welled up in her than it began to ebb, replaced by doubt. *You don't know the first thing about the world,* a sneering voice whispered in her head. *You wouldn't last a day on your own.* And perhaps that was how Rex had always wanted it.

The reason behind Rex's heightened level of possessiveness made itself known one evening at dinner. Rex had his tablet on the table when Annabel sat down; unusual but not unheard of since he sometimes needed to make himself available for work-related correspondence. Annabel took her seat. When Mrs. Lennox appeared in the doorway carrying a roast bluefish, Rex waved her away.

"Mrs. Lennox, a moment, if you please," he said. Mrs. Lennox nodded and returned to the kitchen. Rex turned to Annabel with an unreadable expression on his face. "We need to talk, my love," he said to her.

"What about?" Annabel asked, furrowing her brow, in the hopes that her confusion would mask her apprehension.

"You. Us. You are happy here, aren't you? With me?"

Taken aback by the question, Annabel opened her mouth then closed it again without speaking. "I — of course I am."

Liar, whispered the voice in her head. Annabel felt herself flushing under the scrutiny of his gaze.

"I hope that's true, my love. But lately I've been wondering... you don't seem happy. Not like before."

Annabel felt ice in her chest; she knew he meant when her original was still alive. Even studying the face of her husband, Annabel could not tell whether he was sad or angry. Perhaps a little of both. "Why do you say that?" she choked out.

His mouth tightened, and now Annabel did see traces of closely controlled anger.

"You don't know? I find that difficult to believe," he said in a soft and dangerous voice.

Annabel did the only thing she could think of: continue to feign ignorance. She left the question unspoken, and tried not to look too afraid. After a moment, Rex sighed, and the anger seemed to leave him, replaced by pain. He tapped his tablet then wordlessly spun it around for Annabel to read. It took her a moment to figure out what she was looking at, but when she did, she had to stifle a gasp. Rex had pulled her cell phone records, and the screen showed all of her calls to Arthur Blair, along with her GPS location for the weekend in New York. When she looked up at Rex again, stunned, he regarded her with raised eyebrows. She realized then what he suspected.

"It — it isn't what you think," she said. Her voice sounded croaky and strange. "Arthur Blair is a reporter. The reporter who was writing a feature on the first three clones. I was in New York for them to take photographs of the three of us together. That's — that's all it is."

"That's all? That's all?! Are you telling me that after we discussed this reporter and I told you in no uncertain terms I did not want you speaking to him, you went behind my back and did so anyway?"

"Yes." Annabel whispered, bracing herself for the explosion.

It never came. Instead, Rex buried his face in his hands, running them backwards and forwards, roughly gripping at the skin and pulling it taut with each pass. When he looked back up at her, his hair was standing on end, his eyes wild.

"How can I trust you?" he asked her. "How can I, when you've proven your disloyalty. My Annabel would never, *never* have gone behind my back like this, she'd never have done it." He slammed a hand onto the table, making Annabel jump. "I don't understand. You're supposed to be just like her. I don't understand." He trailed off, gazing around like a man whose whole world had been demolished in a single moment.

"I'm sorry. I'll try harder," Annabel said. She tried to sound as conciliatory as possible, feeling unaccountably guilty. It wasn't her fault that she didn't love Rex as her original had. Nonetheless, she felt responsible, defective. *Will he cast you aside now that he knows you're worthless? Or continue on as if this conversation never happened?* Annabel did not know the answer.

Rex didn't acknowledge that he heard her apology, feeble as it was. He appeared adrift, and when Mrs. Lennox reappeared with their dinner, there was no indication that he even noticed. Annabel served both Rex and herself some of the white wine roasted fish, mashed garnet yams, and sauteed brussels sprouts.

She picked up her fork and began to eat, but Rex didn't so much as react to the food in front of him. After a moment, Annabel laid down her utensils and placed a hand on his shoulder. He jumped at her touch, but seemed to find it comforting.

"Have some dinner," Annabel said gently, rubbing his arm. "Please."

He did as she bid, and even though they did not speak for the rest of the meal, his body language was more relaxed, calmer. It was as though she'd unintentionally managed to reassure him that perhaps things could work between them after all. If only she believed it herself.

46: JAVI

"You realize you're fucking a married woman old enough to be your mother?" Herman said. He lay on his back in their usual spot in the park under the weeping willow tree, inhaling a joint before passing it to Fred.

"Nah, she's not that old," Javi said. His back was to the tree and he gazed around at the park's other occupants in the distance.

"Dude, do the math," Fred said. "She could totally be your mother."

"Fuck you," Javi said lazily.

"D'you know what's a funny word? Foliage," Herman said, gesturing up towards the leaves. "Fo-li-age. It sounds kind of dirty."

Javi snorted. "Only to perverts like you."

Fred and Herman both laughed at that.

"What's the foliage like on your married paramour?" Herman asked.

Javi rolled his eyes. "Why the fuck do you care?"

Herman gave him a mock-pained look. "In case you haven't noticed, I'm the only one here who isn't getting laid. Throw me a fucking bone and let me live vicariously."

"But why d'you want to know about her — her *foliage*?" Javi whispered the word, feeling vaguely guilty for talking about it even though Imogen would never know.

"Peak foliage? Bare foliage? Something in between?" Herman continued, his eyes as bloodshot as Javi had ever seen them and a silly grin plastered across his face.

"I dunno, kind of medium foliage. You happy?" Javi said.

"Why the fuck don't you ask Fred about Violet instead?"

"Violet isn't a married woman," Herman replied, as though that settled the matter.

"D'you have some kind of old woman fetish?" Fred teased. "I'm sure there are plenty of cougars out there who'd fuck you."

"Fuck, I'd be down," Herman said. "Pretty much down for anything with tits at this point."

"Guess you'd fuck Mr. Melcher then," Javi said. Mr. Melcher was their gym teacher, a man with skinny arms and legs, a huge beer-belly and the biggest man-boobs any of them had ever seen. Both Fred and Herman cracked up at that.

"Desperate times call for desperate measures," Herman shot back.

Javi grinned and shook his head. He took the joint from Fred and took a long draw. Then three people crossed into his field of vision and he dropped the joint in his lap.

"Fuck," Javi exclaimed, snatching up the joint again, but not before the lit end had begun to burn a hole in his jeans. At his yell, Bryony Shaw turned and noticed him sitting there. She tugged on her father's arm and pointed. Javi's first impulse was to hide, but of course that was impossible since he'd already been spotted. He did try to hide the joint, stubbing it out in the grass beside him.

"What the fuck —" Herman began, but the rest of his sentence died in his throat as he noticed the little girl ducking under the willow branches to greet Javi.

"Hi, Javi," she said, looking curiously at his companions, both of whom were watching Javi with bemused expressions on their faces. By this time Poppy had arrived, hand in hand with her father.

Theo Shaw was tall with sandy hair, broad shoulders and the beginnings of a belly. He crouched down and peered at his daughter through the willow branches. "Who's this, Bryony?"

She turned to look at him, and Javi had to stifle a groan. "Daddy, this is Javi. Javi, this is my dad."

Javi noticed the recognition flare in Theo's eyes, followed by confusion. "And how do you know Javi, honey?" Theo asked Bryony.

It was Poppy who answered. "He's friends with Mommy," she said in her little high voice.

"Is that right?" Theo said, studying Javi for a reaction. Javi could feel his face burning up.

"I —" he began, but luckily Theo cut him off because he didn't have the faintest idea what he'd been about to say.

"Come on girls," Theo said. "Say goodbye to Javi. If we don't leave now we'll miss our movie."

"Bye, Javi!" Bryony chirped, echoed by Poppy. Theo spared him one last glare before straightening up and leading his daughters away. Under the tree, there was stunned silence for a good minute after Theo disappeared.

"Was that the husband?" Herman asked in hushed tones.

Numbly, Javi nodded.

"Does he know, d'you think?" Fred asked.

"Dunno," Javi muttered, feeling sick to his stomach. "Fuck." He sucked in a deep breath.

Later that night, Javi got a text from Imogen, informing him that Theo had asked how their daughters knew Javi, and she told him about the coffee shop and him stopping by for lemonade afterwards. With difficulty he refrained from texting back, thinking it was likely Theo was there. Javi felt little relief from what she'd told him. Further questions plagued him, and it took Javi hours to fall asleep that night. Once he did, his dreams were a confused jumble of images: masturbating and being walked in on by Theo; running through empty streets naked and shunned by his parents, his friends, and Imogen; Annabel, looking sad and beautiful and disappointed, as she judged him from a high rock overlooking the sea. When he woke up sweating he remembered nothing, but could not shake the overwhelming feeling of guilt that enveloped him like a suffocating cloud of gnats, buzzing in his ears and sucking away at his blood until his entire body was covered with

their tiny, irritating bites.

47: MIRA

Mira was nearly late for the meeting. She'd risked ducking into a bathroom stall in the public library to open the small briefcase she'd been given. It had been surreal to find it stuffed with cash, as though she'd suddenly found herself in an old gangster movie from the 1950s. Ideally she'd have taken it to headquarters to have the bills tagged, but there wasn't time. She did wonder why Harlow didn't simply wire the money to whoever it was she'd be meeting; it seemed unnecessarily risky and inefficient to resort to physical bills. Maybe the man had insisted.

The Metropolitan Museum of Art was surprisingly crowded for a weekday. Mira made her way to the bench in front of Pollack's Autumn Rhythm (No. 30), and set the brief-case down next to her. She pretended to be immersed in the clusterfuck depicted on the massive canvas in front of her in paint splotches of black, white, and beige. Mira didn't know much about art, but she preferred it when a painting actually looked like something. This resembled the artistic efforts of her three year old niece. After a few moments, a man approached and sat down on the bench next to her. He was thin and angular, with sharp features, mousy brown hair and cold gray eyes; the sort of nondescript man who would be easy to forget. It was hard to tell exactly how old he was; Mira would guess thirties but she knew she could be off by as much as a decade on either side.

The man bent down and made a show of re-tying his shoe-laces; he wore faded, scuffed brown work boots that somehow seemed at odds with the studied refinement of the museum.

She noticed with some amusement that he used the bunny ear technique favored by small children to tie his laces, but did not comment. When he was nearly done, he muttered, "You tell Harlow he'd better make good on the other half."

Surprised that there *was* a second half, Mira just said, "I will." The man straightened up and grabbed the briefcase, then stood and walked off without a backwards glance. He left Mira there to ponder with foreboding what it was he'd been hired to do that would command such a fee.

The next morning, Mira woke up to the sound of her phone ringing. Without thinking, she answered it, but regretted her haste as soon as she heard the voice on the other end of the line.

"Mira!" her mother squawked at her. "You've been avoiding my calls."

Next to her, Jack rolled over and groaned. He looked at her curiously, and she mouthed, "my mother" at him. He grinned, and got up to use the bathroom.

"Hi, Ma," grumbled Mira, distracted by the sight of Jack's broad, muscular back and perfectly sculpted ass.

"I hope you weren't still sleeping, Mira, you're a grown woman not some college student. It's three hours earlier in here, and I've already done my gardening and cooked breakfast for the whole family."

"I wasn't sleeping," Mira lied. "I just had something caught in my throat." She reached over to the nightstand and took a swig of lukewarm water from the half-full glass she'd left there.

Her mother clucked her tongue, and Mira rolled her eyes even though she knew her mother couldn't see.

"I bought you a ticket to come home for Memorial Day Weekend. Sylvia's nephew is getting married, and we're all invited."

Mira stifled a groan. While she was happy to see her family, she knew this was part of a scheme her mother had cooked up with her Mahjong friends to set Mira up with some likely suitor.

"I'm not sure if I'll be able to get time off for Memorial Day," Mira tried.

"Nonsense. You work for the government, it's a national holiday. They have to give you Memorial Day. If they don't, maybe I'll have to call your office myself and have a word with your supervisor."

"Ma..."

"I'm only joking, no need to sound so exasperated."

Jack came out of the bathroom, and crawled back into bed next to her. Mira held a finger to her lips, and he grinned again, much more amused by the situation than she was.

"Now, I want you to be openminded at the wedding," her mother was saying. "Sylvia's gorgeous single son will be there —"

"I've already told you I'm not interested —"

"If you just put in a bit of effort — a nice outfit, some makeup, consider growing your hair out —"

"Oh, so you're saying he won't be interested if I don't dress up like someone else?" Jack raised an eyebrow at her, and Mira shook her head in irritation.

"Don't twist my words, Mira. I only said that it would be nice if you put some effort into your appearance for once. Your sisters were all so cooperative, why do you have to fight me on every little thing?"

"Of course, my *perfect* sisters. You'd think six grandchildren would be enough for you."

"Oh, Mira. Now you're just being silly."

"I have to go. I have a work meeting in a couple hours and I need to prepare for it.

"They work you too hard at that job. Maybe that's why you aren't married yet."

"*Goodbye*, Ma."

"I'll be sure to pick up some new clothes in your size, for when you come. That way you'll have something nice to wear when you meet Sylvia's son."

"Please don't."

"You know it's pointless to argue with me about this. If you don't like the clothes when you get here, I'll return them."

Mira sighed. "Fine. Thank you, I guess. I have to go."

"Be safe." Her mother always ended her calls with that. Mira had tried explaining that what she did wasn't that dangerous, but her mother was always watching crime dramas on TV and assumed it was all busting down doors and tracking serial killers.

"I will." Mira hung up.

Jack looked over at her. "I like the way you dress."

Mira elbowed him in the ribs. He caught her arm and pulled her closer. They lay there spooning for a few minutes, and Mira nearly drifted back to sleep. When Jack spoke again, his breath tickled her ear.

"I mean it, you know. I wouldn't change anything about you."

Mira rolled over to give him an incredulous look.

"Why is that so hard to believe?"

Mira snorted, and turned away from him again. She didn't want him to see her blush, but of course he noticed anyway; she could feel his smile against the back of her shoulder.

"So your mom is trying to set you up with some rich bachelor?"

"It doesn't matter, they're all the same."

"All?" he sounded surprised. "How many have there been?"

"I've lost count. Like I said, it doesn't matter. It'll just be a few minutes of awkward conversation at yet another stupid wedding."

"I love weddings. Good food, free booze, dancing. What's not to like?"

Mira laughed. "You're ridiculous."

"I'm not. You should bring me along, I'm a great wedding date. Besides, if I go with you to the wedding, I'll have a good excuse not to spend Memorial Day with my father."

Mira twisted around to look at him again, expecting to find

a smirk. He looked earnest enough, but Mira remained suspicious; surely he must be joking. She didn't know how to react to this seemingly genuine interest. Of course Jack read her mind.

"What can I do to convince you I'm serious?"

"Stop talking." She kissed him.

48: EDGAR PRIME

"Remember, if at any point you feel weird like they may have made you, fuck the footage, just *get out*. Okay?" Noela was as anxious as Edgar Prime had ever seen her. She hovered around Omar nervously in the center of her tiny living room. Edgar Prime sat on the worn couch with a laptop, testing the audio and video quality.

Omar rolled his eyes at his sister. "You worry too much."

Noela's mouth puckered as though she'd swallowed a lemon, and Edgar Prime hastily disguised his laugher as a coughing fit that fooled no one.

"This is serious, Omar. You don't wanna fuck around with these people. Who knows what they might do." Noela began pacing the room, three long strides in each direction before she hit a wall. Luken and a third roommate who Edgar Prime didn't know were both out; Edgar Prime thought Luken had deliberately made himself scarce to further emphasize his disapproval. He was busily planning a rally for the end of the month, and refused to be drawn into what he called their, "playing at espionage". Edgar Prime missed his lighthearted presence; Noela was more tense and serious without him.

"The plan is good," Edgar Prime pointed out. Noela threw him an exasperated look, and Omar nodded appreciatively. "Go into the other room Omar, and say something so we can test the mic."

Omar obediently went into Noela's bedroom and closed the door. Noela joined Edgar Prime on the couch and watched the screen. Omar was walking in slow circles. The camera — hidden inside one of Omar's shirt buttons — bounced with every step, but the picture was sharp.

"I'm gonna talk quietly to see how good this mic really is," whispered Omar. They heard every word clearly from the laptop speakers; through the door they only caught the rise and fall of his muffled voice.

"Got it!" called Edgar Prime. The door opened and Omar reappeared, a huge grin on his face.

"I can't believe we're really gonna fuckin' do this," he said, sounding pleased. He returned to the bedroom to admire the camera in the mirror — it was impressively hidden, the sort of thing nobody would notice unless they were looking for it. Noela turned to Edgar Prime.

"This is a good idea, isn't it?" she said, as though trying to convince herself.

"Yes," Edgar Prime said, even as his stomach gave a nervous lurch. "We don't have any better options," he pointed out.

"You're right," Noela said grudgingly. "I'm just being paranoid."

Edgar Prime thought back to his second meeting with Harlow. They met at the Bronx Zoo, where Harlow had long been a beneficiary. He liked to brag about which animals he personally owned; the rarer, the better.

"It's all set up," Harlow told him as they walked by a lone ostrich staring out at them from behind its glass partition.

"Thank you sir," Edgar Prime said sincerely.

The corner of Harlow's mouth twitched. "Damon, please. 'Sir' makes me feel like an old man."

"Of course, sorry," Edgar Prime said.

Harlow passed him an envelope. "Details are inside. Make sure to follow the instructions exactly. And remember, I won't be taking credit for this mess if it goes south."

"I understand, s—" Edgar Prime stopped himself just before saying "sir", again. Harlow gave him a half smile and shook his head knowingly. They reached an enclosure where a surly-looking trio of lions lounged; two females and a male. Harlow pointed at them.

"Look peaceful now, don't they? I was there when they were acquired. They're smarter than you'd expect — working together and all that. But not as smart as we are."

"How did you wind up on a lion hunt?"

Harlow scoffed at that. "By paying a lot of money, of course! There are few things more thrilling than watching humans demonstrate our dominance over other species, and I had a front row seat."

"Sounds dangerous," Edgar Prime said.

Harlow let out a great, "Ha!" to that. "Part of the adventure, Prime! Always a bit of danger in anything worthwhile, I've found."

Edgar Prime repeated this under his breath to reassure himself, as he studied Noela's doubt-ridden expression. They were doing the right thing. They had to be.

Omar set off a short time later, bound for a warehouse near the river. Edgar Prime and Noela settled on her couch with the laptop on the table in front of them, watching and listening to the bustle of Manhattan as Omar made his way to the subway. At first, Noela barely seemed to be breathing, but she relaxed during the hour it took Omar to reach his destination; the scenes of normalcy were soothing and made what they were doing almost feel like a game.

The warehouse was nondescript, made of dark concrete with heavy steel doors covered with chipped gray paint in what appeared to be an unsuccessful effort at matching the color of the walls. From the outside, the warehouse appeared deserted. After hesitantly wandering around the periphery, Omar went to the nearest door and knocked. The sound was deafening; Noela cringed as it echoed through the laptop speakers. For a long moment, it seemed as though nobody would answer, then the door creaked open to reveal a short man with black hair, pale skin and piercing bronze eyes.

"Horoscope sign?" he asked.

"Aries, but I should have been Gemini," Omar answered. Harlow had warned them that the passphrase must be exact, or else Omar would not be admitted. The man at the door didn't reply immediately, but just as the tension was becoming unbearable, he stepped aside.

"Welcome," he said. Omar followed him inside, and the door clanged shut behind them. The cavernous room was dimly lit, and Edgar Prime leaned forward squinting, trying to make out the dark shapes half hidden in shadow.

"So far, so good," Edgar Prime murmured to Noela. She gave a small nod, her eyes fixed on the screen, her hands clasped tightly in her lap, knuckles white.

"Follow me, please," said the bronze-eyed man. He had neither asked for Omar's name nor offered his own. Omar followed. There was an eerie silence in the warehouse, punctuated by occasional distant booms and clangs. The host led Omar across an expanse of open space into a dim, low-ceilinged hallway. When they reached the last door on the left, the man knocked once then opened the door for Omar without waiting for a reply.

Inside, a woman sat behind a scuffed wooden desk. There were several large file cabinets along the walls, but the desk was empty apart from an open laptop that she closed the instant they entered. She and the man who had greeted Omar looked alike enough to be siblings; her black hair was long where his was cropped, but they shared the same bronze eyes and fair skin. The woman stood up and extended a hand to Omar.

"Please sit down," she said after they shook hands. She gestured to an empty chair opposite hers and Omar sat. The man stepped outside, closing the door behind him.

For a moment the woman did not speak. Edgar Prime wondered whether her silent, appraising stare was as unsettling to Omar as it was to him.

"I adhere to a 'don't ask, don't tell' policy here," said the woman. "I don't want to know what sort of uses you might have in mind for our product. The following are instructions about making your deposit," she handed him a thin manila folder. "Once it's completed you'll receive an invitation to one of our auctions. Bids can be made in the form of cash or wire transfer."

Omar opened the folder to reveal a single sheet of paper.

"That's it?" Omar asked.

The woman smiled slightly. "That's it. Were you expecting a blood oath or a collateral requirement of your firstborn child?"

"I don't have any children," Omar said.

The woman smiled more widely. "We're businesspeople, nothing more. The truth is, we're only interested in your money."

Omar chuckled and lifted the folder. "Paper. Old school."

"You can't hack a piece of paper," the woman replied.

"Fair point," Omar said. He stood up and so did she. They shook hands again and he opened the door to leave.

"We look forward to working with you," the woman said.

Omar turned back to face her. "Likewise," he said. The man was waiting by the door to lead him out.

"That was quicker than I expected," Omar confided as they walked.

"You're not the first one to say that," the man answered. He led Omar all the way back outside, where dusk was just starting to fall.

"Thank you for your help," Omar said.

"Thank you for your business," the man replied. They shook hands, then the man pulled the door shut again with a clang, followed by the scraping sound of a lock sliding into place. Omar set off for the subway, clutching the manila folder. He walked quickly, and Edgar Prime could tell he was eager to get back so they could discuss what had happened. The street was nearly deserted.

It happened out of nowhere; suddenly he was falling until the camera hit the ground with a sickening crunch. Noela gasped and Omar grunted. When he rolled onto his side with a groan, they saw blood on the pavement. Then the camera showed two feet, one of which swung forward and connected with a thud and another cry of pain. Noela screamed as the foot pulled back and kicked Omar again and again, punctuated by yells. Too soon, the reactions stopped. The attacker crouched down as if he was going through an unconscious Omar's pockets. His breaths were short and sharp; they couldn't see his face, only his ripped jeans and dark sneakers. He ran off while Edgar Prime was still dialing 911, feeling zombielike as if he were watching somebody else explain to the operator what was happening.

The assailant left Omar lying still on the curb when he ran off. Noela tried calling him again and again in the hopes he'd wake up, but there was no answer. Tears slid down her cheeks as they heard the sirens approaching, and watched the EMTs put Omar in a stretcher and load him into an ambulance.

49: MIRA

John had set up a screen on one wall for them to watch the livestream. From the looks of it, Omar Kearney was on the subway, heading to the warehouse where the meeting was set to take place. The others looked as tense as Mira felt. She almost reached out to grasp Jack's hand under the table, but resisted the impulse. Warren might have a stroke if he found out about their after-hours activities; it had been several weeks but Mira still considered it far too early to call whatever was going on a relationship. She dragged her focus back to the problem at hand, and watched as Omar exited the subway and wandered down a run-down, mostly deserted street lined with warehouses.

Once Mira discovered what Harlow had planned for the CAN, Liesel had hacked Edgar Prime's computer with ease. While none of them thought he'd allow the CAN to come anywhere near the black market — the fact that he had sent them to a shady warehouse in Brooklyn struck them all as Harlow's idea of a joke — they had decided nonetheless to keep tabs on the video feed so they could continue cataloguing all of Harlow's associates just in case one of them produced another lead.

Harlow's network was proving more layered than an onion, and Mira suspected they'd have a ways to go before they even came close to the man himself. One wall of their office had a massive board with photographs pinned up of all of Harlow's known associates and how they related to the business. They knew they had only scratched the surface. Because the black market transactions occurred on the darknet, many of the individuals involved never needed to come in contact with Harlow at all, or even with anyone who reported to him directly.

Omar had reached a door with peeling gray paint, and knocked. When it was slid open, Mira received her first gut punch: Bob Smith with his easy smile and melodious voice. After their date, he had never contacted her again. She had wondered whether he'd been told not to get involved with one of Harlow's assistants, or if it was just that he'd lost interest. While he and Omar exchanged the passphrase, John voiced what all of them were wondering.

"Does Harlow know we've been monitoring Smith? Is this just him fucking with us?"

"Could he possibly be that arrogant?" Liesel asked.

"Yes," Mira said, without hesitation.

"We should pick him up," Jack said. "Before he disappears."

Warren scowled. "It'll blow our whole operation," he said dismissively.

"Not necessarily," countered Jack. "If Harlow thinks he vanished of his own accord —"

"And why would Harlow think that?" Warren snapped. "Don't think he doesn't have spies of his own keeping tabs on his operation. He isn't just winging it. There's no way we'd be able to get Smith without showing our hand."

On screen, Omar was speaking to a woman with the same black hair and bronze eyes as Bob Smith. The resemblance was uncanny.

"She's new," commented John. He proceeded to search every facial recognition database they had access to; the only name that popped up was an expired New Mexico driver's license with the name "Jane Smith".

"Siblings?" Mira asked.

"I'd make that bet," Jack said.

"Difficult to say," Warren said. "Liesel, see what else you can come up with about the alleged Smith siblings."

"It's probably another alias," Liesel said. "Bob and Jane

Smith are about the most generic names anyone could ever come up with. There'll be so many false hits on any search for either of them. But I'll do my best."

Omar left the warehouse, and was walking off down the block as the sky began to darken into dusk.

"Do you think there's anything in that manila folder she gave him?" John asked.

"Doubt it," Jack said. For once Warren agreed wit him.

"This entire endeavor has been nothing more than an elaborate piece of theater meant to —"

Out of nowhere, the camera shook violently as Omar was thrown to the ground. Mira gasped as a boot-clad foot came into view, and connected with Omar's ribs; the meaning of Harlow's promise that he had something special planned for the CAN had become abundantly clear. Jack called the police, while the rest of them watched the assault helplessly, each kick punctuated by a sickening crunch. The heard sirens approaching, and the assailant stopped kicking the now-still Omar, and ran off. The ambulance arrived a moment later and Omar was rushed to the hospital; he was badly injured but still alive. The video feed went dead, but Jack had instructed the on-duty officer to keep them informed of Omar's status.

They all sat in stunned silence. After a moment, Liesel replayed the last portion of the video, more slowly. Mira gasped again, so loudly the others whipped around to look at her in alarm.

"That shoe," she said. "It... I think it... This morning, the man, I delivered his money and — and —" She was shaking and incoherent. Liesel paused the video feed on a decent view of the boot; brown and scuffed, just like the man from the Met.

"A lot of people have boots like that," John pointed out.

"That's true," Liesel agreed.

"They do," Jack said.

She knew they were trying to reassure her, but it was useless. The guilt felt like a grenade that had detonated in her stomach. She could have prevented this, should have prevented this. If Omar died, it was her fault.

"That'd be one hell of a coincidence though," Warren muttered.

"It's him," Mira said.

"Let's not get ahead of ourselves," Warren said. We'll need traffic camera footage from that area. Liesel, John, see if we can't get a good shot of the attacker's face. Then Mira can see if he's the man she met with this morning."

"On it," Liesel said. She and John both began typing furiously, but it took a surprisingly short time before they had images up on the screen. None were very good, the man wore a hat and kept his head down. Mira took a long look before speaking.

"It's him," she said again, in a quiet voice. She felt hollow now, wrung out and exhausted. "How could we not have seen this coming?" she said.

"We should have." Warren's voice was gruff. "But even if we did, we couldn't have intervened. You don't get a whale like Harlow without any collateral damage. Don't forget about the lives of all the clones that are on the line if we fail."

Mira wanted to argue, but she knew Warren had a point. Harlow would pay for this, she'd make sure of it.

50: ANNABEL

After the initial blow-up about the cell phone records, Annabel and Rex had come to a sort of detente. Neither one mentioned the argument, and both went out of their way to pretend that things were normal. They ate together, slept together and talked in a superficial way. But underneath, there was an uneasiness that belied the truth of their situation: their days were numbered. The end was approaching, it was only a question of when.

There were times when Annabel almost pitied Rex. More often, she felt a detached, faint distaste towards him. How stupid he was to think a clone would be the solution to his grief. Stupid, and stupidly optimistic. But then, if he hadn't been so stupid, she wouldn't exist. Whenever this occurred to her, Annabel's guilt returned and she tried and failed to persuade herself that maybe she still owed Rex. Maybe she should stay after all. Ms. Durant's voice floated through her head telling her that this was her place, her purpose. As Ms. Durant used to remind her, other clones had it much worse than she did. Who was she to complain, or to think she deserved any more than the security she currently enjoyed? After all, there was no guarantee things would get better if she left. In fact, odds were they'd get a whole lot worse.

And yet, she couldn't keep the idea out of her head. She thought about it endlessly, and was on the point of deciding to simply leave, to pretend she was going into town one day and to get on a bus and go wherever it took her, when her plans were temporarily derailed by the publication of Arthur Blair's article. While she had already confessed to Rex that she'd participated in the article against his wishes, he still wasn't prepared for the reality of seeing his name in print. Worse, while Arthur Blair didn't misquote Annabel, he interspersed his own commentary between her answers and his cutting portrayal of the perverted old man who bought himself a wife was nothing short of incendiary.

Even though nobody had bothered to inform her when the article was due out, Annabel knew immediately when she arrived downstairs for breakfast. Rex was clutching his tablet so hard his knuckles were white, and severe frown lines creased his forehead. His expression when he looked up at her was alarming, and Annabel had to fight the impulse to take a step back.

"Your interview," said Rex through gritted teeth.

"Oh." Annabel could think of nothing else to say.

"Sit down, Annabel." There was an edge to his voice that Annabel had never heard before. She obeyed. There was a loud scraping sound when she pulled out her chair, dragging its legs across the highly polished oak floor. Annabel sat perched on the edge of the wooden chair, tense and on her guard. Rex shoved the tablet towards her, and she leaned over to read.

"Aloud," Rex commanded.

Annabel began quietly, and proceeded as fast as she could to get the ordeal over with as soon as possible.

"By far the strangest case of the three is that of Annabel King. She was commissioned by Rex King, husband to the original who died of cancer at the age of thirty. In response to my query about her upbringing — imagine the depravity of one capable of raising a baby as his own daughter only to marry her eighteen years later — Annabel downplayed the strangeness of her situation. 'I was raised by a caretaker, Helena Durant. I didn't meet Rex until our wedding day — he had no role at all in my upbringing.' She explains this casually, as if meeting one's husband on the alter is par for the course. Helena Durant, a former classmate of Rex King's, was responsible for both nurturing and homeschooling Annabel during her

273

first eighteen years. No doubt, this arrangement was put into place to instill in young Annabel a belief system that would cause her to accept her husband without question, and to wed him on the morning of her eighteenth birthday as ordered."

"Stop." Rex snarled. It took Annabel a second to collect herself and take a deep breath before she could look him in the eye. "Now do you see why I told you to stay away from reporters?" Rex said, in a a voice that was full of rage. He leaned towards her, regarding her with cold eyes. His breath smelled like raw onions. Partly to get further away from him, Annabel sat all the way back in her chair.

"I — he — I didn't realize he was going to write about it like that," Annabel said. *Not exactly, anyway.* "Otherwise I would never have agreed to meet with him. He lied to me."

"Did he?" Rex said. His scrutiny became unbearable, and she glanced back down to the tablet. "Want to read the rest? You're welcome to."

"No," Annabel said. "That was enough."

"My lawyer advises that doing nothing would be my best option. Any response might be seen as defensiveness, or validation of the truth of this malicious garbage. I'm not so sure."

"What else could you do?" Annabel asked.

"Sue, of course," Rex said with the air of one speaking to an imbecile. "Or you could publicly disavow the article and denounce this Arthur Blair for twisting your words."

"But the lawyer said to do nothing?" Annabel asked.

"He did," Rex snapped. "But surely that course of action would be unbearable to you. My darling Annabel would never want her devoted husband to suffer for her foolish mistake."

Your beloved Annabel died nineteen years ago. "No, you're right. I'll do whatever you want me to do." *Liar.*

"Liar," Rex hissed. Sensing the impending explosion, Annabel braced herself, and sure enough Rex flung the tablet against the wall with a loud crash, creating a spiderweb of cracks across the screen from the impact. Unsure whether his anger was directed at her or Arthur Blair, Annabel froze, waiting.

"Get out of my sight," he whispered, and Annabel did not need to be told twice. She bolted from the room and up the stairs, into the once-empty room she'd used for yoga and meditation that was now home to several of Rex's still-unpacked boxes. Annabel closed the door behind her, and shoved two of the heaviest boxes in front of it; there was no lock. Her throat was dry and her heart hammered in her chest. She pushed the upper box so forcefully that it fell to the ground with a crash. Fear and adrenaline jolted through Annabel and she stood listening for footsteps, sure Rex would come up to investigate. After a few moments of silence, however, the tension dissipated somewhat. Annabel picked up the box, heaving it back into place, before she opened it to check that its contents hadn't been broken.

The interior of the box was in disarray, a cluster of random items jostled by the fall to the floor. Tennis equipment, about ten signed baseballs each encased in plastic, a couple of small black and white abstract paintings, wrapped in protective cloth that had come partly undone. Amid the mess, Annabel spied a small, metal case. Without thinking, Annabel picked it up and sat down on the floor with it across her lap, once again surprised at how heavy it was. She clicked open the two clasps and lifted the lid. Inside, she found Rex's pistol and a box of bullets. With less hesitation this time, she picked up the gun, feeling the weight of it in her hands. She extended her arms with the gun pointed straight out in front of her, placed her finger on the trigger, and pretended to fire it with a whispered, *bang.*

51: JAVI

"Javi, get down here!" his father called from the bottom of the stairs. It was Sunday morning, and Javi was groggy and not at all in the mood to get out of bed. He ignored his father's continued attempts to wake him for another couple of minutes, then threw back the covers with a groan.

"Coming!" he croaked, pulling on a pair of sweatpants and a t-shirt. "Fuck," he muttered to himself as he yanked open the door and descended the stairs. He found his parents both puttering around the kitchen, his mother making coffee, his father beating eggs.

"What?" he asked, looking from one to the other. "I was sleeping."

"Sit down," his father said, and Javi felt a rush of foreboding. He sat.

His mother turned and looked at him for the first time in what felt like ages. "We read your article," she murmured. Javi's heart sank, and he felt like the biggest failure who'd ever walked the earth. He'd been intending to warn them before it was out, but kept putting it off because he worried it would lead to another fight. And now they had found out anyway.

"Oh." Javi swallowed, throat dry.

"Don't look so nervous," his father said. "We talked about it and we aren't angry. Just disappointed. We wish you'd told us before you did the interview."

Javi looked at his mother, and she gave him a sad smile. "I should have," Javi said. "I'm — I'm sorry."

"No, we're sorry," his father said heavily. "We should have realized — our expectations weren't fair to you. We didn't think — we were just so happy to have you back. I mean, to have you."

Javi found he couldn't look at either of them, instead staring down at a scratch in the wooden table that he'd accidentally made at age seven when his mother had allowed him to help her bake gingerbread cookies. After a while slamming the stainless steel molds down onto the table had become more entertaining than actually pressing them into the rolled dough, and he'd continued his happy rukus until his mother noticed the scratch and sent him to his room.

"About your birthday," his mother started. Javi glanced up and saw that her eyes were full of tears. "What you said to the reporter about not knowing when — about how we always celebrate it on *his* birthday." She took a deep breath. "You were born on April 19," she said.

"Oh," Javi whispered. He couldn't think of anything else to say. Javi wasn't sure exactly how it happened but the next moment found all three of them hugging and crying. When Javi went back upstairs to shower and dress for the day his eyes were red, but the guilt that shackled him and weighed him down had lessened just the tiniest bit.

This feeling of lightness was short lived. His grandmother stopped by later, glaring at him as she always did. She hugged his mother and father, and hissed at him as though she was warding off a demon. Javi supposed that was exactly how she saw him.

"I'm going out," he mumbled. He got up and strode towards the front door, unsure of where he'd go, but knowing he needed to leave.

"Be home in time for dinner," his mother said.

"Okay," Javi said. *Have fun putting flowers on your son's grave*, he almost said, but was grateful he had the wherewithal to hold his tongue. It was too soon to blow up the shaky truce he'd struck with his parents, but it rankled to know that the only reason his grandmother ever deigned to enter his presence was to rub in the fact that he was only the replacement, and a defective one at that.

Outside, he strode towards the park and texted Imogen. As it was a Sunday he knew it was unlikely she'd respond, but he needed a distraction and she was his best option. A few seconds later, his phone buzzed. Her text read, *'Theo and the girls are at the natural history museum, will be gone for two hours at least.'* Javi immediately changed direction and in less than half an hour he was inside her, his mind wiped blissfully clean of all that had been troubling him.

They fucked three times that day, the third of which was perilously close to the time that Theo and the girls were due to return. For some reason this seemed to make it more exciting for both of them, and Imogen was moaning loudly as she rode him hard. Neither of them heard the front door open, nor the quiet steps approaching the bedroom. Even when Theo opened the bedroom door it took a second for either of them to react. Imogen shrieked and jumped up, and Javi rolled off the far side of the bed and yanked up his pants.

When he stood up Imogen was wrapped in a bathrobe babbling to Theo, who looked as though he was carved out of stone. His hand was still on the doorknob, and he was staring at the place on the bed where they'd been a moment ago. Imogen reached out a hand to touch Theo's arm and he flinched away from her, backing out of the room and retreating down the hallway.

"Where are the girls?" Javi heart Imogen cry.

"In the car. I told them they'll each get a special treat if they sit quietly and let Daddy have a ten minute conversation with Mommy," Theo answered, every syllable infused with distain and suppressed fury.

Javi gathered up the remainder of his clothes then trailed behind them, thinking he'd have to escape out the back door. He made it down the hallway and nearly into the kitchen before Theo roared, "And just where the fuck do you think you're going?"

Javi froze, and turned just in time to see Theo's fist coming towards him; the next thing he knew there was blood in his mouth and he was splayed out on the floor. His head was throbbing, and his vision hazy as he looked up at Theo who was shaking his hand out as though he'd broken a knuckle.

"Fuck," Theo muttered to himself. "That hurt more than I thought it would."

Javi had to fight the urge to break into hysterical laughter. Imogen started screaming and shoved Theo against the doorframe. That seemed to jar him out of his trance, and he glowered down at Javi. "Get the fuck out of my house," he said, his voice low and cold.

Javi didn't need to be told twice. He scrambled to his feet and took off through the back door, running flat out once he got to the sidewalk and not stopping until he'd put over a mile between him and Imogen Shaw.

52: EDGAR PRIME

Omar was alive, but barely. The doctors had rushed him into surgery as soon as he'd arrived at the hospital, and Edgar Prime and Noela had spent hours in the waiting room without news. At some point Luken showed up and held Noela's hand in silence. When they were finally visited by a young resident, she told them that Omar was unconscious, and they'd get a better idea of the extent of the damage once he woke. That was over a week ago, and now they were saying that it was uncertain whether he'd ever wake again. Noela's whole family had flown in and were sitting vigil by his bedside day and night. Noela hadn't left the hospital at all, and Edgar Prime knew she blamed herself even though the police told them it was a only random mugging in a bad neighborhood.

Edgar Prime couldn't even bring himself to care that the manila folder Omar had been carrying when he'd been attacked was nowhere to be found by the time the police and the EMTs arrived on the scene.

Edgar Prime had never been more adrift. Suddenly, all their clever schemes to change the world seemed pathetically amateur, and it was hard to remember why they'd thought them so important to begin with. Once Noela's family arrived, he'd felt like an interloper in that hospital room, and had reluctantly returned to his dorm. He attended his classes as before, not hearing a word of lecture. When Patrice texted to invite him to dinner with Dr. Midas and Dr. Yang, he made his excuses, wondering dully how it was that Dr. Midas had managed to get so many chances with Dr. Yang, when Hugo refused to offer Edgar Prime even one.

The evening before Luken's protest, Edgar Prime lay stretched out on his bed staring at the ceiling, trying to decide whether or not it was worth mustering the energy to get up and turn on his lights. It was just starting to get dark when his phone started buzzing. Patrice's name lit up the screen and for a second he contemplated ignoring the call, but knew she'd just keep calling if he didn't answer. With a sigh, he pressed a finger to the green button on the screen, hit speaker and threw the phone down on the bed.

"Patrice?"

"Prime, what are you up to?" Dr. Midas's voice filled the room, jovial and arrogant.

"I thought ... are you on Patrice's phone?" Edgar Prime said, wishing he'd let the call go to voicemail.

"That's not important, Prime. We're coming to get you in an hour. Dinner, with me and Caden. I insist."

"I'm studying. Finals are soon." *Liar,* he thought.

"You have to eat sometime," Dr. Midas insisted.

Edgar Prime heaved another great sigh, knowing it was pointless to argue. "Fine," he said.

"Excellent!" Dr. Midas said, ignoring Edgar Prime's obvious reluctance. "See you soon, then."

The call ended, and Edgar Prime rolled off the bed with a groan and flicked on the light switch.

An hour later he stood on the curb outside his building when the driverless town car rolled up. He walked around to the front seat, and slammed the door closed behind him harder than necessary.

"Good to see you, Prime," said Dr. Yang from the back seat. Beside him was Dr. Midas, and Edgar Prime twisted around to nod in greeting at both of them. The car pulled smoothly away from the curb, and Edgar Prime turned back around and slumped in his seat.

"Seatbelt, Prime," Dr. Midas reminded him.

Wordlessly, Edgar Prime snapped his seatbelt into place. Ten minutes later, they arrived at the restaurant; a pricey sushi bar that Dr. Midas liked to frequent. A smiling hostess led them to a table in the back, and left them to peruse the menus while the waiter brought a pot of tea.

For most of the meal, Edgar Prime was happy to listen to Dr. Midas and Dr. Yang debate the future of genetics or trade gossip about their colleagues. Edgar Prime interjected only sporadically, usually when asked a direct question. They all started with miso soup, then shared several plates of sushi including sea urchin rolls, spicy tuna rolls, avocado sweet potato rolls, and Edgar Prime's favorite, spider rolls. They were all partway through eating their green tea mochi ice cream when Dr. Yang leaned forward in his chair.

"Patrice told us about your friend in the hospital," he said quietly. "Has there been any improvement?"

Edgar Prime felt his throat close, and it was difficult even to breathe. He looked down at the table and shook his head.

"I'm sorry to hear that, Prime," said Dr. Yang. He half-glanced at Dr. Midas and tilted his head slightly, as though they'd rehearsed this conversation and Dr. Midas had forgotten his lines.

"Yes, we were both very sorry to hear of it," Dr. Midas said, in a voice that did not sound very sorry at all. "Always a tragedy when a young person dies before his time. Did you know him well?"

"No," Edgar Prime croaked. "His sister is a friend. And he isn't dead."

"Ah." Dr. Midas gave him a pitying look. "Well, you barely knew him. I suppose that's some consolation."

Edgar Prime goggled at him, not fully comprehending his meaning. "How so?" he managed. His voice was rough.

Dr. Midas shrugged, ignoring Dr. Yang's disapproving scowl. "Be sure to give the family my card. They may be interested in —"

He was interrupted by the loud scraping of Edgar Prime's chair followed by a crash; he stood up so quickly it toppled over behind him, making Dr. Yang flinch and the restaurant's other occupants cast scandalized glares in his direction. Edgar Prime didn't care. He placed his hands on the table and leaned in close to Dr. Midas's face, wondering how it was possible for him to so despise the man whose DNA he shared.

"How *dare* you even suggest that?" he hissed. "Omar isn't even dead yet and you're already —" with effort, he cut himself short, aware of how close he was to losing control entirely and screaming. Dr. Midas looked up at him, bemused and disappointed. There was disappointment on Dr. Yang's face too, but it was directed at Dr. Midas.

"Fuck you," Edgar Prime said, in the most deadly calm voice he could manage. "Fuck both of you." He stormed out of the restaurant before either of them could stop him.

Once outside, he started to run, irrationally wanting to put as much distance between himself and Dr. Midas as possible. By the time he reached campus, he was winded, but he did not stop until he stepped into the elevator of his building. He punched the roof button and leaned against the wall as the elevator ascended, breathing heavily. As soon as the doors opened he tumbled out, striding all the way to the edge. Alone, he leaned on the railing, watching the moon rise in the starless sky until hot tears spilled down his cheeks and his shoulders began shaking.

He heard the door open behind him and glanced around without bothering to hide his face. His heart stopped and stuttered when he saw Hugo standing fifteen feet away staring at him. Expecting that Hugo would leave without speaking, Edgar Prime turned back around and resumed gazing out across the city. He didn't move, even when he heard the footsteps. When the arms encircled him, the gentle pressure made him first tense, then relax. Edgar Prime returned the embrace, squeezing Hugo like a lifeline. They stood there together not speaking for what felt like forever, and yet at the same time it was not long enough.

53: MIRA

It had been hard for Mira not to pummel Harlow with her bare hands when she came into work the morning following Omar's attack. He was entirely too chipper for a man who'd recently put a kid into a coma, and Mira longed to beat the smug smile off his face. She hated him for what he'd done, and she hated him even more for making her a part of it. Inside her head, the assailant's muttered threat repeated over and over in a mocking litany: *You tell Harlow he'd better make good on the other half...make good on the other half...other half...other half...other half...* She couldn't stop wondering whether they'd seen the worst, or if they were still waiting for the other shoe to drop.

By lunchtime, Mira felt strung out and on edge, and she was not at all happy to see Solomon O'Brien making his way to Harlow's office looking much happier than he had on his last visit. *His smile makes him look like Emperor Palpatine*, she reflected sourly. Mira tried to listen in on their conversation but there was something going on with the microphones; the only thing she heard was silence. Mira had a pounding headache by the end of the day, and wanted nothing more than to go back home and curl up in bed. Instead, she made her way to the Chinatown base of operations, to find an atmosphere of muted excitement.

They finally had some good news. The information Jack stole from Deirdre Kirke's hard drive had paid off; Liesel had done the impossible and managed to gain access to one of the clone auctions. The scope was even more limited than they'd originally thought; as an additional security measure it seemed that they ran separate auctions for each individual clone. Even if law enforcement somehow stumbled onto one auction, they'd be unable to get any sense of the scale of the operation. Still, it was a solid lead. The only lead they had.

The auction Liesel accessed was for a single clone living in a shelter upstate, a four year old. The winner was scheduled to pick up his prize in three days time.

An argument broke out around the table: should they hold back and continue observing in the hopes that they'd be able to move further up the hierarchy, or order a raid, arrest the people directly involved in the transaction and close down the single facility they could prove was involved in clone trafficking?

"It's not enough," John said. "Harlow's people will change up their system and we'll be back to square one with trying to keep ahead of it. We'll have accomplished nothing."

"We'll have rescued the little boy who just got sold," Mira said sharply. "And all the other clones living in this shelter, waiting to be sold. That's not nothing."

"Mira's right," Jack said, and she gave him a fleeting, grateful smile. "We can't just sit on this information. We're not giving up on Harlow. Sooner or later he'll make a mistake, then we'll nail the bastard."

"But it'll take that much longer —" insisted John.

"— we can't know —" Liesel started.

"— these are actual children we can help *today*, not years from now —" Mira cut in.

"— but how many are we condemning because we couldn't follow through —" John said angrily.

"Quiet, all of you!" Warren barked, and they fell silent.

Warren glared at them for a moment before speaking. "We're doing the raid," he told them. Mira allowed herself to feel a moment of triumph, even as John scowled in disapproval. The rest of the meeting was planning and logistics.

Mira was at work while the raid took place; they wanted to attempt to maintain her cover if at all possible. It took all of her willpower not to check her phone every ten seconds, and she couldn't stop herself from drumming her fingers incessantly on the desk. At one point she noticed Harlow hurry out of the office with a grim look on her face. Mira took this to be a sign of good news, but she was still on edge, and knew she would be until she heard. Her phone buzzed, and she snatched it up immediately to find a text from Jack. It was only one word: *Victory.*

54: BOB

Bob walked up a familiar path through a familiar garden towards a familiar brick building. Each step increased his sense of dread. He didn't want to be back here again. He didn't want to pick up another little girl to bring to another depraved man who had paid for her on a secret darknet auction.

I could just turn around and leave, Bob thought. *I could leave and get on a plane, and they'll never find me.* Even in his head, the words rang hollow. Deep down, he knew he'd never escape. He reached the front entrance and knocked. Angelica was there, smiling coquettishly and batting her eyes at him. Bob was in no mood to indulge her, and gave her a curt nod of recognition, nothing more.

"Well?" he said.

"I may need your help with this one," Angelica told him. She beckoned him towards the stairs with a sullen look on her face, clearly disappointed that he'd rebuffed her attempts at flirtation.

He followed her, annoyed at the delay. Usually, Angelica had the children ready for him when he arrived. As they reached the top of the stairs, Bob opened his mouth to ask Angelica what was different about this one when — BANG! The door downstairs slammed open and two armed FBI agents burst in guns drawn. Bob heard the back door break open too. Angelica screamed, and flapped her hands hysterically, but Bob didn't waste any time. He ran into the nearest room where several scared-looking children were sitting on the floor playing Monopoly. He slid open the window and swung one leg over the sill. So far as he could tell, they hadn't left anyone outside watching the perimeter, presumably because they thought they had both exits covered. Using the tiny fingerholds between the bricks, Bob was able to descend partway before having to jump. He landed hard and rolled to dissipate the impact. He sprang up and started running, hoping to circle around behind a neighbor's hedge to come out down the road and make his way towards the tiny downtown area nearby.

Bob barely made it fifteen yards before his body seized up and he fell to the ground, twitching in agony. *A taser*, he thought dimly through grunts of pain, *of course they have a taser. Fuck.*

The clicking noise from the taser stopped, but shudders of pain still rattled through his body. The world was blurry, and Bob had never felt so weak. He tried to roll over, but his muscles refused to obey. There were boots walking towards him, but Bob couldn't lift his head to find out who they belonged to. Hands reached down and roughly handcuffed him, then yanked him to his feet. Bob felt clumsy and leaned heavily on his captor. When they made eye contact, Bob started laughing, an out-of-control, wheezy laugh. It was the scowling man who had served as Mira's backup at the bar.

"Shut the fuck up," the man growled, but now that Bob had started to laugh, he couldn't stop. He wondered if this was how his father and mother had felt at their first arrests. Like it was all a big joke. To him, nothing had ever seemed so funny.

55: ANNABEL

"I should never have taken part," said Ms. Durant for the fiftieth time. "Rex will never forgive me." Annabel sighed, and took another bite of her buckwheat banana muffin. They were sitting at their usual table at Seashell Cafe, sharing a pot of jasmine tea.

"It's not you he's angry at," Annabel reassured her, although she wasn't at all sure that was true. Rex had been giving her the silent treatment all week, and had taken to sleeping in the guest room. In truth, she doubted he'd be any more forgiving of Ms. Durant, who didn't even have the benefit of reminding him of the one he'd loved for so long.

"Still. It was terrible what that despicable reporter wrote, just *terrible*. I'm surprised Rex hasn't responded to the provocation. Or sued him." Ms. Durant poured herself more tea from the steaming pot. Overhead, two seagulls were circling, no doubt hoping to snatch up the half-croissant a young child across the courtyard had flung onto the ground in a fit of temper.

"He thought about it, believe me." Annabel muttered.

"I should hope so!" Ms. Durant said, slapping her hand on the table emphatically. Annabel sipped her tea, wondering whether she should tell Ms. Durant that she was thinking of leaving, that the temptation to do so grew stronger every day.

"He may never forgive me," Annabel said.

Ms. Durant's face softened into an expression of sympathy. "Oh, of course he will. There are ups and downs in every relationship, you'll see. Soon enough things will go back to how they always were."

What if I don't want them to go back to how they always were? Annabel almost said, but she stopped herself, knowing there was no point. She felt a dull sense of bereavement that Ms. Durant, who was the only family Annabel had ever known, had more loyalty to her employer than to her former charge. The fact that Ms. Durant regretted accompanying Annabel to New York was obvious, the reason less so. Annabel supposed she had known Rex longer, if less intimately. Whatever her reason, Ms. Durant was unable to offer anything but further aspersions on Arthur Blair, and as soon as they finished the tea Annabel took her leave.

After she said goodbye to Ms. Durant she strolled along Main Street with no clear destination, walking just to walk. All of a sudden a man stepped out of a storefront directly into her path. She had to swerve to avoid running headlong into him, and he her; he made a startled noise and nearly dropped the paper bag he cradled in his arms. It clinked slightly and Annabel realized it must contain several bottles since he had just come out of a liquor store. She glanced up at the man's face to apologize and felt her stomach drop out; before her stood Leon Floros, the handsome gardener who had become her favorite fantasy whenever her husband crawled on top of her. Annabel flushed at the thought.

"I'm so sorry," he was saying. She blinked, and wrenched her mind back to the present, not wanting to seem like any more of a dolt than she did already. "I wasn't paying attention to where I was going. Are you all right?"

"Me? Oh, I'm fine, just fine. Are you? Sorry, it was my fault. At least you didn't drop those bottles." Annabel hated how frantic her voice sounded, and she let out a nervous laugh that caused her to cringe internally. She had only ever seen him in his work clothes before, covered in sweat and dirt, but he looked like a different person now: freshly showered, wearing faded jeans and a wrinkled light blue button-down shirt that brought out the color of his eyes.

"Yeah, lucky." He lifted the bag slightly as if to demonstrate its intactness.

"So you live around here too, then?" Annabel blurted out. "I wasn't sure."

"Yeah, I do," he said with an easy smile. She saw his eyes flicker down her body and back up to her face, and her heart beat faster. "I'm just over on Caster Street, at the corner of Elm. Not far at all."

"Not at all," Annabel echoed. They stood in awkward silence for another second just gazing at each other, then he said, "Well. I've gotta get going. See you around."

Annabel nodded as he turned to continue on his way. He glanced back at her with a smile and a wink, then strode off down the street. Part of her wanted to pretend she had some reason to go the same way he was going, but she dismissed the impulse. She had already made a fool of herself once that day.

As Annabel slowly made her way back home, she thought about what he'd said: 'over on Caster Street, at the corner of Elm'. That's where he lived. Annabel had walked by that corner many times, but had never seen him. *That's because he works during the day, stupid.* Now, she had to fight the temptation to wander past, knowing she'd look ridiculous if he caught her. Then again, he had told her where he lived in much more detail than strictly necessary. He could have just said he lived nearby and moved on, no need to volunteer the extra information. Could it be that he was hinting at something?

Instead of going home, Annabel spent the rest of the day in the park, moving to the public library when dusk began to fall. She knew Rex would wonder where she was, but found herself indifferent to the thought. Hiding in an alcove, she whiled away the hours rereading the beginning of *Harry Potter and the Half Blood Prince*, her favorite book of the series.

Annabel did not leave until the library closed its doors at 8pm. The streets were relatively quiet at this hour during the off-season, with only a few people out strolling after dinner. Reluctantly, she began the walk home, hoping that Rex would already be shuttered away in his office or even better, asleep in bed, when she arrived. When she reached the corner of Main Street and Elm, Annabel stopped. For a moment, she stared up at the street sign, and heard Leon Floros's voice echo through her head, telling her that he lived at the corner of Elm and Caster. A wild recklessness seized Annabel, and she turned onto Elm, striding along purposefully and trying to ignore the hammering of her heartbeat in her chest. He had told her where he lived. That *had* to mean something.

She felt rather foolish when she reached the correct intersection, not having accounted for the fact that there were actually four possible corner houses. Two of them were dark, their inhabitants either out or sleeping. The house she stood directly in front of had a sign on the mailbox that read "Miller", so she continued diagonally across the deserted intersection to the final house. She was in luck; the lights were on and the curtains remained open, giving her a clear view of the living room.

There he was; lounging in an armchair wearing striped blue pajama bottoms and nothing else. He held a tablet in one hand and a beer in the other, and whatever he was reading seemed to have his undivided attention. Annabel merely watched him for a moment, gathering her courage for what was she was sure would be a defining moment in her life. Just as she steeled herself and was about to make her way up the walk to the front door, she saw Leon turn his head and she watched dumbfounded as he was joined by a pretty, pajama-clad woman with dark skin and curly black hair. The real shock came when she approached him and Annabel saw the baby; Leon grinned up at them with such a look of devotion that Annabel felt numb all over, numb and *stupid*. The woman leaned over, and he kissed her on the lips, then kissed the giggling baby on the cheek. The woman vanished again, and after a moment Leon drained his beer, stood up and stretched, then followed her to the back of the house. The light in the living room went off, leaving Annabel alone outside in the dark.

Thirty minutes later she stumbled back home in a daze. Never before had she felt like such an utter fool. *Of course he has a wife and baby, you nitwit. He never wanted you. You're nothing but a stupid little girl.* She closed the front door as quietly as she could, but it made no difference; Rex was awake and waiting for her.

"Where have you been, my love?" he said softly from the living room chair in which he was seated. The lights were dim, and she was struck by the irony of him sitting in much the same position as Leon had been. *So similar, and yet so different.*

"The park, the library. Earlier I had tea with Ms. Durant," Annabel said wearily. Answering his questions was easier than arguing. "I don't know why you care, anyway."

Rex's expression turned incredulous. "Why, of course I care. How could you ever question my devotion?"

"Devotion isn't the word I'd use for it." Annabel didn't know what had gotten into her, but at that moment she wanted nothing more than to smash everything in the house then run away, far away to a place where he'd never find her.

His mouth twisted, and the look on his face could be interpreted as rage or pain or both. "How can you be so hateful? My Annabel was many things, but she was never hateful."

"I'm not your Annabel. Your Annabel is dead."

"My love —" he began.

"Stop calling me that!" She took a deep breath and willed herself not to scream. A strange clarity had emerged from the haze her mind had been, and she did not want him to think what she had to say next was said in anger. Instead, she had to turn herself to ice. "I will never love you, Rex. It's time you moved on with your life, and I with mine. Tomorrow morning, I'm going to leave, and never come back. This is over."

For a moment he only stared at her, staggered. When he stood up his face was eerily still, masklike. It was only when he advanced on her that she felt a stab of fear, and by then it was too late. The backhand knocked her off her feet and made her ears ring; pain radiated out from where he'd struck her cheek and when she tried to press herself up she felt a wave of dizziness. Rex grabbed a fistful of her hair and yanked her back to her feet.

"You're going to leave, are you?" He bellowed, not letting go of her hair even as she tried to cringe away from him. "Do you have any idea — *any idea* — how much I paid for you?" He flung her onto the couch facedown, and the next second she felt one hand pressing hard into her back while the other pushed her dress up roughly to her waist and ripped off her underwear. The act itself was not much different than what she'd endured a hundred times before but the intent behind it — the rage and the possession — seeped deeper into her with each thrust and poisoned her from within. It wasn't long before Rex finished with a final grunt and moan. He collapsed back onto the couch beside where Annabel lay facing away from him, not bothering to cover herself.

"You're mine," he whispered hoarsely. "Forever. Don't forget that again." With that he heaved himself up from the couch and she listened to the stairs creaking as he went up to bed. Annabel lay where she was for a long while before she was able to force herself to get up. She went into the upstairs bathroom and turned the shower up as hot as she could stand, scrubbing and scrubbing, unsuccessfully trying to remove the feel of him, the smell of him from her body. When she finally stumbled into bed it was almost 3:00 a.m. and she fell asleep to the hateful sound of his snores, amid fantasies of burning his house to the ground.

When Annabel awoke the next morning, Rex was already gone. All at once, the emotions of the previous night came rushing back to her; the embarrassment over Leon eclipsed by the rage and shame Rex had left her with. She went downstairs to find him waiting for her looking contrite. The breakfast table was laden with all of her favorite foods: lemon poppy-seed chestnut pancakes, scrambled eggs with kale, cherry tomatoes and pesto, homemade chai tea. Rex drew out the chair beside him with a pointed look and Annabel took the hint and sat down. He placed some of everything on her plate, but she only picked at her food, not speaking except when asked a direct question.

Every moment in his presence was physically painful — Annabel felt like she was choking on her repressed rage, like it was ripping her apart from within. Outside she was detached and unreadable, inside she screamed and screamed and screamed. After what was an agonizingly long meal, Rex kissed the top of her head and went back to his office, leaving Annabel alone. She felt acutely aware of his presence in the house, and no matter how many deep breaths she took, she could not release any of the tension that clenched her body.

Annabel wandered through the house with no purpose other than to shake off some of her pent up energy, and soon enough she found herself in the room that contained Rex's remaining unpacked boxes. As though in a trance, Annabel walked over to the one nearest the door and opened it. She pulled out the familiar metal briefcase, clicked the latches and felt the reassuringly heavy weight of Rex's pistol in her hand. With calm deliberation she slid one bullet into the magazine, then slid that into the gun with a satisfying click. Finally, she pulled back the slide as far is it went, listening as her bullet moved into place. Loading the gun was as easy as it had looked on Ms. Durant's favorite crime shows. She then closed the metal briefcase and returned it to the box.

For a moment, Annabel studied the loaded gun in her hand, then pointed it at her own temple. *Just do it,* she thought. Her breathing was ragged as she tried to will herself to pull the trigger. She couldn't say how long she stayed frozen in that position — it might have been five seconds or five minutes or five hours. Eventually, she let her hand drop, still clutching the gun tightly. She felt herself shaking and cursed herself as weak, too weak to escape. Then clarity arrived, and she realized what she had to do. She got to her feet and left the room, shutting the door quietly behind her.

She found Rex in his study, head bowed over his desk as he read a book. The sound of some jazz song Annabel did not recognize floated through the spacious room, muffling Annabel's footsteps. Rex neither heard nor saw her as she approached him from behind. Before he had a chance to turn or look around, Annabel pressed the gun to his right temple and squeezed the trigger as hard as she could.

The sound was deafening, exponentially louder than she expected, and the recoil was so strong that the gun nearly flew out of her hand as it jerked her wrist upward. Bits of bone and brain matter flew out of the hole the bullet created, and Annabel was splattered with blood. She screamed in surprise, and stepped back as Rex's body fell from its chair onto the floor. She dropped the gun, and leaned her back against the wall for support. The whole room spun and distorted; reality seemed to have given way to a surreal horror show. Annabel felt a mirthless laugh bubble up and burst from her lips. It didn't matter that she sounded completely insane. Maybe she was.

When Annabel saw Mrs. Lennox standing in the doorway, reality returned as abruptly as if a bucket of ice water had been dumped over her head. Justifications floated through her mind but she remained mute, waiting. The older woman stared at Rex's body, then without saying a word she picked up the gun where it had fallen, wiped the fingerprints off it using Rex's shirt, and pressed the gun into his own hand, positioning his index finger on the trigger. Understanding arrived in an instant, and Annabel scrambled over and knelt next to Rex. She cradled his mangled head in her arms — surely a natural act for a woman whose husband had just shot himself — and felt the warm blood ooze over her, masking the initial spray. There was something hard digging into her left knee and she realized with a wave of nausea that it must be a piece of splintered bone. Before the panic could overwhelm her, Annabel pulled out her blood-smeared phone, and called 911.

56: JAVI

"You're not eating," his mother observed.

Javi merely grunted. Coming up with an excuse wasn't worth the effort. He'd already had to lie about the bruises on his face by saying they were the result of a stray soccer ball. His parents accepted this explanation although he doubted either of them believed it.

"Is this about Stanford?" his father guessed. His father's brow was furrowed in concern, but the only feeling Javi could muster was frustration. He wished they'd just leave him the fuck alone.

"Yeah," Javi said. He knew there were better ways to bring this up, but at that moment, he didn't give a fuck. "I don't want to go there. I'd rather go to Georgetown."

He noticed the look his parents exchanged; sad but accepting. *So they already knew.* Somehow, that knowledge made him feel even worse.

"All right," his father said.

"All right?" Javi repeated. "That's it? After months and months of you both making me feel guilty about it, now all you've got to say is 'all right'?"

"What else is there to say?" his mother asked. "You've made your decision."

"Un-fucking-believable," Javi muttered.

"Language!" His mother's voice cracked like a whip.

He threw her a resentful look, but didn't say anything. He couldn't figure out why he was suddenly so angry, when finally they'd capitulated, but at that moment all he wanted to do was upend the table and throw his chair at the wall.

"Can I be excused?" he asked as evenly as he could manage.

"Got somewhere to be?" his father quipped.

Javi closed his eyes for a moment, reminding himself he'd regret it if he lost his temper, even as his frustration peaked. He suddenly loathed both of them, sitting there with their resigned disappointment that he didn't turn out just like their son after all.

"Go ahead," his mother said.

His eyes snapped open and he shoved back from the table. When he reached his room, he barely managed to restrain himself from slamming the door. Inside, he paced relentlessly. Every afternoon since Theo had discovered them, Javi had walked by Imogen's house, unable to stop himself. He noticed Theo's car in the driveway and for that reason didn't knock on the door, instead continuing his brooding prowl down the street. Fred and Herman tried to distract him, but it was an uphill battle. The following night they were bringing him to another party at Violet's house to take his mind off it. *Good luck with that*, Javi thought savagely. He hadn't realized how attached he'd become to Imogen until she had vanished from his life. That night he texted her four times, but received no responses.

To make things worse, he felt a stab of hunger now that he was alone and wished he'd eaten more before storming off from dinner. Much later, when he was in bed staring at the ceiling and trying unsuccessfully to will himself into dreamless sleep, he felt ashamed for how he'd treated his parents. *You really are the biggest fuck-up. No fucking wonder they're disappointed.* It took hours before he fell into a fitful sleep, plagued by one stress-filled dream after another, waking up intermittently drenched in sweat with the covers twisted around him like a python.

The next day he felt like shit. He drifted from class to class like a zombie, barely present. When the final bell rang, he told Herman and Fred he'd see them later for the party, and took off on his usual post-school walk to Imogen's house. When he arrived, he found Theo's car gone. After a split-second of indecision, he strode up the front walk and knocked on the door.

There was surprise on her face when she opened it, followed quickly by wariness. He wanted to shove her against the wall and kiss her until she begged him to fuck her right there on the floor, but before he could act on this impulse she spoke.

"You shouldn't be here."

"But you're glad I came," Javi said in a cocky voice that belied his nervousness.

Imogen crossed her arms. "I don't think you understand."

"Why don't we go into the bedroom and you can educate me?"

"It's over, Javi."

His laugh was hollow and humorless. "Come on."

"This isn't a negotiation. Get out of here before Theo comes home."

"If this is about him —"

"*Of course* it's about him! He's my fucking husband!" her voice rose angrily, but she took a deep breath and her next words were steadier. "Look, I know I owe you an apology. I got caught up in — nostalgia or something. I shouldn't have — we should never have — I don't know what else to say to you. Please don't come back here again."

The facade of calm was slipping away; Javi felt like he was falling with it. "But you loved *him*, didn't you?" He didn't need to tell her who he meant.

She looked miserable, conflicted. But no less resolved. "You aren't him, Javi."

Javi was falling through space, bracing himself for the moment of impact when he'd hit the pavement and splatter apart like a water balloon filled with jello. "You don't mean —"

It was her turn to laugh; it was a cruel sound that almost made Javi cringe. "I don't know how else to say it, Javi. What we had was *not* reality. I won't pretend I didn't enjoy it while it lasted but — " There were tears in her eyes now and, he thought (hoped?), longing too. "It's over now. Goodbye." He saw her face crumple as she slammed the door.

He didn't have a very clear idea of how he got home, only that it seemed to take forever and no time at all. By the time Fred picked him up for Violet's party, he was already so drunk he was slurring his words.

"Fuckin' fuck," he mumbled to himself as they drove. Herman was telling a story and Fred was laughing, but Javi wasn't paying attention. His bad mood soured even more when they reached Violet's. Javi lost no time in filling up a solo cup with beer from a keg in the back yard, but the moment he turned around he slammed into a hulking figure standing behind him in line.

"What the FUCK?" Javi yelled, staggering and drenched in Coors Light that had exploded from the solo cup on impact. It was only then that he recognized the person he'd run into as Kato Barre.

"Dude, chill out. It's only beer," Kato said, even though he was as drenched as Javi.

"Fuck you, man." Javi said, swaying on the spot. The world was blurry and spinning, and the nausea welled up just before he vomited all over the grass. Kato jumped back just in time to avoid the spray, and Javi was dimly aware of a group of people whispering and giggling to each other nearby.

Javi kept retching until his stomach hurt and his throat burned with the sour taste of stomach acid and half-digested food. There was nothing Javi wanted to do more in that moment than lay down in the grass and sob, but instead he stood up unsteadily. Gentle hands took his arms and guided him around the house to the street out front, supporting his weight as he stumbled along while the world rolled and pitched with every step.

A car door was opened, he found himself sitting in the passenger's seat. *Whose car is this?* Javi wondered, as the door closed. Two figures stood talking on the sidewalk, and he realized one of them was Stella. A wave of humiliation swept over him, and he fumbled around trying to open the car door. Before he could, however, Kato Barre got into the driver's seat and turned on the ignition.

"Put on your seatbelt," he said brusquely.

Javi obeyed, leaning his head against the window and closing his eyes.

"We're here," Kato's voice sounded like it was a long way off. Javi blinked his eyes open, confused for a moment about where he was, before scattered memories from the party crashed over him, and he wished he could shrivel up and die.

"Where?" Javi asked. His tongue was clumsy and his breath stank.

"Your house," Kato said with a bite of impatience. "Stella told me your address. Do you need help getting inside?"

"No," Javi replied, but that soon proved to be a lie. He managed to take off his seat belt and open the car door on his own, but the moment he stepped out of the car he keeled over onto the grass. He heard Kato sigh as he came around the car and pulled Javi back to his feet. Kato brought him all the way inside and deposited him on the couch in the living room. His parents had left a few lights on for him, but had already gone to sleep. *Small mercies*, Javi thought to himself ludicrously.

"Where's the kitchen?" Kato asked, not unkindly. "I'll get you some water."

Javi gestured vaguely towards his left, unable to find the words to refuse. Javi heard Kato open the fridge and pour. A moment later, he returned and handed the glass to Javi.

"You should be fine since you puked already," Kato said. "But you're gonna have a hell of a headache tomorrow morning."

"Thanks," Javi croaked.

"Don't mention it," Kato said cooly. "I'm gonna take off."

Javi nodded and sipped his water. He heard the front door close and the car drive away. It barely took five minutes before Javi passed out.

The next morning he woke up with his head splitting open,

to the sound of knocking on his bedroom door. He had a vague memory of stumbling upstairs sometime before dawn after he had woken up with a painfully full bladder and a rancid taste in his mouth. It was only after he'd finished pissing that he realized he'd forgotten to raise the seat and had sprayed all over it, unsteady as he still was. He had wiped it off with some toilet paper, then rinsed his mouth out with Listerine (he hadn't been up for brushing his teeth; the bright light of the bathroom made his head throb). As soon as he reached his bed he'd passed out again, and had never been less happy about being disturbed from sleep.

"What?" he yelled irritably. Judging from the bright light filtering through the window, it was late morning or early afternoon. Javi expected one of his parents to call back asking if he was all right, but instead the door opened to reveal Stella. Javi yanked the sheets up to his chin reflexively, wishing he could hide beneath them until she went away.

"Oh," Javi said stupidly.

"I hope it's okay that I came," Stella said, closing the door behind her and approaching his bed. His face felt hot and he tried not to think about how he probably looked to her. The shame of having to be driven home by Kato hovered over him like a demon, stabbing him with a trident and laughing in his face.

Seemingly oblivious to his discomfort, Stella sat on the edge of the bed and held out a large bottle of coconut water and a wrapped bagel.

"Best hangover cure there is," Stella said.

"Thanks," Javi managed to reply, taking both from her. He sat up awkwardly, dragging the covers with him, aware that he was still wearing the same rumpled clothes from the night before and that he probably smelled. "D'you mind if—I really need to brush my teeth," Javi said apologetically.

Stella gave him a rueful smile. "I know that feeling. Go for it, I don't mind waiting." She got up off the bed and sat down at his desk chair, pulling out her phone. Javi got out of bed unsteadily, and grabbed a change of clothes before going down the hallway to the bathroom.

He looked even worse than he felt; dark circles under his eyes, the crusted remains of what look suspiciously like dried vomit in his hair. "Fuck," he muttered. Fifteen minutes later he was stepping out of the shower with his teeth freshly brushed and his hair now vomit-free. He felt a little better once he toweled off and pulled on clean clothes, but the pounding in his head didn't abate. He arrived back in his room to find Stella spinning absentmindedly in his desk chair while she texted. She looked up and smiled at him when he closed the door and crossed to the bedside table where he'd put the coconut water and bagel. He took a sip.

"Drink all of that and you'll feel a million times better," Stella told him.

He nodded dumbly, and sat on the edge of the bed facing her. "Thanks," he said, while thinking *why are you here?*

"I wanted to check that you were okay after last night," Stella said, answering his unasked question.

"Oh." The shame returned and Javi stared at the floor, taking another swig of coconut water so he would have an excuse not to speak again. "Yeah. I am."

"I can see that," Stella said, and he couldn't tell if she was mocking him. Javi took a bite of the bagel; it was sesame with butter and avocado. *My favorite*, he thought.

"It's good," Javi said. He took another bite. "Look, if you've got somewhere else to be, you don't have to —"

"I don't," Stella interrupted.

There was a brief silence in which Javi chewed his bagel, drank his coconut water and wondered why Stella Castell was in his bedroom. After a moment, she spoke again.

"How did Kato seem to you, last night?" she asked.

"Nicer than I expected," Javi said, surprised by the question. "I guess that was your doing."

"Nah, he's a really nice guy." Stella sounded sad, but Javi couldn't think why she would be.

"I'm glad you two are happy together." The words almost stuck in Javi's throat but he forced them out, trying his hardest not to sound jealous.

Stella's eyes welled up, but she did not let the tears fall. "We're not," she said. "Together. He broke up with me."

"When?" Javi asked, aware that his heart was suddenly pounding.

"Last night," Stella said. "After he got back to the party. He only agreed to drive you home because he felt bad. For me, I mean."

"Shit," was all Javi could think to say.

Stella got up and began to pace. "This morning Leila texted me to say she saw him holding hands with Zoe over brunch. He couldn't even wait twenty-four hours before — before —" she stopped, once again holding back her tears. "Goddamn him! And her! She always pretended we were friends." Stella sounded forlorn as she sat down on the bed next to him, close enough that their knees were touching. Javi felt like an electric current was pumping through his body from the point of contact. Her face was close enough that he could see a few faint freckles he had never noticed before sprinkled across her nose. Her unshed tears glittered as she looked at him, and without meaning to he suddenly felt himself lurch forward and plant his lips on hers even as his hand wound itself through her golden hair.

It was a chaste kiss without tongue, but it seemed to go on for ages. When she pulled away, he knew immediately that she was embarrassed for him.

"Sorry," Javi mumbled, looking down at his lap. "Sorry."

"It's okay," Stella said. She slid away from him but did not leave. Javi glanced up to see that she was looking down at the floor too. Her cheeks were red and her hands clenched together. "Javi, listen. I really — I care about you a lot. As a friend. I'm sorry if I gave you the wrong impression. I hope this won't — make things awkward."

You might as well hope the sun doesn't rise, Javi thought bitterly. "It's not — don't worry about it." Javi couldn't meet her eyes, couldn't bear to see the pity there.

"It's not you, it's me. I'm just not ready to start anything new right now, Kato and I literally just broke up. I just — maybe it would be easier if you and I didn't see each other for a while. Just until — until things aren't so confusing. I really do want us to stay friends."

Fuck friends. "Sure. Whatever you want," Javi said dully.

Stella stood up, hesitated a moment then leaned down to give him a quick hug. Her hair smelled like lavender. "Feel better," she said, and once again, he nearly broke into hysterical laughter. Before he could come up with an appropriate response, she was gone.

57: EDGAR PRIME

When Edgar Prime woke up naked in an unfamiliar bed, it took him a moment to remember what had happened. Hardly daring to open his eyes lest it all turn out to be a dream, Edgar Prime rolled onto his back and found a pair of beautiful green eyes watching him.

Hugo leaned over and kissed him, and for the next hour Edgar Prime lost himself in a state of bliss where nothing mattered but the taste of Hugo, the feel of his skin, the sound of his moans, until ecstasy descended on them both. Afterwards, they lay together with their arms and legs intertwined, soaked in sweat. Their foreheads touched, and Edgar Prime thought he could stay like this forever.

Somewhere on the floor, an alarm went off. They both ignored it for a moment, then Hugo groaned and extricated himself from their embrace to silence it. Edgar Prime watched him bend down to pick up the phone, admiring the profile of his lean, hard body, and feeling himself stiffen once more.

"Come back to bed," Edgar Prime murmured.

The look Hugo gave him was at once amused and alluring; he glanced down at his phone then back at Edgar Prime.

"I've got an RA meeting," he said, and Edgar Prime's heart sank. "Then again, it won't be the end of the world if I'm a little late." They both laughed as Hugo yanked away the covers and dove back into bed.

Forty five minutes later Hugo rushed off for his meeting, promising to catch up with Edgar Prime that afternoon at Luken's protest downtown. Edgar Prime went back to his room to retrieve his towel and soap, then headed off for a shower. He had always thought those cliches about "walking on air" were ridiculous, but today that was the only way he could describe the floating euphoria he felt, so complete that it was as though he might spontaneously combust with the power of it.

When he returned to his room, freshly showered and feeling that at last, all was right with the world, he received a text from Noela saying that she wasn't going to make it to the protest, and that he should give Luken her regrets. Like a candle being snuffed out, the joy of the last twelve hours fled, leaving shame in its wake, shame that Edgar Prime could so easily forget Noela's grief over Omar's hopeless situation. Now the heady feeling of contentment warred with the more familiar self-loathing, for how could anyone as selfish as he was ever hope to deserve the happiness he'd experienced with Hugo. *You don't deserve it*, said a sneering voice in the back of his head that sounded like Dr. Midas, or perhaps even himself. It was difficult to tell the two apart sometimes.

He pulled on jeans and a black t-shirt, and headed out to the subway. On his way, he dialed Harlow's number, expecting to get his secretary. To his surprise, it was Harlow's own voice on the other end of the line.

"Hello, Prime," Harlow said. "I gave orders for all your calls to be put right through to my personal line when I heard about your friend. How is he?"

"No change." Edgar Prime fought to keep the bitterness from his voice, but was unsuccessful.

"Terrible, terrible. To be the victim of such senseless violence at such a young age. I'd completely understand if you wanted to abandon the plans we discussed, in light of what's happened."

"No." He would not give up on this, especially now. He owed his continued resolve to Omar, for his sacrifice. "I'm not abandoning anything."

"If you say so," said Harlow, surprise and skepticism evident in his voice. "We'll speak again soon, I expect. Enjoy the protest, today."

"Thanks," Edgar Prime said, slightly taken aback. He wouldn't have expected Harlow to be aware of any protest, especially one so modest. They ended the call just as Edgar Prime reached his subway station and began to descend into the earth.

It wasn't a large protest — no more than a few thousand people milling around Zuccotti Park when Edgar Prime arrived. After greeting Luken, he mostly paced around the periphery of the crowd snapping photos for social media. The crowd had the purposeful, jubilant air of people who believed in something and felt they had the potential to affect positive change.

It began with a rally; a few speakers introduced by Luken but nobody very famous. As always, Edgar Prime was trotted out, standing awkwardly before the gaping crowd as they cheered for the novelty. Then the others came, mostly college professors who spoke about corporate ties to the clone black market, human rights and the injustice of being in a legal gray zone. Edgar Prime found it difficult to concentrate, his mind kept drifting back to Hugo and replaying memories from the previous night and that morning. He mentally chastised himself, and tried to remain focused, but in truth he was eager for the protest to end. There was a while to go however; after the speakers there would be a march, and Edgar Prime had to stick it out for at least another couple of hours.

Finally, the last speaker handed the microphone back to Luken, and they all set off up Broadway. Sullen police officers lined the route, and after a while Edgar Prime found himself surrounded by strangers; Luken kept stopping to chat with various others and Edgar Prime was too antsy not to keep going. His mind had just slid once again into a fantasy about what he'd like to do when he saw Hugo again, when a movement on his left side caught his eye.

Edgar Prime turned his head and saw a thin, severe-featured man with mousy brown hair and a sweaty face approaching from a side street ahead. For some reason the man made him uneasy; ridiculous because Edgar Prime was certain he'd never seen the man before, and he was in the midst of a large crowd surrounded by police officers. Even so, Edgar Prime felt a chill run down his spine. The man was getting closer, and they locked eyes just as the man reached inside his jacket.

It's way too hot for a jacket, Edgar Prime thought ludicrously as the man pulled out his gun. Before Edgar Prime could react, the gun was pointed his way and there was a deafening bang. Edgar Prime felt the impact in his chest, just before he slammed back onto the blood-spattered pavement. The man stood over him now, swimming in and out of his field of vision as he was nearly blinded by the pain ripping through his entire body. There were two more bangs in quick succession, followed by a feeling of falling, falling, falling. His last thought was of Hugo.

58: ANNABEL

The tears had come easily — how were the police to know they were tears of relief not tears of grief? The entire investigation hadn't taken them more than ten minutes. They had accepted her account of what happened without question, and they conducted only the most cursory interview with Mrs. Lennox. The old woman corroborated Annabel's story, and when they officially ruled Rex's death a suicide, Annabel felt waves of gratitude crash over, even though Mrs. Lennox had scarcely said a word to her since.

At the funeral Annabel wore sunglasses to hide the fact that her eyes were dry. It was a small funeral, and tasteful. Ms. Durant cried silently through the whole thing, her shoulders shaking and her face red and splotchy. The casket was closed for obvious reasons, and afterwards Rex would be cremated.

Annabel didn't hear two words of the ceremony. When it was over, she accepted condolences mechanically. If any of Rex's mourners found her manner odd, they did not say so. Perhaps they thought it was her way of processing the loss. Ms. Durant stood by her side sniffling and dabbing at her eyes with a white silk handkerchief.

"I just can't believe he's gone," Ms. Durant choked out.

"Me neither," Annabel replied. She was telling the truth about that; the idea that Rex was truly gone took some getting used to. *I'm a widow*, she thought, and had to fight back a sudden, irresistible urge to laugh.

"Oh, my dear," Ms. Durant said, enveloping Annabel in a hug. The older woman had apparently taken her strange expression to be a precursor to sobs.

"I'm all right," Annabel said. She patted Ms. Durant on the back dutifully, allowing her mind to drift. The air was hot and sticky, and Ms. Durant's deodorant appeared to have worn off. Oblivious, she kept squeezing Annabel tight to her chest, her tears falling all over Annabel's shoulder. With a sigh, she pretended Ms. Durant's embrace wasn't suffocating her.

Afterwards, Annabel went back to the house alone. As the sky darkened, she stood on the deck and looked out at the waves crashing onto the rocks along the bay. She knew she should feel happy — *free* — but she didn't. At night she still dreamed of Rex, and woke sweating with the sheets tangled around her as tightly as his embrace. She wondered if she'd ever truly escape him.

One morning, about a week after the funeral, Annabel felt more listless than usual and decided to walk to the beach. In truth she didn't know what to do with herself anymore, now that she could do anything she liked. The loneliness pressed in around her in a way it never had before. She found herself thinking of Javi as she kicked off her shoes and strode across the sand to find a solitary spot to lay down her towel.

She couldn't figure out why her mind kept returning to the boy she'd only met once, the boy who'd never contacted her again. *He doesn't want you*, she told herself firmly. *There's no point in wishing it were otherwise.*

To distract herself, Annabel pulled out her tablet and started flicking through her email. In addition to several messages reminding her that she had missed multiple assignments for her online coursework, she came across an email from Midas Laboratory with the subject line, "Can You Put A Price On Grief?". Frowning slightly, Annabel began to read:

Dear Mrs. King,
Deepest condolences for your recent loss. While once there was no solace for those in your position, Midas Laboratories now has the power to offer individuals and families the chance to reconnect with their lost loved ones through the use of our cutting edge clon-

ing technology. Please contact us today for more information.
 Most Sincerely,
 Patrice Zhao, Ph.D

Annabel reached the end of the email and flung the tablet away in horror, earning her several scandalized glances from the beach's other occupants. Her heart thudded in her chest and she felt like an invisible hand had just punched her in the gut. When she got over the initial disgust at the gall of Midas Labs to email her like that, she calmed her breathing and tried to slow her heart rate. She forced herself to get up and retrieve the tablet, smiling sheepishly at the nearest couple, both of whom appeared to be well into their seventies.

As she sat down on her lonely towel again, Annabel stared unseeingly at the ocean, the endless ebb and flow, the power and the beauty of it lost on her. She looked back at the older couple to her right. They were smiling and laughing together as he waved his hands around, telling a story that Annabel was not close enough to hear. And as she stuck the Midas Labs email in her spam folder, the tiniest bit of pity for her late husband crept into her heart. Who could say what she'd choose if she ever learned what grief truly felt like.

59: JAVI

D. C. was hot as fuck, and the humidity made Javi feel like he was being continuously molested by a sweaty giant. From the moment he left the airport, the heavy, stagnant air weighed him down. By the time he arrived on campus, lugging his two largest suitcases, he was out of breath and bad-tempered. His brain had melted in the heat, and all he wanted was to throw himself into a bathtub filled with ice.

After a few wrong turns, Javi found his dorm. The seventh floor room was cramped, with barely five feet between his bed and his roommate's, a tiny closet and two desks shoved into a corner. His roommate hadn't arrived yet, so Javi threw his stuff onto what he deemed the better bed (though in truth there was little difference between them), and sat down on the plastic mattress. He ran his hands through his hair and heaved a heavy sigh, wishing Herman and Fred were here with him, and feeling a stab of jealousy that the two of them would be rooming together at Berkeley.

Saying goodbye to his parents was harder than he expected. They both went to see him off at the airport, after he'd insisted that they not fly all the way to the east coast just to help him move into his dorm. Now that he had arrived all alone, he wished he'd been less stubborn. When they hugged him goodbye outside the security line, both of them had tears in their eyes.

"I'll be *fine*," Javi insisted, embarrassed they were making such a scene.

"Don't forget to brush and floss your teeth," his mother said tremulously. "And be sure to eat some vegetables once in a while. You can't just live off bagels and coffee. And try to get enough sleep."

"Don't do anything I wouldn't do," his father said with a guffaw, and Javi smiled in spite of himself.

"Study hard," his mother continued. "Make sure you don't miss too many of your classes."

Javi rolled his eyes at his father, who chuckled again.

"He'll be all right, Jo," his father said softly to his mother.

"I know," his mother said, but from her tone Javi thought she had her doubts. "Be safe, Javi."

"I will." He gave them one final hug, then turned away. He didn't look back until after he got all the way through security. He wished his heart didn't sink slightly when he saw that they were already gone.

Through the open door, Javi could hear raucous discussion and laughter coming from the common room diagonally across the hall; it made Javi feel as though everyone else already knew each other. He knew he should go introduce himself, but something held him back. The idea of pretending to be excited seemed like far too much effort after battling the horrible weather. To his frustration, all Javi could think about was Stella, Imogen and even Annabel; all the women who didn't want him. *And why would they? Why would anyone?* Javi didn't have an answer to that.

After a while he managed to psych himself up enough to go to the bookstore, even though it meant leaving the air conditioned dorm and braving the elements outside again. Javi wandered down the hall and took the stairs to the fourth floor where the hillside building exited to a small quad.

Though not large, the campus was full of dead-ends, alcoves, and circular paths making it harder to navigate than Javi anticipated. Just after leaving the dorm he came across a small courtyard with a fountain at its center. A group of students stood near the fountain and one of them — a bold-looking girl — climbed up and waded through the shallow water, imploring her friends to join her. The others looked around as if to check that campus security was nowhere in the vicinity, then clambered in after her with huge grins plastered across their faces.

Soon shouts and laughter split the air while they splashed each other, unconcerned that they were all fully dressed. Javi watched them from a shadowed archway across the court-yard; he had never felt more lonely in his entire life. He couldn't say how long he stood there, but after a time a girl walked right up to him and interrupted his reverie, making him jump. She had long, dirty-blonde hair and sympathetic brown eyes that regarded him curiously.

"Are you lost?" she asked.

He blinked. She wasn't as pretty as Stella or Imogen or Annabel, but he felt drawn to her nonetheless. "Yes," he said, and she smiled.

60: MIRA

After the raid, they'd all been drunk with their success, even John who hadn't wanted to do it in the first place. Drunk and arrogant, thinking they'd managed to win something tangible, to make a dent, however tiny, in Harlow's black market clone trafficking enterprise. They had good reason to celebrate, of course; the raid had gone better than they'd hoped. They'd managed to apprehend the buyer, a blonde man in his fifties who had made his fortune importing precious gems, the staff of the shelter, and Bob Smith, who had presumably been there in an advisory capacity to facilitate the transaction. They were particularly excited about Smith, who was sure to be a gold mine of information if only they could get him to talk. They had also safely relocated the twenty-six clone children ranging from newborns to young teenagers, including the four year old boy who had been auctioned. All in all, it had been a good day. A victory.

Then Edgar Prime had been murdered, shocking them all. Even with everything Mira knew about Harlow, she'd never dreamed he'd go that far. The gunman was identified as Graham Sheehy, the same one responsible for Omar's attack. There'd been no opportunity to question him; he'd been shot to death by police on the scene. Mira threw a chair at the wall when she found out. It took all of her effort not to scream, and when Jack put a hand on her arm in an attempt to comfort her, she wrenched away from him and stalked out of the office. It was pouring rain outside, but Mira didn't even attempt to shield herself and was drenched in seconds. By the time she got back to her apartment she was shivering, and she stripped off her wet clothes and huddled under a blanket, unable to sleep, unwilling to do anything else.

She silenced her phone and ignored Jack's calls until he showed up and began knocking on her door. She didn't answer, pretending she wasn't home. Eventually he left, but the worried text messages didn't stop. When she finally responded it was just to tell him to leave her alone. Mira couldn't forgive herself for not figuring out what Harlow was going to do, for not stopping it. She had failed, and Edgar Prime had died for it. For the first time, Mira seriously considered quitting her job at the FBI. Clearly she wasn't cut out for it. Even in the midst of her swirl of guilt and rage and grief, Mira registered how thrilled her mother would be to hear that Mira had given up on her wholly unsuitable career, and that made her even angrier. They hadn't spoken since Mira abruptly canceled her trip home for Memorial Day. She'd lied and said she needed to work overtime on a case that weekend, but in truth it was because she couldn't face them after her abysmal failure.

The morning after Edgar Prime's death, Harlow gave Mira a massive file room and told her all of it needed to be resorted and organized by the following day; an impossible task for three people, let alone just one. Mira set to work, and wasn't even a quarter of the way finished by the time she left the office twelve hours later. She spent every second of that day seething with rage, fueled by fantasies of shoving Harlow off the roof of the seventy-story building. By the following morning, she felt empty.

Mira had only been at work fifteen minutes when Harlow called her to his office. She stood waiting as he scrutinized her from behind his massive desk.

"I think you know why you're here, Mira."

"I don't, sir."

That seemed to amuse Harlow. "Then allow me to enlighten you. You're fired."

Mira blinked, dumbfounded. "Why?" she managed.

In answer, Harlow opened a desk drawer and pulled out the

tiny microphones she'd placed around his office shortly after beginning work there. Even though her heart skipped a beat, Mira kept her face as neutral as she could. "I don't know what those are."

Harlow quirked an eyebrow. "I'd have expected someone in your line of work to be a better liar," Harlow said. "If you want another reason, fine. You fail to complete assigned tasks in a timely manner."

"No one could have reorganized those files faster."

Harlow shrugged. "Security will escort you from the building. Your things will be delivered to the address we have on file."

Mira wondered if he was subtly hinting that he knew where she lived. She glanced over her shoulder, and saw two armed security guards standing just outside the door.

"Good luck with your future endeavors, Mira," said Harlow. "I do hope they're more fruitful than this one has been."

Mira's mouth twisted like she'd just taken poison, and suddenly it was too much. "How can you live with yourself? I know you killed him. Edgar Prime."

"His death was a tragedy, but it was the work of a madman, a radical fundamentalist in the anti-clone lobby. The small consolation to those who knew and cared for him is that the man was brought to justice."

"Killed before he could testify against *you*, you mean."

Harlow gave her a concerned look she saw through at once. "You're not making sense. Perhaps you could do with a nice long vacation. You seem to be hysterical."

"You paid him, to do a job. You had me deliver the money."

"I hired him to oversee the landscaping of my summer house in the Hamptons. Imagine my distress upon hearing that the very same man was responsible for such an atrocity. I really should begin running background checks on my employees and contractors."

"Enjoy your freedom while it lasts," Mira spat. "You'll be rotting in jail soon enough, wishing you were dead too."

Harlow had the gall to laugh at that. "If you're the best the FBI has to offer, I'm not worried. Now get out." He nodded to the guards, who took Mira by the arm and led her away. She was shaking from suppressed anger; her cover was blown and Harlow was still free. The whole investigation had been for nothing.

The guards deposited her on the sidewalk and warned her that they'd call the police if she tried to enter the building again. Mira started walking, and a half hour later was surprised to realize that she'd made her way to Jack's apartment without thinking about it.

She felt a chill of trepidation; she wasn't sure Jack would want to see her after the way she'd behaved the other night. When she knocked on the door however, he opened it and immediately pulled her into a hug.

"I was worried about you," he told her.

She stepped away from him, and sat down on the couch. His apartment was far more organized than hers was, here everything had its place. Jack sat down next to her, waiting.

"I'm sorry," she mumbled. She couldn't even look him in the eye.

"I understand," he said.

Mira grimaced. "Harlow won."

"He hasn't won. We haven't stopped. We just haven't won yet."

"What if it takes ten years for us to find anything on him? Fifteen?"

Jack shrugged. "Then it takes ten years. If we're lucky one of his competitors will take care of him before then."

"Then we'll just go after the next one and the next and the next... it'll never end."

"You knew that when you started this job."

"I did."

"But you wanted to do it anyway."

"I did. I do."

"What we did wasn't meaningless. There were twenty-six

kids at that shelter. This'll make a difference in all their lives. And who knows? Maybe one day one of them will grow up and decide to do her part in making the world just a little less evil. And that'll be a win for us too."

Jack took Mira's hand and gave it a squeeze. The empty feeling eased just the tiniest bit. Mira still felt sad and disillusioned, but she knew she couldn't dwell on it. There was always more work to be done.

61: BOB

Bob sat in his cell, staring at the ceiling. Tomorrow morning he was going to tell them everything. With any luck, they'd be able to rescue little Dolores from whatever hell he'd left her in, in that surgically clean apartment in Rome. He still saw the look of betrayal on her face every night in his dreams.

It was too quiet in the jail, and Bob was itchy. He wished he could take a shower. He'd been placed in the cell all the way at the end of the hall, so he couldn't see or hear anything that was going on in the rest of the police station. Bob stood up and paced, and rubbed at where the handcuffs had chafed his wrists.

He heard the door at the end of the hall groan open. Bob tried to look, but the angle was wrong and all he could do was listen to heavy footsteps thudding louder and louder as they approached him.

Finally, an officer came into view. He was tall and brawny with a deep tan and cropped black hair. The man stopped in front of the cell door and gave him a scowl. Bob stood in the center of the cell, hands raised, watching the officer quizzically as he turned the key and stepped inside.

"You're on suicide watch," the man informed him. "Take off your belt."

Bob obeyed, moving carefully so as not to cause alarm. The officer took the proffered belt and began to walk a slow circle around Bob. He slid out of Bob's peripheral vision, and the hairs on the back of his neck stood up. He resisted the urge to turn around with all his might. Then all of a sudden, the belt was around his neck. He tried to pull it away, but the officer was fearsomely strong. He tried stamping the man's feet, elbowing his ribs, reaching up to claw at his eyes. It wasn't long before spots of light began popping across his field of vision. His efforts were futile; the man was too strong. It was an eternity, and no time at all. Bob was in agony by the time the darkness descended and he was pulled into the abyss.

EPILOGUE

"Why?" Dr. Edgar Midas ran a hand over his face wearily.

Across from him, Harlow shrugged. "He was meddling."

"*You* encouraged that," Edgar pointed out. "You told him what to do. You said that you were behind him."

"A test," Harlow said. There was a pause. "He failed."

Edgar exhaled. He had never felt more exhausted in his life. "And the others?"

"If they're smart, they'll have gotten the message," Harlow said. "If not, well . . ." He left the threat unspoken.

"You're a monster, Harlow."

Harlow seemed to find that amusing. "I prefer to think of myself as pragmatic."

"I need to get back to the lab," Edgar said. *If I spend one more minute in your company, I may strangle you.*

Harlow leaned back in his chair and actually grinned. "Now *that* doesn't surprise me one bit."

Edgar stood up. The calm order of Harlow's office offended him. "Was it all about the money?"

Harlow laughed. "Come on, old friend. You know me better than that."

Edgar turned and left, to keep from launching himself across the desk and pummeling Harlow to death.

Outside, his car was waiting. He got into the back seat and called Caden.

"Well?" Caden asked him, answering after the first ring.

"I'm sure you can imagine." Edgar was so very tired.

"I never liked him." Caden's voice was bitter.

"Will you stay tonight?" Edgar asked.

"Now you want me to stay?" Caden said.

"I've never not wanted you to stay," Dr. Midas objected.

There was a rueful laugh that didn't suit Caden at all. "That's not how I remember it, Edgar."

Edgar clutched the phone like a lifeline, hardly daring to breathe. He'd always known there was a possibility that Caden would decide it wasn't enough and walk out of his life forever. But he wasn't sure he could survive that today.

"Please, Caden." It was barely a whisper.

There was a long silence, so long that Edgar was afraid Caden had hung up. Then a sigh. "Of course I'll be there, Edgar."

For a moment, Edgar couldn't speak. "I'll see you later, then."

He hung up before he could say too much.

When he arrived at the lab, he called Patrice into his office. She hovered by the open door.

"There's an irony in all this, you realize," Edgar said to her.

"Irony?" Patrice repeated, a blank look on her face.

Edgar waved his hand; she was being stupid on purpose. "With Prime," he said. His voice almost broke when he said the name, but he managed to control it.

"I don't understand," Patrice said.

"Midas Labs primarily makes clones for people who've lost loved ones," Edgar said. "People who are grieving — we're the cure. And now, I've lost my clone. It's a vicious fucking cycle." He never swore, but no other word seemed appropriate in this instance.

Patrice's expression softened into sympathy, but she did not speak.

"Whatever you were doing this morning, give it to a research assistant. I need you to get started on this immediately," Edgar said.

"On what?" Patrice asked. She looked annoyed at being pulled off her experiment, but knew better than to grumble about it.

"You'll need to prepare my sample for implantation in a

surrogate — make sure to pick the best one available —"

"You mean — you want to make *another* clone?" Patrice interrupted.

Edgar stared at her, confused by her reaction. She looked horrified, but how could she not see? There were no other options.

"Of course I do," he said. "I'm surprised you haven't figured this out already, Patrice. It's the only logical action given the circumstances." *As if this is about logic. He's dead.*

Patrice stood gaping at him, as he took another deep breath to steady himself.

"Now, get to work," he told her. "There's a lot to be done, and I'd like a summer birthday for Double Prime."

She just stood there, eyes welling up, looking as though she might shout at him. But instead she fled, before the tears had even begun to fall.

ABOUT THE AUTHOR

M.A. Gelsey is the author of *CLONE*, a novel that explores the unintended consequences of human cloning set in a near-future world. She also authored the *Green Sleuths* short stories, featuring Detectives Shea Harper and Jiro Winter as they attempt to solve the strange crimes of an east coast suburb called Purgatory. By day she is a software engineer and when not coding or writing she practices yoga and Brazilian jiujitsu.

www.ingramcontent.com/pod-product-compliance
Lightning Source LLC
Chambersburg PA
CBHW021532250626
47154CB00006BA/2086